Joseph A. Gobineau

Typhaines Abbey

A tale of the twelfth century

Joseph A. Gobineau

Typhaines Abbey
A tale of the twelfth century

ISBN/EAN: 9783742860330

Manufactured in Europe, USA, Canada, Australia, Japa

Cover: Foto ©Andreas Hilbeck / pixelio.de

Manufactured and distributed by brebook publishing software
(www.brebook.com)

Joseph A. Gobineau

Typhaines Abbey

TYPHAINES ABBEY:

A TALE OF THE TWELFTH CENTURY.

COUNT A. DE GOBINEAU,
AMBASSADOR OF FRANCE AT RIO JANEIRO.

TRANSLATED

BY

GHAS. D. MEIGS, M. D.
OF PHILADELPHIA.

PHILADELPHIA:
CLAXTON, REMSEN, AND HAFFELFINGER,
819 AND 821 MARKET STREET.
1869.

COUNT AKTHUR DE GOBINEAU, •

AMBASSADOR OF FRAMCR AT RIO JANEIRO, BRAZIL.

Sm:—

I would not, at my advanced age of seventy-eight years, have thought of taking the trouble to write and publish a romance, even were I endowed with genius and learning sufficient to qualify me to produce a picture so admirable as this tale of the Twelfth Century, composed by you while lately Ambassador of France to the King of the Hellenes, at Athens; but I felt constrained to make this translation solely as an act of personal homage to you, and as my most sincere expression of gratitude for many hours of happiness, and for much instruction that I have derived from the perusal of your works on Ethnology and other works of various research.

Your Abbaye de Typhaines appeared to me, too, less a romance, than a history constructed on the same basis as that adopted by your admirable countryman, the late M. Armand de Menteil, in his History of the French during the last five centuries. I know nothing to compare in vivid truthfulness of representation with your Typhaines Abbey like the old Cordelier's letters to Frfere Andr6, in M. de

1* (O

Menteil's first volume, written from the Chateau de Mont-bazon, and which, though pure fictions, serve to impart to us a true picture of life in the seigneurial castles of Frauce in the thirteenth century; just as your story is a pictograph, a broad and beautiful translation of the inner-life, the sentiments, aspirations, and actions of peoples of every social rank, high and low alike, in western Europe, at the epoch of the Crusades; an epoch most interesting to every reader, not only as to its romance, but by the real influence it exerted and continues to exert on the condition of the entire Christian world.

It was at the outbreak of our late rebellion and wars that I came into possession of your " Essai sur l'liiegalite des Races Ilumaines,·· and which I read in my sequestered country-home with a delight I have no words to express.

The dogma on which that work hinges is, that peculiar races of men, and animals as well, are imbued with instincts, peculiar and special to each, and by you applied as interpretation of the instinctive and inevitable tendencies of man's action in all ages of the world, past, present, and to come: that principle, or law, which you was the first to discover, and which is true as Kepler's or Newton's, was carried out by you to times even beyond the origin of the Yedic hymns, and so closely followed down to the actual present, that it seemed to me you must have planted your foot, so to speak, in every track left by our race in the secular migrations, changes, and combinations of the various peoples of the world; so that, as if you had been eyewit-

ness of the ages, the " Essai" seemed to me an absolute
Baconian induction from all the FACTS of history, annals,
traditions, monuments, and philology of our race, so far as
they have been hitherto made known to us. All this had
been a myth and a mystery to my understanding until you
came to shed on the long story of man the light of your
scholarship. In saying this I am very far from the least desire to disparage the labors of other illustrious benefactors
of learning in the same fields—the Niebuhrs, Bunsens, Karl
Ritters, Lepsius', Lassens, Bournoufs, Movers', and Sehaf-
faricks, and numerous other writers, none of whom appear
to me to have founded their interpretations, as you have
done, upon the physiological and spiritual principle of an
original and imperious natural instinct: still the world
owes those remarkable scholars a debt of respect and veneration forever impayable, for the resurrection they have
effected of long buried and forgotten nations and *quasi*
civilizations, that, like the silent remains in that old valley
of the dry bones, have waked again, risen up and been
clothed upon, and now speak to us with fleshly lips to tell
the long mournful story of man's origin, progress, and now
partial triumph in learning, and science, and civilization.
Avicenna is reported to have said of the works of Galen:
" Sexies legi, et iterum vellera legere." I can say of the
"Essai sur l'In£galit6 des Races," that I have read your
four volumes not sexies but decies, and that I hope, aged
though I am, to read them again and again, as leading me
to springs of living waters that are both refreshing and
strengthening to my spiritual life.

*

As I am trying to explain to you and to my friends at
home why I, so old a man, was led to make this Translation of a romance, let me further say that I was won over
to a sort of enthusiasm on the subject of Persia, so long
ago as 1829, by obtaining possession of good old Sieur
d'Aubaiue's curious and instructive account of his travels in
Persia and India, and that, so far as I know, I have perused
all the documents on Persian history and story that have
since come into my hands. But I ever read Persia as in
a mist; I found nothing clear, defining, or penetrating like
the lenses in a modern perfected microscope, until I became
acquainted with the " Trois Ans en Asie" (a work of research), which was the result of your protracted sojourn as
Minister of France at the Court of the Shah, at Tehran.
Then came your " Philosophies et Religions dans l'Asie
Centrale," and your, to me, amazing interpretations and
criticisms on the Cuneiform Writings at Khorsabad, Bisu-
tun, Persepolis; on Babylon-cylinders and bricks; on
Abraxas and Talismans. Before I read your writings, I
say that I read Persia in a sort of mist—but now, any
man may read her as under a lime-light, so clear and dis-
coverable have you made that wondrous land and story.

I have, too, your " Aphroessa," freighted with pages that
appear to me far to surpass, in many respects, the effusions
of your Clement Marot, your Racine, Voltaire, and Delislc.
Your " Achilteide" contains as charming passages as some
of the choicest phantasies of the JSneid ; and lastly, your
work, written in German, and just published at Leipzig,

serves as the complement-evidence of your most ripe scholarship and philosophy, I mean the "Untersucbungen uber Yerschiedene Aeusscrungen des Sporadischen lebens."

Am I not your debtor, then, and deeply your debtor ? and have I done a thing *non s&ant* for seventy-eight, in translating your story of the twelfth century, though standing, as I do, on the outer verge of existence ? I cannot think it; particularly, when I remember that the good man and philosopher, Herr Fichte, tells us that the Scholar is man's teacher and guide, ever discovering to him, and inviting him to partake of his well of living and sweet waters ; waters springing up to cleanse him of ignorance and error, and strengthening him to fight the good fight, to keep the faith, and finish the course that leads to victory at last over the world, sin, and death.

Men should adore their Scholar-class—I do—and I lay this labor of my hands on the altar of your scholarship as my oblation of unreserved respect.

But who is a Scholar, most worthy Sir? Every man who upholds and gives aid to religion and morals; every man who, by example, teaches others to be good citizens; all founders of schools, inventors of steam-engines, mills, ships,—every ruler of an honest Press; every farmer who 6hows how to make two blades of grass grow where one only could be grown before; wise and upright judges, statesmen, lawyers, physicians, and civil and military officers; such are of the Scholar-class, and such should be, and forever held in both public and private respect.

I admit that personally I have had pleasure in the task —for you made me fall in love with your beautiful Damerones the Rose of Typhaines; and dear Monseigneur Philippe de Cornehaut has a place in my heart by the side of my great-grandchildren.

And see, your Excellency! what a strange thing!

You had buried the Commander of the Temple-Order with his valiant brother Payen, by his side, on the banks of the Orontes, by Antioch! The saintly relics of Damerones the sweet Rose of Typhaines, too, were calmly reposing, by the side of the unfortunate Eteloise, at the convent of Paraclete. But by your permission I have clothed them in a new American dress, and if my countrymen should give welcome to them, they will long be seen traversing this new world of our American civilization! We shall perhaps see the knight and the heroine, and even Mahaut— and Fulk, all flying at a speed of forty miles the hour from Boston to San Francisco; scurrying away along the banks of our ocean -rivers to their very spring-heads; scattering tens of thousands of stampeding buffaloes from the railtrack on the prairies, and hurrying along by myriads of toppling-down prairie-dogs on their cones; looking out at the swarthy, stalking forms of impassive Arapahoes and Camanches; rushing beneath the towering heights of Pike's Peak; scorning the foul Mormon, and breathing warm breath on their frozen fingers by the shores of our Alaska, and our Behring's Strait. When I start for San Francisco and Oregon, I will be sure to have, as part of my company,

the Good Crusader and all his cortege; and to make sure
that he is a portrait, and not a *schema* of a portrait, I will
have with me this *Sirvente* (which I beg your leave to
add), the Troubadour, which is said to be by the hand of
Bertrand de Born, Comte de Hautefort en P^rigord, in the
twelfth century, at the very time the cloth-merchant was
plotting against your holy Abbot Anselm at Typhaines.
This Sirvente is given by Mr. Roscoe in his translation of
Sismondi's literature of the Middle Ages, who says he was
indebted to the translation out of the *langue d'Oc* into
English, to a friend.

You, sir, are not a writer by profession; you are a French
noble, *"de la vielle roche,"* and if I have made free—perhaps too free—to express in this manner my poor private
opiniou as an American of your worth as a philosopher
and scholar, I am only the more confirmed in my boldness
and gratified to hear that the government of your sovereign, the Emperor Napoleon, has authoritatively acknowledged your literary and philosophical pre-eminency so
far as to take charge of and to print and publish, at the
expense of your nation, the four volumes of your " Histoire
des Perses," the result of fourteen years of labor, with its
numerous inedited manuscripts in Sanscrit, Zend, Arabic,
and Persian, with all which languages, as well as with
Cuneiform writings, the classics and the modern languages
as well, you seem to me as familiar as I with the New
England Primer, that taught me in 1797 that

> " In Adam's fall,
> We sinned all."

I have the happiness to possess the first 199 pages of that precious boon you have just bestowed on the world.

It is an honor and a homage to every true lover of learning when such testimonials are given by great Nations like yours to those who are in truth man's teachers and guides.

Farewell, most excellent sir: that honor and happiness may attend your every step, is the prayer of

Your most respectful and

most grateful servant,

CH. D. MEIGS, M. D.,

Emeritus Professor in Jefferson College.

1210 WALKUT STREET,
PHILADELPHIA, February 18,1869.

TYPHAINES ABBEY.

CHAPTER I

AN August sun was pouring down vast floods of radiant light and heat all over the wide-spread glade that lay there bounded by a lofty and dense wall of oaks, chestnuts, birches, and other secular giants of that dark and gloomy wold.

The huge forest trees were crowded to their topmost spray with a maze of vines and creepers and twisted climbers, whose thickly tufted volutes gave intenser expression to the shade below, where beneath their verdant canopies sprung in wild profusion, myriads of grasses, weeds, and tall ferns that half buried the prostrate trunks of mighty ancient monarchs of the woods, now mouldering there under a pall of exuberant vegetation. Here might be seen a huge rock lifting its enormous rifted summit all over mottled with many-hued lichens from among the decaying trunks at its feet, while there an ancient fir looked not unlike a broken bridge just where its top was still upheld by a couple of great ash trees as aged as itself. And all around these monuments the place was thick sown with bushes, ferns, heather, and tall wild weeds that seemed inclined to emulate the lofty columns above them, so vigorous was their green and luxuriant growth.

In all this majestic solitude not a sound fell on the ear

2   13

save the silver song of a streamlet, clear as purest crystal, as it fled hastily onwards, wiuding in and out over its bed of bright sand, gleaming, hiding, and flashing out by turns, now plashing among many colored pebbles and stones, and again rushing among broken masses that vainly strove to check its mutinous career.

The spring that gave birth to the brook lay off at some distance over the green, where it burst forth at the foot of a low hill.

The rude workmen, of many centuries ago, had covered in the fountain by means of three tall unhewn stone slabs, two of which served as walls, and the third laid across the top as a solid roof, which rustic though it was stood nevertheless a mark of their respect. So then it seems that this daughter of the wild woods must have had friends of her own, even so long ago, among the children of men ! Yes, friends—and better than that, timorous worshippers ! a ready inference—seeing the care taken by the clergy of old, who had set up on the roof a rude stone effigy of the holy St. Procul, who was the original missionary and apostle of conversion to that idolatrous population, centuries ago.

In those remote ages, the wild sparkling fountain, free as its own bright element, might well have dispensed with a patron saint. She was a divinity in her own right. Under the outward form of a beautiful girl, she was said to have made these woods a fearful place, by seducing any too rash invading huntsman, and even by now and then drowning one of her lovers. A reputation so equivocal as that might have well drawn on her the suspicious regards of the ecclesiastical authorities, nor was it less than sound common sense to provide the fair maiden with a powerful meutor, who might put a bridle on her extravagances. Even Saint Procul himself was nothing more than just equal to the task; his very cross and stole could hardly keep her quiet to her work, so that even now people shivered as they told how master Luke, the carpenter, brother Maclou, the bailiff, and (horresco referens) one of Lord de Pornes' own sons, happening most rashly to pass after sunset, too near the fairy's spring, were suddenly plunged heels over head into the water, and almost strangled to death !

Now, what could blessed St. Procul be about, while his neophyte was playing such wicked gambols ? It's quite clear that a saint, such as he, must have had charge of more than a bare one penitent, and so the mischievous fairy might take advantage of his occasional absence to indulge in her diabolical pranks. At last, about the beginning of the twelfth century, when Louis VI., commonly called Louis le Gros, was king, and in a remote corner of the Nivernais, where it bordered on Champagne, where our story is laid, things had reached such a pass that to brave the vicinity of St. Procul's Spring after sundown, was considered an act of temerity that might well lead to the most disastrous consequences.

It was on that bright August day, then, at about three o'clock in the afternoon, that you might have seen strolling along the blind path that led across the green prairie from out the dark and dreadful wood, a well-made active-looking man, who seemed to be walking slowly onwards, and very busily looking all around, as if in search of something. Anywhere else than in so desert a spot he would have hardly attracted a look, but in the midst of such a solemn vast and silent nature, the appearance of any human being is a thing not to be disregarded even by the haughtiest and most disdainful observer. The coming man was dressed in a black and white goat-skin frock, with the hair outside. The rude garment was close drawn about his

waist, by means of a yellow leather strap, at which hung a
scrip, a sheaf of arrows, and on the left side a long bare-
bladed knife, with a wooden handle. The rawhide sandals
on his feet gave a moderate protection against the briers
on his path. As to his head, there was no other coveriug
but its forest of crisp chestnut curls, that certainly had
never known the comb. The savage-looking huntsman
held an ashen bow in his hand. There's little to be said about
his features, which conformed with the rude appearance of
his arms and dress; they were rough enough, and clothed on
with that subdued gravity so characteristic of a sort
of majestic stolidity in the being whose face is ever un-
moved by the variable emotions of an intellectual soul.
He looked as if between twenty-five and thirty years of
age. The light red beard was as matted as his hair; long
mustachios giving a brutal soldierly look, reached their sharp
points as far down as his shoulders, after the fashion of
our Frankish ancestors; and lastly a pair of dull gray eyes,
announced a creature devoted to the superstitions no less
than to the impetuous passions of the savage.

While we are looking at him, he has strolled across the
wide green meadow, got beyond the golden sunlight, and
was already in shadow close to where the path led into the
heart of the wood, when suddenly he stopped short,
and his strained eyes took on a terrible expression of
mistrust and rage.

" What are you about there, you thieving villains," cried
he, passing his bow instantly from the right to the left hand,
and clutching the knife with the right.

"Well, what then," said an insolent voice; "are people not allowed to walk about in these woods ?"

"Walkabout? Yes; but not to cut down the limbs,
and steal the wood, and that's the very thing you are
after."

Hardly had he spoken, when a dozen stout fellows sprang to their feet out of the thicket, and hurried forwards to support the man who had answered our traveller so boldly. They all, as they stood there in their coarse gray smock-frocks, looked stout and strong, while the chopping axes in every man's hand, and their great bushy beards gave them a very determined look.

Standing with his band around him, the wood thief spoke again.

" Come now, Rigauld ! don't be cross. It was only yesterday and you might force us to look at the forest as a thing of terror, and we would no more have dared so much as to touch it than were it the shaven crown of the very least of the Abbey brethren over yonder. To-day, things are on another footing; so, lest you should take the trouble to get into an unprofitable passion, I'd have you to know that threats and wrath are not worth a rush with a set of men determined to make use of their hands to show who is the stronger, you or we here. Eh 1 by my truly, Rigauld; people iu paradise used to cut their wood wherever they chose ; there were neither Abbots nor mouks in those days."

"You lie in your throat!" briefly replied the hunter, without regard to the number of his adversaries, " and you shall soon find out in the Abbey dungeon, that such scum as you are not allowed to lay their hands ou what belongs to their betters."

The jeering peasant at once began to make his axe fly round and round above his head.

"Oh, ho! Rigauld," said he, "you think to make a dozen such stout comrades as we all tramp just as you please! Were you monseigneur the Count de Nevers himself, on his biggest charger, wrapt all up in mail, you couldn't speak out bolder. Come on, then, you braggart, and let me show you that your knife isn't master, face to face, with a dozen chopping-axes!"

Rigauld shook his head like an insulted bull, and with a single bound fell on his opponent, who, unprepared as he was for so sudden an assault, felt the terrible grip of his enemy at his throat; he was choking already: at the same instant, that sharp uplifted blade was about to strike him dead : the other peasants rushed up quite sure of at least avenging their spokesman by exterminating the Abbot's bold huntsman, when all of a sudden there rose up from the tall grass, near by the angry group, a strange figure murmuring with a strangling voice !

"Help! Rigauld l Help."

To this outcry the peasants responded by exclamations of terror, and suddenly turned and fled. Rigauld's hand dropped down without striking, and let go the fellow he was choking, who as soon as he was free, and active as a deer, plunged at once into the thickest depths of the forest. As to the guard, there he stood stock still, his mouth agape, his eyes bursting from their sockets, his face all horror-struck, and he unable to move a single step.

But no fear of a mere mortal enemy could have troubled him so. He had just thrown himself without the least fear on an antagonist supported by a dozen comrades. One champion more to fight, would have been nothing to make him give back. No l but the voice he had just heard was so strangling and hoarse, so strange—that lump, or whatever it was, lying there in the tall grass, and which his horror-struck eyes could not make out—looked so sinister— and what'8 more, it was such a fearful place, this St. Procul's Spring, that it were hard to feel surprised at the appearance of even the most dreadful apparition. That it was that chilled the very blood in Rigauld's veins.

Meanwhile the terrible phantom that had fallen back

again among the tall herbage, uttered no articulate sound; nothing save low and plaintive moans. In the course of a few moments, Rigauld, who found that he had as yet suffered no attack, began partly to recover his presence of mind, and with a trembling voice, asked—

" Art thou man ? art thou ?" murmured he. 44 Art thou demon ?"

14 Help!" replied the lugubrious voice. 441 am an unfortunate monk; they have murdered me."

The suspicious forester muttered twixt his teeth :—

44 It's one of the demon's tricks; if I go near him he will iump on me and strangle me to death."

Had he dared to run, it is likely that he would have asked no questions, and fled from the haunted spot, but he was afraid to retreat lest he should be assailed in the rear, and so he spoke.

44 Monk, who was it murdered you f'

44 The robber band in the woods there:—art thou not Rigauld f "

441 am Rigauld," answered the woodman, and venturing a few steps nearer, the better to see the object of his terror: he cried out in his astonishment:—

44 Why I it's father Nicolas 1"

Before him lay the horridest sight his eyes had ever beheld. The poor Monk's frock was all rent and torn in a thousand places, soiled with earth and mud, and bits of grass and broken reeds, as if he had been dragged along the ground, and had not fallen without a struggle. His naked breast was gashed with a blow from a wood-axe. Numerous wounds of the head and neck made it almost impossible to know him, so steeped and stained was he with his still fast flowing blood. On his hands, his arms, and legs, Rigauld saw nothing but gashes; they had chopped him to pieces.

" It is father Nicolas," repeated he. " I know him by his long gray beard."

The sight of the Monk all hacked as he was and horrible to behold, were a mere trifle to the savage forester in comparison with the very smallest of the devilkins in the bottomless pit.

He kneeled down among the ferns by the Monk's side and spoke.

" Were you fighting with the peasantry, father?"

" No. I was riding along on my mule;—they were cutting down a noble fir ;—I tried to strike them ;—they have murdered me—I am dying now."

" Who struck the first blow ? Tell me, for I will revenge you."

" It was,"—said the Monk in a feeble tone," it was Pierre the blacksmith at Grand Clos."

" I," said Rigauld," recognized Eustache the ploughman among them."

" Yes, he was there too. Ah, Jesus, my God! I shall die without confession."

" If you had only had a little more patience," said Rigauld," I would have killed him for you ; but as soon as ever they heard you speak they all ran off, no doubt because they thought you were coming to."

" Oh!" spoke the Monk, his eyes already beginning to glaze, " why must I die out here;—which way is the Abbey ?—my own cell! I would like to die in my own cell!—My sins are great—but I have expiated them all —*Miserere Mei Domine* !"

He sighed heavily, and crossing his hands on his breast began a fervent prayer.

Rigauld kneeling in the grass bent over his form.

"Father, shall I carry you to the Abbey? I can carry

you on my back, and perhaps we may get there time enough."

"Two long leagues!—No.—I should die on the road. No. It's too far!—Oh, my Holy Patron! who would have thought of all this *f*"

" At any rate," resumed the forester, " you shall be sorely revenged. The Typhaines peasantry will talk for long about your death! His reverence the Abbot will not let a scamp of them go unpunished !"

"No!" replied the Monk with difficulty.—"I forgive them.—I am now under the religious habit.—But it is a very hard thing for a man of my lineage," and the aged Monk began to pray again in a low tone.

" I'll go to the spring and get some water for you, and wash off some of the blood from your face, father."

" Go, my son, and if you find me dead on your return —bear witness that i fell a martyr in defending the rights Of the Church.—My God! this is a great grace thou hast vouchsafed unto me!"

Father Nicolas began to pray again. Rigauld rose from his knees and ran to the spring, whence making his scrip serve by way of bucket, be brought a supply of the liquid. The Monk was still alive, but his eyes were closed, aod his lips, that alone were moving, murmured a whispered Orison.

" If only some one would happen to come by," thought the guard, " we could soon rig up a stretcher, and by a fast walk or even at a run an hour would be enough to bring us to the Abbey, and console this poor father who is dying here like a mere infidel, without the least bit or crumb of absolution."

Rigauld looked all around, but not a soul could he see in the whole immense clearing; and now the hunter, finding himself alone in this way, began to grow uneasy again.

Just as the thought struck him, the father once more opened his eyes, " Give me—some water," said he.

Higauld took up a few drops in his palm and poured them on the dying man's lips, and next tried to wash away some of the blood that begrimed the whole face and head. This process, which gave him a clearer view of the horrible wounds made by the peasant's chopping-axes, convinced him that it was no use to stay any longer, and he expressed his wish to be gone.

" You can't live much longer, father; I can do you no good, and as for you, in a few minutes you'll have nothing to fear. Let me go then, and do you die here quietly; your murderers shall get their dues, I promise you, and that is a thought that ought to comfort you, say what you will about it."

" Don't leave me," replied the Monk in a suppliant tone.

" I can't do anything for you," rejoined Rigauld with a frown, and casting a timid glance towards the witches' spring.

" It is hard to die here alone"—and a moment afterwards —"you are right," said he. "Go, then—take a packet of letters out of my frock.—That's, well—that's the one! Carry the letters to the Reverend Abbot—he will find that I did fulfil my mission; I should have been happy could I have met with a better success.—Go now—my death is but the beginning of many crimes. The Lord's House is in danger; tell the Abbot I die a true believer in all the Church teaches. Tell him.—Begone, the day is closing. Perhaps the Abbey is already in peril. Run—tell the Abbot to have prayers said for my soul."

Rigauld thought the poor father must be raving; he put the letter with its red seal in his bosom, and went off without once looking back and without the least remorse for the cruel precipitation with which he had left the dying man all alone. The fact was, he saw the snn was near going down, and though night was not on him quite yet, he dreaded the idea of being caught by the twilight in such a fearful place. So he hurried on in the gloomy track as it wound beneath the limbs of the trees, and unhesitatingly plunged into a dark labyrinth in which he felt far safer than he would have been near that limpid spring.

He went onwards until he came to a cross-roads, and there, as he heard the tramp of several horses on the 6bort greensward, he turned and saw advancing on his right four cavaliers that he who was in the habit of meeting all the gentlemen hunters in the neighborhood, could not make out as belonging to that part of the country. For some time he gazed at them with a distrustful curiosity.

At the head of the cavalcade rode a handsome young man, for he looked not more than twenty-five or twenty-six years of age, who wore a hauberk of iron mail, over which was a surcoat of green cloth with a small red cross sewn on the shoulder. The Knight, for from his equipment he was evidently a Knight, was coiffed with a black plush hood; on his neck was a gold chaiu and heavy gold spurs at his heels. A broad heavy high hilted sword hung from an embroidered leathern belt. His hands, as well as his thighs and legs, were encased in mail. No one ever beheld a more resolute and spirited physiognomy than that of this handsome Seigneur; large, dark, beautiful, well opened eyes, nearly on the face level, and bright as a brand, were all aglow with intelligence and fire; exquisite teeth; cheeks imbrowned by the wind and the sun—all these and a close curling beard—he looked the very model of a warrior.

Next behind the Knight, mounted on a vigorous Flanders roadster, came a big burly looking individual, stout and square of build, and blind of one eye, who seemed to be not at all inclined by any evidences of good temper to evince

his gratitude to his mother nature, for so large an endowment with brawn and bone, or the incomparable strength
revealed in every iota of his outward man. This giant,
this Caligorant's crabbed sullen visage was half hidden in
a thicket of red beard. Like his master, he too was covered
with mail, but wore no surcoat. On the right of his amiable figure was an enormous dagger, and on the left a sword
still more enormous; while a massive battle-axe swung
from the pommel. His dexter hand bore a couple of spears,
one of which surmounted with a blue pennon was blazoned,
a lion rampant argent, his master's arms; with the left
hand he managed his powerful steed.

In the rear of this tragical looking figure, and in evident
awe of his vinegar scowl, came on a pair of pages, one of
them thirteen or fourteen and the other of some sixteen
summers, bearing the Knight's helm and buckler blazoned
like the pennon.

The two boys, who when out of the old squire's sight, must
have been a precious pair of blusterers, also wore armor of
mail and had steel caps on their heads.

As soon as he observed Rigauld, the gentleman put
the question that never fails the lips of a traveller upon
meeting a countryman.

"Halloo, fellow," cried he, "how far to Typhaines
Abbey ?"

" A league, monseigneur. "

" Thank you, we shall get there in time then. But, God's-
blood! what is all this I see, master rascal ? Blood on
your dress *t"*

" What 1 Blood I Have I blood on me ?"

"You are all covered with it," rejoined the Knight.

The fact is, Rigauld could not have been kneeling down
by the dying Monk without staining his clothes with great
staring purple splotches.

44 He's been killing and robbing some one," pot in the old Squire in a sententious tone.

14You lie!" replied the guard; "you are more of a murderer than I am."

44 Shall I split his skull open ?" inquired the giant, passing his hand towards the battle-axe.

44 No, Fulk, not just yet, let me interrogate him first."

44 Answer me now, whence this blood that stains you so?"   :

44It's a Monk's; it's father Nicolas's blood, who was murdered just now, about a league from here, close to Saint Procul's Spring, by a set of mutinous burghers, and I am on my way to the Abbey to tell them about it."

44 What 1 How long is it since your yilains hereabout broke out in insurrection ? God's-death 1 I am sorry for you all; l am familiar with that kind of scourge and know what it costs with vermin of that sort. No reasoning for them equal to blows."

44 That's the very fact," muttered Fulk, in his moustache, nodd:)g his head with an air of conviction.

The Knight resumed

44 Thou shalt show me the way; I am going to the Abbey too; walk close to my horse."

44 Willingly !"

This brief reply, given with no hurry or the least sign of confusion, seemed to lessen the Knight's suspicions, who began a familiar chat with the forester.

44 So then, you say your burrougbmen are in a state of mutiny! Are they already crying out for the *commune* ?"

44 Commune ? what do you mean by commune ?"

44 He knows nothing about that," said Fulk, with an indulgent glance at his master.

44 The commune, my lad !" cried the Knight. 44 Why, it is the most abominable invention that the devil ever let

3

loose in the world for the eternal damnation of poor peasant folk. Whenever the Tempter gets very hungry for
Jacques Bonhomme's soul, he begins to whisper in his ear,
telling him what a nice thing it wonld be to have no more
taxes to pay, to be ordered on no more corvees; not to be
compelled to obey anybody; to walk abont, right or left,
just like a gentleman or a clerk. Such an idea being pure
and simply scandalous and absurd, of course he takes it up.
So the clodpolls with commune in their heads run about
preaching that all men are equal—one man just as good as
another. To all this I have only one answer, and that is
that the bishops should excommunicate every propa-
gator of such lies, that nobody believes in, not even the
insurgents themselves."

" They don't believe a word of it," said Fulk.

" As soon as the demon's suggestions have got fair hold,"
continued the Knight, " the clodhoppers begin to stir, and
it naturally follows that their Seigneurs can't allow them
to keep such notions in their numbskulls. So they go to
work, snatching at any weapon in reach of their paws, and
as if really possessed by the devil, crowd to their towns and
burghs, running hither and thither, and howling out 'Commune! commune!' The more they shout the more people
they massacre: they devour little children; rip up women's
bellies, and behave just like excommunicates, as they are
in fact."

" They've killed father Nicolas," muttered Rigauld, in
corroboration of the Knight.

" They've played the devil wherever they happened to
break out. Look, my lad, they put out Fulk's eye there
only five years ago."

" They put out my eye," gravely added the Squire.

" Then we shall have a fight; so much the better," put
in Rigauld.

As the travellers were talking in this way, they issued from the forest, and coming to a heathery plain, looked out before them and beheld, on a rocky eminence, the Abbey of Typhaines, and the Burgh far below, that looked as if it were crawling at the feet of the sacred edifice.

CHAPTER IL

A SINGLE glance at the Abbey might well satisfy the highest expectations of an approaching pilgrim to that holy sanctuary.

At the summit of a rocky hill, where the two branches of a broad valley came down to spread over the wide fertile plain, it stood all alone, like a strong fortress resting as it were on a firm pedestal. Its massive belfry, towers and lofty walls of reddish stone, filled the beholder with respect, while his admiration swelled at the aspect of the wide and varied landscape, that stretched out in every direction at the feet of this venerable house of God. To the west, the sloping hill fell downwards to the margin of a deep, narrow stream, whose banks were choked with reeds and rushes, and other aquatic plants, the favorite resort of thrushes, fish-hawks and various birds, among them an occasional heron, that rose heavenwards with flapping wings and loud screams, as he sought the airy fields above. A bridge with two narrow and strong arches, for it was built of huge blocks of hewn stone, served as communication between the abbey and its town below; for the Burgh of Typhaines was on the farther shore of the stream, —grouped in the broader plain, its narrow streets crowded with the abodes of the burghers and peasantry that seemed as if shrinking into the smallest possible magnitude, like a man panic-stricken or suffering under the condensing power of an ague-fit.

It certainly was a considerable town, and really deserved to be called a city, for from the height down whose slope the Knight, with his companions guided by Rigauld, was now descending, among the cabins of the rustics and other more pretentious buildings, they looked down on two larger structures that alone evinced the importance of the Bourg de Typhaines. One of them was a small church edifice, the other a stern square structure, which was neither more nor less than the Abbey-gaol; to deserve a more honorable title, nothing was wanting to the Burgh but a proper provision of ramparts fit for offence as well as defence. The view before him of the Abbey, the town, and flourishing fields, so much better cultivated than lands belonging to the secular seigneurs of the time—the whole scene, indeed, heightened the Knight's rapture and admiration so, that, checking his steed, he exclaimed, in his enthusiasm:—

" Good God ! This, then, is the celebrated Abbey of Typhaines ! This the abode of that holy Abbot, Anselm ; the spot so renowned by that virtue and pure piety of his ! Yonder, too, stands the glorious church, the tomb of so many venerable personages, so many illustrious knights, and, among them, even as many as three of my own honored ancestors ! As for me, I can now well comprehend that love that impelled so many gentlemen to enrich the worthy monastery, and I cannot die in peace unless I too shall be enabled to bequeath her some portion of my own domain. I suppose, forester, that the whole of the country before me belongs to yon glorious Abbey ?"

" Oh, monseigneur," replied the hunter, his eyes sparkling with pride, " though your view extends very far from this spot, yon cannot yet see the outer bounds of our fiefs !"

" I am glad of that," growled the man-at-arms ; " never can the masters be as rich as I could wish them to be—and it's safe for you to say, they have not a warmer friend or more devoted servant than I am. And so, yonder auda* cious Burgh is so bold as to venture into a quarrel with this noble mansion, and insolent burghers dare to threaten its holy monks l Will they go to murdering their pious seigneurs ?"

" Have a little patience," rejoined the hunter. "I know the names of the guilty, and the reverend Abbot will surely have them all executed. Besides, in case he should hap* pen to forget the knaves, didn't I promise Father Nicolas to take vengeance for him ? I swear to you that his poor soul need not give itself the trouble to come back to this world and put me in mind of my engagement."

" You'll be a lucky dog," said Fulk, "and your Abbot too, if the rustics who committed that crime should agree to be captured like sheep, and suffer their throats to be cut, without a single bleat. As to me who am pretty well acquainted with that sort of cattle, I rather think Master Jacques Bonhomme has a very sharp set of teeth, and knows how to bite too. Try him, and you'll be ready to swear that the idolatrous Saracens themselves have the most angelic tempers compared with a set of peasants and burghers in open insurrection."

Rigauld appeared to not very clearly understand the Squire's meaning, or at any rate, to care very little what he was talking about. At first he looked at him with an air of surprise, and then, after shaking his fist, turned away and began to whistle.

Again the Knight broke the silence

" Tell me now, after all, what about this Abbott Anselm, who, after what I have heard about him, I am ready to pronounce a great saint and the very best man in the whole world. I must confess, bold huntsman, that I am on my way to yonder Abbey for the purpose of treating with him about a matter of great importance to myself, and I would explain it to you if I had time. I wish I could satisfy myself beforehand that I am to meet a hearty welcome and my business too."

" Faith I" responded Rigauld, " provided you don't know Abbot Anselm better than that, there must be very little news where you came from ! Ah, you ought to have seen the Abbey when under Abbot Ranulph's charge, if you would know the difference. Abbot Anselm certainly is a saint, a real saint I Whenever I find myself in his presence, I begin to tremble as if in the presence of God himself. E verybody knows he is wiser than any magician, and that if he chose to do it, all he would have to do to summon before him all the devils in hell— only just let him open one of his big books. It is a fact that he has worked miracles. I am not going to tell you about them, for here we are at the gate—but he did work miracles ; so, if what you want is all square and fair, you may feel quite safe—for he will do it for ye in a trice."

" Thank you for your information," answered the Knight " And to show you how well I am pleased with the good hopes you give me, here, take this purse, and buy you a good sheaf of arrows, or a pot of wine—what you will."

The forester put the money into his scrip, and the little troop, now at the summit of the rock, pnssed on through the great gate, into the interior of the wealthy Abbey of Typhaines.

It was easy to perceive at the very first sight, that Rigauld had by no means exaggerated the hospitable disposition of the Monks within. Two of them, though still environed by a mendicant crowd, were busily engaged in the yard with the stated distribution of provisions, and the wretched gang were dispersing, some carrying off their jugs of beer, their loaves, their fruit and slices of bacon. Farther off, you might see people on crutches, and all sorts of lame folk just coming, with bandaged head or arm, out of the leech's office, who was still busy giving and enforcing his last injunctions, as they crawled on with that piteous look so peculiar to a clodhopper when he thinks he is sick.

On discovering the Knight, two of the lay brethren hastily advanced to greet him.

" Brethren," said the Kpight, " I salute you. I have to beg your hospitality,, which I venture to hope will not be refused me."

" This holy house is never so unjust as that," replied one of the monks. " How then should she dare to refuse a soldier of the Cross? Come in, Monseigneur, come in with all assurance of welcome. Pray, alight, and while the Father Abbot gives welcome to you and your company, allow me to take charge of your horses, and see them well cared for."

The Crusader did not give the Monk the trouble to renew his invitation, but leaping to the ground, and his men, as well, they followed one of the brothers appointed to conduct them into the presence of the great ecclesiastical lord.

The travellers followed their guide through long, low, dark cloisters, and mounted more than one stairway. The Abbey had not been built by a single architect, nor in accordance with a single plan, so that, at various periods, new buildings and even entire wings had been added to the original pile. To effect easy communication betwixt the old and the newer parts of the monastery, it must have severely taxed the invention of the new builders to supply infinite passages, corridors, and stairs. They had almost converted it into a labyrinth.

On the second story, at the end of a wide gallery looking out on an inner court, the lay brother opened what looked like a cellar door, to give admission to the newcomers. It opened into the Abbot's room. A look showed what the abode of that puissant dignitary was. It was a stone cell, some twelve feet square, with a ceiling so low as to prevent any one from standing erect in it. The light came in through a loophole in a very thick wall, and let in an oblique and imperfect beam. Beneath the pale ray of light was an oaken table unfamiliar with the plane, standing on rough posts, and loaded with huge volumes, diplomas with their parti-colored seals, and parchments, some of them still blank, and others covered with that large, strange, angular writing characteristic of the age. A few pens, ink-stained and ragged, sticking in a vast leaden inkstand enthroned above the chaos, imparted a proper finish to its severe physiognomy. In front of the table stood a wooden stool, quite as rough as its major pendant. Off in the darkest corner of the room lay a couple of bundles of straw upon the stone floor, which was deemed bed and pillow sufficient. A wooden crucifix secured to the wall dominated above this terriblo couch, and a discipline garnished with long, sharp iron points, hung close by the image of God the Saviour.

As the visitors made their appearance, they saw the Father Abbot, who, doubtless deep in meditation, stood leaning against the wall, his tall figure bent forwards, the arms crossed on his bosom, and the eyes downcast towards the flagstone floor. The A bbot, seeing the strangers, with a grave smile at once advanced to meet them on the gallery, where they had kneeled, so that, stretching forth his hands above them, they received the benediction.

" Holy Father," said the Crusader, " I am come hither to commend me to your good grace, and demand a boon at your hands, the very greatest the world could give me. But God's work should take precedence of mine, and here is a forester whom I met on my way, and have brought hither to disclose to your holiness a sad and most dangerous event."

At these words, and as if news of a new misfortune might be by no means unexpected, the father turned towards Rigauld, who stood humbly in the background at the end of the gallery, holding in his outstretched hand the blood-stained missive of Father Nicolas.

" Well, Rigauld," said he, " what is this letter and what the misfortune you are come to announce ?"

Rigauld presented the letter, and said :—

" Father Nicolas has just now been killed by some of the burghmen."

The lay brothers turned pale. The Abbot displayed no sign of emotion, or at most, an imperceptible tremor might be seen about his thin, compressed lips. He opened the dispatch, read it rapidly through, and then slowly folding it again, turned to address the Knight:—

" You are come to our house, my son, at a painful moment. Be not, however, less welcome on that account, and whatever may be the motive of your visit, if a poor monk, as I am, can do anything for your contentment, I promise you beforehand that your wishes shall be gratified. I shall give orders to let you want for nothing here. But the duties of courtesy may not, by your permission, compel me to postpone others not less imperious for persons of my rank in this Abbey. When I shall have performed a painful task, I shall be ready to hearken to you." He next spoke to Rigauld:—

" Take with you four of my valets, and let a couple of the lay brethren accompany you to find and bring in the body of our unfortunate brother, in order that it may receive burial in conformity with the rites of the Church."

As the Abbot uttered these words amid the profoundest silence of every auditor, loud outcries suddenly broke on the ear, hurried footsteps resounded along the cloisters, and, mingled with groans of distress, rose up and reached even the distant cell of the Christian priest.

The Knight, his head stored with souvenirs of burgher insurrections, cried out:—

" How now, hoi 7 father? Can it be that your townsfolk have broke out in sudden rebellion ? As I passed by near the outer town, I observed nothing calculated to excite suspicion."

''Let us not be alarmed," quietly spoke the Abbot.

" Let us go forth, and learn the meaning of this tumult. "

11 If your serfs break out," said the Crusader, striking his portentous sword with bis hand, 41 you may count upon her, holy father. Rudaverse is a good Christian, and she won't sleep quiet in her scabbard."

" There's nothing I'd like better than a chance to teach the clod polls what a nice thing it is to have only one eye left," added Fulk.

"My dear children," responded the Abbot, "I give thanks for your zeal; but, no doubt, we shall not be under the necessity of putting it to the proof. Patience and mansuetude are arms stronger than yours—follow me."

The tumult was still swelling, and, step by step, ran through every portion of the monastery. As he passed onwards along the cloisters, the Abbott saw door after door opening, and the astonished and terrified monks coming out of their cells to join him and ask for information from their spiritual father.

" I know no more what it all means than you do, my children, but we shall know what it is in a few minutes."

In this way, surrounded by his flock, and attended by the Knight and his people, the Prelate stepped out into the yard, where a scene was presented fit to melt all hearts. Lying on the ground, surrouuded by lay brethren and valets, who were lifting up their hands to heaven and uttering lugubrious cries, lay stretched a corpse dressed in the monastic frock of the order, that had been just brought in by five of the townspeople. One of them, who appeared to be their head man, was holding a horse by the bridle.

To understand the course of this history, it is indispensable for the reader to take a good look at the last-named personage. He wore a coarse, brown serge dress, and was armed with merely a short cutlass with a born handle. A leathern purse hung from his belt, close to the warlike implement, and he is coiffed in a red cloth hood of the plainest sort. Although dressed in this humble guise, which announced nothing more or less than a merchant of the period, the man, who looked some fifty years of age or more, evinced in the traits of his countenance a firm expression of rude boldness. His darkly tanned features, massive and square, embrowned by exposure to the sun and the wind, are lighted by piercing eyes, that look fearful beneath their restless gray eyebrows. He is not a tall man, but visibly he is strong as an athlete, and his motions evince a quickness amounting to temerity. Seeing the Abbot come forward, he uncovered, but did not bend the knee, a thing that excited universal surprise there, and gave rise to some murmuring.

"Holy father," said the burgher, not in the least embarrassed, "as I was on my way home from the fair at Troyes, we foimd this monk in the woods, and thought it best to bring him"here to you. He was dead."

"Are you very sure of that?" asked the Abbot, in a severe tone.

" Do you mean that you are suspecting me ?" the merchant spoke out haughtily.

^ " God forbid," returned the priest, " that I should accuse any man, save upon clearest evidence, you or any one else, of having taken the life of a human being; yet, and I tell you frankly, I do not hold that the man alone that drives the steel is a murderer; the evil counsellor guides the arm, and is no less guilty of the crime than he who stabs."

"I understand you not, holy father," replied the burgher, with the same provoking tone. "Besides, I am nowise disposed to hide my thoughts. Perhaps this monk here drew down upon him his misfortunes by some insolent act of oppression."

" Shall I strike him down ?" said Fulk, looking at his master.

The Knight arrested his squire's hand, which was already on the dagger-hilt with a clutch, and in the mean time the Abbot gave answer to master Simon, the cloth-merchant, in a gentle and sorrowful tone.

" Learn, my son, and meditate on these words of Holy Writ, 'Woe unto him by whom offence cometh !' You have just now insulted the memory of our unfortunate brother lying there, and I, as your temporal Lord, might lawfully execute justice on you for that outrage. I know, too, yes, I well know, the seditious harangues you often make to excite our burghers and serfs against us, breathing with all the power you can wield, an evil spirit into their feeble souls. I fear much that the demon has blinded your heart and mind, to the end that he may at last crush you beneath the ruins of the guilty edifice you are striving to erect. At this very moment, with menace in your eyes, and with insult ready to rise to your lips, you cast down at our feet the mutilated body of one of our people. Take heed—take heed, lest the same stones now red with the blood of the righteous, rise not up at some future day to testify against you ¹"

4

The merchant erected his head with an air of defiance, as he heard these words, and with a contemptuous stare at the monastic crowd around him, he spoke

" Is this then your gratitude ? Menaces when I bring yon body home to you I Bah I The monks, I fear, have forgotten the very simplest virtues, and are greatly in want of some reform."

" By the Holy Cross!" exclaimed Fulk to his master, " I feel I am a sinner until I shall perform some act of faith !"

He suddenly drew his dagger, and stretched out his hand to take hold of Master Simon. But the Abbot 6trode before the squire, and in a severe voice, " Withdraw," he said. 11 And you, Master Simon, go in peace, but if your conscience troubles you, rest assured you shall be punished."

The merchant answered not a word, and at once passed out at the great gate, laughing a^ond, along with his companions. The Abbot and the monks kneeled down around Father Nicolas* corpse.

CHAPTER **in.**

WHILE the monks were engaged in prayer, Rigauld and the other valets following their example, as well as they knew how, the Knight turned to Fulk, and whispered :—

" The good fathers are chanting an office for the dead, but it were quite as well for them to be thinking about some measures of defence. Thou sawest how pleased Master Simon and his comrades looked, and how sure of compassing their ends ? Could we but get a peep into their hive just now, we would find the bees not at work on their honey-comb—but sharpening their stings the rather."

1 think so, too," said Fulk, " and it would be well for us to begin the fray. A few well-put thrusts and cuts readily reduces a mutinous burgher to his duty. They never are indomitable except when they are first to begin. Go and request the Father Abbot to lend you his men-at-arms. "

" He hasn't any," replied the Crusader, scanning the yard and the adjoining walls. " I see no soldiers. Hoods and frocks in plenty, but not so much as a helmet. It seems to me that we happened here in good time—for if there should be a fight, we alone are stout enough to stand the shock, and that gives a chance to do the Abbot such good service that, even were he so inclined, he could not, after the victory, decently reject the demand I came here to make. So everything is in my favor, and please God, I wish the vilains would soon stir. But come, I am cu-

rious to see the poor dead monk that those wretches killed
to try their hands."

The Abbot had risen from his knees, and some of the
lay brothers having provided a bier, several monks respectfully took Father Nicolas up in their arms, and after un-
covering his face, laid him down on it upon a white cloth.
Others stood ready to lift the sacred burden to their
shoulders, while yet others hastened forward to throw open
the church doors. Just at that instant the Knight came
up to look at the corpse.

The feeling that brought him there was doubtless one
of curiosity pure and simple; he had but small tinge of
the horror produced by such sights in our times; the customs of the twelfth century inspired no very great degree
of delicacy. In those old times blood was blood, and
nothing more, that is to«say, a thing of no great importance, only a dead body : nothing but a sad-looking object,
a disagreeable occurrence, which everybody, especially
soldier folk, ought to expect on his own account. The Crusader's eyes, therefore, gave expression to a mere common^
pity when they first rested on the features of the victim.
But scarcely had he begun to look upon it when a sudden
expression of terror, grief, and rage broke forth, and the
Knight's countenance becaino wholly changed.

" Ah !" exclaimed the youth. " Am I gone mad ? Is
it a vertigo I have ? Tell me, is it really a monk, is it one
of your companions I behold here before me ? Answer
me, oh, holy father. Who is this man lying here slain ?
Is it not Messire Geoffroy ? It cannot be my father ?
Oh, monseigneur, my honored parent, it is thou indeed !"

The Crusader threw himself on the body and began to
sob, crying out aloud, weeping and uttering broken words
that could not be understood by the people about him.
Fulk went up to his master like a hound passionately

attached, and he, too, looked at the dead face of Father Nicolas. Fulk nodded his head with a solemn air, and, as if he deemed his master's sorrow too legitimate to allow of his intervention, let his arms drop, locked his fingers, and stood silently gazing on bis prostrate lord.

The Crusader's cries and despairiug gestures were very surprising to the whole assembly of spectators. The monks, lay brethren, and valets began to whisper to each other their different opinions as to an adventure so unexpected ; but the Abbot, laying his hand softly on the Knight's shoulder, said :—

"Have courage, my son. Are you sure that your grief does not deceive you ? May it not be that a false resemblance is the only and frivolous cause of your sorrow ? Are you quite certain that this is your father ? The man you embrace with such filial devotion was known as Father Nicolas, though h£ once bore the name of Messire Geoffroy de Cornehaut."

"Ah, monseigneur, my dear father," resumed the young man, with streaming eyes, "there was no need of further certainty. I knew but too well it was thee whom I hold in embrace on this funeral pall. Oh, most redoubted and dear lord, heaven has punished me now because I did not at once fly to bear you the news of my return, and prefer to your embraces other ties, however legitimate they might be. Ah, my Jesus! Why did I not follow at once the path that led to ray paternal castle ? Why did I come hither ?"

"Because you would not hear a word I said," said Fulk.

The groans of the unhappy young man for some minutes stifled every word he tried to utter, and then he cried again:—

"But it is my father ! I left him full of life and ardor, bearing old age as lightly as his armor ı I left him, a true knight, renowned, illustrious, admired, adding day by day to the honor of our house, and here he now lies, a monk, and a silent corpse I" He buried his face in his hands.

Had Fulk, who was of a calmer temper than his master, been in possession of even a very little power of observation, he would have wondered at the expression of the Abbot's features, while Messire Geoffroy's son was giving way to the bitterness of his sorrow. Father Anselm seemed to be suffering from some feeling that was not sorrow merely, though it looked like a painful state of anxiety; some deep-laid form of thought.

But Fulk's intelligence was not subtle enough, nor sufficiently awake, and he drew no extraordinary conclusion, as the Abbot turned to him and said :—

" So, my son, the knight here is none other than Monseigneur Philippe de Cornehaut ?"

" Certainly it is he—he is no shame to his name 1"

" He is renowned for his bravery and piety," was the Abbot's reply.

" Then renown is no liar," said Fulk, his eyes brooding over his master's prostrate form.

" Is it true, then, that Messire Philippe, at his return from the Holy Land, did not go at once to his castle? At least, had he received no news from home ?"

" Not a word, father," said Fulk, with a shrug. " Not a jot. In that I grant you he was very wrong, but from the very moment of our landing at Marseilles, his every thought was to come hither. What would you have him do with a head crammed with projects, the nature of which he himself will give you to understand ?"

"I can't guess," said the Abbot, talking to himself, " what it means. But, no matter 1 It's God's own cause, and it cannot fail."

He stepped forward to the Knight/

" Have a care, my son, lest this terrible grief should prove to be rebellion against God's will. God's chastisements reach those only whom he proves. Rise—be firm. The man who visits his native land, after a prolonged absence, must expect to meet with more disasters than one." Though Messire Philippe did, perhaps, hear this consolation, he answered not a word, and went on weeping. It was his squire who succeeded in giving his feelings quite a new direction, and that by a single reflection addressed aloud to himself:—

" Such a brave knight—and to be killed by such a low-born mob ı"

These simple words proved more powerful than the Abbot's exhortations had been. The Crusader leaped up at a bound. The tears on his burning eyeballs were dried on the instant. His nostrils expanded in his rage. Bareheaded, for his hood had fallen to the flags, his countenance all ablaze with auger, he flung open the great portal, and looking to the town below, he lifted up his hands on high, and exclaimed:—

" By the Holy Sepulchre, by Mount Carmel, Bethlehem, and the bones of all God's saints, I swear it—I will wear a hair cilicim garnished with iron nails next to my body until the very last of my father's murderers lies before me in his blood I Bourg de Typhaines—oh, thou burgh accursed—should I be forced to tear thee down with my fingers, and stone by stone, I wilf search thee in pursuit of the assassins to the bottom of thy deepest caverns. All hell shall not wrest them out of my hands ı"

As the young man spoke, he shook his arms in his rage ferociously. His hair streamed out on the wind. At other times, and beneath other skies, he would havo been taken for an inspired prophet denouncing ruin to a city. Then, as if some part of his harden of woe had been alleviated by his cruel vow, the Crusader returned to the Abbot, with his head aloft, his footstep firm, and perfectly master of himself.

41 Holy father, you are right No more despairing—no tears—no more outcries. It would be offensive to God, and wholly unprofitable. My cause is yours as well. We are united—allies inseparable 1 My lands are bounded by your own ; and since your burghers are in a state of rebellion, I will, under our united banners, do battle in your cause."

41 Yes, come, my son; little by little, peace shall settle down on your soul. In the mean time, brethren, be it yours to repair to the church, and there set down these precious remains of Father Nicolas in front of the altar. We will pay him the last duties we owe, and then pass the night in prayer for the repose of his soul."

The Abbots orders were at once obeyed. The monks, entoning a liturgical chant, lifted up the body, and marching two by two, moved in procession to the church. The squire and the pages were conducted into the domestic part of the monastery. Rigauld returned to his hut in the forest, and the yard being now quite deserted, the Abbot led the Knight, still torn by grief and rage, into the solitude of one of the inner cloisters.

After taking a few steps in silence on the ringing flagstones, the priest spoke aloud:—

44 You, my son, appeared to be greatly astonished to find your father under the monastic habit of our order. Just now, when I am weighed down by a thousand pressing cares, I am compelled by my conscience to speak to you of yourself as well as of Messire Geoffroy. That venerable seigneur, that holy monk, previous to his unexpected death, had made certain arrangements you ought to be made

acquainted with, and which, though it may occasion you to feel somewhat chagrined, will yet give you an opportunity to show your devotion to God's service. "

" I am prepared to hear you, my Lord Abbot Some great change must have taken place in Messire GeofFroy in the five years I have been from home, to induce him to give up his battle charger, and range himself under the rule of your order."

"You are about to know the whole story," resumed the Abbot. "But, before I begin, answer me this question: When your father commanded you to proceed to the Holy Land in fulfilment of a vow he had made, did he explain the motives of his resolution ?"

"No, indeed," was Messire Philippe's unaffected reply. "My redoubted seigneur was not in the habit of explaining his orders; and when he had once spoken, that was enough—all that was left was to obey."

" Well, then, I shall proceed to lay before you some facts which, if you would know me well, you ought to fully understand. It was more than twenty years ago that Messire Geoffroy conceived the project of assuming the Cross. Although he was a married man, and you only just born, he was desirous to proceed to Syria, and spend some portion of his blood, with the hope of securing in that an eternity of celestial joy. Thinking of nothing but his laudable design, and perfectly resolved to put it in execution, he unfortunately happened to be in want of the necessary funds, and so ho was not only unable to provide for his own proper equipment, but he was obliged to procure a sufficient number of squires and men-at-arms and archers. So he was in great distress, and knew not which way to turn, when one day, a demesne-burgher of his came forward with a proposal to lend a large sum, on condition that, upon his return, he would make a concession of freedom to him-

self as well as to all the mortmain inhabitants of his domain. Messire Geoffroy reflected not so carefully as he
should have done upon the consequences of such a proposal,
and, pressed with anxiety to get off, acquiesced in all that the
people asked for. Consequently the money was counted
down, he raised a fine troop of men-at-arms, and leaving
the Lady of Cornehaut with her infant child at the manor,
set out for the Crusade. He came back at the end of the
third year. He returned alone; all his companions having
perished, some in battle, some by sickness. He came back
an impoverished man, on foot, the beggar's scrip at his
side, and yet, no sooner had he planted his foot on Christian ground, than the idea of recovering his castle and its
domains revived a spark of joy within him.

" But what must have been his astounishment when, after
he climbed to the top of the rock whereon stood his manor
house, he beheld a banner not his own flying from the
summit of the donjon ! It was then he began to feel a
thousand bitter thoughts about your mother and yourself
too. A peasant who was coming down the incline, informed
him that within a few months after his departure, the dame
of Cornehaut had applied to her vilains, who had long
ceased to pay in their taxes; that they now exhibited the.
charter of their franchise and laughed at the lady's impo-
tent demands ; that, in her embarrassment, the chatelaine,
in utter want of the necessaries of life, as she sat within her
old castle walls, had hearkened to evil counsels, and sold
the castle to the peasantry. Within a month they had
entered into possession of the place, and planted the banner
of the commune on the old keep. As to the dame of Cornehaut, she had taken refuge with one of her relations,
some leagues away, and was now living there in a poorish
way, together with her son.

" While Messire Geoffroy was hearkening to this recital, his heart seemed ready to break, and he has since told me that what most deeply wounded him, was not the wretched state of his family, but the sight of a strange banner flying on the abode of his ancestors. He felt as if he had been defeated, and his arms dishonorably 6tained, and gave himself over to the most sorrowful reflections.

" After parting with the peasant who had, without recognizing him, given the above details, he sat down on a stone by the wayside, to eat a miserable bit of oaten bread a kind woman had bestowed on him that same morning. Still, unable to withdraw his gaze from the castle above, and with eyes veiled in tears, he pondered upon the position of his affairs, to find out what it was he ought to do. He was terribly embarrassed, but could by no means comprehend that Ood, whose servant and liegeman he was, could now recompense him for his services by letting him die of hunger and overwhelmed with shame. Just then there came along another man, whom he remembered as one of his stable-boys at the castle Dressed in a new, close-fitting cloth coat, the peasant was riding on a stout horse, with his wife seated on the pillion behind him, and laughing as they went on. Messire Geoffroy could not get rid of the idea that his own wife and son were, perhaps, even at the very moment suffering for want, and was giving way to the sorrowful reflection, when he heard:—

''' There, vagabond, take t h a t a n d a small coin fell at his feet. His former stable-boy was calling him vagabond, and giving him alms 1

" My son, your father was a good Christian—a gallant knight; but in those days, he was still fond of the maxims of the world, despising poverty, and detesting humiliation; he remembered not that, after the coming of Jesus, the greatest saints made it their special delight to be in want

of everything and overwhelmed with opprobrium. He
did not pick up the money, but went off at a hurried pace.

" He soon reached the fortress in which you and the
chatelaine had found refuge. He did not reproach the
lady ; there was none he had a right to make, seeing that
he had left her without any means of support. But he
hardly took time to rest his weary frame, and on the morrow, attended by the lord of the place, he went about,
visiting his relations and old friends and companions,
whom he invited to meet him in arms in a meadow lying
near his old castle. The whole company having assembled
at the rendezvous, to the number of eight knights and
fifteen squires, with their people, amounting to eighty men,
well supplied with swords, lances, battle-axes, bows and
arbalists, your father, who had no armor on, and nothing
but his rags, his cross on the shoulder, and his pilgrim's
staff, addressed the meeting as follows:—

"' My dear relations, my dear friends, and neighbors,
behold what a condition I am reduced to! And you know
I earned these rags, not by harming any person, by attacking my allies perfidiously, or .by betraying those who confided in my honor. You well know that I have ever
endeavored to deal fairly with all men. Now, it is certain
that I could never, unless I had taken up a loan, have proceeded to Jerusalem to fight for the Holy Sepulchre. Was
it just, was it right, then, while I was shedding my blood,
to deliver the tomb of the Saviour—that my peasants, whom
I left in their comfortable houses, busy making money,
should bear no portion in the burden of such a sacrifice as
that ? No. It was not right nor just. Yet they refused
to help me. They declined to give any gratuitous aid in
the way of funds, or follow me to the battle-field! They
sold me their succor at the cost of my rights. Next they
abused my absence, to obtain from the urgent necessities

of my poor wife, concessions that I never did make. In this they have acted like false vassals; and I now ask you to say whether it is fitting that I am to be left to perish with hunger, while my serfs are feasting at the great table, and in the very hall where you and I used to greet each other in bygone times ? ' "

"I can readily describe beforehand," cried Philippe, " what answer Messire Geoffroy's friends gave—that is, if they were gentlemen at heart"

" Ah ! Yes, my son," pursued the Abbot, with a sigh, " men—in a worldly sense held to be high and illustrious, but in my view men of violence and injustice—every man of them standing there in that meadow beneath the willows, were of one mind, that your father and his family, who for centuries had been lords of the canton, could not, by the mere stroke of a pen, and a few silver marks, to be spent in a cause so sacred, be righteously despoiled and beggared. Every man of them declared upon his faith, that the serfs were in the wroug, and deserving of a proper punishment—that a man, a gentleman, situated as Messire Geoffroy was, would think it right to recover by force any domain wrested from him by guile, and that it would be a right thing to bring the serfs back to their duty, at any cost whatever.

" Your father stood waiting for the decision, and then proposed what be thought ought to be done ; to which they agreed, and further engaged to give him such help os might be required.

" After agreeing upon the necessary measures, two of the oldest knights quitted the assembly, and proceeded at once to the town. It is hardly necessary to say that your father's return was already known there. You well know that, in such country parts there are ever idlers to be found who make it their business to run about hither and thither,

5

gathering news of all sorts, and retailing it again wherever they can tind a listener. The knights found the people assembled in crowds in the public square, and among them four individuals dignified with the title of wardens, and who acted as their captains. They saluted the assembly, and declared aloud that Messire Geoffroy de Cornehaut had returned from the Crusade to the Holy Land; that he thanked his vassals for the friendly way in which they had advanced funds for his voyage ; that he would refund them as soon as ever he could provide the necessary means, and that for the present all they had to do was to prepare a reception suitable for the occasion of the seigneur's return to his domains. It was his intention to take possession of his manor that very day.

" Scarcely would the populace allow the knights time enough to bring their address to a close. They began to utter frenzied cries, vociferate curses, and some of the worst of them to gather up stones. But the wardens or captains succeeded at last in quieting the disturbance, and told your father's envoys that the money had not been loaned, but given; that in his absence, they had established a commune, which they intended to maintain, even at cost of their lives; and that the castle was theirs, and they would keep it too. The old knights returned to the meadow, and reported the result to Messire Geoffroy and his friends. Then it was that your father, lifting up his voice, exclaimed :—

You see, my dear relatives, that these people are an unreasonable folk, and that they are determined to live with us on a footing that was never before allowed since the world began. Our fathers and their fathers lived here, ours above and theirs below. I know not whether it may happen some day—whether we, after the loss of our skill at sword-play, may be compelled to put up with such a degradation as that But, as to me, 1 must say, that times of that sort are as yet very far off.*

" They all shouted, ' You are right! You are right V and every soul of them got to horse—your father like the rest; but he had no armor, and said he could do without it in a matter of bringing a parcel of serfs back to duty. Then seizing a battle-axe, and nothing more, he galloped off towards the village, shouting, as he went, his battle-cry, *'Notre Dame ! ifotre Dame P*

" The peasants were taken by surprise, and had no time to run to the castle and shut themselves in, nor even to barricade their streets. In utter dismay, and without leaders, and badly armed, they vainly, here and there, tried to resist the fierce onset of the knights. Though ten times more numerous, they were driven back, surrounded, trampled down, and massacred. There was a great carnage, and the streets and squares were stained with gore. The resistance ceased in the course of a couple of hours, for some were slain, many had fled, and the rest, on their knees, were begging for mercy. Of the four wardens, one had made his escape, the others were arrested and hung on the spot, from the donjon battlements, and after that it was deemed well to spare the survivors.

" In the mean time, Messire Geoffroy had disappeared. They called out his name—they searched for him high and low, but all iu vain. For a while it was supposed that he had been killed in the fray. At length they found him in a house, down on his knees beside a corpse, looking as if he had been stunned. And now it was seen what a fearful crime be had been so unfortunate as to commit—a crime, compared to which, any other is to be looked on as a trifle. In the heat of the fight, he had, without knowing it, broke into the Curate de Cornebaut's house, and as he was killing everything he met, he had killed the priest, like the rest!"

Here the Abbot ceased speaking, as if terrified himself at the bare memory of the event. Messire Philippe bent down his head. He fully understood the grave import of the relation to which be had just hearkened.

" From that day onwards," pursued the Abbot, " there was no more rest for Messire Geoffroy. It's true he re-entered into the possession of his property; he was highly esteemed through the whole province; he became prime favorite to his suzerain, the Count de Nevers; upon a thousand occasions he gave proof of his wisdom and valor; but he was never known to smile, and though he often repeated to himself and to his own conscience, that he bad slain the priest unintentionally, he ever looked on himself as a great sinner, and lived on, overwhelmed with remorse, and in just dread of everlasting punishment. In vain did he erect and endow a chapel; in vain multiply his good works; in vain did he send you, my son, to the Holy Land as soon as you had attained your twentieth year. Nothing could alleviate the burden of his sorrow, and so, finding himself at last a widower, he took up the resolution of seeking the supreme remedy for all his ills. That is the reason why it will be three years next St. Martin's day since he assumed the habit of our order in this Abbey."

CHAPTER *TV.*

THE Abbot bad brought bis recital to a close, and Philippe de Cornehaut, who remained pensive for a while, turned suddenly to the Abbot, and spoke :—

¹⁴ Think you, holy father, that Messire Geoffroy's penance was sufficient to merit pardon for his crime ?"

" I have some reason to think so, my son. Nevertheless, I shall not conceal from you that so precious a result is not wholly dependent on any austerity through which Father Nicolas may have attempted to redeem his error. I have to declare that there is another person who may yet very seriously compromise your father's salvation, and that person is your very self!"

"I!" said Philippe. " I—why, what can you mean?"

" Before I explain myself, and open my whole heart to you," replied the Mouk, in a grave tone, ¹¹ it's necessary, my son, to know what I am to think of you yourself, and to learn whether I am to regard you as a good and loyal knight, or rather, as one of those men without faith or conscience, who, in our unhappy times, seem to make their pilgrimages to Saracen vices rather than the virtues of the Holy City. I shall not hide from you the motives of this prudence of mine. Your father had heard news from you that gave him no little concern; and though the matter was not altogether so bad as was supposed, there was enough in it to justify me in some lingering distrust as to yourself."

6*

At these words, Messire Philippe appeared to be not a little contrite. For a moment or two he was silent and still, and then, making np his mind, he spoke as follows :—

" I am not about to deny, holy father, that there have been some wrong things about me ; but appearances made them out worse than they were in fact, and it concerns me that you should believe so. Besides, as I told you when I entered this pious abode, I did not come to see you merely haphazard, or out of a merely truant disposition. I have a serious matter in hand, and have to ask your consent to what will assure my complete felicity, and to that end it is necessary that you should not regard me as a great sinner or a brainless fool. "

" I am not going to accuse you, my son, without some proof at least. Say, then, what you have to allege in your defence."

"The day," resumed Messire Philippe, "when my redoubted father made me set out for the Holy Land, with my squire Fulk and a dozen archers, I was not, I must confess it, very joyous at the idea of quitting my native land. I was young, and far more in a hurry to go in search of pleasure than to voyage to a country where, as I had heard say, there are more kicks than coins to be got, and I thought it a hard thing to go and haply get myself killed before I had enjoyed any opportunity to win a fair fame among my companions. In a word, I was hardly twenty years old, and reflected but little on the consequences of my actions. And so, when I had gone but a few leagues away from the castle, instead of pursuing my route southwards to embark for Palestine, I turned right about, and went northwards towards Cambrai, where I had a great desire to go.

" My squire, I must do him the justice to say, did all in his power to dissuade me from such disobedience, but finding me very much bent on my project, and that all his persuasions went for nothing, he chose rather to go with me, than leave me to follow my inclinations all alone, and so pay a visit to countries that excited my curiosity far more than Palestine."

"I can hardly understand all this in a gentleman such as you are," responded the Abbot. "To me it seems that no land should appear more attractive in your eyes than one where you was to expect glorious battle-fields; you ought to have preferred the battle, and not your private gratification."

"I was a madman !" replied Messire Philippe. "And perhaps, too, I had hearkened too eagerly to the counsels of my companions, no wiser than I. I had no fear of hob-goblins either, as you perhaps may find. I was sure that without going to sea, I should find, my good lance helping me, a thousand chances to win both booty and renown. Just about that time a quarrel had broken out for the second time, between the Bishop of Cambrai and his burghers there. Reports had reached our province to the effect that the good bishop was imploring all knights and sergeants-at-arms to give succor in his distress; that all his attempts had failed to bring them to their senses, he proving wholly unable to convince them that peasant-folk are born into this world to the sole end of paying due obedience to their seigneurs. Further, that stiff-necked race still refused to hearken to their rightful Lord and head, and were actually, at that very time, crowding to the brink of the castle fosse, and howling out that odious cry, * *Commune! Commune!* a sound that, once heard, never ceases to ring in one's ears. Thus there was nothing to be done now but to make use of some force that might compel those deaf brutes to hearken to his paternal ex-hortation. The bishop promised good pay, booty, and such indulgences as holy Church usually concedes to all true Christians who fight against excommunicats in her defence. It boots not, of course, that I should tell you the commune had already been struck by an Interdict.

"Your holiness is probably aware that Cambrai is a large trading town where young people find plenty of chances to enjoy themselves, and that consideration determined me to proceed thither, and there make my first proof in arms.

" On joining, we found that we made up a force of some two hundred knights and squires. I am not going to trouble you with details of our splendid fights at that town. The bnrghers and peasants fonght like so many real devils, aud we had no little trouble to hold our own against them. My poor Fulk lost an eye in one of the frays. But at last, after many a conflict and with the help of our courage, we succeeded in putting an end to their obstinacy, and that gave us a good three whole days of plunder and booty —days, the like of which I can never hope to Bee again."

" Have a care, my son ! Have a care! For, although yonr cause was a just one and sanctioned by heaven, never forget that military excesses are odious and accursed by more than one holy council."

" I assure you, holy father," replied the youth, " if you had only been there, with a trusty horse under you galloping through streets of flame, with a good lance in your grip, among swarms of people running, praying, screaming, crying for quarter, some shouting for gold, some for silver; with exquisite tapestries or beautiful clothes and furniture flying out of the windows for whoever chose to lay hands on them, you'd hardly have found time to think about councils and all that. Besides, don't you be scandalized about it, for when I was at Jerusalem I did full and complete penance for whatever I happened to do that day at

Cambrai; and it was even the Archbishop of Tyre himself who gave me his absolution for it, when he saw how I wept over my sins in the Church of the Holy Sepulchre there.

⁴¹ After a stay of two months at Cambrai, and when the bishop had thanked and paid us for our services, besides arming some of the best ot us knights, of whom I was one, I took my leave, and turned my face towards Champagne, hardly knowing as yet what I was going to do, and persecuted by Fulk, who was always insisting on my going off at once to fulfil my father's vow, in Palestine."

⁴⁴ It seems to me that you have a good servant, in that man," said Anselm.

⁴⁴ Excellent. Rather talkative, but a capital soldier, and remarkably obstinate. We were travelling along one day, side by side, and talking away about a matter that was always nearest my heart I had left my heart behind me in Cambrai. I was in love with a dame of high lineage, and instead of proceeding to the Holy Land, I should not have deemed it a very 6ore disappointment if I could have stayed and got a chance to perform a few nice exploits, the renown of which might perchance reach her ears, and at the same time hold me at no too great a distance from her beautiful eyes. I confess that the lady in question was not wholly insensible to ray friendship ; that with the consent of her guardian, we exchanged our betrothal rings. But the lady had never been apprised that I had assumed the Cross, for I had carefully kept that matter a secret from her, for fear that she, a very religious person, would take a dislike to me, in case she should happen to find out how wretchedly I was procrastinating the fulfilment of ray father's vow. It was Fulk's opinion that I was in the wrong to dissemble with her, and indeed that I was always in the wrong, do what I might; that some misfortune

would be sure to overtake me, unless my patron saint or
the holy virgin herself should take pity on such blindness.
I certainly was somewhat shaken by Fulk's discourse, and
was trying to give him an answer of some sort, when we
were overtaken by a man, who I at once recognized as
valet to the lady I served. I eagerly demanded what he
wanted, and whether he was looking for me.

"'Yes, Messire,' was the reply; 'and I am sent by
Madame to say that le Seigneur de Pornes has made oath
to her on the holy relics, that you secretly assumed the
Cross, and the reason why you did not quit the country
was to be found in your want of courage, and nothing else.
Further, she charges me to demand whether that is true or
no; and in case she had not been deceived by the Lord
de Pornes, then she requests you to send back the ring, and
think of her no longer.' While so saying, the messenger
had drawn the gold ring out of his purse, and tendered it
to me.

" Ah! holy father, on hearing words so unexpected, I
seemed turned to stone. But my wrath soon got the better
of my shame, and I said, ' Carry the ring back to your
mistress. Tell her that if I did not set out for the Holy
Land as soon as I perhaps ought to have done, it was out
of my love for her; but that you saw the Cross on my
shoulder, and I on my way thither.' So saying, I took out
the Cross from my bosom, where it lay concealed, and
placing it on my shoulder, I added :—

"'Further, you shall say to your mistress, that in case,
before I return, or the coming of no assured news of my
death, she, without a motive, should fail in her pledged
word to me, I will wage war to the death on the man, whoever he may be, that shall have traitorously espoused her;
and that she herself shall never again find rest in this
world from my just revenge, nor in the next from the

demons who are appointed to pnnish perfidy like that." I
then dismissed the messenger, and for this time seriously
set out for Palestine. I arrived there; I fought there; was
wounded there; made prisoner, redeemed, aud then taken
ill, nursed and cared for by the Knights Hospitallers of St.
John; and concluding I had done enough, ruined, emaciated,
and exhausted, I set my face homewards, along with my
faithful Fulk, quite as worthy of pity as I was myself. In
this condition we reached the kingdom of Naples; and you
may rest assured it was by no means a pleasing spectacle
to see us in our rags, half naked, with our miserable beggar's scrip, and asking alms at the hands of the poor
vilains.

44 One day, sitting by the margin of a spring, and trying
to soften our black bread by soaking it in the water,

144 Dost thou think,' said I to Fulk, ' that it would be
sfant in us to return to the Nivernais, in a pitiful equipment like ours ? As for me, however much I long to see
my betrothed again, I must say I should blush with shame
at the thought of appearing in her presence in a condition
more like that of a brute beast than a Christian knight.'

44 To this Fulk made answer:—

44 4 If you have any skill to mend our fortune, why not tell
what it is ? And tell it quick ; for I am quite as tired as
you can be of the way we are getting on.'

44 4 All that's necessary,' said I, 4 is to enlist in some
leader's service and do battle for him until our pay and
booty suffice to make us better off. I am aware that years
peijiaps may elapse, but what would you have ? I cau
never make up my mind to appear before Mahaut in the
guise of a miserable beggar.'

44 Fulk approved my advice, and the heavens smiled on
ns. We took service under a Neapolitan prince, who furnished us with numerous opportunities to repair our equip-

ments; and, to be brief, when we took leave of him, I was in a most flourishing condition. I had won good clothing for Fulk and myself, flue armor, and fifteen hundred silver marks, besides the honor. I set out for France. At Rome I received the Pope's benediction. At Marseilles, where I left nearly all my followers and baggage, I learned from a Champenois that my betrothed was still waiting for and expecting me, but that I could not apply to her uncle now, as he was dead, but to you, holy father, who are her new guardian. Then I came hither, and I now demand your pupil, Mahaut, in marriage."

"Was that demand," said the Abbot, rather incredulously, "the sole motive of your visit to me ?"

" I have none other. But why are you so astonished ? In that marriage there is nothing but what is right and wise; at least so I think. Madame Mahaut's lands and mine adjoin. Numerous alliances have heretofore united our families, and you ought surely to know that her uncle, the Bishop of Cambrai, had sanctioned my suit, provided my father should approve; an approval I can no longer hope for, since Messire Geoffroy is dead."

For sometime the Abbot was silent

Philippe, who was impatient at getting no answer, could not restrain himself, and he cried out:—

" By our Lady, I don't understand, holy father, why you make me no answer ! Is it because you have some favorite of your own on whom, and to my detriment, you would prefer to confer the Dame of Cornouiller's hand ?"

"Not so, my son," responded the Abbot. " I have no thought of doing you an injustice. My reflection was not such as you suppose."

" What were you thinking of, then ? Why not give your consent at once f"

44 Is it the part of a faithful guardian to marry a wealthy heiress to a knight her unequal in fortune ?"

44 You must be jesting, holy father. The lands of Cornehaut, if that is your way of looking at such matters, are one-third larger than the domains of Cornouiller. And as to revenues, you should know that a charter conceded by Monseigneur, the Count of Nevers' grandfather, greatly augmented them some forty years since, as compensation to my grandfather for signal services to him rendered."

"I am aware of all that;" and stopping, the Abbot put his hand on the young man's arm, and then proceeded to say: 41 But did I not tell you there was something still left for you to know ? Have I here before me a good Christian, or a Pagan—one hard on Holy Church ?"

11 How you do drag!" cried Messire Philippe, stamping with his foot so as to make his heavy sword rattle in its iron scabbard. 44 How you do drag ! Know you not, holy father, that I am one of Christ's vassals ? a man who has shed his blood in his cause ? and is there any occasion, then, for you to ask me whether I am a miscreant? Make an end. Tell me, and that quickly, what you have to say to me, and let us get back as soon as possible to the only subject that I am interested in—my prompt union with Mahaut."

The Abbot shook his head. His companion's vehemence didn't half satisfy him ; yet he armed himself with resolution, and, with a sigh, delivered himself as follows:—

" My son, when your father entered this Abbey, he was shone on by a ray of divine wisdom. He was a priest's murderer, and deemed that nothing he could do would be too much by way of appeasing the vengeance of heaven. He dreaded lest the penalty for his crime might extend even to you; yea, even to your descendants ; and besides,

6

he felt some remorse on account of the way he had adopted
for the recovery of his estates !"

" What 's the meaning of all this ?" said Messire
Philippe, with frowning brows. " Are you goingto attack
Monseigneur, ray father's reputation ?"

" God forbid!" was the monk's soft and gentle response.
" God forbid that I should ever dream of disturbing that
valiant gentleman's memory—a monk so holy I The fault
he had committed he had, indeed, most nobly expiated and
redeemed; for the demesne he had recaptured had been
the cause of so many misfortunes—that, too, he expiated
by making a solemn donation of it in full and without re-
striction of any kind, to the holy Abbey of Typhaines."

" My father did that ? My father gave away my estates ?
What, my father leave me without an inch of land of my
own ?"

"Your father ransomed his own soul," was the monk's
response.

To portray the expression of blind fury that brought instant change on the Knight's features—that would be a
thing impossible. He stood there unable to speak. His
eyes darted out flames, and his crisping fingers had clutched
the heavy haft of Rudaverse. A mere nothing—a bare
word, and less than that—a movement of the Abbot's eye
—might have been enough to extinguish the very last spark
of reason in his soul—and then what would have been the
monk's fate ? Messire Philippe was in one of those
paroxysms common enough among the redoubtable men
of that epoch, in whose hearts an all powerful passion might
hush down even religion itself, though far more powerful
than reason or experience. Had he discerned in the Abbot's features the least indication of a menace, or any sentiment of aggression, or even of flight, certainly it would
have been ail over with the priest, and Philippe would have

laid up for himself a store of terrible remorse, such as often iu those days gave rise to penitential sufferings as dreadful as the very crimes themselves. But, by the energy of his courage, the Abbot first restrained, and at length subdued the fiery rage of the laic before him. It would not be going too far to say that the Churchman actually fascinated the Chevalier. He held him in arrest by the calm intrepidity of his gaze long enough to allow the Crusader's emotions to subside by gentle degrees ; the fingers on the hilt gradually loosened their hold, and the face grew less stormy and threatening.

"Messire Priest," said Philippe in a choking tone, " it 's your good pleasure, then, to plunder an orphan, and turn me out of doors at my ancestral home ?"

"You are too angry just now to hearken to words of wisdom," was the Abbot's reply. "At a future moment, I shall be able to show you "

" Falsehoods !" shouted Philippe, ready to burst again into another towering, furious paroxysm. "Ha! You churchmen! you did mighty well to invent the notion that to smite such as you is a crime of the deepest dye. Yes, that was well, for you often conjure up the temptation to do it."

The Abbot smiled a little, looked down to the ground, but said nothing.

The Knight madly hurled his steel gauntlet at the stone wall.

" I will deny God, if But I am gone mad I You arc in the right, sir, and all this does no good. Let's talk —let's talk calmly. Do you really propose to keep possession of my estate ?"

Monseigneur withdrew some ten paces from the Abbot, and stood there, leaning against the cloister wall. He fixed his eyes on him, and waited for the reply.

" Should you," so spoke the Abbot, "should you, to the
eternal damnation of your soul, strike down this miserable
body of mine, that would not help to put you in possession
of a domain that is not mine—for it belongs to God's
Church. Cease, then, to regret the past. You are too
young to nurse a sorrow far fitter for an old man. Think
of the future, when the powerful influence of the Abbot
of Typhaines may, without any fault, either on his side,
or your own, brilliantly repair all the losses you are now
deploring."

" Ha !" broke in Philippe. " If but only you weren't
a priest 1"

The Abbot, not in the least disturbed, was about to make
answer, when one of the monks entered the gallery, drew
near him, and said:—

" Holy father, here is Master Simon come with four of
the boroughmen, to confer with you on some business
about the Commune!"

" The *Commune I*" cried Philippe, at the top of his voice,
forgetting at once the loss of his estate, his father's murder, and all thought of his betrothed.

" The Commune 1" said the Abbot. " What, already !"
in a lower and troubled tone.

" Yes, they said the Commune," continued the monk,
all of a tremble. " They did utter that execrable word.
Am I to guide them hither, or send them away?"

The Abbot paused awhile to think. He looked askance
at Monseigneur Philippe, who had advanced to the door
to have a look at the five deputies, and then spoke:—

"Yes, go, brother, and beg those poor deluded people to
come hither, when their Seigneur will try to find some way
to cure them of their treasonable designs." The monk
bowed low, and withdrew.

CHAPTER V

Let us leave Abbot Anselm and the Knight of Cornehaut waiting for their visitors, and return to the moment
when the five Typhaines men, after they had brought in
the remains of Father Nicolas, had left the Abbey court,
and were taking their way down again to the Burgh. The
monks were lookiug on with indignation, as they moved
down the steep rocky way, laughing aloud, and shaking
their fists at the sacred pile behind. But it was too far to
hear what Master Simon and his friends were saying.

" There they are," said one of them. " There they are,
those monks. They really 6eem to think that the whole
world belongs to them !"

" Ha!" spoke one of the party. " What would you
have, Payen ? My father lived at their feet, and they have
got it into their heads that I'm going to do so too."

" Well said, Antoine," rejoined a third. " Those insolent
monks there, hard as any of the secular lords, treat us poor
burghers like slaves. They claim to make not a bit of
difference between us and the very glebe-men. But upon
my faith as a Christian, it is not going to be always so,
and I rather conceit that I know the whereabouts of a good
sharp knife that is getting to be very restless in its sheath."

" Listen to me, Endes, and listen well—you, too, Antoine, Payen, and you, Jacques," said Simon. " You are,
all of you, neighbors of mine, and to-day is not the first
time we ever groaned together over the wretched lives our

seigneurs compel us to drag on with. You, Antoine, old
crony, are quite right in what you say. Knight or abbot,
squire or prior, sergeant-at-arms or plain monk or seigneur,
all the same: all of them are just so many Herods—all
hungry and athirst for our money and our blood. They
know very well—for the very children at the breast know
it—that we are no slaves, no miserable creatures like their
field hands. Whenever we tell them that our forefathers,
in the olden times, were as free as they, they don't deny it,
and couldn't if they would ; and yet they never put a stop
to their oppressions and intolerable exactions. They tell
us, to mock at us, I suppose, that they are all our protectors, and that they defend us against the chatelains of
other demesnes, but what is it to me, whether I am pillaged and robbed by my seigneur's neighbors or by my
seigneur himself? No ! By all the saints, no ! Must I
go on repeating, all I have been saying, day after day, these
two years past ? But we have broken the ice on this miserable theme, and it's time for us to stand shoulder to
shoulder like true brothers. I must repeat it! If you will
go on living along in this wretched way, you are no better
than so many dogs. You are as servile as they are,
and every kick you get, I tell you beforehand you well
deserve them. I tell you now, for I—you know it full
well—am preaching not my own merely, but your honor
and your advantage, far more than any of mine. I am
above their insolence—those mqnks up there—as a stranger in this demesne, and being monseigneur the King's
burgher, I am independent of them: they are neither my
seigneurs nor my judges. I've a right to come and go—
buy and sell—it's no affair of theirs, and when I've paid
up my regular taxes, I'm just as much my own master as
the proudest knight or vainest prelate of them all. Like
any other gentleman or clerk, I depend on the royal suze-

rainty, and on nothing else. Whether you lose your patience at last, or stay as quiet as so many sheep, with your masters' knives at your throats, I 've nothing to lose by that. When I am trying my best to make you look inwards down to the very bottom of your hearts for some faint spark of courage there, you ought to know, and that full well, that I am speaking for you and for your wives and children."

After speaking as above, in an animated tone, the merchant ceased. The men kept silent around him, and for some time not a sound was heard save their great heavy shoes, as they went tramping downward on the stony road, and the horse's hoofs that Master Simon was leading down hill behind him. At last thus spoke out one of the Typhaines men :—

" You are a very lucky man, neighbor, very lucky, indeed; and upon my word, if, as you did, I could possibly make out to buy a royal charter to get me out of the power of the monks, I swear to you that the money wouldn't be slow at coming out of my purse. Tell us, for the love you bear us all, what can we do to secure such a boon as that ?"

Master Simon merely shrugged his shoulders, and then said:—

" The thing you want—that you 'll never learn from me —No 1 Never will I show how you can betray your relations, your friends and neighbors—every soul that has as good a right as you have to live free, rich, and prosperous ! And though you. see me here, far away from my native land, don't go to think I left of my own free will : I was driven away from home by evil fortune. And this title of kings-man, that you are envying, please God Almighty, I'll change that some day for public liberty in this Burgh, and for yours among the rest I It's a poor mat ter, believe me, to be the only fortunate man where slavery weighs down all around you, lands and men alike 1"

" That 's so," was Payen's instant reply, as he boldly raised his head. "You talk as a brave man should talk, and I answer you in a like strain. The bare sight of those monks set my very blood a tingling. What you told us on our journey to Troyes' fair, about those splendid communes at Aix, Narbonne, and Toulouse, made my blood boil, and my heart choke. In the devils name, let serfs be serfs if they like, but not us burghers though I The men of Noyon have set up their commune, and the Rheims men are at it too. The people at Laon made no bones about massacring their gentlemen, or even their bishop. Ton my soul—let 's have a heart; let's pluck up our courage. We have arms and legs and blood to boot. Whenever I fire my arbalist, I can make nine out of every ten bolts drive the one last before it Whenever I fence with the trained-band sergeant, I always make him give back. Holy Cross of Typhaines 1 My mind is made up ! I am not the poor devil I used to be 1"

" Listen to me," said Antoine. " Don't let us be in too much of a hurry."

Antoine was a man about forty years of age, a cooper by trade, somewhat stooped by hard work, lean, sharp-nosed, and sharp-eyed. But there was no smack of meanness about him. It was only that prudence and cunning were his predominant characteristics.

" Don't let us be in any hurry as yet. If we can provide us with some good friend and even some powerful ally, it would be all the better for us. Money can do anything, and I am ready to loosen my purse-string, that I am, and let the shiners sparkle in his eyes, whoever the good knight may be, that comes to our'help."

" Let us understand each other," resumed Master Simon, hooking arms with the cooper, "and you'll find Payen not far in the wrong to be in a hurry."

"Certainly I am not wrong in that," said Payen, with a toss of his head. " Let me have a talk with neighbor Antoine. Yon know, Antoine, that for several months past we've not been slow to speak out what we thought about the monks and their seigneurage."

" Yes, I know that And to tell the truth, a little more care would have done us no harm."

" That's your way of thinking. It'8 none of mine, though. Nor theirs, either"—pointing to the other men. " Ifthere '3 any harm in it the mischief's done already, and you heard iust now that the Abbot knows all about us. Is it your opinion that it would be a wise thing for us to wait quietly till they take us to the abbey gaol ?"

" They sha'n't take me," cried Jacques. " Crime of rebellion ! No pardon for that! Once you are shut up, there's an end of it; you '11 never get out again."

"That'8 not the whole of it," pursued Simon. "If Father Nicolas really was killed, who do you think did it?"

" Some discontented or drunken serf, I suppose," replied Autoine; " as I told you when we were coming away from the woods."

" I let you talk then," said Simon, " but you was under a mistake. He was killed by some one of our young fellows here. Our talk, my good friends, and it's a lucky thing, too, has set all their hot heads a burning."

To this, Payen and Jacques both nodded assent.

" If that '8 what you think about it," said Antoine, "you must have been a set of big fools to carry the dead man home to the abbey with your own hands; why, they will accuse you of being accomplices at least."

" Good !" said the king's burgher, with a smile. " Did you suppose I had any motive but that, when I took you up to the abbey ? Liberty or the rope, friend Antoine, that's all there is of it for you, just as you stand there—other chance have you none 1 Hanged, or free men ! And that's where I want to see you; and I in your company too. Don't be uneasy, neighbors. You were talking of succors, and succors shall not be wanting."

As Payen and Jacques walked on, they went rubbing their hands at such delightful news.

Antoine hesitated for a while, and then spoke :—

⁴⁴ Well, well I What is done can't be done over again. I should have rather gone not quite so fast. But as you have managed the affair in another way, you 'll find me as stout as the best of you." *

Just then the four burghers had crossed the bridge, and as they strode into the principal street, Simon stopped, took every man's hand in his right, and joining and covering them with his left hand, said, in a solemn tone:—

⁴⁴ Go home, all of you. Go in peace. It shall not be long before liberty and franchise shall be your own. And trust me, though the danger seems dreadful now, if you will but meet it with a bold front, one-half of it will vanish at once. All I now ask is, give me a few minutes to go home and embrace my wife and child, and that over, we will leap to our arms, and use them, too."

⁴⁴ Well spoke," replied Payen. ⁴⁴I am off at once in search of my crossbow and my iron head-piece."

The conspirators grasped hands for the last time, and without further speech went off, every man to his own dwelling. As soon as Master Simon found himself alone, his face shone with the light of his haughty, savage joy. He strode on, light and happy as a youth to his first love meeting. Looking at him, you would have said that his trade had just brought in some enormous profit. And so he went on to his doorstep and drew the latch.

His home was a thatched house consisting of one very

large room merely, and a low-roofed garret above. The
only outside decorations of the rustic dwelling consisted in
a wooden bench and a rampant grape-vine at the door. In
the interior there was a clay floor ram'd, solid, and smooth.
An opening in the roof furnished vent to the smoke that
was floating upwards from a stone hearth planted on
the clay floor in the middle of the room. At the further
end of the apartment stood an immense wood and osier
bedstead, with lamb-skin bedspreads, and closed in with
serge curtains. An enormous chest and a bread-locker
flanked the huge couch. Great rolls of cloth of every
pattern and hue stood piled on the shelves that lined the
walls, while a dozen wooden stools were scattered here and
there throughout the great living-room, whose sole orna-
mentation depended on a holy-water-font and a copper
crucifix of curious workmanship that hung at the head of
the bed.

So moderate was the luxury permissible for a king's-
borough man in that age ! a position which, ambiguous
though it was, yet served at least Master Simon's turn.
In the apartment were two women, both of them seated,
and twirling their distaffs near the firo on the hearth where
supper was cooking. They both put aside their work, and
advanced to meet him. One of them gave him a kiss, and
then spoke:—

" Ah! you are come at last, husband!"

The other one kissed him, too, but uttered, in a tone
fer gentler :—

" Welcome home, father !"

He made an affectionate return of their caresses, and
taking a seat between the two, a hurried conversation commenced at once. Master Simon's wife, Jeanne, seemed as
if she might be about his own age, if we may judge by the
grayish hair that was escaping from the edge of the matronly

cloth coif on her head. She looked like a fitting companion
for a man so resolute as he, her face expressive of a sort of
severe and hard temper; her blue eyes cold and determined in their outlook, and her stout, heavy frame bore
witness of a vigor that was not belied by a pair of big
hands, made coarse and hard by work. She was well
dressed for one in her condition, in a brown linsey-woolsey
gown and a black mantle. Truth to tell, she would have
best been compared to a furze-bush, yet even then it must
be admitted that on her rude, ungainly stem a fair and exquisite rose had bloomed.

Her daughter was as tall, delicate, and slender as any chatelaine in the whole land. Damerones* face and hands were
all of a delicate blonde, wherever the hues of health were
not seen burning. The candor and brilliancy of her glorious
blue eyes were unequalled. She was a marvel to look upon!
I may well add, that of all this she herself entertained no
shadow of a doubt, for the whole village had long been
telling her so, evening and morning, and the lads of the
town all assumed to be as amiable as possible in hopes of
winning her good-will. Nobody, not even Master Simon
himself, had ever been able to resist the charm, for it
was the universal opinion at Typhaines that it were impossible for him to refuse anything whatsoever to the fair
Damerones. Though it was a work day at the time, she
was dressed in a woollen gown, sky-blue, neither more
nor less than an exact counterpart of the Holy Virgin's
effigy, where it stood there in the old abbey church on the
rock ; and to carry out to the very full such audacious co-
quetry, a scarlet mantle, the edges bound with silver cord,
gave a perfect finish to the likeness. Temerities of this class
are adapted to none but beauties perfectly sure of themselves ; but like everything else about Damerones, she never
seemed in the wrong, and even that very day no less than

three of the most splendid young fellows in town, one of Antoine's nephews, Eude's eldest son, besides Jacques' second son, the very flower of Typhaines youth, one and all, as they passed by her doorstep, where she sat spinning by her mother's side, had assured her over and over again that she was the exact image of the Queen of Heaven up yonder in the old minster. But it was no use, for she had long been perfectly *bla&te* as to such compliments as that.

Simon smiled benignantly as he kissed his charming daughter's brow, and then drawing his purse from his girdle:—

" There, my dear Jeanne," said he, " lock up this money for me. The cloth had a capital sale at Troyes. Be quick about it. I 've something to say to both of you."

The housewife took the money, counted it with a pleased look, and then went over to the corner of the room behind the bed, and opening a hole in the darkest part of the room, she poured the coins out, which fell ringing on a pile of their fellows that had long been stowed away as clear gain in the same hiding-place. The joyous sound seemed to add not a little to Master Simon's cheerfulness, for he tapped his danghter on the knee, and said :—

" Damerones, do you know you '11 have a very nice little portion ?"

" Do you know," said his wife, " that there's great news here ? Father Nicolas, from the abbey yonder, has been killed by some of our folks. "

" That's a very good thing," replied Simon, rubbing his hands together.

" Yes," continued the womaa, " it makes one seigneur less, anyhow. But the lads that killed him are at their wits' end, and don't know what 'b to become of 'em—people only whisper when they want to tell what they've done, and, in fact, everybody is frightened. There's not a soul

7

to be seen in the streets, for everybody is gone home, and shut the door—and as you was away, we did just like the neighbors, though it's such a splendid day."

"People that hide to-day will soon show their faces again. —Listen to what I say, Jeanne; you, too, Damerones. This is a great day for Typhaines. It's all over with the abbey; aud as to Nicolas, the monk, whose other name you know so well, 'twas, I—yes, I—that gave orders to have him killed, just as I was setting off for the fair at Troyes ; and I want you to know it."

"What a brave fellow," said his wife, looking at him proudly.

"But, father, you will be excommunicated !" said the maiden.

"I expect so, my daughter," said he, " but one must risk everything for liberty."

For a while he sat pensive. His brow was lowering, for the thought just presented to him by his daughter gave rise to some sad reflections. He soon drove them out, however, and then went on :—

"After two whole years, I have succeeded at last! The whole population here are of my way of thinking, and ready to follow my lead. Perhaps there may be some blood shed; but I care not for blood if it only flows for the good of the public."

"You must hate our seigneurs very much," said Darae-rones.

"Simon has good reason to hate them," said Jeanne ; and she squeezed her terrible husband's hand.

The merchant was just about to impart to the two women an account of his conference with the four burghers in the morning, when indistinct sounds, as if of a distant tumult, were beginning to be heard in the street. Damerones and Jeanne rose. Simon kept his seat, but smiling the while, his head turned to one side, as if listening. The noise growing louder and louder, came nearer and nearer to the huge hovel where he sat.

" Go sit down," said Simon, in a severe tone. They both obeyed him, and the door suddenly opened. A great multitude, burghers, peasants, women and children, with alarm painted in their faces, were crowding about the doorway with moans and cries of distress. Antoine, Payen, Jacques, and others from the crowd came into the room.

" Comrade !" exclaimed Payen, " up with you, up at once, or we are all lost men !"

"Not so," replied Simon. "We are saved men, even now." He rose from his stool.

" Dost thou know," said Jacques, " that the monk was slaughtered by our own friends, our own sons, nephews, aud cousins ?"

" They are brave fellows !" Drawing his knife, he strode to the door, brandished the blade, shouted to the crowd, and exclaimed—

"You people there I choose what you will have, and choose at once. Are you willing to see your friends, the men who rescued you from the grasp of your masters and tyrants; are you willing to see them put to death without justice or law? If not, to your knives, to your knives, then !"

The whole crowd shouted their approval.

" Have no fear ot the monks," continued he. " A monk's frock is no armor of defence !"

" That's true ! That's true !" they cried. " Down with the monks! Down with the monks! Away with them !"

" A paradise on earth is liberty to do as you like ; to he master of your own property. What are you worth, mise rable slaves as you are, bowing beneath the yoke of a master ? You can neither go out nor come in, nor marry, nor

inherit, nor bequeath without buying beforehand the consent of a master, most of them knowing no name of pi;y I
It's time to put an end to such a miserable state of things.
Let us set up our commune. You are no slaves 1 To your
knives 1 To your knives ! Let us all combine and let us
set up our commune, and th&n neither monk nor knight shall
prevail against us 1 How many strong, able-bodied men
do I see before me, every man fit to bear arms ? Two
thousand at least!"

" Yes, and the women besides 1" rung out a thin, shrill
tone from the distant outside of the crush.

This interruption carried the public enthusiasm to its
topmost height: shouts and cries and clapping of hands
and bursts of laughter showed forth the common devotion
of the people to the common cause.

"Now," shouted Simon, "men, women, all of you; we
are ready 1"

"Yes, yes, we are all ready!"

" Let us to work, then, at once. I rejoice to see you
so brave ! You are free men and free women from this
very hour, and I proclaim that you are just as noble, this
day, as the knights and seigneurs themselves. But courage
is not the only thing we want—we want prudence as well.
It *s well to be prudent. It 's your business now to select
your leaders. Choose out the best and bravest among you,
the wisest you can find, and let them take care that all the
cunning and skill of your enemies may attempt in vain to
subdue you."

This proposal was received with acclamations, and, as is
usual under such circumstances, they elected their chiefs
on the spot. As soon as that was done, Simon, who was
the first on the list, ordered the mob to retire peaceably to
their homes, and wait for further orders. He then invited
his colleagues into the house, and sending his wife and

daughter away, shut himself in with the rustic senate—which consisted of the four burghers who had come back with him from the abbey, and who were of the richest and best of the townsmen of Typhaines.

The whole affair did not detain them for more than half an hour. In all revolutions of the sort, liberty is only the word, the thing is ever a dictatorship, and all that Simon had to do now was to state his opinion—it was adopted unanimously; and so the door was thrown open again, and, standing at the head of the new council, he addressed the people as follows :—

" My friends, ail we people here are men of peace, and all w'e ask is justice. We shall first seek Heaven's favor by bearing to the Lord Abbot a pacific proposition. Should he prove to be a wise man, what we propose in your behalf may be accomplished without a struggle. But if his pride should mislead him, and it comes to a matter of force, I am ready to shed my blood, and I doubt not you will pour out yours in the common cause."

"Yes, yes, Simon. God's blessings on you ; God save you, Simon!" Amid such shouts, and pouring down blessings on his head, the crowd followed their chiefs to the great abbey gate. The lay brothers and valets, see-iug the approach of such a host, became panic-struck, and hastily closed the portal, where they remained until, after much parleying on both sides, the gates were opened by the Abbot's order, who consented to admit the five deputies, and them only: the burghers were led into the cloister, where Abbot Anselm and Messire Philippe de Cornehaut stood waiting for them.

T*

CHAPTER YI.

IT was doubtless involuntary—but Antoine, Jacques, and Eudes stopped at the cloister door, and cast their eyes downward as they stood there before the cold looks of their ecclesiastical and temporal lord: not so Simon ; followed by Payen, he advanced with intrepid step, and when near enough gravely saluted the Abbot, and then spoke:—

" Holy father, this morning I did you a service for which I got but a poor acknowledgment. I knew not then that I should so soon return as bearer to you of the just demands of the good people of Typhaines."

" Say on," coldly said the priest.

The burgher looked distrustfully towards the knight, at the men-at-arms and the monastic crowd around him, and then went calmly on :—

"You, my Lord Abbot, know better than I do, that Adam and Eve were created free to do whatever seemed good in their sight, and that we—all of us—children of the same parents alike, are lawful inheritors of their rights. It nowhere appears in the Holy Scriptures that knights and clergy are descendants of a human family superior to that of the glebeman and laborer, bound by birth and lineage to obey and to suffer for their betters who can claim a veritable right to command them."

Here Simon stopped to see what effect his reasoning had had, but the impassible Abbot merely said:—

" Go on."

[11] As the unhappy burghers and peasants of Typhaines are your veritable, your true brethren born, they havo decided to leave the best portion of their celestial patrimony no longer in your hands. They cannot think it just and right to toil on forever in your service; and following the example that has been set by many cities in the realm of France, in the County of Flanders, and in the country of Lauguedoc, they have adopted a resolution to combine together in the form of a commune, and they now require of you an acknowledgment and an approval of their design."

Master Simon here paused again, and his eyes, like all others in the assembly, were bent on the countenance of the Abbot.

" Are you done ?" asked the ecclesiastic.

" Not yet. The inhabitants of Typhaines are a peaceful folk, and loth to engage in a quarrel with your lordship. They request your friendship, and in return therefor, promise to supply you with a hundred sheafs of wheat, a flock of fifty sheep, eight oxen, and a caparisoned horse, in consideration of which you shall hold them quit of all taxes, ordinary and extraordinary; and also of all compulsory service. Further, they do not refuse to pay you down a reasonable sum in money, by way of redemption of any ancient seigneural rights of yours. Make answer now, holy father, for I have spoken."

The Abbot straightened himself, like a bold champion entering the lists, and spoke as follows :—

" My son, to all you have here advanced I have but one reply to make. Holy Church, who is the spouse of God, and my sovereign as well as yours, forbids me, by the voice of her Pontiffs, to yield up any of her lawful property to any earthly greed whatever. Were I a mere lord temporal, I know not whether my sincere love of peace might not prevail on me to accede at least in part to your demands; but the property you covet is not mine to give ; it belongs to this holy abbey, the guardianship of which has been confided to my hands, in order that, as a vigilant watch-man and steward, I might preserve it, and at my death restore it, augmented perhaps in value, but never dimin-ished. Know, then, that never while Abbot Anselm enjoys authority in this house shall the least iota of her rights be wrested out of her hands. I believe that you are a poor people misled by vain desires—but if you will persevere in your sacrilegious enterprise, you shall come to loss in this present world, and what is far worse, in the world to come. And were you the Count of Nevers or the King of France himself, all your power would become as nothing in presence of the power of God."

" Reflect, holy father. Remember that your only means for resisting our will consists in your orisons and the ring-ing of your bells. You have no sergeants-of-arms here, nor crossbowmen, as in the days of Abbot Ranulf; and I must inform you that your neighbor, the Count de Nevers, will not take sides with you."

The Abbot, in spite of his firmness, turned pale—but he soon recovered.

" What know you of that!" said he. " That pious noble-man is not in the habit of abandoning the feeble clergy to the furious cravings of the laity !"

" Oh, holy father," returned Simon, with a laugh, " it's useless to feign. We know full well that you have received from the noble Count letters less than pleasing—and, more frank than yourself—we beg to show you this."

Drawing from his bosom a parchment-roll, he put it into the Abbot's hands.

The priest read the document, and then raising his eyes

towards heaven, exclaimed, with an expression of distress he no longer pretended to conceal:—

"Jerusalem ! Jerusalem ! Is it thus thy princes and chief men abandon thee ? I have seen the time when princes and knights would have blushed to not lend their swords and their lances to the Church's cause. But now they not only leave her in the hands of her old enemy, but attack her themselves. Hearken, my brethren, hearken my children, to the words of the Count de Nevers He, the son of an illustrious house, even he takes no shame to write to the insurgent serfs of a holy abbey

"Raoul, Count of Nevers, to his feal and good friend, Simon, merchant; salutation in our Lord. Say unto the good people of Typhaines, that, in consideration of a monthly payment of twenty silver marks, I will lend them fifteen knights, thirty squires, and two hundred crossbow-men, to defend them against all and every, without distinction of person or condition."

While the reading of the parchment-roll was going on, the three peasants looked proudly on the assembly around them, and the monks and servitors began to moan and tremble, as they heard the dread detail. Great tears were falling down the Abbot's now wrinkled cheeks. At this spectacle, Messire Philippe felt his heart swelling with emotion, for though his eyes had been witness to many dread disasters, it was still open to impressions of pity. He was preparing to take part in the passing scene, when the Abbot, brushing away his tears with his hand, exclaimed:—

" Oh, man of little faith that I am I Oh, my brethren, imitate not my example. Can you, like your cowardly pastor, forget that against our Holy Church the gates of hell shall never prevail 1 Oh, my friends, let us be prepared

to suffer martyrdom if we must, but let us never desert our
holy cause."

Then Anselm, turning an angry scowl on Simon and his
colleagues:—

" Think not, oh miserable men, that I stand here de-
fenceless. In vain shall the Count de Nevers lift his lance
against this holy house. I will raise a tempest against
which his buckler shall prove no shield for you."

" They are far away—those clouds you threaten us
with," said Simon, insolently, " and your mutinous people
are thundering at your door even now. Who is to guard
you against them ?"

" I—in Christ's name. I, miserable vilain," cried Monseigneur Philippe, stepping towards him. " And the holy
Abbot needs but make a sign and your riven skull shall
never go out hence to preach sedition again !"

" Ah ! Is it your voice I hear, Monseigneur Philippe
de Cornehaut ? Robbed of your estate by these greedy
monks, are you about to take their part in this quarrel ? Ah!
If yon are the man I named—and I know you are he—you
must be signally degenerated from the pride of your race, to
undertake the defence of your cruellest enemy 1 Or perhaps, think you, this monk, rescued by your hand, will restore the plunder. Ask him, Monseigneur, and you will
speedily find what his gratitudo comes to:"

" By all the saints in Champagne," said Messire Philippe,
laughing aloud, " for a poor vilain as you are, you can talk
like a bishop, and your counsel is so good that I will certainly follow it. Come now, holy father, be frank. If I
and my squire there, and my two pages, and my two archers,
will undertake to defend you to the death, will you restore
ray manor and lands ?"

Like a man on a wreck, and seeing his last hope sinking
beneath him, Master Anselm cast a look fraught with an-

gnish and terrible reproach at Simon, and then murmured :—

[14] Oh, my God I wilt thou abandon thy children ? Shall
the snares of the devil prevail against us ?" He wrung
his hands, and then, with a suddenness unequalled, threw
himself on his knees at Messire Philippe's feet.

" Ah I my son," he cried, " bethink you. Think of my
old age—think of my misfortunes, and behold how I kneel
before you I No I You will not suffer me to be taken in
the snares of the enemy of Christ I It is in vain that yonder man stands flattering himself for his hideous triumph.
Neither you nor I will ever betray our duty. I have confidence in my Master. All this wickedness must come to
naught And I have no thought to mislead you. What
belongs to the Lord, cannot return to secular uses. But
if you will defend the Church, and protect her ministers,
temporal blessings can never fail you—nor happiness beyond the grave, as well. Ah I my son, do you frown upon
me ? I conjure you 1—I implore you, tarnish not the honor
of your good name ! Cast me not bound into the inexorable hands of these rebels !"

A violent struggle broke out in the soul of the Chevalier. The fury he felt when, not an hour ago, he first
learned the fate of his demesnes, broke out afresh on hearing the heroic though imprudent avowal of the Abbot.
Yet the sight of that old man, whose trembling hands were
clinging to his knees, and his respect—he could hardly
quell it—for that holy personage; all these varied feelings
and emotions triumphed at last on seeing how Eudes and
Jacques put their arms akimbo, and laughing, with a sneer,
in the very face of their rightful lord on his knees before
him.

Monseigneur Philippe instantly raised the Abbot to his
feet, and said

" Holy father, what will yon have me do with this rabble ?"

Prompt to avail himself of the change;

" They are bad advisers for my serfs," said he, " and I have every right over them to prevent any evil of their concocting. Seize them, my son !"

Philippe, without a moment's hesitation, dashed forward to take Simon by the throat. Fulk and his men followed his example. But Simon, who was on his guard, instantly drew his cutlass, leaped aside, and began to retreat with his comrades, who had put themselves, like their leader, on the defensive. Had the cloth-merchant not missed a stroke that Rudaverse aimed at him, it is likely his career would have come to an end on the spot. Luck would have it that an agitated monk just at the very moment stumbled against the knight, and his terrible sword swerved lrom its path.

" Accursed race that ye are!" said Simon, as with a backhanded blow he tumbled on to the stones one of the lay brothers who was pressing on him with a hayfork: once fairly in the court-yard with his comrades, they readily reached the great gate, and finding it shut, they shouted to the multitude outside :—

" Help, good people ! To the rescue 1 They are murdering us here !"

The appeal was heard, and a terrible uproar of voices arose from behind the walls. It was a howl of rage, more furious than any war-cry, that music of the battle-field, and mingling with the tempest, arose the bellowed sounds, " *Commune 1 Commune /*" and then the sharp stroke of axes fell thick as hail.

" They are shouting out * *Commune /*' " said Fulk, stopping still just as he was pressing full sore on Eudes, who had found it a very hard task to keep him off.

Making this reflection, Fulk scratched his ear with his

finger quite thoughtfully, and then went up and took his master by the left elbow.

" Monseigneur," said he, with that calmness that never deserted him, " the rabble are hallooing out ¹ *Commune P* We are not strong enough to stand up against such a cry as that. The door will give way in a few seconds more. Are you not of the opinion that it would be well for us to retreat with the father Abbot and his monks, to the inside of the convent, where, at any rate, seeing how few we aro in number, we might make a better defence than we can out here *t"*

¹¹ You are right, Fulk," replied the knight " Fathers, retreat—and be in a hurry, for the gate is giving way ; a great piece of the splintered wood showed how true that was, for at the sight, the whole monkish crowd began to hasten forward, terror-struck, after the Abbot: the soldiers formed a rear-guard, and in less than a minute the whole great court-yard was cleared ; not a soul was left in it save the leaders of the Typhaines communeers, who at once went to work assisting their friends outside to break down the obstacle between them, and so shut off all access to the convent To that task, well fitted to be called homicidal, Simon addressed himself with an ardor and passion that left far behind the less impetuous though still excited zeal of his confederates. The man worked as if endowed with superhuman strength and activity. He was, visibly, one of the race of the strong, who are born to command all that come within range of their will.

As the peasaut crowd rushed into the abbey court-yard, brandishing axes, sharpened stakes, scythes, and every form of offensive engine they had snatched up in their haste, Simon dashed into their midst, and succeeded in pre-venting them from separating into small squads, as they

8

were just about to do, ravening to break into the monastery, and lay hold on the monks.

" Dont separate ! Keep together ! To the cloisters ! To the cloisters !" he shouted, in a ringing tone. " Run to the cloisters ! *Commune! Commune!*"

The whole crowd poured on at his heels, and the doors soon gave way as the portal had done just before. The assailants, dancing and bounding with delight, threw themselves bellowing into the vaulted corridor, and soon reached the end, whence a spiral stairway led up to a higher floor. The unreflecting peasants pushed onwards and got jammed in the dreadful gulf. No sooner had they begun to ascend than two arrows, rapid as a blast, overthrew two of the excited mob, and tumbled them back at the feet of their friends, yet a third mounted over the corpses of the slain, and fell back with his head laid open by an invisible battle-axe. Others continued to climb over the prostrate carcasses, only to meet the like fate, hewed down by a formidable sword. In such a labyrinth, the besiegers scarce got a glimpse of their adversaries.

The attack began to grow cold. Simon saw that to persevere would be to compromise the enterprise, and expose his party to disasters that must tend to cool their ardor in the cause.

" Back, neighbors !" he shouted. " Back ! Don't go and get killed ! Don't go into that rat-trap. Our enemies can't escape. In a few minutes we'll have 'em at a cheaper cost. *Commune !* Hurrah for the *Commune !*"

The peasants now gave back, and went out to crowd the court-yard. There Simon selected fifty of the most vigorous and best armed among them, who were put under Payen's orders, with instructions to keep vigilant watch and ward over the lawn and the outer walls, to prevent any soul from escaping to seek succor for the beleaguered pile. Simon then withdrew the rest of his men, and went down the rock to Typhaines. As he marched onwards, he established a post, consisting of about twenty men, at the bridge, to secure his communications with the besiegers in case of a sortie by the monks or their defenders, and then entered the town.

The women, who had, at a safe distance, been following the insurgents, testified by their shouts and congratulations, what a part they had taken in what they supposed to be a victory, although it had not been crowned by a great success. Husbands, fathers, and brothers were loaded with compliments, and embraced as if they were so many heroes. Simon himself accepted the congratulations of his wife and daughter.

"At last, at last," murmured Jeanne, as she squeezed her husband's hand, and with a singular expression of her countenance.

"Damerones," said he, "rejoice, oh, my daughter, rejoice, Damerones; never more shalt thou be poor girl, receiving no respect from the high born, and exposed to danger by thy beauty. Henceforth thou art become a lady, and thy presence shall inspire with respect all that come into the presence of a powerful burgher's child."

"It is well, father," she coldly replied.

"Now, my daughter, and thou too, my Jeanne, go, like prudent women, to your bed. I must return to my colleagues, for I must acquit myself of some heavy duties this night."

He departed—he was transported with enthusiasm ; ho seemed as if endowed with the energy and the will of two ordinary mortals. He thought not of hunger or of thirst, or rest, or sleep, and though just returned that day from a long and difficult journey, he was insensible to any signs of fatigue.

It was now dark night, and no moon in the sky to shed
down a cheering light. By Simon's orders large bonfires
were kindled in the streets and squares. He then went to
the abbey gaol, henceforth to be dignified with the title of
townhouse, where a council was about to be held, and which
was to serve as the town hall, until, according to onstom,
a proper city hall and belfry, to be built out of the public funds,
should arise. In the course of that night, he demanded, with
a spirit unequalled save only by his colleagues, that every
man should hold himself ready to spend his all in the good
cause. Every man of them declared his acquiescence. In
the borough which had grown rich by its trade and agricul-
ture, and where the numerous pilgrims of Typhaines had been
long in the habit of depleting their purses, there were many
wealthy people, but not a single egotist It was not the
chiefs alone who returned the exact amount of their estates,
but other people of flourishing means came forward with
offers of all they had for the public weal. Simon settled
the figures of every assessment, and then charged himself
double the sum due by any of the others. Other resolutions
adopted by the meeting clearly show the prevailing state
of burgher feeling of the time. It was resolved that a
commencement should be made that very night of a military
fortification by which the whole town was to be surrounded
and secured. Next, laborers were to be brought in from
all the country round about, to work on the walls and fosse,
with towers from distance to distance. The city hall and
belfry were to be commenced without delay. Two commissioners were despatched to Troyes for arras and warlike
munitions, and a courier to the Count de Nevers, to request
him to promptly send forwards his promised succors. Finally, the number of supreme communal chiefs was defi-
nitely settled—they were to be five in all—and Simon,
Payen, Jacques, Eudes and Antoine, in imitation of the

southern communes, assumed the sonorous appellation—
consuls.

After all these resolutions had been adopted, and announced to the assembled populace, Simon and his colleagues went forth to visit and inspect the posts. Again
and again they made the complete tour of the abbey. It
was a dark and moonless night, yet they hearkened, as they
went along under the outer walls, to the chants of the monks
within, celebrating as usual their nocturnal ceremonies.

" They are celebrating mass for their dead," said Payen.

" Never doubt it," said the consul, squeezing him by the
hand.

So passed the night away. For the insurgent communeers it seemed to be the best night they had ever
known, and when the sun arose in the morning it shone
down on them gayer and stronger than the most perfect repose could have made them.

8*

CHAPTER YII.

AND now, every brain in Typhaines was intoxicated with
the enthusiasm of liberty. The people who the morning
before bent to the knee at the passing by of the very least
of the brethren on the hill out yonder, were proudly smacking their lips at the delicious savor of their new-born
happiness. Every order that came forth out of the old
abbey gaol, now the city hall, but added to their delirious
joy, and they were continually, in this exaltation, uttering
cries which rose upwards on the wings of the breeze, to
be transported thereon to the now silent and solemn abode
of the professors of a holy religion—sad warning to the
ears of the venerable Abbot and his devout children and
servitors.

" They '11 soon come out of their rookery up yonder,"
cried many a villager, as he pointed to the lofty walls and
towers above, and then shook his fist at them. " They '11
come down by 'r Lady; and even should we let them alone,
without another assault, hunger will soon force them to surrender. When that happens, won't these ehopping-axes
that have split their wood for so long, have a good pay
out of their necks ?"

So spoke the peasants in their revolt; and he who could
find the most violent, ferocious, and insulting expression,
was chosen favorite for the occasion. Gathering around
their street fires, mixed up with women and children, the
burghers kept up these atrocious conversations, which are

the usual pride of insurrection days. The sun's return, that had put to speedy flight an August night, had but added vigor and intensity to these terrible apostrophes to the desolate abbey.

And yet the abbey, ever since the close of Simon's vain assault, had given no outward sign of life within, save that gloomy nocturnal chant and invocation. Those night-songs might well, in that distant century, have passed for angel's voices wafted from on high by immaterial forms, and certainly, had any sincere partisans of the good Father Abbot been surprised by those pious wailings, they never would have failed to spread abroad the rumor of a miracle. But we have seen what a sinister reflection it was that was aroused in the minds of the patrolling consuls, as they fell on the ear in that dark and starless night.

The pious abode, then, was silent without. Within, the monks and their servants, not to say the very men-at-arms, were far from being as cheerful or joyous as the townsfolk below. The fight was hardly over, when the knight hurried up the winding stair, and approaching the Abbot, returned his sword to its scabbard, as he found him and his people engaged in prayer, on the landing above.

Monseigneur Philippe's face was radiant and bright, and a smile played about his lips. The genius of battle lighted up its areole on that bold and hardy front, that had been all uncovered during that short but rude melee, for the knight had not taken time to snatch either helm or buckler. He approached, as I said, the Abbot, who, as he was looking at him, could not keep down the secret thought that Gideon himself, armed for the Moabitish fray, could not have appeared brighter or more terrible.

"Well, now, holy father, I rather think we have had some pretty good sword play. You can get up, now, and leave off praying. The rascals are gone, save some few

who fell down stairs there, and I suppose are just ready
to give up their last breath, so Q6 never to give you; any
more trouble in. this world."

[41] Yes, my son, next to God himself, this holy house owes
its safety to you ; and never will I be unmindful of that
service. But would it not be insensate to abandon ourselves to joy so soon ? Though repulsed now, our serfs
will come back to-night or in the morning, and then "

[44] Then," said Monseigneur Philippe, " they shall find a
like reception. Still, you speak like a wise man. It is
not time as yet to glorify ourselves. As I am the only
knight here, I think it would not be presumptuous in me were
I to assume the command of the garrison. Let us go and
make all the necessary arrangements that are now possible.
And to begin with, holy father, is there any other entrance
but this winding stair to the interior of the abbey ?"

[44] Yes, my son, there is the great church door, though,
to be sure, it is defended by a battlemented wall, but I know
not whether, weak as we are in point of numbers and courage, our servants are enough to garnish the wall."

" To garnish walls with the small force at our disposal
seems to me not a very easy thing to do," replied Philippe.
"But show me your wall, and I will do the best I can
with it."

As he was moving off, he charged Fulk to keep a strict
watch, and calling his two pages to follow him, accompanied the Abbot to the point which was likely to prove most
critical in the coming operations for defending the place.

The church façade, consisting in great Roman arches,
was pierced for three doors spacious enough to admit, on
grand festival occasions, of the entrance of the entire population of Typhaines, the good people of the neighboring
villages, and the crowds of pilgrims, in one serried mass.

Whenever the Abbot, surrounded by his monks, appeared

officiating before the sacred relics, clothed in his whole pomp of dress, such was the nature of the architectural arrangements that the ecclesiastical dignitary was enabled to cover with his edified gaze the whole vast crowd that crammed the whole church, filled the lawn, and even hung around on the rocky slopes of the hill. But a wise and prudent forethought had considerably modified so sumptuous a disposition of the sacred spot. The abbey had, in the rude war times of old, been menaced with conflagration by whirling firebrands from without, to the great peril of the monks, as well as the church itself, and it became necessary to renounce some portion of a magnificence so perilous. Guided by the best military skill of the age, a wall fifteen feet high had been traced on such a plan as to protect the entire front by means of its solid battlements. The only entrance now consisted in a passageway some eighteen inches wide, and so low that one had to stoop in going through the defile.   *

There is no doubt that though the religious display lost something in point of splendor, the abbey got a large gain in the matter of security.

No sooner had the Crusader got on the top of the wall thai) he began a rapid reconnoissance, and at the very first sight he laughed out for joy.

" You are not going to expect me, holy father, to defend this rampart? Had we a dozen men-at-arms the task, even then, would be a hard one, for I see no ditch here, and the wall is a low one. Why, Charlemagne and his nephew to boot would never agree to take charge of such a post! Never ! But let us do better than that; let us give up the church, and be satisfied with working hard all night to wall up the passage that leads out of the church into the monastery. By so doing, we should have absolutely nothing to do but guard our winding stair—and I swear 'pon my honor that a whole army could never get up there I"

The Abbot looked resolutely at the knight:—

You may be in the right, my son. To me it seems as it does to you that we are too weak to save our church ; but if, in these days of disaster, my blood must be shed, let it flow out on the very threshold of this holy house. No! Never will I abandon to profaning hands the sanctuary of the Lord, the chapels where so many sacred relics are reposing, the tombs of the Abbots who have gone before me, nor the very pavements where so many of the faithful once trod, honored and made sacred in my eyes. What is there in this whole inclosure that is worth saving at the cost of bloodshed ? Our cells, the cloisters, the corridors, the chapter-halls ! Nay, my son, the church is all in all, the rest not worth thinking about. And I tell you truly, that if my monks and I can find no other way to save our miserable lives but by betraying our altars, think no more of it, for we are ready to perish."

The knight made no answer, and thought the Abbot was not far wrong People in those times had none but absolute sentiments, unreasonable reasons, such as impel men who put them into practice up to the very palm of heroism or to the disasters of madness. In a less barbarous age a captain would have tried at least to convince the Abbot that there might be no great harm in transferring the relics and other most valuable objects in the church to the interior of the cloister, at the risk of being obliged at some future day to purify the church, if the rebels should dare to profane it. But Monseigneur Philippe found the Abbot's views on that subject so just and natural, that he made no attempt to change it, and without decreeing a crown to himself for the bright thought, he simply replied:—

" Yery well. We 'll try to defend the wall. Now, holy father, come, and let us have a talk about a very serious matter; and yon, my pages, do you stay here. Should the rabble down yonder behind the ruins of the great gate show any signs of coming forward, call me to the rescue." So sayiug, the Chevalier led the Abbot away; and after they had got into the interior of the monastery, said :—

" What have we to eat, to-morrow, next day, and the next day after that ?"

The Abbot crossed his hands, and made no answer.

14 H m !" said Monseigneur Philippe. " Yet people generally do brag a good deal about the good cheer to be found among the monks."

"I have been improvident."

" Yes ; your charity to the poor people has carried you too far, holy father," replied the knight, with great respect. " Still, we may expect a crust of bread and a cup of wine for to-morrow ?"

" Yes, you can have that; but nothing more."

" So, we have a chance to hold out till to-morrow evening," pursued the Crusader. " Let us make use of that to secure our last chance for safety. One of your people must devote himself, get out of the convent, deceive the vilain guard, and go to demand succor from the nearest neighbor you have."

" You are right," said Anselm. "I will at once write to the only person who can help us. The Count de Nevers[7] vassals are all around us. Their fidelity due to the Count, will prevent them from doing us anything but mischief. There is only one support I can rely on, and that is the Lady of Cornouiller."

" Ah! holy father," cried Philippe, all red with emotion, "is it really possible to inform Mahaut of what is going on here ? By the Cross, you redouble my courage, and I beg you, when you write, to put in that I am here with you."

" I shall do so."

" But don't delay I The night favors us; the moon is not up yet; perhaps we could not find a better time to make the attempt."

" I believe you, my son, and I 'll go directly and write to the only person who, at this time, can possibly come to our assistance in this terrible misfortune of ours."

They now separated: the thought of Mahaut's being speedily apprised of his return from the Holy Land, and the danger that threatened him, awoke a most delicious feeling in his soul. A few words that had fallen from the Abbot's lips left no doubt that the affair of his marriage was in a much better train than what concerned the restoration of his domain, and as, after all, love and war of all else in the world were what he most delighted in, he rather thought his prospects not altogether of the gloomiest. As far as to any checks probable, or merely possible, we must do him the justice to declare that he never so much as thought about them, for he was a real soldier to the fullest extent of the word, and improvident as a child.

Filled with the most flattering hopes, he went out to join Fulk, whom he found, his drawn sword tucked under his arm, leaning against the wall of the winding stair, and giving a lecture, in a savage tone of voice, to the valets. In his master's absence, he had issued his orders. They were all to go and arm themselves as best they could ; and when Messire came up, his eye fell on some twenty of those unvalorous rascals, not a bit fond of fighting, but furnished far better than could have been expected, with rusty swords, bows, lances, not to add, here and there, a helmet.

" If we were out now in the open country," said Fulk,

" I know very well that we should be obliged to march in
the rear at these fine fellows' heels, to keep them from running away. But here, behind these stones, and a little
bit out of danger, we may get some good out of them in
spite of their villainous mien."

Messire Philippe detached fifteen of them, and ordered
them to join the two pages on thefa9ade rampart. He left
Fulk and the two archers at the important post at the
stair, stationed the five improvised militia that were left,
as pickets here and there where a good view could be got
of the country, and the burgh especially, from the belfry,
for example, and when all these dispositions had been
duly made, he lay down on the flagstones, wrapped in his
cloak, to catch a few moments of rest he was much in want
of. Then his thoughts wandered to his betrothed, to his
murdered father, his stolen goods, and the splendid fights
that he was about to enjoy, and musing so, he waited until
the Abbot could get his letter written.

Think, then, whether any man whatever, speedy to think
and prompt to decide, would not be likely to grow confused,
wandering among such a variety of subjects of contemplation, and judge whether or not the good knight, with
his wild imagination and hot, impetuous brain, might not
be utterly lost among so many blind paths. Yet there
were two dominant points in his reflection. One was Mahaut; the other, an ardent desire to bring the revolted
clodpolls back to their duty. The very word " *Commune*"
was to him instinctively odious, and the behavior of the
Count de Nevers was, to his loyal soul, so utterly inexplicable, that he conceived a feeling of contempt without
bounds for the name and character of his suzerain.

While the gentleman was thus giving aloose to his
imagination, the chief and lord of this place of prayer had
proceeded to his cell, and when there, and the door closed,

9

had thrown himself down on his straw bundles in an attitude of the deepest discouragement. Father Anselm took
a more discouraging view, no doubt, than the careless and
turbulent knight had conceived. He knew far better than
the man-at-arms did, the power of the shout, " *Commune!
Commune !*" which was heard at that period in almost
every region in Europe, sounding out from the throats of
the mainmontable crowds wherever they deemed it a possible thing to publish their will to the world. He kuew
that the coming strife must issue in the abasement of all
ecclesiastical power of his, or the massacre of the burghers
who had been for so many centuries the docile instruments
of the grandeur and wealth of his abbey.

In the Abbot's grief there was no element of a narrow
minded and scandalous egotism. To glance merely at the
poor, miserable living room he had constructed in the very
centre of his splendid monastery might well convince any
one to the contrary. Certain it is that throughout the vast
extent of the demesnes of Typhaines there was not a peasant, nor in the whole expanse of all Christendom, a hermit so poor as not to have been shocked at a view of the
wretchedness by which Abbot Anselm was perpetually
striving to augment the rigor of his surroundings. A disciple, and a beloved disciple, too, of Saint Bernard, though
Anselm had risen to the very highest rank to which his
talents, the elevation of his character, and his devotion to
the Church, had carried him, never did he, in that eminent
station, lay aside the virtues, the asceticism, nor any part of
the inflexible that had made him dear to the founder of
Clairvaux.

But though hard on himself, and more than disinterested,
he became an ambitious man whenever a question arose
involving the interests of the cause or the wealth of his
abbey. He had meditated bravely upon the passing events

of the age. He had seen, whether in France, in Champagne, or on the domains of other lords; bishops and abbot's despoiled by submissive servants to their time-old authority, and had done all that in him was to divert from his own monastery the advent of days so evil. He had made every effort to win the confidence and love of his vassals. As far as possible, he had lessened their burthen of taxes and corvees. His immense charity had gone forth far and wide, to seek out and to solace every wretched soul. His seigneural granaries were found ever empty from the generous prodigality with which he ever succored the poor. And he hoped to find safety in this policy, sacred in itself considered and in the protection that his personal austerities and the virtues of his monks, so submissive to the rigorous discipline of his order, must constrain the bare justice of heaven to vouchsafe. Distrustful, as well he might be, of the secret intentions of his illustrious neighbor, the Count de Nevers, he had endeavored, with Father Nicolas' help, a man known to have been held in high esteem by the bold suzerain, to turn aside the threatened storm ; in short, all that the most prudent provision, all that the most ardent and truest devotion could prescribe, that he had done; but prudence, devotion, charity, all had failed in face of the secret persistency of the glebe-men, who, more than charity, more than affection, more than justice itself, cherished and henceforward would insist on, liberty.

At length, after a moment surrendered to what the Abbot considered as his human frailty, he took up a fragment of parchment, wrote a few words to his pupil, and went back to seek the chevalier. The youngest, most active, and boldest of the abbey valets was selected, for he was familiar with all the paths that led down to the town, and put in charge of the message. The Abbot made an appeal to his devotion, gave him his blessing, with a promise of liberty and a farm, provided he should return on the morrow as guide to the Cornouiller men-at-arms, and lead them up to one of the abbey towers.

To prevent him from being observed by any of the enemies^ pickets, he was lowered by means of a rope from one of the windows farthest away from the burgh, where their vigilance was supposed to be least keen. It was an anxious time they spent there, watching his proceedings, as he was carefully looking all about him, and at last began to creep down. They watched him as he disappeared in the dark, and then the Abbot, quite composed, as a man in command ought ever to be, said:—

" If that man should succeed in putting my letter this night into the Dame of Cornou'.ller's hands, our deliverance is made sure. The rebels are not strong enough to stand fast against the smallest squad of cavalry, and I do not think the Nevers ment-at-arms have joined them as yet. Let us hope on, my son."

" I do hope," replied the Crusader, suppressing a formidable yawn. " But, if you please, holy father, I* 11 go and stretch myself down on the rampart, and sleep a few hours. It will enable me to handle Rudaverse so much the better, when the assault does come."

" Do so, my son," rejoined the monk, inwardly envying the laic's quiet way. " In the mean time I will go and unite in prayer with my people, and invoke's Heaven's pity on us all."

While Anselm was on his way to the church, the valet who had charge of the precious message went forward at a good pace, with his face townwards, where he speedily arrived, and put Mahaut's letter into Master Simon's hands.

CHAPTER Yin.

THUS, it appears that when the sun of the new-risen morn was beginning to gild the walls of that terror-struck though still hopeful abbey, every chance of escape was clean vanished and gone.

The garrison were soon apprised of the miscarriage of the missive. About an hour after sunrise, the knight, leaning on one of the battlements of the facade wall, saw the serfs, who still occupied the lawn, running about and uttering loud shouts, and gathering in crowds round the ruins of the great gate. At the same time a crowd of people issued from the burgh, and crossed the bridge, headed by Master Simon and Payen, armed with hauberks, just like so many knights; and they all began to climb the hill. Meanwhile, a still more considerable mass of the populace, consisting in the main of women and children, spread themselves out on the plain, and with picks and spades and barrows, set about tracing and digging out the ditches that had been ordered by a consular decree, for the purpose of completely inclosing the entire town with fortifications.

This second troop made no great impression on Monseigneur Philippe. He cared but little, and, sooth to say, not in the least about what the Typhaines folk might be about at home, for he considered the only important matter was what they were proposing to do at the abbey.

9*

He didn't wait long before he could find out what Master Simon was going to do.

In the first rank marched a number of men bending under the weight of their long ladders. Behind them came peasants, armed with bows and slings. Others advanced provided with scythes, and a few of them had long lances.

The knight sent for Fulk.

" What thinkest thou is going to happen ?"

" Nothing at all," replied the giant, " only we may have a rather tiresome forenoon."

" Tiresome I Why tiresome !"

" Whenever I come to a quarrel with communeers, I'm sure to meet some sort of ill luck. It seems to me I'm going to lose this other eye of mine."

" Not at all—not at all. You 'll be quits for a finger or some other trifle of that sort," said Messire Philippe. " People never are hit twice in the same spot."

"1 'm rather inclined to the opinion," 6aid Fulk, while that other eye of his was always turned towards the advancing mob, " that we are not going to get out of this alive. The Saracens do, at times, give quarter—but peasants, never! I'm sorry we didn't take some other notion in our heads, instead of coming here."

" And I—I'm delighted with perhaps a fine opportunity to do what nobody ever as yet attempted to do. Dost thou opine, that since the days of Baron Olivier and the twelve peers, any man-at-arms has by himself, alone, ever defended a fortress ? 'Pon my faith, if I should even happen to be killed I'll leave a good renown behind me ; and Mahaut will have far to seek before she 'll find a successor fit to take my place. As I am only doing this exploit out of love for her, this old monk here ought to have thanked me; uot robbed me of my domains. I'd have served him right had I let his serfs have the pleasure of cutting his head off."

" Do be reasonable for once in your life," said Fulk; "and let 's get out of this. It's mighty fine, I suppose, to leave a fellow's poor bones bleachiug about these walls in the rain ! Pshaw !"

" Go to the devil with you," said his master. " I sent for you to ask whether you are williug to trust our two pages so far as to leave them alone to guard the stair. You and the fifteen vilains would be a marvellous reinforcement just here."

"Very well. Send the pages," replied Fulk. "I think I can stay with you."

As he was talking, a man made his appearance on the lawn. He proved to be Master Simon. He stopped about twenty paces in front of the wall, and raised his hand.

The knight stepped forwards to the edge of the parapet, and said:—

" What is it ?"

"Monseigneur," replied the man, "we are just about to give the assault."

" Give it."

" Before we begin, I have to say that you should not deceive yourself. This is not to be a fencing match, nor anything of the sort. • If the Typhaines burghers should scale that little wall of yours, they 'll slaughter everything that's before them, monks, abbot, valets, knight, men-at-arms, the children, the women, and the dumb beasts, too, if they find them there !"

" Use your pleasure," answered Philippe de Cornehaut.

" Consider, monseigneur, that those brave fellows I seo behind you, looking as valiant as you are yourself, will probably run away as soon as the fray begins—the only thing, be it said, they can do, to save their lives."

Messire Philippe involuntarily turned his head to look at his garrison—and the fact is, that every mother's son of his raw recruits, on hearing what Simon had said, turned remarkably pale, but that didn't prevent his making answer.

" You can massacre them, if so please you, but you 'll have to get in first, won't you ?"

The consul bit his lips. However, he once more resumed :—

"Monseigneur, you are but a young man as yet, and you ought to cling to life rather than risk it in the defence of the worst enemy you have in the whole world. I have but one word to say to you, and perhaps that word may induce you to decide. You are relying on the speedy arrival of succor from the Lady of Cornouiller. Yery well, then. This is the Abbot's letter to her—you may see it is so by the seal. Your messenger came, like an honest man, to join his brethren in town, and delivered it to me. Will you still hesitate ?"

" No; sir vilain," replied the knight, as he was crossing his arms on his breast. " Such as I do not hesitate. Men of my lineage never go back on their word when once it is pledged. I promised the Abbot to defend him, and I shall defend him, and now I have to give you notice that in case you should venture to come within bow-shot, my only answer will be an arrow."

" Begone, then, wretched fool that you are," cried Simon, in a towering passion that showed how false and seeming his mansuetude had been. " Begone—and rest assured these flagstones shall soon be wet with your infamous blood, and that you'll have no one to blame for it but yourself." With these words Simon withdrew.

" How tiresome all this is," muttered Fulk. " What a wretched day! I begin to think, for want of something better to do, it wouldn't be a bad notion to throw all these rascals here oyer the battlement. When we get to business with their village friends down there, they '11 be sure to attack ns in the rear."

"Not a bad notion that," responded the chevalier, looking fiercely at the garrison behind him. " What say you to that, my masters ? Don't mind now. Do you mean to behave like that infamous scoundrel who has just betrayed your master ? Speak out I But only take notice that the very first knave that seems wanting in will or courage either shall find out how heavy Rudaverse is !"

The valets—the whole of them—on seeing Rudaverse aforesaid flaming in the knight's hand, were suddenly seized with a violent enthusiasm for the monastery. An enthusiasm, I say, that rendered them utterly intrepid. They had discovered a great difference between the rusty old scythes, and sharpened stakes, down there in the lawn, and the flaming brand in the chevalier's hand, as well as the ponderous battle-axe of the burly squire. It was a very questionable matter with them whether the burghers, numerous though they were, could ever succeed in carrying the wall against a gentleman clad from head to foot with iron mail. All these considerations filled their hearts with boiling ardor, and they began, of their own unbiassed will, to salute the approaching crowd with most energetic shouts and imprecations.

" Stand fast, Fulk I Stand firm, brave vilains," cried Messire Philippe, at the top of his voice. " Notre Dame de Typhaines and Cornehaut!" he shouted for his battle-cry. There's enough in that to startle better men than that scum."

The threatening crowd came on the while, laid three ladders to the wall, and at once began to climb. Philippe struck but three blows with his ponderous blade, when

furions lamentable cries, screams, and groans, told the tale.
The ladder was lying at the foot of the wall, with every
soul of the poor men that had rushed to claim the privilege
of mounting first to the assault. The Crusader flew to the
next, but the work was already done. Fulk had knocked
over the foremost assailants, and broken the ladders to
pieces. Such success carried the valor of the gallant fifteen
to the topmost height of delirium: they screamed like so
many possessed; they brandished their swords over the
wall, and poured forth volleys of abuse on the crowd below.

" Keep cool 1 Keep cool!" growled Fulk, as he saw
more ladders coming up, dragged forwards by the furious
mob.

" How disagreeable!" muttered the squire.

The second assault turned out no better for the besiegers
than the first. It 's true the burghers did succeed in laying a dozen scaling ladders to the wall, and that four of
them made out to get a footing on the battlements, but the
weight of the scaling parties that crowded the rungs, broke
three of them, carried to the ground all bruised and bleeding every soul that was eagerly striving to reach the top
of the wall, and then the valets began to behave like heroes,
while the knight and Fulk were knocking down, slashing
and hacking every man bold enough to come within theii
reach.

This time they didn't wait for their adversaries to renew
the assault. They poured a storm of crossbow bolts and
arrows on the rabble; they picked up enormous fragments
of the battlemented walls, great paving-stones they had
piled up at hand the night before, and dashed them down
on the miserable wretches still lying at the foot of the wall.
Then rose up a fearful cry most piteous to hear. Tho pocr
creatures, tumbled all wounded, broken and dying, from
the fallen scaling ladders, uttered dreadful screams and

groans, till the terror-stricken mob, seeing their friends squirming and convulsed and howling with pain as the rocks and stones rained down from above to dash out their brains and cover them with gore—the crowd, I say, struck with horror, began to give back as their impetuous ardor grew cool. They now felt how much it would cost to carry the terrible height. Monseigneur Philippe de Cornehaut, his armor all blood stained, his vizor down, and helm closed, lifting up and then casting down huge fragments of rock on the ruined masses below him, looked as if he might be the fatal genius of that miserable race.

Eudes and Antoine, in utter disorder, rushed up to where Simon stood.

"Wretched man!" they cried, "see what you have brought us to ! Our men are all driven back in terror ! That kniglft must be the devil—and we Ve done our best : neither prayers nor threats are of the least use to persuade the very bravest of them to face his sword and the rocks he is showering down."

" Oh !" said Simon, as he stood wringing his hands. "You are in the right there; that dog is indeed a child of the house of Satan, and till we can get him into our hands I shall never have a happy hour. But to suffer a defeat would be fatal—it is impossible to submit to it—it would be the ruin of the commune. The abbey must be taken! Don't answer me! Don't speak to me ! Victory is as necessary for us as life itself. Do you suppose the state of the abbey can remain long unknown in the country ? No ! To-morrow, or the next day at the farthest, succor will come from some quarter."

"But remember now, Simon," replied Antoine, "the Nevers men will be here in four days' time, and with their help we can do better than we can alone."

" How blind !" cried the Consul. " Do you think those

allies are going to be your servants ? They '11 help you to
carry the abbey; but the entrance once forced and the
Abbot and the knight fairly in their hands, you don't suppose they will be handed over to you to have justice done
upon them. No ! They '11 keep them themselves. They'll
send them to the Count. They '11 feed us on hope, and I
tell you now, that so long as the Abbot is alive and the
gentleman can wield a sword, neither your liberty nor lives
are safe. No ! not if you should reduce them to beggary!
Believe me then, dear friends—my dear neighbors—if you
do love the commune for which you took up arms, and for
which you swore to die if needs must—to the assault I to
the assault! Never let your courage fail. Never despair."

So speaking, Simon's soul was deeply moved. He ges-
ticulated, he shouted aloud. Great tears rolled down his
cheeks. He seemed on the point of casting himself down
at their feet. Payen, with a wound of the shoulder and
his dress all torn, his steel head-piece broken in, just then
came up: the blacksmith had succeeded in struggling for
a few moments with Monseigneur, on the top of the wall.
Jacques, who had just escaped by miracle from a blow aimed
at him by Fulk's battle-axe, seemed somewhat cooled.
Still Simon's impetuosity and his supplications won them
all over at last.

"Well, then, once more," said Jacques.

" Let's try it," shouted Payen.   *   %

" Brave fellows !" cried Simon. " God will bless you.
Come on—I '11 lead you."

He laid hold of a ladder and began to draw it along
at a run, shouting, " To the wall I To the wall, good men
of Typhaines I Vengeance for our friends 1"

The spectacle of their Consuls returning to the fight
aroused something of vigor even in men who seemed to
have lost it all Some of his comrades seized the ladder

that Simon was drawing after him, and many a combatant came up to the rescue.

"Here comes the most tiresome part of the whole affair," said Fulk to his master. " I doubt whether we shall get well out of it."

" Never doubt it," replied the knight.

Seeing Simon come on, Messire Philippe grasped his hilt with a force so great that no human power could have torn it from his hand ; the sword and the man looked as if made of one single piece of iron.

Fulk's prediction was not very wide of its fulfilment. Three of the valets were down already at the first shock. Simon, who now faced Mouseigneur, parried his strokes so skilfully that he succeeded at last in planting one foot on the battlement, while the other stood on the upper rung, aud he had nothing to do now but leap into the place to win au entrance. The man was so vigorous, so hardy, so intrepid, so adroit, that the gentleman thought he had got at last a foeman worthy of him. Yet Messire was not in the least disturbed at that; but, seeing the danger was pressing, he determined to not yield an hich, and sooner than that, die on the spot.

And he was very near doing that very thing. Master Simon's sword had cut his buckler in two, and wounded him on the arm. In the hurried 'melee, which allowed no time for a regular duel, victory was about to declare for the peasants, for Fulk and the valets were finding it nearly impossible to drive them off, when the youngest of the two pages darted in to take part in the fray, and snatching up an axe that a dying peasant had dropped, he struck the Consul such a furious blow, that he stumbled on the wall, threw up his arms, fell backwards, and toppled down to stretch himself on the pile of dead and wounded men at the foot of the rampart.

10

"Well hit, my little fellow!" cried Messire Philippe. The whole garrison gave a shout of triumph.

"The stones ! The stones 1 Take to the stones !" roared Fulk, seizing a broken flagstone to crush Simon's body below. In the wild confusion and amazement of his men, Payen, who was the most intrepid man among them, had presence of mind enough to dash into the very heart of the turmoil, raise the stunned body of his friend, hoist it to his shoulder, and carry it off at speed. Without a signal-call, and at the same instant of time, the whole rabble, the whole Typhaines army took flight, and ran like a flock of frightened sheep out of the fatal courtyard, where so many bold peasants lay dead or dying.

The fight, with its repeated attempts to scale, had lasted not more than an hour.

" It's my notion," said Fulk, " that it's over for to-day. I should not refuse, just at this time, to eat a bit of bacon, or even to have a stoup of wine. Such a runuiug about in this hot weather makes a fellow thirsty."

" Hush, you brute !" said Philippe, as he was unlacing his helm to get* a little breath : " there's nothing here to drink but water, and as for bacon, there's hardly enough to last till sundown : don't set all those scamps to shouting ⁴ famine.' "

The caution came too late; the valets had overheard the squire's proposal, and a hubbub broke out euough to deafen one's ears.

'My throat's on fire. Halloa ! Wine! We want some wine ! Let's go to the cellar ! Wine—and of the best! Haven't we fought—and well, too ? Good God, how I did fight! I've got a sprained wrist, and my shoulder's out of joint!" " As for me, I have sprained my back so bad, that I '11 never get over it in all my born days 1 Did you see me plant that rock in the very pit of that big fellow's stomach, there? And would you believe it, just as he was tumbling over, he said I was an awkward dog ? Were you hit ? Has your axe got such a nick as mine here ? What a thump I did give him, hai ? 'Twas on the top of the wall, just as I was knocking over that grand Clos carter fellow. Drink, give us something to drink ! Give us something to eat!"

"My darlings," said old Fulk, rolling his cyclop at them, " it 's quite clear you aren't much used to fighting, and that you've been having a very good time of it in this old minster. You never stump your toes, you don't; for you 're always sure you 'll make good time. Why you ought to know that the very worst thing a man can do is to drink when he's too warm. All the doctors will tell you that; and there you are now red as lobsters, and sweating like a spring-head. It's my mind that you won't get a driuk till supper time."

"I 'll die if I don't get a drink."   *

" If you do drink, you 'll be sure to die of the fever—a bad cold, and a thousand other disorders," said Fulk, " and besides, Monseigneur wants you, and wants you strong and sound, too. So, now, the very first man of you that even squints at a visit to the cellars before I say he may, shall have a talk with me. Do you hear that:"

The squire was busy in this way quieting the very legitimate claims of his infantry, and the knight on his route to the church where the Abbot had gathered his monks before the fight broke out, and was still engaged in offering up such prayers as would seem best fitted to draw down Heaven's blessing on the arms of their defenders.

Upon the chevalier's appearance at this end of the nave, the chants of the monks suddenly ceased, giving place to silence the most profound—a silence of expectation and anxiety. Leaning over their stalls, the monks, with open mouths and straining gaze were hearkening to what the warrior might have to say. The Abbot was the only person to feel encouraged by his appearance in the church, for he well knew the Crusader was not the man to quit his post merely to carry useless news.

" Well, fathers," said the gentleman, " for once more, the assault has failed, and the enemy haven't got into your church."

A murmur of satisfaction ran through the meeting. All those cenobites seemed to have got a new lease of their almost expiring breath.

" My son," said Anselm, "think you our persecutors will renew the assault to-day ?"

"No," responded Monseigneur Philippe. "If they are wise, if they've got auy seuse, they '11 let us waste away on our poor victory. If they should come back, Rudaverse here will be ready to receive them. But if they keep their distance, and only continue to surround us, we are but lost men. There's nothing to eat now, or next to nothing; to-morrow it will be a complete famine. Our messenger has betrayed us and the maiden of Cornouiller knows naught of our straits. To speak frankly, holy father, I must repeat it because I believe it—we are lost men." As the knight spoke these words very calmly, he walked on and sat down in one of the stalls, and folded his arms across his breast.

A monk now rose. He was the Prior of the community. He was ninety-two years of age, at least, and was still in the practice of austerities so great that it was the general opinion that not a soul in the convent, except the Abbot himself, could be considered more of a saint than lie. The white-bearded old man then rose up in his stall, and humbly demanding his superior's permission to speak, he said:—

" In the time of your predecessors, I mean the one before the last, a great conflagration broke out in the northern cloister. All appeared to be lost. But holy Gilles de Gouron, who was governor of the abbey at the time, ordered the reliqnaries to be placed in front of the flames, and the fire stopped. Inasmuch as temporal means can't save us, it appears to me the part of wisdom would be an appeal to the goodness of God. "

" Yes," said Philippe, " a miracle, or we are lost without recourse, and every man of us massacred !"

" Come, my brethren," said the Abbot, with a loud voice, " let us see what the bones of the saints will do for us in our extremity. That is indeed our last resource."

CHAPTER IX.

THE reader, no doubt, remembers that while the monks were moving towards the great church with the remains of poor Father Nicolas, Rigauld, finding he was of no further use at the abbey, had set off for his sylvan abode. The path he took led him quite clear of the town, for, turning his back on Typhaines, he strode down a narrow, scarce discernible track, and was soon lost in tho depths of the forest.

The duties of his office, which at times obliged him to repress and even to punish the burghers and peasants for infractions of the abbey rights by plundering their wood and stealing the game, had ended in making him an object of universal detestation to the townsfolk. His name was hardly ever mentioned without an accompaniment obligato of insulting epithets. He, too, serf though he was, treated the raainmontables very much as if he really belonged to the master-race. Governed by these hostile feelings, repelling and repulsed alike, he had gradually laid aside all connection with his own class, and as he could not fray his way to a full companionship with monks and squires, he had come at last to lead the life of a hermit in the woods; and yet no one had ever heard him complain about that. It often happened to him to spend days and even whole weeks, without once opening his mouth to speak, and if he should occasionally discover a person, he rather avoided than sought for a meeting with such fellow-being. It was very natural that, under such circumstances, mixed up with other charges against Rigauld, the Typhaines people should accuse him of being a sorcerer, and as he was always going about scouting every portion of the forest, not only must he have come across legions of hobgoblins, but must have made familiar acquaintance with Satan as well; and, in fact, had sold him his soul; and in this they were not so very wide of the truth. The hunter, in fact, showed that this must be so—and every one knew it must be so, judging merely from the supernatural weight of his ponderous fist.

Rigauld, then, had returned to his hut, where it lay half hidden in the densest thicket in the forest. On his way home he had never even looked towards the burgh, and so his disdainful indifference led to his total ignorance of the events that had transpired at the abbey since his departure for the woods. But after a sound sleep on his moss bed, and his awakening by the morning light and the chirping of the birds on the surrounding bushes and spray, he was not long in learning the terrible tale. This is how he found it all out.

He had traversed, during his morning scout, a considerable portion of his official domain, and came at last to the edge of the vast, expanded glade where this history began. He had come to the very spot that had long been the object of his respect as well as his terror, and in order to continue his course, had been compelled to jump across the haunted mutinous brook, and tramp onward through the tall ferns and bushes on its banks.

Had it pleased kind heaven to rid the place of St Procul's Spring and all its diabolical surroundings, Rigauld would have been lifted, by the change, to a state of supreme felicity. The fact is, he once told the Prior at Typhaines Abbey that he certainly had never in his life caught a distinct view of anything to really justify his terrors, and just now as he happened to strike on the spot, the hour—about six in the morning—was not a very unfavorable time, for it is well known that spirits, demons, and goblins are not half so lively in the morning light as they always are in the dark. So Rigauld walked on till he found himself on the short rich greensward of that fair and wide roeadow-land near St. Procul's Spring. Just at that very time he heard himself called by name ! He started, and turned suddenly round, and saw .   .   fifteen years subsequent to the events related in this book, Rigauld turned pale whenever he ventured to give an account of tho incidents of   that   memorable   morning   ...   he   saw, then, relieved against the east stone slab that inclosed St. Procul's Spring, what seemed the likeness of a beautiful girl, dressed in a green robe. He couldn't believe that it was a real, natural woman that he saw there. Besides, he hadn't got a fair look at her, because, as soon as he turned his head, the apparition had swiftly drawn down a rather thick veil, and hidden her face, so that he couldn't make it out very well. The terror-struck forester fell on his knees.

44 Hunter !" cried the strange creature, the spectre, 44 approach me not 1 Hearken to my words ! Listen well 1 The burghers of Typhaines have revolted, and unless succor comes and comes soon, the abbey will be taken this very day. Thou lovest thy masters. Tarry not—look not behind thee—ask not who I am. Ruu—run without stopping an instant. Hasten to the Chatel de Cornouiller. Demand succor for the minster—prompt succor."

Rigauld felt ready to faint: his whole body was in a tremor of alarm. His gross imagination, excited to the highest pitch by his habitual loneliness, and a continual sense of the presence of invisible ghosts and hobgoblins at his side, made him susceptible to boundless fears, while his Absolute belief in them developed a feeling of curiosity that

gave him some little courage. Passing, as he did at Typhaines, for a sorcerer, there really was, in his very inner
man a violent temptation to become a wizard, that gave
him some small endowment of courage. Hence, he tried
to see who the vision was, and said:—

" You won't hurt me ?"

The apparition replied :—

" Get up, and go in peace, to do thine errand. Thou
hast nothing to fear."

" You ain't a wicked fairy, then ?"

This question appeared to anger the vision, which answered in an angry tone :—

"I have nothing to tell thee. Thou hast lingered too
long already. Remember, thou wretched serf, that thy
master and a nbble knight are at the point of death. Haste
thee to Cornouiller thou babbler, or thou shalt pay for thy
disobedience !"

Rigauld made an effort to rise, and though pallid, with
hair on end, half stunned with dread and scarce master of himself enough to find the path, he moved, as the
phantom pointed with outstretched hand, towards the castle
of Mahaut. Though he fairly flew over the plain, scarcely
lmd be reached the margin of the woods when he turned
his face towards the mystic spring to get another glimpse.
The three stone slabs stood there, and the stone effigy of
St. Procul at the top. The vision was gone. Fear gave
wings to his speed, and Rigauld darted on as if the goblin
was at his heels in chase.

As he could not see the witch at the spring, his frantic
imagination made him sure she was following, and off he
went like an arrow, winding on in the dark narrow path
obstructed with trees, and bushes and briers, and as he
bounded onward heard gibbering howling hissing noises,
mysterious and awful, above, below, and all around him,

that hurried on his rapid flight. For all the demesnes of Typhaines, for all the wealth in the world; hardly to win a paradise in the next, would Rigauld have checked his career for an instant long enough to catch his breath, for he seemed to feel that the claws were already clutching at his hair, to punish his least act of disobedience. Driven forwards At this flying rate, he soon passed the wood, and was now out in the open country, where he began to feel not quite so distressed, like a poor soldier flying from a lost battle-field from the swords or pikes of the panting cavalry behind. Though in a race of two leagues he had run himself quite out of breath, he dared not stop, and continued at a fast walk for four leagues more. He had just done two leagues in the woods, and his legs were now all bleeding and lacerated with brambles and thorns. He was impelled by terror, but a strong motive for his haste sprung from the dangerous posture of affairs at the abbey. Rigauld was the most faithful of servants.

It was ten o'clock when he descried on a lofty rock the buildings that constituted the Chatel de Cornouiller. Built in a preceding century, the fortress exhibited the same dark and rugged aspect that still continues to impress us with a feeling of respect for the ruined donjons of our feudal ancestors. It was a square tower that rose up above the peaked summit of a steep rocky acclivity that seemed to make it all one with the living stone. Windows, narrow and few, and loopholes, gave admission to the light of this sombre abode. The entrance-gate was narrow and low, and had no drawbridge, for such a form of defence was useless, so difficult was the scarped ascent thus made secure by its original constructors, the seigneurs of old. In war time, all that was wanted was a proper supply of huge pieces of rock to roll down the narrow ladder-like track, by which alone access to the tower could be gained, and which could instantly be swept clear of any assaulting party, should due vigilance not be wanting.

An inclosure, consisting of a thick battlemented wall, surrounded the donjon, and in this outer inclosure were stables for horses and great shed9, under which, in case of a raid, the villagers and peasants might find a safe refuge.

Rigauld, a man well known through all the country side as abbey forester, had no difficulty in making his way within, for one of the guard at the gate opened for him, and as he said his message to the lady was very urgent, one of the men went up to announce his arrival and his pressing haste. He soon returned to the courtyard, and led Rigauld up to the great hall, where the Dame de Cornouiller was seated in the third story of the tower.

In the great hall, when Cornouiller had a master, and where the gentlemen of the surrounding region used to meet round the massive table still standing there, Rigauld beheld a large company assembled—a large company, it should be said, considering the strict seclusion in which the maiden mistress had lived so long.

In the first place, there was Mahaut herself, seated in her grand seigneural chair, with its high carved back, surmounted by a little canopy. She was a very beautiful girl, and of a noble and imposing air. Her gown was a rich purple sandal silk stuff, worked in large golden silver and azure flowers, and her light golden hair was confined by a veil of marvellous fineness, which was attached in front to a circlet of gold. It was a mass of rich and multitudinous curls, close and thick.

When Rigauld entered the hall Mahaut's elbow was resting on the arm of her sofa, and the chin in the white palm, in a listening attitude of concentrated attention. She was hearkening to a personage sitting in front of her, and dressed in the apparel of a regular canon of the time!

Behind her were seated her serving-women, all twirling their spindles, and listening, with attention wrapt as her own, to the disconrse of the venerable personage. Ranged along the wall stood a number of men-at-arms, some with their arms crossed on the breast, and some with hands down and the fingers locked in front, all imitating the contemplative air of the feminine portion of the audience.

"Come in, Rigauld," said the chatelaine, turning her face towards the forester. " They tell me you demand to speak with me."

" Lady," responded the hunter, throwing himself down on his knees, " the father Abbot of Typhaines is sure to perish unless you give him instant succor. Attacked as he is and almost captured already by his rebel burghers and peasants, for the love of the Holy Virgin make no delay."

" What is it you say ?"

" I saw naught of it myself, my lady; but one, whose name I dare not repeat, appeared to me at St. Procurs Spring, and despatched me to you. Ah I madame I Give me your men, or monseigneur the Abbot is lost!"

Every soul in the hall now looked in his neighbor's face, and in an instant nothing was seen except the whole crowd making the sign of the cross. They little doubted the truth of the forester's story. In our own day, perhaps, the mere fact of intervention by a being so widely known as St. Procul's fairy, in favor of an abbey, might have had something of a squint in it. Why, and to what end should hell intervene for the protection of God's servants and the property of the church ? This was not the way they saw things in those times; on the contrary, they supposed sprites, goblins, and ghosts, to be rather fond of looking after the affairs of the seigneurs, and even of ecclesiastics too, and so, of upholding and maintaining their authority in thc'land.

Madame Mabaut rose from her sofa.

" What is to be done, master ?" said she to the canon.
" You are aware that the Seigneur de Pornes has already
made two attempts to capture the chatel by surprise and
carry me off to force a marriage with his eldest son. If I
lend my men-^t-arms now, I shall be left here without any
defence ! yet, on the other hand, as the Abbot of Typhaines
is my guardian, I owe him succor."

The priest replied in a strong German accent:—

" My daughter, you mustn't be frightened. The Seigneur
de Pornes, doubtless, has no idea of what is going on, and
even if he does know it, and in spite of his disloyalty to
you, instead of coming here to assail your house, he 'll do
all he can to defend the holy abbey. And, besides, your
chatel is such a strong one ! If yon keep up a strict watch,
who can capture it f But if you can't feel easy, call your
serfs into the fortress; they'll be enough to guard you
for a short while, till your soldiers come back ; and that '11
be very soon."

"But," cried Mahaut, " I must either send them all, or
keep them all here ! The Typhaines folk are thousands,
and it would be a difficult matter to defend the Abbot with
only my poor ten men-at-arms and some twenty sergeants.
Of course, the Abbot hasn't a single lance I"

"Oh 1 lady," answered Rigauld, " by God's mercy it was
only yesterday forenoon I guided a knight there. He had
just come back from the Holy Land, and he and his squire
and pages will fight for the minster—of course they will 1"

" The Holy Land ! What did you say ?" cried Mahant,
her face all flushing. " Know you the knight's name ?"

"No ! but he's a brave gentleman."

"Tall?" said Mahaut.

" Yes, truly ; tall and generous looking."

" Has he brown hair ? Has he blue eyes ?"

" I can't tell about that."

" Stupid creature 1" cried the Maid of Cornouiller, stamping her little foot. " But, at least, you must have seen the sign on his pennon—his armor and shield ?"

" It's a—" putting his finger to his forehead, and trying to remember: " oh, yes 1 it's a lion argent; the rest is blue—yes, I think it's blue."

" Holy Virgin!" screamed an old waiting-maid, and dropping her distaff. " Our master's come home 1"

Mahaut now quickly turned to the old canon.

" Master," she said, " Monseigneur de Cornehaut, my betrothed husband, is at the abbey; and I have reason to dread a great misfortuue. He is just come back from the Holy Land ; and if he has gone there to seek Master Anselm, it is probably because be has found out about his domains. In that case, he will be very angry, and join the burghers."

" Do you judge him capable of so black a crime as that ?" said the priest.

" Passion," replied Mahaut, with a shake of her head, " passion knows neither crime nor virtue—neither good nor evil 1 But we mustn't allow Monseigneur Philippe to bring dishonor on his fair fame. "

" I am far more afraid he '11 perish along with the Abbot: those rebels will be very furious. He '11 perish just as those gallant gentlemen did at Laon, who flew to defend Bishop Gaudry against his burghers."

" I 'in not so uneasy on that score," she said, with an air of scorn. " Monseigneur Philippe isn't the man to escape the sword of the Saracen and come here to get killed by a swarm of low peasants. But don't let us talk about it. To horse, all of you, my men 1 to horse 1 and hold one in readiness for me too !"

" For you 1" cried the canon. " Are you going mad, my

child ? It is only a moment ago, and you was afraid to lend a few of your men to holy Father Anselm in his distress, and now you are going to take horse yourself ! Do be a little wiser ! Do as I advised you to do, and while your people are away to deliver the holy abbey and Mon-seigueur Philippe too, from the hands of thut rabble, do you stay here with me and hear the rest of my holy exhortations that I so delight to lavish on you."

Mahaut, while he was talking, went on giving her orders without attending to what the canon was saying; but when he had made an end at last, she apostrophized him as follows:—

" How is this, Master Norbert ? You, a servant of God— are you going to give me such timorous counsels ? Is it the fashion in your country of Cleve for women to care not a rush about their husbands and betrothed lovers in peril ? Do you know that I have been patiently waiting here for mine these five long weary years ? that, deaf to the whisperings of my own grief, I—yes, I—sent him to Palestine where so many of Christ's gallant soldiers have been ? He might die ; and do you suppose that I am going to let him stain his illustrious name, or die in my sight ?"

In spite of a retort so lively, venerable Norbert would take no discouragement, and seeing the Lady of Cornouiller about to leave the apartment, without hearing his answer, be seized her by the mantle, and in a severe tone said:—

" Stay here, my daughter ; I command you, out of my affection for you; it's not seemly for a young lady to be galloping about the country and affronting perils fitter for warriors, and not for women ! Shall I, who am ever striving to keep churchmen far from the battlefield, shall I allow a lady, and my own penitent too, to give way to the same blindness !"

Master Norbert held fast to the mantle, as he spoke

to the chatelaine in a tone half indignant, half suppliant.
But he clung to the hope of making her hear him, little
knowing the haughty temper of his spiritual child. She
looked about her, and seeing that the men-at-arms had
all gone down the donjon stairs, leaving Rigauld at her
side, she looked at the man in an imperious way, and
then said:—

" You I Here, take this monk, and shut him up in the
great hall I"

Scarcely were the words uttered, when, lifting the old
man in his arms while she twitched the mantle, to which
he still clung, out of his hand, the wild forester bore him
off, and set him down in the arm-chair where he first found
him preaching to the lady. That done, Rigauld went out
at the door and rejoined Mahaut.

Meanwhile pious Norbert, left alone among the waiting-
woraen, gave himself up to, probably, not his first series
of reflections on the savage independence of his contemporaries.

He, whose mission it was to soften their manners, and
recall priests, women, and seigneurs to practices less violent and sinful—he, who by the church has been honored with
the title of saint for his life-long labors in the cause of reform—he found his work every instant balked and even
nullified by the violence of a race that he found it very hard
to bend to the light yoke of the evangel. How tenacious
this barbarism was ! Ever since morning, with what pious
meditation and sincere enthusiasm she had hearkened to his
counsels 1 But now, a mere circumstance was enough to
put to flight all he had flattered himself for having effected
in her, and her women iu waiting, as well. Yet, be it said
again, Norbert was not a man to be discouraged in any
work of love or mercy : he meditated for a few minutes,
rose from his chair, went out for his walkiug gear, and, his

long staff in hand, went forth to join Mahaut, who by this time was far away.

For her to change her worked veil and mantle for a red cloth cloak, to descend the steep stair to the court-yard and spring into the saddle, and give the order to march, was an affair of but a few moments.

Rigauld, mounted behind a trooper, gnided the party by the shortest though not the safest paths, in obedience to Mabaut's orders, and a few hours would have brought them to the towers of Typhaines but for the compulsory delays of the tired footmen, who compelled the men-at-arms to implore her not to hurry them on at such a rate. In spite of her anxiety, Mahaut felt obliged to yield to the necessity of the case, so that the sun was sinking low down in the west as she caught sight of the distant abbey, half drowned in the many-bued mists of the coming eve.

To look through the dim vapors at the spot where her lover was, rendered the maiden's anxiety almost intolerable. In spite of the prayers of her men, she ordered the knights to follow at a gallop, and recommending the best speed to her infantry, she struck her horse with the switch and flew over ditches and hedges, and soon reached the foot of the mount on which stood Typhaines. She was about to press her steed up the rocky side, when Rigauld, who had leaped to the ground, darted suddenly at her bridle-rein and turned the horse's head just as an arrow whistled close by her 6ide, and f}ew to bound away again from a rock hard by.

"Frontless vilain I" she cried, as she lifted her rod to smite him.

Tho men-at-arms uttered a startling cry.

"We are too late !" spoke an old knight—the seneschal.

It was too true. Mahaut descried a troop of peasants at the bridge, who, on seeing the lady, began to hoot and shout aloud. She looked with scrutinizing gaze to see if glint of helm, or spark from lance and pennon, might be in the crowd, and seeing none :—

" Then he is dead or a prisoner !"

Insisting, as she did, on knowing something clearer on this lamentable subject, Rigauld asked for nothing better than a permission to devote himself, and they allowed him to take his own way. He climbed to the top of the ascent, and cautiously made his way into the great court-yard, where he saw a great many dead and wounded men, the latter striving by their lamentable cries and moans to secure his pity and his help, but it was to take trouble to no purpose ; the forester, descrying none but Typhaines men among the poor wretches, paid no more attention to their appeals than he would have bestowed on the bleating of so many half butchered sheep. lie next came to the postern in the fa9ade-wall, so long defended by the valorous knight and Fulk, his squire. It was not broken down, but stood wide open. Passing through to the church, he beheld the two pages stretched on the pavement—the brave boys !— one with his head laid open, and the other with a couple of arrows deep sunk in his breast. Rigauld got into the nave —then into the choir, where he found nothing but solitude —no wounded, no corpses—neither abbot, knight, nor squire. He thought that was enough done, and so went down the mount again.

" What of it ? What did you find ?" said Mahaut.

" Nothing.—Nobody 1"

" They are prisoners," she said.

No doubt that such a thought was less lugubrious than others she had allowed to torture her imagination, as she was hurrying along the road thinking to find her lover dead or dishonored. Yet that thought was fraught with its own bitterness, too, for to become a prisoner, he most have begun with a defeat.

Perhaps," she murmured, " he made his escape."

But the seneschal shook his head doubtingly.

" That's hardly possible," said he. " The peasants are too many for that."

ll We can inquire about it," said she.

" It would be far better to make our way to the chatel. Look you, lady I That rabble there are running to their barricade in crowds. Should it, perchance, be a sortie they are thinking of, your presence, with our small numbers, will put us to a great disadvantage."

"No matter 1" said Mahaut. " Do what I order you to do—and at once. After that, you can use your pleasure."

The seneschal put his horse at the walk, and so advanced alone towards the bridge, and when at ear-shot, he cried:—

"Messieurs burghers and peasants of Typhaines, the Lady Mahaut of Cornouiller requires to know whether truly your Abbot and Monseigneur Philippe de Cornehaut are prisoners in your hands, and in case they are so, then at what ransom do you hold them—each of them ?"

He waited, expecting one of the armed burghers or peasants then gazing at him to make answer to this polite invitation ; but all of a sudden the crowd opened, and an interlocutor made his appearance whom he by no means expected to see in such a place as that. He was none other than a herald-at-arms, bearing the blazon of Nevers, who cried aloud:—

" Messire Seneschal, make known to the Dame of Cornouiller that, in the name of her seigneur, the Count de Nevers, she stands prohibited from undertaking any enterprise in this place; and that she shall retire without delay, under penalty of forfeiture of all her fiefs 1"

The seneschal, utterly confounded though he was, would gladly have argued the point, or at least repeat his question, but as the peasants replied only with hootings, he hung his bead, and, with a heavy heart, rode slowly back to the lady.

CHAPTER X.

YES, the seneschal was compelled to return to his mistress. The poor old old gentleman, who hadn't much heart for the affair, was very naturally clearer headed than she on the question—a very serious one to him—of the material interests involved in the case. To carry on a quarrel with a set of burghers and serfs at Typhaines was one thing, and though a rather foolish piece of business, considering their recent success, it was quite another matter to fly in the suzerain's face and make war on his allies and even run the possible risk of being obliged, some day, to pass your sword-point right through his own banner, an enormity not to be for a moment thought of by any person, even one moderately schooled in feudal principles and usages. Certain it was, that the Maid of Cornouiller wasn't on such a footing as that in her relations with the Count de Nevers.

The old soldier had a very piteous look when he came up to the lady and told her and the men-at-arms that stood round her, what had just happened—for he was still fearful of some intemperate bit of obstinacy on her part.

Mahaut looked down, and kept nibbling her glove finger.

It's time for us to go," said the seneschal. " It's near night already, and if the peasants should happen to make pursuit, and we should meet any of Seigneur de

Pornes' forces, it would be a hard matter to defend ourselves."

" If Messire Philippe is a prisoner, what will they do
with him ? they '11 kill him !" said she.

" They wouldn't dare do that," rejoined one of the
knights.

" They will set a heavy ransom on him," sighed the old
seneschal. " Let us be gone."

Mahaut put her horse to a gallop—but she drove at the
barrier. The men stopped her;

" Suppose you too should be taken prisoner ?" asked
the seneschal. " Do you think you'd get the chevalier off
any the sooner for that ?"

Mahaut made no reply: she was a sensible young
woman, and so found nothing to object. Yet she sat
there, gazing intently at the crowd in town. She shed
no tears; nor did she make any wild, passionate display
of her feelings; but when Rigauld, at a signal from the
seneschal, took hold of her bridle-rein and turned the
horse's head towards the chatel, she drew a long sigh, and
that was all.   -

The foot-soldiers had now come up and joined, and the
whole band, infantry and cavalry, being made acquainted
with the state of the case, took the road to the castle in
a very bad humor, for they had a march of six long leagues
before supper-time, and so they went trudgihg along the way
with a hang-dog look that showed how disappointed they
were. As many as could do so, got into the rear-guard,
where they could swear and curse to their heart's content,
without any risk of offence to the Maiden of Chatel-Cor-
nouiller.

I know not whether it was that heaven was now touched
by the dolorous tranquillity of that fair maiden and the patience of her submission to so distressing a lot, but the

fact was, that at a turn in the path she met old Norbert stalkiug forwards along the dusty way, with his long staff in hand.

" Well, daughter !" said the canon, " has any good come out of your violence this morning ?"

" Master," responded Mahaut, " God has justly punished me, and my sin requires a penance. Holy Abbot Anselm and Monseigneur Philippe have been taken prisoners by the rebels; and Monseigneur de Nevers is their declared enemy. He has joined the rebel party."

" Don't despair," cried Norbert. " Neither your violence nor your arms can avail anything here ; but the word of the Lord can open every door unto me. You, lady, have greatly sinned against one of the servants of the Most High. Repent!"

" I do repent," she said, submissively. " And I am ready to do whatsoever you may order me to do."

" You come of a hard and a violent race," resumed the saint, " and bone and flesh are ever driving you on into the snares of Satan. Go npw, in peace ! Return to your manor, but go on foot, and tread, as I have done, the dusty road. Alight from your horse, and humble yourself, if such a thing as that is possible. Let it be your duty to wait with patience and in fasting and prayer for the success of the attempts I am about to make in your behalf."

Mahaut made no remark whatever. She quitted the saddle, and made ready to prosecute the journey as modestly as she had been commanded to do by the canon; and according to the usage of that age, her entire suite at once imitated her example. Norbert stood until the whole sad party of penitents had defiled by him, and then set off for the Burgh of Typhaines.

The attempt he proposed to make was not devoid of great peril. Though by his preaching he had endeared himself

to the commonalty and the seigneurs through the length
and breadth of the land; though his piety bad begot
uuiversal reverence, he well knew the men of the time to
be as variable and capricious as any barbarian people whatever, and that in their paroxysms of ferocity, even the
most cherished objects of their devotion lost much of their
sanctity in their eyes. As he had just said to the Lady
of Cornouiller, they were a hard and violent race of men
he had to deal with; and to trust to the passions of the
laity was, sometimes, to expose one's self to the cruellest
fate. Yet, in all ages, one excess gives rise to its antithesis,
a great vice oftentimes giving birth to a greater virtue',
and though knights, burghers, and serfs were terrible
scholars, the church was wise and skilful enough to set over
them a class of preceptors whose pious intrepidity refused
to go back in presence of any menace whatever. Besides,
they too, those hardy preceptors, they were a stiff-necked
and impetuous generation: naught but the direction they
gave to their passions could have sanctified and made
them venerable.

Norbert went up to the barricade, and presented himself at it with as much quiet assurance as if he had himself
been one of the consuls of Typhaines—and right before the
eyes of the crowd, who were astonished at his audacity,
knocked at the gate with his long staff; it was a sort of
postern they had constructed among the stones, beams, and
great heaps of barrels.

" Come, open to the servant of the Lord! Open at once !
Let not justice languish for admission !" cried Norbert.

Norbert was well known, for he had been travelling the
country there for six months. One of the burghers on
guard at the gate went hurriedly away to call Payen, who
was commander of that important post. The consul came

up, and respectfully inquired of the pious canon what his
object might be in a visit to the burgh.

" What means this insolent language ?" haughtily asked
Norbert. " And how long is it since the sons of sin began
to question the will of the Most High f I know thee. Thy
name is Payen—and pagan thou art, no doubt, and well
deserving the stake shouldst thou dare detain me here!
Open I"

And the saint struck the door heavily with his long staff
again.

Norbert's pious double entendre produced a great impression on the consul and his attendant crowd. A pun
in those days used to be accepted as an unanswerable argument. In the schools, in the pulpit, in the books of the time,
the power of a pun was daily tested, and whoever he might
be that was successfully hit by one, was obliged to confess
the triumph of his antagonist, provided he failed instantly
to reply by a successful thrust in point, and to the very
purpose. Payen (*gallice*, Pagan), who never could have
so much as dreamed of chopping logic with such a gram-
matical host as the canon, judged there was nothing left
for him to do but open the wicket and let the master in.

" Come in, holy father. Perhaps my colleagues will
blame me for admitting you within the burgh without first
ascertaining the nature of your business here ; but provided
you will only pray for me, I '11 try to bear it."

"Yes, 111 pray for you, provided and on the sole condition that you are not one of holy Abbot Anselm's murderers."

"Would to God," replied Payen, with a sudden change
in tone, " you had to absolve me of a crime like that I May
I be excommunicated if I might first stamp my foot in his
gashed throat—that false traitor, that wicked seigneur I

12

But the cowardly villain still lives, for his master the devil tore him out of our hands !"

Norbert raised his arras towards heaven, his face radiant with joy, and utterly reckless of his surroundings, cried aloud :—

" Blessed be God who hath delivered his servant out of the hand of the impious ! Come, then, thou hardened sinner, tell me now what miracle it was that rescued that venerable father from the jaws of death, reserved for him by such as thou. And then say what thou hast done with the brave knight, Philippe de Cornehaut."

" I shall tell you nothing about them" retorted Payen, in a very bad humor. [14]I am afraid I have betrayed my duty already. As some Reparation for that fault, I shall take you to the council chamber, at once, and my colleagues may do as they, in their wisdom, may think befitting."

"Come on at once! You anticipate niv wishes;" and the canon, though burthened with a weight of years, exhausted by the heat of that August day, and his walk of six leagues from Cornouiller, kept step with his guide, and in a few minutes reached the coramune-hall.

Payen pushed open the door of a large room, and led Norbert in, where one glance showed him the tragical nature of the scene before him.

At a large table were seated the consuls, Simon, in the centre, seeming to direct all the proceedings. Two knights were seated with them, who, no doubt, were the representatives of Count de Nevers, and also a sort of scribe, bending forwards over a parchment, ready to engross the verdict about to be pronounced by the judges. Yerdict is the word, for Messire Philippe, then and there on trial for his life, was sitting on a wooden stool in front of the table; he was laughing as the venerable canon entered the hall.

The aspect of the crusader was enough to tear the heart-strings of them that loved him. His surcoat was all rent and torn ; and poor Rudaverse, where was she ? but the sorriest sight of all was Messire Philippe's head, wrapped in a coarse linen cloth all stained with blood, which, together with the extreme pallor of his face, showed that the chevalier had not been taken without knowing why, and that his defence must have cost somewhat to somebody.

The appearance of Norbert interrupted the proceedings in council. Payen went and whispered to Simon about whom the members and the commissioners from the Nivernais now crowded, and as the rapid conference went on, a deep shadow fell on the face of the cloth-merchant. At length the magistrates and their allies resumed their seats, and Simon addressed the pious canon:—

"We know not the cause that has brought you hither; yet we hold your sanctity in respect, and out of our veneration, we beg you to be seated with us and assist us in the trial of yonder knight."

Norbert without answering him, took a seat by the clerk's side and put himself in a listening attitude.

Simon now addressing Seigneur de Cornehaut, said:—

" Knight, you will not deny that you have done battle against the Commune of Typhaines without pretence of right to do so, and solely moved thereunto by your malice ?"

"Messire vilain," responded the crusader, "I was laughing, just now, with all my heart at the sight of a parcel of rascals like you setting themselves up as judges in the case of a gentleman; bqt really this is no laughing time, for I plainly see that what you want is to take my life, and I've no disposition to let you have it. Therefore, I now declare—if you do not know it already—that no man can be tried save by his peers, and that peasants, even rebellious peasants, are no peers of mine 1"

"Don't be so bold," said Jacques; "a burgher's axe is as sharp as your sword, and please remember we are masters now, and we intend to try you by our laws !"

" I believe you," responded Philippe. " And because I fear your vengeance, more than I confide in your equity, I '11 not be tried by you. I did defend the Abbot of Ty-phaines ; I could not suffer him to be butchered before ray own eyes. He is my betrothed wife's guardian, but at bottom he is my enemy, and had I happened to be two leagues away instead of at the minster, and knowing that he had taken possession of my estates, I swear the quarrel might have fought itself out for all I cared."

One of the knights now rose, and said :—

" Messire, your suzerain, the Count's law would be harder on you than that of Typhaines. You have defended his enemies, and killed and wounded several of his allies. For all these offences, you deserve to be punished I"

" Messire," said the knight, " make these fellows set me at liberty, and I will then make answer as is befitting;" he made a scornful shrug; it was clear that the verdict was made up before the trial.

Simon was gazing the while at the soldier, with eyes burning with hate ; and sentiments equally sinister were legible in the faces of his colleagues. Yet, as if the legal formalities of a trial, ill observed as they had been, were still in their way, Antoine struck his clinched fist on the table, exclaiming:—

" There's been too much of this already 1 Are we going to spend the whole evening, and the night, too, to fiud out whether that knight there is guilty or no ? Are we a par-cel of children to amuse ourselves with such nonsense ? I say he did defend the Abbot—that with his own hand he put many of our friends to death, and wounded more of them, some mortally, and others now doomed to be crippled as long as they live, and had it not been that the valets at the abbey opened a window for us to get in, we should be this very instant exhibiting the shameful spectacle of a whole army fighting against one single man ! Isn't this enough of his misdeeds ? What more can you want ? I know that he got the Abbot off to levy whole armies of our enemies ; and now you have got him fast and safe in your hands, you are not goiqg to put him to death I"

"Antoine talks like a sensible mansaid Simon, "and if you '11 believe me, the knight ought to die."

Norbert rose from his stool.

" So," said he, " you are preparing to carry on war like a troop of brigands V*

" No," replied Simon, " like trodden down men who want revenge ! Master Paul, write down that the consuls condemn the prisoner to death !"

The crusader stretched forth his hand.

"It can't be," said he, "you are about to use me so harshly as that! Don't kill me! Set a ransom on me."

" Your ransom!" cried Simon, shaking his fist at him, "your blood's your ransom !"

Here the knights of the Nivernais broke into a coarse laugh.

" What a pair of base scoundrels !" cried poor Philippe, staring in their faces.

Just then he felt the weight of two heavy hands pressing on his shoulders, and looking back, saw an immense savage of a serf, who said :—

" Kneel down ! Lay your head on the stool 1 I won't hurt you much."

The crusader's eyes were drawn towards a glittering something behind the peasant; it was a ponderous axe.

Norbert seized the gentleman's hand.

" Don't be afraid," said he.

12*

" Do I look like it ?" replied the crusader.

" Isengrin, make him bend his knees !" shouted Jacqnes. " Let us have the pleasure of seeing how a gentleman looks when he 's begging for pardon !"

This lucky thought delighted everybody except Philippe and the canon, who at once jerked Philippe out of the executioner's hand, and then stood in front of the victim.

He stood betwixt the prisoner and the serf, and boldly he spoke as follows :—

" If you are to cut off any head here to-night, it shall be my head—and I am a priest—and your souls shall be damned if you do that I"

The hangman rubbed his ear, and then turned to his masters with a hesitating look; but not waiting to let some one else get the floor, Norbert exclaimed:—

" You have said enough, and done enough in this busi- ness already. I forbid you to go any further with it. I prohibit you ! You know perfectly well that God and the Virgin are now here 1—Yes, now 1—invisible, at my side 1 Were you a band of pagans you wouldn't dare execute what you purpose ! Why ? Because you are not a gang of fools. Come now—merciless men that you are—come now, let me teach you something. Why did you take up arms ? Did you do that to have the pleasure of murdering people ? No ! You did it to set up your commune, and live under it in liberty and your own laws. How can you hope to succeed, then, if you will persist to rouse horror-struck reprobation and the justest vengeance on you and your people ? Messire Philippe, who you are wanting to butcher—Messire Philippe, whose life you are now seeking, has relatives and friends who will not patiently submit to see him butchered. His suzerain, the Count de Nevers, is not so base a man that he too will not be angered should you traitorously shed this gentleman's blood. I clearly discern that you are stimulated to commit this rash act by interested persons: yes, thou base and unworthy knight—thou wicked Baldwin de Pornes, thou art the man; thou art the false gentleman that art cunningly driving these poor people on to the commission of a crime that may serve to remove the worthy rival of thine own son !

" But if they are wise men, they will not venture to enhance the dangers that surround them to please and serve 6uch an one as thou. Come, then, my masters, try to understand what I am saying clearly. I say that if one hair of Messire Philippe's head should fall by any violence of yours, I will go forth from this place and in the public square of Typhaines, in the "presence of the people, I will call down vengeance on your heads and all your abettors. If they refuse to hear me there, I will traverse the whole of the Nivernais aud Champagne; I will visit Burgundy and France, if it must be so. Against you I will league knights, communes, and the king himself. If they will not hearken to my voice, I will preach a crusade against you, and in a week's time, you shall be found standing among the ruins of your houses ; and you shall weep, and others, if left alive, shall weep and repent for your mortal ferocity !"

Simon now cast a scrutinizing glance around the company, where the only individuals he could deem firm to their purposes were de Pornes and Simon himself.

" Master Norbert," said Baldwin, " you had no occasion to threaten us so sorely! You ought to know that the consuls of Typhaines both respect and obey you."

" Let them make proof of that, then. Set a ransom on the prisoner."

" Never !" shouted Simon. " Never, while I live ! I took that young man with my own hand. Ho is ray own prisoner, and so I will hold him !"

Philippe, who for a moment Had felt that he was about

to be liberated, lost hope once more and sot gazing at the axe.

" What then, will you cede me ?" asked Norbert. " Are you rallying me ?"

" I never rally any person," replied Simon. " For the present, I concede you his life. Isengrin, take the prisoner back to his dungeon."

Messire Philippe now stepped to the edge of the table, and in a grave tone, quite conformable to the serious nature of his position, he said:—

" Sires vilains, I comprehend marvellously well what is about to happen to me. For the present, you are afraid qf this venerable canon here, to whom I would now gladly promise a long and grateful remembrance, though I know him not. But as soon as he is out of sight, you will recommence your trial, now only suspended. Yet I desire to make known unto you that I hold you to be a band of traitors and brigands, and that . . . . It seems I have nothing more to say."

Messire Philippe deemed that by this speech he had acquitted himself of what was due to his self-respect and his good renown: the scruple, honorable though it was, failed to subject him to the rather uucharitable will of either Simon or his friend, de Pornes. Norbert, after pronouncing a benediction over him, at once addressed the council with a view to obtain some rather better condition. In the mean time Isengrin led his captive away.

If there really does exist one moment in the course of a man's life in which it would be most particularly disagreeable to him to die a violent death, it must be the one in which he is not only wounded, but humiliated by defeat. Depression of spirits and bodily exhaustion are ill preparations for the heroic appearance, without which it is a most painful thing to stand face to face with one's avenging enemies. So the poor crusader, who had been most cruelly beaten, bruised and wounded, while resisting the crowd of peasantry who were admitted by the infamous valets into the interior, aud who, besides, had had nothing to eat since the morning before, was only so much more to be admired for bis haughty courage on the occasion. Under other and more favorable circumstances, it would have been a mere frolic for him ; but the effort he made to carry on with a high hand, must have cost him not a little.

When he had got into the dark corridor that led towards the descent to his dungeon, he had nearly fainted with weakness. Loss of blood and starvation had made him more sensitive at the sight of that great, horrible axe, and now he could hardly stand: still, his courage forbade him to call on Isengrin for help, and letting the jailer walk on ahead, he stopped to lean for support against the wall. As he stood leaning, giddy, and ready to sink to the floor, he suddenly witnessed a scene within a couple of paces of him, which passed so rapidly that at first he thought it must have been a dream.

To reach the dungeon he had been confined in, and where he was now going, you had to pass along a dark corridor, and then down a 6piral stair, which came winding down from the upper stories, and so clear down to the dark prison below. Isengrin, who supposed the prisoner was coming along behind him, had already begun to go down, with a lantern in his hand imperfectly lighting with its red glare the secular darkness of that awful hole, and was carefully stepping down the cold and slippery stone stairs, when Messire suddenly saw something darting down on him from the ascending part of the spiral—or rather, a man falling on him as sudden as a flash of lightning, who gave him a blow, thanks to which, our acquaintance with that amiable personage is here brought to an instant close.

The effect of the blow was so prompt that, without uttering a sound, the jailer threw up both arms and fell head
foremost dowu the winding gulf in which he was very
carefully picking his way. He reached bottom with a
heavy thud, and as Philippe was steppiug forward to see
what had happened, Isengrin's murderer rushed up to him,
seized his arm, and whispered :—

" Silence ! Not a word ! you are free ! follow me!"

The unknown snatched a cloak from the foot of the upper
stair, threw it over the knight's shoulders, and holding
tight to his arm, began to drag him away. Poor Philippe
could have asked nothing better than to get away from
that sorry abode, but he needed help to walk. The unknown hurried him on, and as he knew nothing of Monseigneur's weakness, grumbled at him for being so slow.
In this way, they came to where a door led into the
council-hall.   .

Messire Philippe cast a side look at that terrible door,
out of which might suddenly start a new horror of captivity
and all its sinister cortege. Of course then he tried to
make as little noise as possible; but that precaution was
not needed, for the honorable consuls, the brave knights,
and the venerable canon, were mixing the loftiest diapason
up with an inexplicable web of retorts, questions, outcries,
and apostrophes, with, perhaps, some few curses, that swallowed up the sound of footsteps in the passage.

His conductor turned, and suddenly said :—

" Either walk faster, or stay here by yourself: may the
devil smother me if 1 'm going to stay and get butchered
for your sake!"

" Don't you see that I am badly wounded ? Have patience. I'm going as fast as I can."

By this time they had got to the front door of the townhouse.

" Wrap that cape about you. Pull it over your head," growled the savage.

44 It 's done," said Philippe.

" Corae along, then."

The two fugitives now got into the street. The night had shut in, and though many torches were burning here and there, the crowd was so thick that they ran very little risk of -observation. Besides, round every one of the torches, some provident burgher, combining profit and patriotism in one, was serving out drinks at his improvised bar, whether bench or a wine-cask with its head stove in, to the intrepid victors of the day, who were busy eating, drinking, and paying each other compliments on their splendid deeds. The Burgh of Typhaines was too busy just then to be thinking of trifles.

This proved to be the poor gentleman's safety ; for lie was so weak, and his gait was so awkward, that he certainly would have attracted notice in a less enthusiastic crowd. But he did go on, and without any mishap reached a small alley, where his guide stopped at an old thatched building, and said :—

" This is the place 1"

44 This ! What do you mean ?"

44 The place we are to stop at."

14 What, brave vilain, are we not to get out into the country?"

44 You'd look nice in the country, and especially with a long tramp before you—you would—particularly as you are looking just now. Come this way; you can rest a bit aud 1 '11 get you something to eat."

The knight looked round about him, and did not feel quite satisfied.

44 My good fellow," said he, 441 don't think I ever saw a more sinister, cut-throat spot than this is. Are you quite

certain you haven't made me exchange a chop of that axe for a stab ? The fact is, that betwixt the two, I shouldn't choose either of them."

" Here's a great talk about nothing," said the man.

" Go in, or devil take me if I don't make you I"

CHAPTER XI.

THOUGH he was a good tempered man and naturally inclined to be grateful, Messire Philippe felt somewhat vexed
by the words as well as the tone of bis guide. Yet, as he
on all occasions trusted more to his strong arm than to his
eloquence, he turned round and raised his fist with a mani-
fest purpose of driving it at the vilain's face, but the fellow
suddenly stepped back, and said :—

" Monseigneur, if you strike me, I >11 rip up your belly ;
and that would be a pity, for I have nothing against you."

" Then give me a better lodging than this house here."

" Monseigneur, we have no other choice; anywhere but
here you 'd be retaken, but there—Dame Dieu !—you '11 be
safe enough. Come, make haste I Sick, wounded, and
hungry, as you are, what could be better for you than to
go and get a little rest ?"

" If I had a good horse under me, I could ride to the
world's end."

" But we haven't got a horse."

" I don't like this hole of yours."

" Oh, you '11 do very well. But I must beg to say, Monseigneur, if you won't go in with a good-will, you '11 have
to go somehow, and I should be sorry to hurt you."

The chevalier looked at him, and saw the gleam of that
very same short, bright blade that had just worked such
wonders on Isengrin.

" Not such a fool 1" said Philippe ; "1 don't run a risk

13

of getting butchered without a chance to kill somebody myself; so, comrade, open the door, I 'll follow you."

The man didn't wait to be asked twice. When he opened the door it was pitch dark, bat the serf drew him inside, shut the door behind him, and then Philippe couldn't have seen his hand before his face.

" The devil!" cried the knight.

" Take care you don't fall," said the guide, pushing him before him to an invisible stair, where he gave him a shove that sent him slipping down several steps, until he lost his balance, and then rolled down the rest to the bottom.

He rolled down at least a dozen steps, and had it depended on himself, would have gone on rolling, but he did reach bottom, and was brought up against a wall of some sort.

" Where am I ?" grumbled the knight, as he was trying to get on his feet, " in a hole, a cellar, a cave, in a cata-comb, or in some new dungeon worse than the other ? Worse! No doubt of that, for in that old one I could see a little. May you be executed, you traitor vilain, for bringiug me here ! But where the devil are you now ?"

He raised his arms as high as he could, to feel if there was anything above him. At length, high above his head, he heard the guide say:—   ,

" You are safe enough now. Be quiet. Don't get angry—it's no good to heat your blood so. Besides, you've nothing now to fear as to your life. Good-night!"

Messire Philippe now heard a dull sound, as if some one was shutting down a trap-door and then shoving the bars. When that was over he heard not another sound.

What he did next was so natural, that in all ages, before as well as since the twelfth century, everybody of 6uch a temper as bis did do, does now, and shall do hereafter. Against the walls of his new prison he launched volleys of oaths most terrible, most redundant, most splendid, each more frightful than the last. Thanks to Monseigneur's travels, he had been so fortunate as to adorn his memory with choleric invocations, arranged in a multitude of languages, so that had a philologist happened to be at hand there, he might have enjoyed the pleasure of picking out from among the various formulas of French blasphemy, many rich gems in Latin, Langue d'Oc, Flemish, Italian, Greek, Catalan, and Sarrasinese, that would have left him nothing more to wish for, in respect at least of their extreme energy.

After some time, he found how wrong his behavior was, and so falling on his knees, he recited, with equal warmth and impetuosity, not less than a round dozen of paternosters to the saints, the virgin, and to God himself.

But, alas 1 his prayers availed no more than his oaths had done, the walls being as solid as ever, not even opening to let him out, nor allowing a single beam of light to come in, was it but to show how thick the darkness was. Messire had now become completely discouraged, and thought he had better sit down ; but he must first have something to sit on. He thought of the steps down which he had just tumbled at such a rapid rate: holding out his hands before him, he started to find them by feeling after them, and got stopped by a wall. He turned a little to the left, and hit his shin, and stooping down to find what it was, he felt a great plank or beam, perhaps, sticking out from the wall, which reached onwards he knew not how far. Tired of groping for the stairs in this way, he took a seat on the piece of timber: his heart seemed choked up—and he began to bemoan himself as follows;—

" How was it that Monseigneur, my father, sent me to the Holy Land, instead of going himself? Had he done that, I might have stayed at Cambrai, where, after making a good number of thrusts and cuts to gain a stock of renown, I could have been married like a brave knight, to Mahaut. After that, I might have gone back home, and being a young, and a rather sensible person too besides, I might have found some way to hinder Monseigneur from giving, not himself, but my property to that abbey that has given me such a world of trouble of late. But I 'm wrong to blame my redoubted parent. He is not the only guilty one in this matter. Just look at me here ! If the truth was told, what have I been doing except behaving like a mere fool ? Why I had got that splendid chance of coming back from Syria far better off than most of the folks that have ever been there; I hear that my sweetheart is still perfectly faithful ; and with not a bit more sense than a starling, I plump right into a net! Donkey that I was, I take it into my head that everything is working like a miracle! I go to Typhaines, get her guardian's consent, take him with me to Cornehaut, and we two are to persuade Monseigneur Geoffroi to agree. And then we all three start for Cornouiller with followers, with troops of friends, and then I get married to Mahaut, all in a sea of pleasure and joy. What infernal troubadour was it that put all that nonsense into my poor head ?

" Yes, Fulk was quite in the right. If, instead of taking up the notion of giving Mahaut a surprise, I had only found out that those monks had ruined me, and that, but for my booty that I luckily left behind at Marseilles, I was without a sou or a maille, most certain I am that I'd never have gone to the old abbey, and of course I shouldn't have been a prisoner here this day."

Had Messire Philippe gone on in this rigorous course of self-examination, it is very likely he would have gone mad with rage against his own self and others as well. But his holy patron saint gave his thoughts another direction.

" I must confess, though, after all," said he, " that if I had not come to Typhaines, I should have missed some most splendid cut and thrusts with poor old Rudaverse. That defence of the church is a thing that's not going to disgrace me —at any rate, I don't think so, and I certainly did give about one dozen points and as many backhanded blows that it isn't every man you'd expect to see do the like. Corps St. Denis! I can see right here, that poor clodpoll I tumbled off the top of the wall with a cut in the shoulder that went half way through his breast! How well poor Rudavers did behave I It was a most lucky thiug for me when I whirled her up in the air, just as those thousand devils of vilains laid hands on me. She got caught on a gargoyle, poor thing, hard and fast, and it's to be hoped I '11 get her down again one of these days. Why not? You are not going to suppose any peasant is fit to handle her? Yes—and thanks to me, the abbot's safe, for Fulk was enough to get him out of the scrape. Yes, indeed, 'pon my soul that was an elegant exploit, and 1 'd be sorry enough if anybody else had accomplished it."

This new perspective opened up a very smiling scene in the crusader's future prospects. He nearly forgot that he had lost his father, his castle, his liberty, and his good sword Rudaverse, that he was not sure of saving his life from that axe, and, battered and wounded, and aching with his broken head, poor Messire Philippe at last stretched himself down on his plank, in this act of doing himself justice on the score of his being by no means a mere vulgar sort of a knight, drew a deep sigh, and, oh, marvellous power of vanity ! fell asleep !

While this most valorous of champions was, contrary to all manner of hope, thus taking a little rest, the consuls the Nivernais knight, and Canon Norbert, were going on with their conference.

Norbert had soon made out that the members of the

council were not all alike eager to put Philippe to death.
Payen would vote for his execution ; but it might be a possible thing to bring that bold burgher over to a more
moderate way of thinking. Eudes, Jacques, and Antoine
talked very loud, wearied themselves with threats against the
sanguinary warrior who had wounded and killed such numbers of their friends; but still they had an eye to the real
interests of the commune; and so the three magistrates
were to be looked on as men not wholly unchangeable in
any resolution of theirs on the subject of Messire Philippe's
destiny.

One of the knights of the Nivernais, Anseau de Loysel,
a sort of impudent, debauched imbecile, and son-in-law to
de Pornes, seemed to have no decided opinion on the subject—and the rest consisted only of Simon and Monseigneur Baldwin. But those two were raging, savage, obstinate, for good reasons, no doubt; but whatever those reasons
might have been, they were fully determined agaiust the
knight's release. Messire Baldwin was a great wheedler,
cunniug, a cheat, and wicked to a degree, according to the
general belief. There were rumors current about things at
his castle-dungeon that looked very bad. The condition of
ills maiumontables was such that none of the surrounding
serf population were at all envious of them. Nobody ever
could think, without horror, of the condition of his *(ailla-
biles de alto et basso ad voluntatem,* and his people used
to talk about them with tears in their eyes. It was no
secret in that region, that the amiable chatelain had been
soliciting the Demoiselle de Cornouiller's hand for his eldest
son, and had been refused by Abbot Anselm, and that
another more formal demand, addressed to the lady herself,
having met with a decided refusal, he had twice attempted
to scale her walls at night, and carry her off, to compel her
to marry the youth. From all this, the iuterest he so

warmly took in cutting Messire Philippe's head off seems quite plain, as one chop of that axe would take off, at a blow, a head and a rival too.

None of those people were able to find out Master Simon's real motives; but the man was always such a mysterious person, that no one could from his mere silence, conclude he had any personal spite against the crusader. Besides, he disguised his own sanguinary designs under the cloak of good of the commune, and was always talking of the necessity there was for a public example, one that might well strike such terror into the hearts of the neighboring seigneurs as to keep them from making any attempt on the commune.

In the face of two such opponents, any one but Norbert must have given way. But he too was ardent, he too was firm, and influence was by no means wanting, and that to a great extent and at his command.

In that remote age, it was not a rare thing for a person in a fit of furious rage, to venture an attack on some churchman, but as soon as the fit was over, the madman cast himself down more prostrate than ever before, at his clerical adversary's feet.

Besides, the canon was not Seigneur de Typhaines, and was generally looked upon as far superior to holy Anselm in the business of miracle working.

"No!" cried he. "No! every sensible man in this council will take good care not to commit the crime that is being urged upon them. You have already in a tumultuous way, set up your commune—and that, in the sight of God, is an execrable piece of business, of which, sooner or later, you will all have to repent. Yet the very children of darkness have some sense left! Instead of irritating the nobility, all of them connected with the Cornehauts, don't you think you 'll have enough to do to defend yourselves against all Abbot Anselm's power, and the indignation of every bishop and prelate in the whole land ?"

⁴⁴ But, holy father," replied Jacques, somewhat troubled in mind, ⁴⁴ you should remember we have the support of Monseigneur, the Count of Nevers. The presence here of these two honorable knights is proof enough of that."

⁴⁴ As for these two seigneurs, I know them, and know them well, too !" looking contemptuously at them. ⁴⁴I know all about them ; and to send those two persons here as envoys shows very plainly what kind of succor you are to get I Though your affairs are nothing to me, my advice to you is to keep a strict watch on those two men, and weigh well any advice they may give you. But even admitting, if you please, that those gentlemen have cojne hither full of zeal, and in good faith, know you not how precarious is any assistance they can afford you ? As long as you continue successful, and are stronger than your adversaries, those traitors who go so far as to desert their own cause in your behalf, will divide the booty with you, only they will always take the better half of it—but wait till defeat comes, and see if they, like all traitors, will not be the very first to turn their backs on you f Never do more than half trust in the promises of refugees, aud don't be like that old king of Assyria, whose pride grew so high that it turned him into a brute beast I"

It is clear that the Sire de Pornes and Monseigneur Anseau de Loysel would hardly suffer themselves to be handled in this way, without some reply. One of them, who had too correct an appreciation of the saint's influence to treat him with open disrespect, tacked about, looked humble, and defended himself, though pretending submission. The other one, who was not so crafty, was not sparing of abuse, in trying to defend himself. Simon, however, endeavored to refute the canon's arguments, turned them over and returned them, and twisted them in every direction, in hopes of preventing his colleagues from hearkening to the good man's advice, which tended to nothing less than the immediate release of the prisoner.

After a long and violent discussion, it was resolved that the accused should not be immediately sent to execution, and that was the utmost concession Norbert was able to obtain. It is very evident that the lords consuls were not very distinguished for what is called mansuetudo.

Norbert now loaded the knights and the burghers, too, with reproaches, and got up to leave the hall. The consuls eagerly made tender of their several houses for his lodging that night, but he roughly declined the invitations, saying, he preferred to ask hospitality of the very first serf in the street. As soon as he had withdrawn, the council set about establishing the terms of the proposed treaty of alliance that the two Nivernais knights had come to solemnly ratify between the Count de Nevers and the commune of Typhaines. That being over, and the document or charter as it was then called, drawn up in due and acceptable form, by the clerk, the whole party affixed their signatures or their marks, and sealed it with their arms, such as had any, leaving a large vacant space for the great seal of the commune, which was not to be finished until the next day. It might be as well, just here, to say, that the engraver was to make a figure of St. Procul, with the legend, *Communia Burgensium Typhanie7isium"*

The treaty being concluded, the assembly next passed on to the consideration of a question not less pressing in its present, and much more so in its prospective influence on the future of the communal charter, to wit, the liberties, immunities, duties, and obligations of every burgess of Typhaines. In form, the consuls in this matter were to be looked on as the mere registrars or secretaries of the com-

mune, though, in fact, they knew quite well that any proposition of law to be now drawn up by them, would meet
small opposition at the crisis of the grand ratification day.
The proceedings were carried on, therefore, with a manly
and perfect confidence. As the two Nivernais knights were
indispensable confidants, they were invited to seats at the
board, with the right of discussion on all questions to come
before them. And so they went on, all night long, inquir-
ing into the terms on whicli the emancipation of the
burgh of Typhaines was to be finally settled.

Thirty years ago, in France, people had forgotten that
the spirit of liberty had its representatives among the noble
classes in the sixteenth century, but they entirely ignored
the existence of the same spirit in the burgher classes of
the twelfth. A few scholars who had been greatly surprised
at the revelations made to them in old musty tomes, could
hardly believe their own eyes, and pondered over statements
that they could not but regard as exorbitant, incredible, and
contrary to nature itself. As they knew not how to proceed
in publishing and securing any faith in them, they kept
them for themselves, as a secret of their own discovering.
But at the present day, we who are so familiar with the
behavior of people in great crises of political excitement,
find it by no means a difficult task to conjure up a picture
of the interior of a communal council-hall, even so far back
in time as the twelfth century.

Let any one, then, figure to himself our five consuls,
dressed like plain working-men, just as they are, in their
coarse cloth coats and cloaks of felted wool, with their
square-built faces, coarse, heavy features, and yet with eyes
flashing with anxiety to comprehend everything well, to
express their thoughts clearly, and enforce the adoption of
them. Look at them, as they go on discussing there, with
the vigorous thought that God had endowed them with,

the various questions about the prejudices of the age and the principles on which the communal system they were building up ought to be founded.—Look especially at Simon, the ablest man of them all, ever making the balance incline to his opinion by his ready citation of authorities, such as the communal charter of Laon, Amiens, or Cambrai. Simon, it is clear, was the politician for Typhaines; he was the knowing man—the bold brave guide of public opinion there; Payen, the generous soul—Jacques and Antoine are the timorous minority, the men who make up majorities.

As for the two Nivernais men, they only looked at each other and smiled, and now and then shrugged their shoulders, though they were always ready to applaud anything their allies thought right.

The consuls were in the height of their work, very busy in elaborating a difficult and important article, when a dozen wild looking men rushed into the hall. The discussion was broken off at once.

The new comers were great stout fellows, dressed pretty much in Rigaud's style, except his arms, for they too wore wild beast-skin clothing. Their great-coats—such as had great-coats—were worn-out coarse rags. They made up a burly, dirty, and dangerous looking set of people.

One of them went yp to the table; he was the spokesman.

¹¹ Who are you ?" asked Simon.

" Me ? Why, I 'ra Joslin," replied the giant " Me and my comrades here are De Pomes' serfs, and we Ve hearn how you are making up a commune here, and so we've come to join you in it."

" One minute !" cried Messire Baldwin, " are you joking now, you scoundrels? Oh, yes, I remember you now— you, Joslin—yes, I remember the whole of you 1 To the

glebe with you, villains I back to your glebe, and to-
morrow you shall have a talk with my seneschal I"

We aren't going to have anything more to do with
glebes," said Joslin, drawing back a little from his seigneur's stare. "We know the Cornehaut serfs have been
with you this very morning, and got a welcome, too.
We 're quite as good as them I"

"But," said Simon, rather confused, "but that's a different matter. Monseigneur Baudouin is one of the commune's friends, and we are not going to ruin him—we '11
defend him against all and every; you didn't know what
you were after, my friends; you've been far too quick in
this thing."

The serfs began to grumble, and Joslin, on finding them
ready to stand by him, returned to the charge.

" There's only one word to be said about it," he added.
" You've freed serfs already, and you '11 have to free us
too, just the same I"

"We are not a band of robbers," rejoined Payen, in a
passion. " Begone with you I Off with you, rogues I"

" My seneschal—yes, my seneschal," said Messire Baudouin, with a quiet smile, " will tell you what affranchisement means."

" Hang the seneschal I" boldly replied Joslin. " Here,
you Typhaines-men, don't go to be so hard on us. I and
mfr comrades have lots of money, and we can put up
houses here as well as any Cornehaut fellows can. They
told us that's one of your conditions of admission."

" He's rich, that scamp is! Just look at him I and
yet people say I don't treat my serfs well! My good
friends of Typhaines, please to have those fellows taken up
at once I"

" To be sure we will," said Simon ; " their impudence
deserves to be chastised."

" Now don't refuse us," answered Joslin, " for we have it in our power to get all we want out of you. We have a good security for that."

" Security or not," cried Antoine, "get out of this, and go right back to De Pornes, and leave us to take care of our own business—which is none of yours."

The serfs grumbled loudly, and Joslin again spoke :—

" As to sending us back to glebe, don't think of it, for we won't have it. We are quite as good as you are at shouting out * *Commune! commune !'* But here, we haven't come to you empty handed. Look but for yourselves now !"

" Money 1" said Monseigneur Baudouin. " When did you steal that from me ?"

" No, not money," retorted the serf. " But if you should happen to find out that you hadn't that prisoner of yourn in the dungeon, now I maybe you might happen to ask what's become of him, and maybe I might be able to tell you."

At the idea that Messire Philippe had got away from them, Simon and the Seigneur de Pornes both uttered ejaculations of agony. They jumped up as if mad, over-setting their stools, and looking—it is not too much to say it—like a couple of ferocious, threatening tigers, so frenzied were their gestures.

They would certainly have strangled Joslin on the spot, if they could but have got hold of him, but as the huge table was between them, the serf had time to reach the door, and rush out into the street; the other-men, while Simon was thinking of nothing but Joslin, got away, followed their spokesman, and became lost in the crowd.

Seigneur de Pornes, whose gait was made awkward by his armor of mail, and Simon, who began to reflect on what was due to his station as magistrate, stopped at the door-sill, for they soon found it to be in vain to follow the run-

14:

aways, and so they went back to the council-chamber, where they found their colleagues looking as much disconcerted as they were themselves.

" Bah!" cried Anseau de Loysel, breaking out into an uproarious laugh. " Bah! gentlemen, don't worry yourselves about such a fellow's lark. You '11 find the fool soon enough in some old Typhaines thatch. All you have to do is to look him up and then hang him and his fellows at the first limb you come to. Ah I do you know, now, that if all the serfs on our lands should take it in their heads to walk over here to your burgh, we should be a couple of nice donkeys to come here and defend your cause 1 Don't you think so ?"

"All this talk is of no use," said Simon—"for if what that serf said is true, then where is our prisoner, where is our revenge, where is our hostage ?"

" Let us go and look at the dungeon-lock," said Payen.

"Yes; make haste," Antoine said, as he seized a pine torch that was flaming from an iron ring in the wall; and the whole party followed ^im, with anxious looks. The honorable council and their allies went down the damp dungeon stair, at the bottom of which they found Isengrin, with his legs upwards on the lower steps, a wound in the back, penetrating deep into the chest, his head split open by striking in his fall one of the sharp stone angles, a wound that couldn't have hurt him, after the deadly stab in his back. Simon examined the door. It was close shut. He picked up the keys out of a puddle of blood, drew back the bolt, and went in. There lay the straw bundle and there the mug of water—there was nothing else. The prisoner was gone !

Simon turned pale as death, and could not find a word to say. He turned back, and met Monseigneur Anseau in the passage-way, who was standing by Isengriu's corpse, and just saying to Jacques :—

14 You must get another .hangman, for this one is quite out of office now !"

He went up the stair, followed by all the rest of them, took bis seat at the table, and when they were all seated in their places, in profound silence, he wiped his forehead of the cold sweat that stood on it in drops, and with a firm voice, he said :—

"We were discussing the question as between our burghers and the serfs of the neighboring seigneural domains ; we had resolved that no serf of ours should intermarry with neighbors' serf-classes, save by consent of the proprietor, where such proprietor should have subscribed to our commune—Let us proceed."

In this way Master Simon set the very first example of civil courage and strength ever seen at Typhaines.

The discussion was now resumed and continued.

At about three o'clock in the morning the meeting adjourned its long deliberations with the recording of a resolution that on the morrow the population of Typhaines should be convened in the square, to decide on the fitness of the laws projected, then and there to be reported in their presence. And the consuls went forth into the night to go the rounds of all the posts, and see what advance had been made in the work on the walls and ditches that were going on in pursuance of orders issued by them. The two knights did not accompany them on these grand rounds, but went home to the lodgings prepared for them by Jacques.

It was a splendid night, warm and calm. The consuls found everything going on well, the people at work, and perfectly cheerful. The diligent sentries looked about them as they patrolled their beat up and down to see that all was well. The pioneers were hollowing out the great, wide, deep ditch, with a speed never wanting, and only to he found in the first days of a new revolution, when every-thing seems delightful to everybody, so that the consuls were gratified at the prospect of finding their burgh inclosed by an enormous earth-wall and fosse.

Probably even all this joy was insufficient to calm the deep-laid sorrow in Simon's breast, for when he got home to his own house, he did not go to bed, but seating himself by the embers on his hearthstone, he buried his face in his hands, and burst into tears.

CHAPTER XII.

STOON sat there in silence, weeping. His tears ran down between his fingers, and fell dropping, oue by one, on the ashes of his own bome-fire. By the hearth-flame, Jeanne, half raised up in the immense bed> and leaning on her elbow, was intently gazing on her husband, and wondering what it all meant.

" What art thou doing there, Simon ?" said she. " Why dost thou not lie down ? The hour is late."

As Simon made no answer, she got carefully out of bed, for fear of waking Damerones, who, as was the custom of that now distant age, was lying across the foot of the bed, and buried in tranquil sleep. Jeanne crossed the room to where the consul sat, bent over him, and discovering the reason of his silence, said:—

" What 's the matter with you, Simon ?"

" Speak lower," he whispered, looking askance to where his daughter was sleeping. " Speak low. My misfortune is so great that I would fain no ear save thine should hear it. Indeed, I am in the wrong to sit here crying like a child. But after so many years of suffering, such repeated cruel disappointment, to find, at last, a traitor in one's own house, is enough to plunge one into despair, and put to flight forever the most resolute and unflinching courage."

" I hardly know you, Simon !" said Jeanne. " It's not your way to give up like this !"

" When I made up my mind to attack the abbey," he

rejoined, " I trusted to the suddenness of the assault for laying hold of the monks there, before any news of their peril
could reach the surrounding country. But not so. It was
by mere chance that I did succeed. Who was it, do you
suppose, that warned the Lady of Cornouiller ? To be sure,
when I had got that miserable Philippe into my hands, my
heart was ready to dance for joy ! I felt at last that that
vile heart's blood of his would soon gush out at my heads-
man's stroke, and the last living drop of that infamous line
of the Cornehauts should sink into the earth ! Who warned
the canon ? Whoever did that, will defraud me of my
revenge, and ruin our commune, as well!"

" Neither one nor t' other," replied Jeanne. " What you
call treason was probably a mere accident. And besides,
arn't you master of the situation ? Philippe is in your
power."

"Not so. No ! The serfs of De Pornes have carried
him off, and refuse to give him up to me save at one price
—one only price—and that's their enfranchisement 1 What
am I to do ? Can we venture to anger our only feal supporters, Baudouin and Anseau de Loysel? Not a singla
nobleman in the whole country will raise a lance for our
side, except those two scoundrels ; and everybody is aware
that they always lead the Count de Nevers by the nose—
he never does anything but what they tell him to do."

Jeanne was shocked, and held her peace for a while At
last she spoke again :—

" And so, then, our enemy is to go on living still ? Our
dangers are gathering about us again, Simon ! And you,
husband, after so many escapes, through such miracles of
your address and courage, from the rope, the sword, and
the dagger, if I am to see you again safe, it must be in
exile, in poverty, and wandering ! Ah I what a miserable

life! How it tires me!" Her tone was very low and mournful.

" Hearken, Jeanne. Listen to what I must tell you." And he looked hard towards the foot of the bed where Damerones lay sleeping, with her face covered over with the bedclothes. " I 'll not hide from you, even the very bottom of my thought. I believe I know who it was that betrayed me!"

" Then let him find no mercy!" she said, in a ferocious tone.

" Dost thou remember how Philippe found a mug of poisoned ale at his bedside, one night, when he was a boarder at our house in Cambrai ?"

" Pretty poison, indeed, that! We got nicely cheated that time—for it was nothing but some stuff as weak as water!"

" You are greatly mistaken there," said Simon. " The poison was good, but Philippe never took it I Was he warned, do you think ? The ale was emptied out on the ashes: if 'twas he did that, then he must have been told about it. If it was some otLer person, we were betrayed all the same."

While they were talking in low voices, a slight tremor was observable in the bedclothes where Damerones lay, and Simon, starting to his feet, darted to the foot of the bed, and began stripping the covers from off Damerones· face.

"You miserable wretch!" he cried, "you are trying to save Philippe's life !"

Jeanne, who stood petrified at the action and words of her husband, seemed at first as if she would seize his arm to stop him, but she couldn't stir—and there she stayed, mouth open, and eyes all on a gaze, like one fascinated.

Damerones' fair face now seemed changed, and she looked

pale as a corpse. Her clenching fingers vainly strove to draw back the clothing and hide her face again. She would put you in mind, as she lay under her father's stare, of a poor little lark, all palpitating with terror under the statue-like gaze of a trained pointer, as she lies helpless and fascinated there, half hid, half disclosed, in the tall meadow-grass.

^ The terrible moment was soon past and gone, and it was Damerones who put an end to it.

" Father," she said, in brief and tremulous words, " what is it you have against me ? What is it? Accuse me at once ! I will make answer."

" Was it you that saved the knight at Cambrai ?"

" Yes, I saved his life there."

" You wretch!" almost screamed the mother.

" You infamous girl!" muttered the cloth-merchant, and he ground his teeth in his fury. " You infamous girl, you have sold your father, your own mother, and the memory of all your people butchered at Cornehaut by this very villain's father—the inhuman beast 1 It was you, too, no doubt of it—you, too—that sent for succor to the Cornouiller men-at-arms!"

Damerones no longer stood with downcast eyes before the scintillations of his glaring balls. Ou the contrary, she seemed to borrow half their fiery energy.

" 'T was 11" she answered resolutely.

Simon's hand moved slowly to where the handle of his dagger hung at his girdle—but the hand stopped short of the haft.

" It was you, too," still more agitated, "'t was you that tanght the serfs of De Pornes how to carry their point by wresting Philippe out of my grasp: you thought that was the way to save his life. Was it so ?"

" I did it!" she replied, for the third time.

" When a man finds a viper under his hearthstone, you know what he does with him l"

" Listen to me, father," replied Damerones. " Threats are of no use now. You are not going to kill me, I know that; you are my own father ! Just at present, you know not what to do l But you love me, and you are not going to slay me ; I tell you so, again ! What's the good of all this violence ? Think you I am afraid of you ? Before I laid me down to rest, I made my prayer to God, and he, I know it, will not desert me now."

" What is that Philippe to you ? Are you bis mistress ?"

" His mistress I No ! By the blessed Virgin, no l But if you will, I would be his wife."

"His wife I His *wife!"* roared Simon, and burst into aloud laugh. "Do you forget, then, who you are ? Do you think that a son of old Geoffroy de Cornehaut is going to offer his hand in marriage to a maiden of your class ! If ever you spoke to him of such a dream as that, and he did not hoot at you, 'twas because he adds to the other vices of his family, the basest hypocrisy."

" I never did speak to him about it," responded Damerones very calmly. "I know not, indeed, whether he ever looked at me, or if he knew of my existence even. But I —yes I—do know that marriage of such as I into noble houses is not a thing impossible. Didn't we see merchants' daughters at Thoulouse who became wives to noble knights ? You know we did."

"Thoulouse!" impatiently responded Simon; "Thoulouse is not a French city, and people on this side of the Loire differ from them on all points. But to let you know —and know it well too—your projects are impracticable ones, I tell you that if Philippe were to throw himself at my feet, to beg your hand in marriage, I'd spurn him. I '11 have uothing of that man but his heart's blood. Never can there be betwixt him and me any sentiment in common but one of irremissible hate; so you may drive all this nonsensical stuff out of your poor brain ; and if the thought of them proves bitter as wormwood, may the bitterness long remain as a punishment you well deserve ! You said well— I will not slay you ; the new commune must not be founded on a crime detestable alike on earth and in heaven. But by all God's saints and all the wounds of the crucified Lord, you shall be disappointed if you hope I 'll ever forgive you !"

Damerones threw herself off from the foot of the bed, and stood before him, with an intrepid countenance.

" I don't ask yon to pardon me, for I am fully resolved to compel you to desist from the pursuit of what you call your just revenge. You shall not take Messire Philippe's life; that I swear here, before your face, father! And against all your hateful oaths the only barrier I set up is the true devotion and holy love I have in secret sworn for him. Yes, father, in your own words, ⁴ by all God's saints and all my Saviour's wounds,' I swear it! You shall not pour out the heart's blood of the man I love ! Raise but your arm to strike him down, and my bosom shall be a safe shield for his life ! If you know what it is to be implacable, I, too, know, and know quite as well, how to guard the life I love so well from every threatened peril !"

"By the souls of my fathers," cried Simon, " 'twas a lucky thought of miue, that day when hell breathed into me the idea of putting you in the Archdeacon of Cambrai's hands, to make an educated woman of you ! That dreadful knowledge—how you bring it to bear, this very hour, on the fondest hopes of thine own parent I See how full are thy words of the perfidiousness and malice of the demon ! Oh ! Damerones ! Damerones I Child of my heart! Is it thus I must gaze oil mine only child—in open rebellion against my house, and serving my most mortal enemies ? Oh, Damerones ! my child ! my child 1"

During this terrible struggle with his daughter, the only being for whom he ever indulged a feeling approaching his all absorbing devotion to the freedom of his class, Simon had gradually subsided from the towering height of maddened passion, to a sort of miserable depression and languor. He clearly discerned that there could be no issue to the quarrel. As Damerones had boldly told him, he could not stab her with his own hand, and yet the maiden's offence was one, the consul thought, to be fitly punishable by death alone. And so, finding that nothing in the world could ever make Damerones give way, he left off speaking to her, and stood still in an attitude of doubt and wistful hesitation. His face was painfully expressive of his mental agony, and cruel conflicts seemed raging among the hard, coarse features of his countenance, just as the tempest-tossed ocean lifts and by turns lets down the angry waves. Damerones, partly from her tender nature, and partly from policy, offered to clasp him round the neck with her beautiful arms. But, for the very first time in his whole life, Simon pushed her away from him, and with frowning gray eyebrows, went to sit down on his stool by the hearth. Jeanne was still leaning against the wall in a dark corner of the room, praying in secret and from the bottom of her heart, that nothing ill might befall her child, though at the same time cursing her fatal perfidy. Damerones sat down on the foot of the bed.

The consul's hatred of Philippe de Cornehaut and his love for the new commune were so blended into one ; they sprung so absolutely from the same source, that the two sentiments mingled without mutual discordancy, in his 6oul. To abandon the hunt for the blood of Messire Geoffroi's line, or to yield one hair's breadth of the interests of Typhaines, would have been, in the eyes of the old burgher, equally base : and yet his daughter's crime made it an impossible thing henceforth to nurse his schemes of vengeance and for the good of his city too. He could not but admit that the Abbot's flight from the minster was a misfortune far more serious than Messire Philippe's evasion, for the ecclesiastical dignitary might, by force or cunning, at least so be flattered himself, as to be led to agree to a concession of communal rights. In those olden times, no person, no burgess, however powerful he might happen to be, ever dreamed of what we, in our own day, call a radical revolution. All that they could expect was to buy their freedom from the suzerain seigneur, and in case of his refusal to sell on any terms, they endeavored to extract the concession by force. Still they never did conceive that violence of any kind could abrogate the old-time laws of suzerainty; and even when oppressing one of these seigneurs, they never went further than the putting, by main strength, into his purse, a sum of money estimated as a proper equivalent for rights they thus wrested from him. Should they, in the tumult of an attack or a resistance, happen to do *meshaing* on him, or to *meshaing* him, as they called it, so as to wound or kill him, they never considered themselves, on that account, absolved from obligation of seigneurage; and it was with the new master they had to treat for ransom, and for the reserved rights of the commune, outside of the true suzerainty. Under these circumstances, as Simon had not the abbot in his power, he must, perforce, treat with the prelate at a distance, and so felt all the difficulties of his position. Besides all this, other cares came in to assail him.

The Count de Nevers was not the man to give the burgh a gratuitous succor, ne, too, had claims which, if not ponderated by the legitimate rights of the abbey, might prove to be dangerous ones. While Simon was in treaty with that puissant neighbor for a mutual alliance, he found that by only half breaking the monkish yoke, he must wear the other half of it as a shield against the pretensions of his protector, who might well some day lay the weight of his hand on the commune itself, in case it should ever come to belong to no one but itself alone. But now, the Abbot being fled away, and it being probable that no power could be brought so to bear on him as to make him yield one poor inch, he might possibly find it necessary to throw himself much farther than prudence would admit, into the wiley counts arms. It is quite clear, then, that the consul's affairs were as various and as serious as those invariably appurtenant to states of a far higher range than his poor Typhaines. There was yet another awkward incident.

The serfs of the De Pornes estate, and Joslin their leader, by holding the prisoner as hostage, had shown that they too could rise and strike for freedom. Yet the commune could not, without very great risk, make them such a present as that; scarcely could sho now hope to save her own affranchisement. How, then, could she lend a hand in the cause of other men, without drawing down innumerable dangers on her own ? While still busily at work to found her own institutions, and offering to swear a mutual support with the surrounding nobles, was that a fitting moment to rob them of their working-men ? Simon did not even for an instant pause on that point, so inadmissible did it seem in his eyes ; and yet what could he do to recover possession of his captive, provided ho would not turn a listening ear to Joslin's proposals; but on the contrary show him that on no account would he do anything for him or in behalf of his village? He finally made up his mind to come to an understanding with Monseigneur

15

Baudouin, who, deeply interested as he was in the affair, ought to have got hold of some scheme by this time, for getting himself and his Typhaines friends out of the difficulty. Monseigneur Baudouin was well known for his talents in the way of finding out expedients as well as for the elasticity of his conscience on all occasions : effective expedients, right or wrong, were alike acceptable. There is a manuscript genealogy on parchment, and written in characters apparently of the early part of the thirteenth century, in which that eminent personage is called *Baadouin III. the Trickster*, showing that his contemporaries were men who did full justice to his abilties..

The dawning morning had now begun to light up the scene of that mute consternation, wrath, and concentrated anger, that had transpired during the night, in the abode of the most eminent of the five Typhaines consuls. The silence of that chamber had not been broken by either of its unhappy inhabitants ; and it can scarcely be said that either of them had stirred during that whole long time; sitting there in their different attitudes, they might have been taken for so many statues.

The morning light seemed in some degree to relax the tremulous tension of Simon's heart-strings, and he gradually grew calm under the influence of the growing light, as it came in through the narrow windows to disclose the furniture, the floor, and the three unhappy souls that sat there. Simon turned a side look to where his daughter sat, and saw her so changed that his paternal love was shivering in the profound deep of his soul, whither it had been banished by the raging passion that had crushed it back and trodden it down there. The voice of his old blind love for Damerones, the only child now left to him in the world, began to sing and be musical once more, amid the tumult of passions far more austere.

Master Simon moved ; he turned towards his child, and stretched forth his arms. He stretched them out to her with a look so humid, so passionate, indeed, that she saw he was pardoning her misdeeds, and that, implacable by nature though he was, yet he was now softened by the magic power of affection. Damerones threw herself down at his knee.

" You know I love you as much as you love me, father; I well know my faults are many, but you won't have Messire Philippe put to death, will you, father ?"

" Damerones, even while I am embracing you, you can think of nothing but that detested crusader!"

"Yes, I am always thinking of Monseigneur Philippe."

" You love none but him ?"

"No; I love you and my mother too; and you are both ever present in my heart, even though you be not at home."

" But you prefer Philippe to both of us ?"

" I love him more than the whole world besides!"

And now came another dreadful, silent pause.

" Suppose the knight should happen to die: what would you do then ?"

" If I died not myself, I would put on sackcloth next my body. I would go on foot to Compostella, to Rome, to Jerusalem, praying, ever praying for the repose of his soul, for yours and mother's, and so would I continue to do as long as ever I lived !"

" See, Damerones, my anger is gone, and my heart full of tenderness and pity. For you, my daughter, I desire nothing but your good, and I pardon you many, ah! many things. Speak to me now frankly, and answer me truthfully in everything. Does the knight know that you love him so ? A little while ago you told me ' no,' but perhaps you were not sincere."

" He knows it not, father; I swear it in your presence, and know it he never shall, unless ho should ask my hand in marriage. But let me alone about that. What I wish for must happen. Father, I am not a giddy girl."

" Then 'twas you that got Joslin to carry him off?"

"Yes, father, 'twas I."

"How could you have given such order to that vulgar brute ?"

" I have been acquainted with Joslin this many a day. He used to come to Typhaines to sell his fruit of different sorts, and we bought of him more than once. It's a good while ago, but he told me he was well off; that under the wood-pile in his cellar, he had put away about a hundred gold bezants, a part of which had been bequeathed by his father. As he says he wants me to be his wife, he often tells me about different projects of his. I saw him yesterday and told him he never would gain his freedom, nor his village either, unless he got a hostage from you."

" That was a cunning device of yours," said Simon, nodding his head, and smiling. "And so Joslin took possession of Monseigneur Philippe ? You and Joslin make a pair of cunning foxes. It's a very ticklish thing to have a couple of enemies of that sort ahead of you."

" You are smiling now, father; and you terrified me so all night long ! You wasn't so angry as you pretended. Eh ?"

Damerones, lifted by her father's own hand, was by this time sitting on his knee, and he tapping her soft cheek with his great, rough lingers, and Jeanne, seeing that concord was now restored, came forward in great delight, and leaned on her husband's shoulder, hearkening, but not interrupting, and joyfully savoring to the very centre of her soul, as if it were a delicious restorative perfume, every qnestion and retort, that filled her poor heart with its old joys again. To his daughter's question, Simon replied :—

" Don't you think that. I was angry, and I am so yet. A maiden, methinks, however knowing she might he, can never be truly wise, or you would not ask me a question like that. But to an ill that can never be cured, there is only one thing to be done, and that is to submit to it at once. Now perhaps, if you and I could have a good understanding together, I might, maybe, not go on blocking your project. In what you was telling me a while ago about Thoulousc and other places, there was one thing that struck me very much, and that was that the nobles at Verpignan and Thoulouse really do make no -difficulty about marrying burgher-girls, and it's just as easy, too, for their burghers to marry into the families of the gentlemen there."

" To be sure, father, and why shouldn't Monseigneur Philippe, who has travelled so much and knows all about those matters as well as we do; why shouldn't he want me to be his wife, once we could but know each other better ?"

"You forget," rejoined the cloth-merchant, with a cruel smile, "a thing you thought about only a little while back, and that is, that the Dame de Cornouiller is Philippe's lover!"

Damerones proudfully and confidently tossed her head. That toss, those eyes of hers, that smile, all combined to show forth the confidence in herself that every woman has when none come near but to praise and flatter her and fast fix in her very nature the conscious power of her charms.

. " Well, then," resumed Master Simon, "as you are so snre of making Monseigneur Philippe bend to your will, from this very moment I will make no further objections, and I consent to all that is honorable and just on his side ; and now, to prove my good-will, I must tell you thnt of all asylums in this world, the one where you've put Monseigneur Philippe is the most dangerous one. This commune never can or will agree to affranchise Joslin and his comrades, for silver or gold, for Philippe's life—no, not even for the life of Monseigneur, the King of France, himself! Never!"

"Now, what's that to me,?" said Damerones, smiling the while, and with a little saucy shrug.

"You talk like a child ; yes, just like a mere baby," continued Master Simon, as he went on caressing her cheeks again. " Don't you know that as soon as your allies are forced back to their glebe, and Joslin ready to hang on Messire Baudouin's gallows-tree, there will be oniy one real satisfaction left for the wretches ?"

" What satisfaction ?" cried Damerones.

" Eh ! a very simple one, truly," said Master Simon, quite jovially; "why, of course, they'll be quite delighted if they put your nice knight to death, and they '11 be sure to do it, too."

"I don't believe one word of that!" replied Damerones, very dryly. "No! they'll set him at liberty in hopes of his helping them-to their freedom."

" I see how little you do know about those brutes of serfs when their passions are once roused on the liberty question. They haven't half as much sense as you think ; and what's more, you surely ought to know that if Joslin should take it into that blockhead of his to even talk of such a thing to Messire Philippe, the knight would think himself dishonored by the very proposal."

Here Damerones fell into a deep.reverie, and she answered not a word. At last she said :—

" He's in great danger, then ? You are not deceiving me, father ?"

"Judge for yourself," he replied. "Only weigh what I

told you. and you can't differ from me on the subject; no, you can't, at all."

Damerones sat still, thinking again, and Master Simon twiddling with the little silver cross hanging on her neck.

" I am afraid to ask advice of you, father, you hate Monseigneur Philippe so!"

" Yery well, then, don't you see, child, that as you are determined on having him for a husband, I am obliged to change ray mind, whether or no."

" Come now, father, since you do know that Monseigneur Philippe's life and mine are bound up in one, tell me how I can get him out of Joslin's hands ?"

"There's only one way."

" And what is that way ?"

" Tell me where they have put him, so that I can get hold of him again!"

Master Simon, as he uttered these words, involuntarily equeezed Damerones' hand hard, his eyes grew flashing bright.

Damerones screamed.

"You are deceiving me I" she said—and she pressed both her hands on her father's shoulders, and sat staring him full in the face. Simon bore the inquest steadily, desperate though she looked, and went on playing with her fair cheek.

" Ah !" she said, tears in her eyes, and her voice tremulous with emotion. " Ah ! can it be possible you are playing a mere game with your Damerones' life, and falsely giving me hopes that you disavow in the bottom of your heart, father? Tell the truth now, are you deceiving me? Do not ask me to deliver Monseigneur Philippe into your hands to put him to death, and for that only. Only think, what a crime ! I—yes, I— would be his base betrayer into the hands of the executioner I And do you suppose, or can you dream that I could ever pardon you for that, in this world or the world to come ? Oh ! rather But do you really, truly mean to abuse your daughter's dear love?"

"If you think that," said Simon, very simply, "all you have to do is, don't tell me your secret. My vengeance will be paid by the serfs who have him, instead of by my own hand, and you 'll have, nothing to blame for that but your distrust of your own father. That's all. So do as you like."

Damerones got off his knee, and he rose and stood up.

" So, you won't tell me," said he, muttering.

" I 'll think about it."

Just then, a rather imperious knock at the door was instantly followed by the appearance of a mail-covered knight, none other than Monseigneur Baudouin himself.

" Ah, Sir Consul!" said Baudouin, with a courteous mien, " up already, and your women, too ? Here, come this way, I've something to say to you."

"Yes, I know,"said Simon, smilingly. "It's that business about the serfs that gives you such an early start."

" My serfs ? that's the word. And I hope you are going to be all fair and square about that."

" Never doubt it. But let's go out. Good-bye, Jeanne. Damerones, you had better think about what I was saying, and quickly, too. I shall come back in about an hour to hear what you have decided on."

The knight and burgher left the room, and there sat Damerones, lost in a mist of painful hesitation and dread.

CHAPTER XIII.

AND SO, the consul's daughter sat alone, lost in contemplation. Given wholly over to a passion, which in people of her class might seem an enormity; traitress to her own father; enfranchised, though so young, from the notions of the time that required and expected an absolute devotion to the opinions and will of the house-chief—children and servants alike—she must henceforth live, and ever be, a stranger in her father's house and heart. The burgher being gone, Jeanne at once went to work to put her housekeeping in order; but though she passed and repassed again and again the place where her poor daughter was sitting in sorrow, she spoke never a word to the child, and the only sign she made was, every now and then to give her an angry scowl that did not go far towards raising the maiden's downtrodden spirits and courage. Even if Damerones chose to forget her duty, she, Jeanne—yes, she—had ever clung to it, without having one self-reproach, all the days of her life, and that, too, without one moment's hesitation. This perfection of married love and obedience only served to make her just now utterly intolerant, especially of a love affair so doubly criminal as poor Damerones'. Had her child's life been in danger, she no doubt would have interceded for her, but as all that was now over, she gave full swing to her ill-temper.

For some time Damerones sat there, worn down, miserable and weeping, and trying to catch her mother's eye.

But when she at last found that she had nothing to
expect from Jeanne's commiseration, and that she was
left to struggle all cjone against her father's secret wiles,
she suddenly recovered all her courage and •nergj, and
then wiping her humid eyes, leaned her forehead on her
hand, and began to reflect on the situation. Jeanne, in the
meantime, had gone out of the room, and shutting the
door behind her, left her daughter alone there.

Monseigneur's Philippe's protectress, finding she was no
longer watched, immediately walked across the floor, opened
a small door, and stepped out into a garden where there
were a few trees, some piteous-looking cabbages, a few pot-
herbs, and a bunch of summer-flowers here and there. She
went rapidly forwards, and came to a hedge between that
and the neighboring garden. Damerones looked all around
her with anxious care, but her face soon brightened up as
she discovered Joslin stretched on the grass, on the other
side of the fence. As soon as he saw her he got up.

" God's blessing, and all his saints' too, be on you, Damerones!" said the de Pornes serf, as he saw, with scintil-
lating eyes, the fair maid of Typhaines. "I was wishing
from the bottom of my heart you'd come to me, for our
affairs don't get on as I expected. Your father isn't a man
easy to deal with !"

"I am aware of what has happened, Joslin," replied
Damerones, gravely; " but father hasn't said his last word
yet."

" Your father ? Yes, maybe that's so; but since I saw you
last, I barely missed falling into the seneschal's clutches, who
has been chasing me, and his two men-at-arms to help him.
If those men-at-arms were not on such bad terms as they
are with the Typhaines people, and afraid to go into
the houses, they'd have followed me here, and hung me,

too, by this time, all the same as the burghers hung that poor abbey-baily yesterday morning."

" Don't you be afraid, Joslin ; ycur prisoner is your safeguard Monseigneur Baudouin is quite as much afraid of losing him as father is ; he's a good security you have in hand."

Joslin shook his head, as if not so sure of that.

" I rather think you are mistaken, Damerones," said the serf. " The consuls and Monseigneur, too, would far rather let that poor devil of a prisoner get off than lose a chance to hang a dozen revolted serfs. As for me, my mind *s made up now."

"And might a body know what that wise ' made up' means ?" said Damerones, pretending to smile.

" Oh I I've no secrets with you, sister," said the giant. "I am going to knock out the fellow's brains with my axe here, so os nobody shall get him, and then my comrades and I are to make for the woods, and there we are going to live like bold robbers until some Free company comes by, and then we '11 all enlist in the corps. I intend to soon be a captain, and as soon as I get that, come back here, burn the town down, and carry you off with me I You shall see what a nice time you and I '11 have together !"

Damerones on the instant saw that, even if Simon was trying to cheat her, his purpose was in a fair way of being served by the circumstances. She had been acquainted with Joslin for a good while, and knew that nothing could equal the brutal obstinacy of the fellow who was brave to rashness, and of a ferocity unparalleled.

To this happy quality it was that he owed the honor of being frequently called on by Messire De Pornes, a circum- stance that gave him a high standing in his village, and so made him ambitious.

" Joslin, I should like to have a talk with your prisoner."

" That 's rather a surprising notion," replied the brute;
" and what might you happen to want with him ?"

"Well, I guess he's a kind of a man that's likely to
have his money hid somewhere, and if he'd only tell me
where, don't you see what a capital thing that would be
for us both ? Why, you could go right away and buy you
a splendid horse, a nice set of armor, and then, of course,
you'd soon get to be captain ! Don't you see, man ?"

Joslin's eyes were now gleaming with greed, but he sud.
denly thought of a better way.

" You needn't trouble yourself talking to him, Damerones. I '11 go bring Allard and Thierry, and we three
will make him feel so bad that he '11 be obliged to tell us
all about his business before we kill him !"

" I forbid that 1" cried the consul's daughter. "And if
you should even dare touch Monseigneur Philippe "

She stopped short, feeling that such warmth was but
ill suited to effect the desired conversion in her brutal
lover, and likely at best to arouse suspicions very dangerous to the unhappy Philippe.

" You are too bad, Joslin. I pity the woman who's to
have you for a husband, ready as you are to strike and
torture your neighbors. I've no idea of getting myself
damned by doing a wrong thing when there's no use in
doing it."

" Then your notion is that you can make Messire Philippe
give up his money ?"

" Easy," replied the girl.

" But you'd be frightened at the sight of him," cried
Joslin. " He was severely wounded in the head, at the
capture of the abbey, and he's all over bloody and pale as
a corpse, and I really have had too much to do to get time
to take him anything to eat yet."

Damerones answered very quietly:—

" Yoa are very hard hearted, Joslin, and if you go on this way, making such complacent exhibitions of yonr wickedness, I shall hardly be able to love you very much. I '11 go to the honse, and get some bandages, some bread and a flagon of wine, and I *11 take them to the prisoner. "

 " Very well. Do as you like best, Damerones. By the blessed Virgin, you are the only soul I do love. I'm entirely besotted about you "

Damerones hardly heard these last words, so hurried was she to get back to the house. But Joslin was quite sure she not only heard them, but had them packed away in the very hollow of her little heart. Joslin, notwithstanding his athletic form and his broad back, thoroughly versed as it was in the delicate attentions of the De Pomes' seigneural baton, was a rare specimen of what they call a great big fool. Some little good fortune as a beau in his village, and his renown for strength and brutality, had made him so bold as to lift his eyes to the cloth-merchant's daughter, though the fact is that, until the morning before, never had she given him even a civil reception; but that was enough for him, and he thought he might venture to declare to himself in terms used to express one's good opinion of himself, in those times, namely, that he really was and intended ever to be the lucky and irresistible scoundrel that he had been all his life long.

In about five minutes Damerones came back. She was hurrying along as fast as she could walk, with a jar of wine and a great roll of bread on her head, and bandages, thread, scissors, and a small jar of balsam in her hands.

" Come !" said she to Joslin.

" That's the place. There in your neighbor Lienard's cellar. I hope when the knight has done eating, you '11 give me something too, for I'm half starved."

16

"I promise you. Is this the place—this little alley, where you and your comrades always hide ?"

" Yes, always. And here we intend to stay till we make for the woods, and that we shall do as soon as we are sure the Typhaines people won't take us into their commune."

As they were talking in this wise, Joslin led the way to an old shed, at the farther end of which was a trap-door, hidden beneath a pile of fagots, that led down into a deep cellar.

" Is this the place where you put Monseigneur Philippe ?" asked Damerones, in trembling tones.

" Yes; this is the place. Ain't he well hid ? I'd defy the devil himself to find him. But stop, let me light my lantern for you. There, take care you don't fall—the steps are steep, and very slippery. If you come out before I get back, you must pile up the fagots again; for I must go and send Lienard into the town, to find out the news this morning."

Damerones went down the dark steps.

The place looked like the inside of a sepulchre. Notwithstanding the season of the year, the air inside was very cold and damp. She wept carefully down the steep, slippery steps, and when at the bottom, she found she was in a confined hole not more than fifteen feet square, and very deep.

Upon a large wooden plank that might, perhaps, have been put there as a shelf to stow away the peasant's provisions, lay Monseigneur Philippe, stretched on his back, his hands crossed under his head, for a pillow, and fast asleep. Damerones scarcely could recognize, in the unfortunate prisoner before her, the brilliant young seigneur she had seen five years ago, prancing along the streets at Cambrai with his mailed companions in arms, and fell in love with, then and there. Somewhat embrowned by the Syrian sun, the features of her beloved had lost the freshness of the juveuile bloom of that old time. And that was not the saddest part of the change. He was deadly pale now, and his bloody head wrapped in a coarse, ensanguined cloth, and signs of great suffering, fatigue, and misery, all of them sad presages of what was to come for the man she loved, were enough to rend her very heart-strings.

She put the lantern in a hole she saw in the wall, and then stood still, gazing intently on the knight's countenance.

Five years of absence, especially absence in one who never showed you any particular preference, is so rude a love trial, that few persons in our busy and enlightened age could stand it; but in the Middle Ages, when once a maiden had hugged one dear thought to her breast, common opinion ever blamed her if she let it go, and on the other hand, applauded her if she proved to be unchanging and true, for there was then no such word in love as "forget." In the lives of people so little hurried, carried out in a sort of unchanging uniformity from beginning to end, you \1 have far to seek if you would hope to find a case of inconstant love; and so, Damerones· whole nature was love for Philippe, as fervid now as the first day she saw him at Cambrai, riding among his men. The only change that had taken place in her feelings all that long time was but an. increase in their intensity.

In this miserable funereal cavity, on that rustic beam, in spite of his pallor, in spite of the blood that begrimed his face, in spite of Syrian suns that had embrowned him, Damerones saw Monseigneur Philippe more beautiful than ever before. At that spriug-day of her existence, Damerones looked on him as a youth, fresh, rosy, fair, just out of pagedom, and just entered on his career as a bold lancer. Now she looked on him as a knight well proved in the dust and blood of the battle-field; a crusader; God's avenging hero; a defender of the holy sepulchre; one of tho&e intrepid knights-companions far famed for courage, and just returned from the field of victory. Sick though he looked, lying there asleep, he yet looked so strong, so firm, so puissant by nature, that Damerones imbibed a feeling of respect and reverence that came to take place along with her constant, glowing affection for his person. She felt, in a measure, sorry to wake the soldier, and she hesitatingly touched his shoulder, and gave it a little push.

Monseigneur Philippe opened his eyes wide, and gazed with surprise on the beautiful maid of Typhaines.

¹¹ God's name !" said he, with a sweet smile. " This is a rather more gracious waking than I thought for when I fell asleep here. I must be well off, so it seems to me, if they give me such jailers as you are."

" Don't think that, Monseigneur," replied Damerones, " for you are in the power of the very wickedest people on the whole earth, and unless the blessed Virgin guards you, this very day you must die."

¹¹ All right, then, and I sha'n't die at all, for in all my life long I certainly never did give holy Mary the least of-fence—that is, as far as I know of."

" Monseigneur, if you have any questions to ask, I can answer them just as well while I am dressing your wound. Let me take off the bandages from your head. We had better make good use of the few moments I have to spare here with you." And so saying, she at once began to remove the bandages from his brow.

" True, now ! Mademoiselle, who are you ? Don't de-ceive me, for I never have been forgetful or ungrateful, wheu people have done me a kindness."

ʰ Do you remember the burgher at Cambrai where you lodged five years ago ?"

"Remember; why certainly I remember. He was a cross sort of a man. 1 never could get a civil word out of him !"

" He had a daughter," pursued Damerones, as she went on with her surgery.

" Oh, yes! A little girl about fourteen. Yes, I remember her."

" Hardly, I should think, Monseigneur. But ray memory # is better than yours. As you was going away, you gave me a silver cross, and asked me to pray for you ; and not a single—no, not a single day has come and gone since— but I prayed * fervently for you !"

" Ah 1 what a brave child V' cried Philippe, drawing his head backwards in spite of Damerones' endeavor to make him hold still, and not see how she was blushing. He looked steadily at his consolator, far more than he had done.

" I remember you now!" with a face lighted by the frankest smile. " How beautiful you've grown to be ! Why, you are a miracle !"

Damerones went on washing off the hard, dry blood on his brow, and exclaimed :—

" You '11 soon be well again. This cut they gave you isn't very deep."

" Burghers and peasants, lucky for me, don't know much about sword-exercise. Had I raised my hand as high as the knave did that gave me that blow, I'm sure I'd havo cut him right in two. But, my dear, did you happen to think while you were so kind as to get ready to come and cure me, that I am a little hungry or so ?"

" To be sure, Monseigneur. See, here's some wine, and here's a nice buttered roll for you."

" What a good girl you are ! I '11 go on with my breakfast, and you please to tell me all you kuow about my affairs at Typhaines, and why those people are so bent on taking my life? By the Cross, I never was guilty of the least disloyalty as to them. All I did, while fighting them, was the mere, plain duty of a good soldier."

" What you ask me to tell you is what I do not know myself," said Damerones, " but certain it is, you have some violent enemies here, and had you not got out of that dungeon, you must have been dead by this time. I it was, who bad the happiness to get you out of it."

" What, Damerones ? Is it to you I owe my rescue ? I promise you—yes, I promise by my poor Rudaverse, and by my spurs too, I *11 never forget it. How comes it that you could desire to do me so great a service, for you are not a vassal of mine ?"

Monseigneur's question was quite a natural one, but the gentleman hadn't as good an opiniou of himself as Joslin had. As the consul's daughter made no answer, but merely went on with her charitable ministrations, Philippe de Cornehaut began again with:—

" But, my pretty child, from what you've been telling me, I seem to have got out of one danger only to fall into a worse peril I How are you to get me out of that ?"

"I know not as yet, Monseigneur; and, indeed, I must confess that I have been thinking about it this many an hour. Let me make you fully acquainted with the situation, and then see if yon are luckier than I at finding expedients."

" I hear what you say, but I wᵀant you to know that I'm no great matter of a clerk; where address is wanted, or cunning, wisdom, or what they call prudhomie, I haven't much to boast of, and I guess you are better at all that than I am: anyhow, go on, and tell me all about it."

" Monseigneur, if you were in the hands of the Typhaines people, they would put you to death at once I"

"Good; I know that already."

" And now, if you continue to be held as hostage for the serfs, you must die as soon as ever they find that the consuls will not let them join the commune !"

Damerones now entered on the detail of many subjects already known to the reader, for the purpose of clearly explaining to the knight the pretensions of the De Pornes serfs, and the indispensable necessity for the rejection of them by the burghers.

"I it was," said she, closing, "I it was that put you into the power of that frightful wretch, Joslin ; but, trembling as I was for your life, what better could I do, Monseigneur ? I tried to ward off one peril by interposing another not so near at hand."

" You did quite right, sister," answered the crusader. "Yes, a thousand times I say it, and all the days of my life I will hold it in faithful remembrance. Wouldn't anybody think I am looking for a long life to hear mo talk so ? and why not, indeed ? God will save me, Damerones ! In fact, now that there's an end to my abstinence, and having drunk up your wine to the last drop, and swallowed the very last crumb of that nice roll of yours, I find my heart 's got back to its old place again. Sit you down here, close by me, and let us have a talk about it all. So, you say Joslin and his fellows are coming down here directly to break my neck, in case you shouldn't forestall them by handing me over to your father ?"

Damerones nodded affirmatively.

" It's my opinion that we had better not decide on such a poor recourse as that, until we Ve tried some other way. Go and get me an axe, a ploughshare, or even a good club; anything that comes to hand, and when Messire Joslin and his friends come down to pay their ugly visit, I 'll hold such a conference with them as may show them how very much they are in the wrong."

"1 believe your courage is very great, Monseigneur, and your strength as well; but if you should not be killed by a dozen serfs as strong and better armed than yourself, the survivors will deliver you to the Typhaines men, or,' possibly, shut you down in this hole to die of starvation. If, on the other hand, you should defeat your assailantsi what will become of you ?"

"I'll get out of this dungeon," said the knight, "and try to get clear of the town."

"You couldn't do that. There's a deep, wide ditch around the whole place, and eveiy issue is strictly guarded. Of course, as you look like no other person here, and are totally ignorant of the roads, you would be retaken at once."

" As that is the case, sister mine," said Philippe, " give me up to your father, then. After all, it may be that the pious canon, who has already saved me once, will make his appearance again, just in time to deliver me from the jaws of death."

" That's a very feeble resource," murmured Damerones, moving her head from side to side.

"It's a thread, at least," continued the knight, "and that very thread may turn into a cable, to hoist me up to a place of safety. Anyhow, though I must say it annoys me to think of dying in this unlucky adventure of mine, I trust I shall do no dishonor to my name or my knighthood, nor to friends that love me—nor you either, Damerones."

The young girl raised up her beautiful eye6, all wet with tears, to the knight's, who, when he saw her admirable face 6o brimming with passionate expression, felt softened and went on, without thinking the least evil:—

" Dear sister Damerones, what a pity it is you are a burgher girl ! For you have a heart equal to the noblest maiden's in the land. How glad it would make me to see

a gold crown on your brow! Still, all that can't prevent me from repaying your friendship with lasting grati •
tude. Pray, believe, Damerones, that I truly love you for
your faithfal souvenir of me."

So strong was the poor girl's love, that she could desire
nothing better than to yield to its illusions. Without any
idea that the gentleman's affection was in the least of the
like nature with hers, she felt that she would willingly sacrifice her life a thousand times over for his dear sake. True
love asks but little.

She rose from her seat.

[41] Adieu, Monseigneur !" she said. " Adieu 1 I know
not what I am about to do. I will go pray to the blessed
Virgin for enlightenment; but be sure of this, you shall
not perish 1 I '11 find resources that a vulgar affection could
never dream of. Perhaps I shall not see you for long—
for very long should my father keep watch over me, or
confine me to the house, so that I could not get out you
know, to come back again. But believe me, I shall always
think of you, and believe, pray, there's one devoted heart.
Ah, Monseigneur Philippe, if you should die, do not blame
me—and wait for me a little while in heaven 1"

Damerones burst into tears.

"You love me too well, sister!" said Monseigneur,
deeply affected at the scene. " I don't like to see you weep
so. Because I am so unfortunate in this affair, that's no
reason why you should weep for me. Many a better knight
than I am has perished from the earth, and yet nothing came
of it; the world goes on all the same. I understand very
well how sorry it makes you to think your father should behave in such a cruel way to me ; but what would you have?
'tis a very uncommon miracle where a rebel burgher shows
any courtesy and goodness of heart. Don't you worry
yourself about it; you are not to blame, and I love you all

the better for what you have done. Farewell, sister; and try, if you can, to let me see you anywhere else than in this hole. It would please me well if I could see the suu shine once more, before I set out for eternity."

Damerones had by this time taken up her lantern. She cast on the kuight a woe-begone, despairing, burning look, as a mother's when quitting a child with but a frail hope of ever seeing it more. She made no answer to the knight, save by movements of the head—her heart was too full. To speak, would be to burst into sobs. She went up the stairs, raised the trap-door, and went out, leaving the prisoner alone in the dark. When he got back, by groping his way, to his beam, he sat down, and began to think about Damerones and the great love she had shown for him.

Good Monseigneur Philippe felt convinced that that young maiden was moved by her pure and warm piety to act as she had done, and that her father's brutal conduct was driving her almost to despair. It was to this filial sentiment, and to her fears for the future state of her father's soul—so black was it—that he attributed the warm expressions of Damerones. He remembered at last quite clearly how he used to give her ribbons, at Cambrai; and another thing that had wholly slipped his memory till now, how he one day knocked down a gay page he caught trying to kiss her by force. He thought of the sweet smiles she used to lavish on him ; but he did not dwell very long on those, to him, insignificant reminiscences.

" How is all this to end ? 'Pon my faith, I feel very well, and in good heart too; but when I think how sadly I lost monseigneur, my father, without counting in my other mis-ventures, I am really mad at myself for being so lively. Never mind, 1 hough. I '11 do penance for all that as soon as I get a good opportunity."

He was reasoning in this way, when the trap-door was raised again, and looking up towards the light, he saw several faces stooping and looking down at him, and then some one said :—

"Monseigneur, come up l"

CHAPTER XIV.

MONSEIGNEUR Philippe, on seeing so many people bending forwards to look below for him, and whose hands he
doubted not, were ready to lay hold on him, stood for a
while, thinking what was best to be done. It was a difficult problem; nor is it surprising to find that he was
putting off the crisis as long as possible, and trying to make
up his mind. Let us leave him for a while standing down
there, his arms crossed on his breast, and he looking np
at them, trying to make out the physiognomies of the newcomers, and threshing his brains, in hopes of beating out
some liberating idea, some miracle, in short. In the meantime, we will go back to Master Simon, who, as we already
know, had been called on by Monseigneur de Pornes, at
an early morning hour.

"I have a great deal to say to you," was the opening
remark of that gentleman.

" And I have none the less to talk about," replied the
cloth-merchant.

" Let me begin first, comrade," rejoined the knight, " for
what I'm going to say will certainly make you open your
eyes to the course of conduct of these Typhaines affairs.
Messire Anseau de Loysel and I are quite determined that
you must not receive our serfs into your establishment, and
that is what I want you to understand most clearly. I
hold so strongly to that condition of friendship, that I
would rather even sacrifice my rancor against Philippe, just

and right as that is. Let him escape, let somebody rescue hiui, let him get out into the country—I even prefer such a misfortune as that to the loss of my serfs. What could I do if my peasants, one and all, should make for your village ? Who would supply my corvees ? Who would pay my taxes ? And when taxes and corvees have been paid, should it unfortunately happen, as it always does in fact, lor me to want a little money, who would be left for me to tax over again at my good discretion ? No I I'll not let my servants, my mainmortables go, and whole squads of my vilains I No ! rather than that, I'd renounce my homage to my suzerain, the Count de Nevers. Now you see, sir burgess, that I 6ay just what I think; and Messire Anseau de Loysel is exactly of my way of thinking on this matter; exactly."

" You have no occasion to trouble yourself in this way," coolly replied the Typhaines functionary, "or to threaten us about the matter either, for all we want is justice and the good of all concerned. We are neither heretics nor Saracens: we are perfectly loyal to our friends and allies. Your serfs are serfs, and, please God and his angels, serfs they will be to the day of judgment, before the Typhaines folk ⁄\\ meddle with the subject; and this I am ready to swear on any relic you choose, or on the holy wafer itself, if you ⁄d rather have that."

" Meanwhile," said Monseigneur, smiling, "you are all of you here in a state of revolt against your suzerain, serfs and burghers and all, and I see a good many of the former in town, who have run away from their masters, and yet you keep them here! What does that mean ?"

" Monseigneur," added the merchant, " if you will attend to your own business, we will take proper care of ours. Provided we are willing to receive the good people from Cornehaut or the abbey-lands, and the demesnes of Cornou

17

iller, what difference does it make to you ? You are our
ally, and have nothing to fear from us."

" I should be much gratified," said De Pornes, with a
wink at him, " if such fine words as those could be put into
the body of that charter you are making."

"They shall be, for we as a people are brave and
loyal, and there shall be no cause for any dispute between
you and us. Now you are satisfied, I suppose, and it's my
turn to tell you something."

" Do so, then."

" I 'll begin with one question. Is it a matter you care
much about whether you hang Joslin and his comrades to-
day or to-morrow, and rather to-morrow than a week
later ?"

" Certainly. Good workmen don't like to have their
business put off; they are never well served if not promptly
served. "

"I agree with you as to that But suppose the question
to be to recapture Monseigneur Philippe, and by a little
patience have him and your serfs too, safe in hand ? It
seems to me it would well be worth the trouble of waiting
a little."

" Oh, ho ! you are a very knowing sort of man, Master
Simonand his eyes blinked like a cat's at the thought;
" you are very kuowing; and if you can procure such a
twofold pleasure for me, I 'll esteem you and honor you
more than any man in the whole world."

"I am sure I can do it. Do you ouly feign to be fond
of your serfs and quite ready to forgive them. Let it be
bruited abroad that a few silver marks often settle the very
worst kind of trouble. Tell how well you think of Joslin;
aud in fact do your best to make him and his comrades
think that the word you said yesterday wasn't your last word
about it."

Monseigneur Baudouin had so high an opinion of all sorts of trickery that he always was suspecting everybody else, and the consul's remarks rather tended to renew his doubts.

" Comrade," said he, " if I could but see a little further into your projects, and understand what they are to end in, I might say, 'yes ;' but just now, you seem to be demanding a rather extensive credit."

"Iam surprised," replied Simon, "you don't see into my perplexities : am I perfectly sure of what Joslin and his fellows will do with Philippe ? It may be that they will allow him to escape, to checkmate you, especially if they have got him out of town already, and that they might have easily done last night, and even yet, seeing how much disorder there is in the borough. If I could be sure they could be in such a rage as to kill him outright, though I should regret not to have a hand in it, I could be consoled about it, I suppose; but who knows what such a set of brutes might do ? I shouldn't be surprised if they'd take him straight to the Lady of Cornouiller, and then he would begin to carry on a war with us, that wouldn't be very good for our side."

" You are right, comrade," rejoined Baudouin de Pornes. " and that, too, without taking into account how his marriage to the Lady Mahaut would block my game. In that event, my poor boy Enguerrard would fail of getting possession of those splendid tracts of land of hers that dovetail so nicely into ours. Hurrah, then, Master Simon, you must carry out your plan, of course ; and in case of need, I promise you I '11 kiss Joslin on both cheeks the first time I meet him!"

"One word more," said Simon. "We must also lay aside all appearance of animosity against Messire Philippe 1"

"A capital idea that!" cried the knight, misconceiving

Simon's purpose. [11] It will be an excellent way to keep Canon Norbert's tongue still. That old creature might possibly come up once more and worry us, and I wish he was further off. He has converted Monseigneur the Count de Nevers three times already, and it might do me considerable damage if he should go and convert him for the fourth time."

"Now that that's settled," said Simon, "let us go and look at our workmen and the fortifications."

When the consul and knight reached the scene of the works opposite the abbey where the ditch and wall had commenced, they were delighted to find a wide, deep fosse and an earth rampart, completely finished, at the most important point of all. Without doubt, the whole town would be completely inclosed before sunset, so eager were the people to complete the works of defence.

Baudouin and Simon soon met with Payen, who had just come from handling the pick-axe for a quarter of an hour, by way of example and encouragement.

"All's well," said the blacksmith; "and now we shall have to distribute the arms, but I wanted to see you, Master Simon, before I would make up my mind about it, and Eudes and Antoine thought just as I did, so did Jacques. There's no doubt the coats-of-mail will be here this evening, and the bows, too, and above all, the lances we ordered from Troyes; however, I don't think we shall be in any great need of them to-night; I went to see the abbey yesterday, and found them all panic-struck up there."

" Where is the canon ?" said Simon.

" He spent the night iu an old woman's thatched hut in town, and then went out to inquire after the monks; he was told they were all quite quiet in their cloisters; but without saying one word to the crowd, who pressed around him to beg his blessing, he only answered by threatening scowls, and proceeded to the barrier, where the guards were afraid to refuse a passage. De ⁷s at the abbey yet/*

" I wish he would stay there, and die there, too," exclaimed Messire Baudouin. " If people would only be of my mind, those chattering priests wouldn't be allowed to tramp about the country, frightening old women and fools !'>

" Master Norbert is a saintly personage," said Payen, respectfully, and at the same time makii g the sign of the cross, "and I don't advise you to say hard things about him, in this town, for you '11 find few people to agree with you. It's true we are at war with our Lord Abbot, but we are no misbelieving Turks, for all that."

"You are in the right there, master," said Simon, in a conciliatory tone; " still, it must be confessed the canon has worried us not a little, and 'twould be better if he would put off his visit here to some other time, for in case we recover the prisoner, it is absolutely indispensable to keep it from him."

"Just as you please," replied Payen. "You hold to the execution of Philippe de Cornehaut, and I suppose you have your own reasons for that, and I shall not meddle with it. But let us have an end of it some way, for it would be a very unpleasant thing to me to get cursed by so holy a man as Norbert is."

The conversation now took a political turn, and the three personages were joined by Anseau de Loysel, who according to usage was already well advanced in his customary intoxication, though it was an early hour. That amiablo seigneur had given himself quite over to the tuition of his father-in-law, De Pornes, and his touching confidence in his wife and parent had been rewarded as might be naturally expected. The chatelain of De Pornes had put a g*arrison in De Loysel's castle, and on his own private account touched a special tax on the property. Anseau was not an unhappy person, for he always had wine enough and of the best; and as his father-in-law had no further fears of him, he treated him with the greatest joviality and good humor, over their daily wine at the dinner table.

Ansean planted himself close by his father-in-law, and with his usual stupid laugh, begau:—

"Ventre Dieu ! Monseigneur, so we are going to have a grand time here to-day, eh ? I Ve just come from the square, where they are putting up a scaffold of beams and planks. Are they making a platform to receive the abbot of Typhaines' benediction ?"

"Nothing of the kind," answered Jacques. "We are going to read the articles of the charter to the good men of Typhaines. We drew it up last night—you was there, and Monseigneur Baudouin, too."

"It will be a splendid spectacle," Payen said, with a very serious air. " I Ve been looking forward to see it this many a month, and hardly ventured to hope I 'd ever live to see it 1"

"You are a strange set of fellows, you burghers are,'* replied Anseau, with his half drunk look. "You really do get novelties into your heads that nobody else even so much as dreams of."

"Very well. Let all that pass, and we41 now go and make proclamation in all the streets and lanes, that any serf or serfs who will deliver to the public authorities the person of Monseigneur Philippe de Cornehaut, shall be made a freeman, and a citizen of this commune. You, Monseigneur Baudouin, are acquainted with the conditions, and know that nothing shall be done in conflict with your rights."

" I think I can guess what it means 1" said Payen, "but I don't like to have a lie told to auy man. Kill the knight, as he is an enemy of yours, and I see no harm in that. But don't go and deceive the poor serf-folk."

" Bah!" rejoined Monseigneur Baudouin. " Do you suppose that castles and communes are to be managed as you manage your shopkeeping ? You've a good deal to learn, if you do, friend blacksmith!"

CHAPTER XV.

THE consols and knights, after addressing and encouraging the workmen, now quitted the rampart, and moved
forwards to where the old abbey-gaol stood, on one side of
the square; there we shall for the present leave them,
while we repair to the presence of Saint Norbert. That
saintly man's object in going to the abbey, was to offer
some consolation and encouragement to the poor distressed
monks; but a still higher and more pressing consideration
for him was to provide lest the depression of spirits and
the terror naturally to be expected, after the late events,
might, in some small degree, influence the rigorous observance of the discipline of the holy sanctuary, or weaken the
force of the order, even for ever so short a time.

On entering the great court-yard, he noticed the signs
of disorder there, that have been already described. The
church, though utterly deserted, was intact; and the old
priest went and kneeled on the flags at the entrance of the
choir, where he made a long, fervent prayer. Pressed
though he was, to fulfil the task he had undertaken to perform, he concluded, in common with the generality of
clerics of his times, that there was not in all the world a
precedence over that, the most rigorous of obligations, and
so, for a whole hour long, he continued on his knees on the
hard stone floor, praying and utterly absorbed in devotion,
just as if he were not the only human being in the vast,

solemn pile. He ended his prayer at last, and rose to his feet.

The canon discovered a small side door behind the choir-stalls, opened it, and stepped into a long, low, narrow, vaulted corridor, lighted by dim dormer windows. At the end he found a spiral stone stair that went winding down deep below into the bowels of the earth. He stopped to listen. A low' sound, like a psalmody, convinced him the community must have retreated into that dark abode. At once he went along the passage, and then down the winding stair, until he found himself at a strong oak door. He struck the door with his staff. The psalm went on; yet an aged voice from within inquired :—

" Who art thou that coinest to disturb God's poor servants in their morning office ?"

" I am Norbert, Canon of Treves, and I bring you such words of consolation as I have. Open !"

At these words the bolts were drawn, and the lay-brother who had been posted as watchman at the only opening by which the poor monks had been momentarily expecting to see the mutinous crowd rush in upon them, was hurriedly thrown open. The name of Norbert was at that day a thing of power and public respect throughout the west of Europe, the like of which is nowhere to be found at the present day.

The canon pronounced a benediction over the kneeling brother, and moving forward, a few steps brought him into the middle of the crypt or subterranean church of the abbey of Typhaines. The aspect of the place was an imposing one.

Though an image of the catacombs in which the early Christians took refnge with liberty, religion and life, the cavern was not a very extensive one. It had in ancient times served as a habitation for St. Procul and his pious com-

panions, when fleeing from the Arian persecution for refuge
there. Situated far down below the church pavement, it
received its light through a small iron-grated window, that
was partially obstructed with ivy and other climbers, all
green and vigorous, that had pushed their ambitious shoots
and tendrils even into the interior of the apartment. Still
through the narrow opening the joyous light was dancing in
between the bars and tendrils and leaves, to play gayly ou
the paved floor below. There, in its pure rays, on a stone
altar where the sainted bishop used to celebrate the holy
mysteries, the abbey-relics were now reposing, and surrounding those rich treasures, the fifty monks, kneeling in
their white cistercian garments, were performing the offices
of the order and with all the fervor inspired by holy Anselm's recent reforms, were trying to save their souls at
the very moment when, as they apprehended, their bodies
were threatened with imminent peril of death.

The canon was made happy by seeing that not a soul
moved from his knees to give him welcome. He took a
low place in the assembly and joined in with the chants of
the congregation. At last, when the ceremony came to a
close, all the people turned their faces towards him, and
the prior asked :—

" Holy father, what news is it that you are come to announce to this unhappy flock ?"

" First of all," said Norbert, " where is holy Abbot Anselm ?"

"He is no longer here with us," replied the prior;
" while he was busy yesterday giving directions for the
transportation of the holy relics to the church rampart,
the Typhaines rebels were admitted by the valets through a
window they were appointed to guard ; they got next into
the cloisters: in obedience to our superior's orders we
crowded round the martyr's bones and hurried here with

them. We then heard loud shoutings; and brother Gilles saw Monseigneur de Cornehaut's two pages fall at the church steps; he saw the knight lift the Abbot in his arms and bear him to the stables, and while the valiant gentleman's squire was bringing out a couple of horses, he looked with admiration that nailed him to the spot, at that noble gentleman holding his ground, and with his single arm keeping the whole wild crowd of vilaius in check; the Abbot and Fulk went off at speed, but Monseigneur Philippe, when he in turn atttempted to vault into his saddle, was grappled by the raging masses of peasants, dismounted, and thrown to the ground. Doubtless that noble knight must have met his death in the melee, but God will have found him a place already in his paradise between St. George and St. Alexander."

" He is not dead," replied Norbert, " and if I can trust the previsions I have acquired from on high, that champion so illustrious and terrible, so proved by Saracenic steel and Syrian suns, is not doomed to fall like a hired infantry man, by the knives of those rebel peasants and serfs ! No ! let ns have no fears for him, my brethren, for he lives still. I saved him last night, with God helping me; the celestial puissance fell on my tongue last night, and that forced his murderers to give back. Since that hour, Monseigneur Philippe, by some miracle, has escaped from the hands of his persecutors, and even if they should succeed in retaking him, I '11 be there again to wrest him out of their power. But let us dismiss all thought of him for the present, as he has no pressing need of our assistance. Let us think rather of you, my brothers."

" What will become of us ?" cried the prior, with melancholy accents; " the flock hath lost its shepherd, and will perish in the wilderness."

"I hope that you are not like so many sheep with neither

forethonght nor courage! I know Abbot Anselm right well; he is a man of a rare lirmuess, an intrepidity equal to any danger, and totally incapable of resigning a single one of the rights of the church to any emissary of Satan whatever. Either I aui greatly mistaken, or he decided as he fled, to what door he should go and knock for succor. Honored as he is by the whole church of the Gauls, alike dear to the bishops and legates of the holy Roman See, your superior, my brothers, is not a champion to be braved with impunity. Should the proud Count de Nevers, emboldened by his temporal puissancy, send aid, as 'tis said he will, to this impious commune, Anselm will be sure to put a stop to all that. Fear nothing then, and meditate in all confidence that sacred word, that buckler of holy Church : [4] the gates of hell shall not prevail against her.'"

The canon's words restored a small measure of energy to the poor monks, who had courage enough to die under the blows of the rebels, but not enough to struggle for their own lives. The new perspective opened by Saint Norbert revived the dying spark within, and concluding there was no danger now of a massacre, they pressed round the saintly canon, supplicating him to direct them in the way of duty.

" Your duty, brethren, is very simple," replied the priest. "The Typhaines' burghers may revolt, they may utter threats against you, and they are actually in possession of some temporal power, and might, in a fit of satanic rage, put you to death ; but never can they, save with your consent, give to their commune the rights indispensable to secure its existence. It can never exist in truth without your sworn consent. This is the reason why the communes succeeded at Amiens, Soissons, Laon, and Noyon : without the Seigneur's consent, no commune; that is the law, and the law it will ever remain. If your insurgent burghers had to deal with masters temporal, they might find some way to frighten them into a concession by threatening them with the destruction of their race, or by placing themselves under the protection of another seigneurage, but where is the daring suzerain to openly accept a domain robbed from the Church ? So, you have nothing to fear. To any and every demand they may make, you have nothing more to do than refuse compliance with it. Be firm, immovable in your answers ; but, at the same time, be kind and moderate; for you, brethren, are stronger than lance or sword. Be then wise as serpents, but harmless as doves. Your Abbot is the only person who has a right to give orders in this place, and it is yours to refuse every proposal that may be made in his absence. "

The monks gave thanks to Norbert for his advice, recovered their outward appearance of calm, and followed him out of the crypt to make a beginning of putting things in the grand court into their usual order. The dead w'ere taken away, washed, and deposited in the church. The lay-brothers commenced repairing the broken gates, and a lay-brother was despatched to the town to say that, if they desired their dead to be honorably buried, the monks would willingly give the assistance of their prayers. This proceeding exhibited an air of humility about it that was very gratifying to the canon, who conceived it as likely to substitute the rule of negotiation for that of violence. Norbert, therefore, urged the prior, over and over again, in no case to step beyond the bounds of true prudence and patience, and then, when he had given the fathers his blessing and advised them never to lose sight of their rules of order, in any tribulation whatever, he set off in haste for the Burgh again. Monseigneur Philippe, in case of a recapture, might possibly once more rccpiire his intervention.

As the canon passed into the street, where all who met

18

him went humbly down on their knees, he saw Master
Simon, who seemed in very high spirits; he was just
parting with his daughter Damerones and approaching
Jacques, to whom he spoke with a vivacity and sprightli-
ness that led the old canon to suspect something amiss.
For a moment the old man hesitated ; but suddenly giving
way to one of those interior inspirations which his ancient
zeal had always induced him to respect as if they were
heaven sent, he moved off in haste and at last overtook
Damerones.

CHAPTER XVI.

WHEN the holy canon had come within a few paces of Damerones, who was walking onwards, absorbed in reflection, he cried—

" Stop, young woman ! I have something to say to you : don't kneel to me ; I am but a poor sinner myself, and we have no time now to lose in vain demonstrations. Art not thou consul Simon's daughter? I think I saw thee a month ago in his company, and heard thee call him father."

"Yes; you are not mistaken in that. I am his daughter. What would you have with me ? Pardon me, I am in trouble; my soul is more tossed than a bark on the sea in the angriest tempest."

" Never mind your troubles; the question now is neither more nor less than a knight's life."

" A knight?" cried Damerones. "What! Messire Philippe's ? Is it possible ray father has deceived me, then ?"

" I know not what you mean, but this I must tell you. You are young yet, and your heart, no doubt, is not hardened to crime; you are a woman, and you can't be happy at the sight of bloodshed. Now I am come to implore you, yes, old as I am, to implore you to intercede with your father in Philippe's behalf, if it's true, as I suspect it to be from his joyous air, that he has got the knight into his power again."

Damerones uttered a cry so dolorous, so agonized, at this

intelligence, that the moving crowd in the street stopped
to look at them, and pressed round her to ask what could
have so disturbed the rose of Typhaines, the powerful consul's child; but Norbert dismissed them with an angry
scowl, and they went on their way thinking that it might
be a matter of some penance, some bizarre act of devotion,
not uncommon in that age; and as they respectfully withdrew, the old man took Damerones' arm, drew her to a
lonely alley, and there they both sat down on a stone seat.

" What's the use of all this despairing?" asked Norbert,
tenderly.

"I, yes, I am the cause of Messire Philippe's death:
'twas I who to save his life led him into a danger from
which it became absolutely necessary to rescue him. Yesterday evening I tore him out of father's hands so save his
life when the danger was most pressing; and to-day I was
obliged to wrest him from the power of the de Pornes serfs,
because a moment more might have insured his death.
Ah, holy father! I trusted to father's promises; I allowed
me to give way to the oaths he swore; twice did he return to the charge, and at last made himself master of my
secret. Ah, I have murdered Monseigneur, for I have
just confessed where he may be found; ah, Philippe 1
Philippe 1"

The poor girl's despair was so real that Norbert, ascetic
though he was, and habitual despiser of all sorts of passions and the language of them as well, was unable to keep
down the emotions of sympathy for the beautiful maiden
that her anguish inspired. He ordered her to be calm,
and give him a circumstantial account of the whole matter,
which, as yet, he had no clear idea of. She obeyed, and it
was easy for Norbert to comprehend that it was a sentiment
far livelier than one of simple piety that so stirred the very
depths of grief and remorse in the soul of poor Damerones.

Bat that was no time to talk what they call moralities to
her; and so the canon, as soon as he had gathered all she
knew on the subject, rose from the stone bench, and 6aid :—

"Go, daughter, go home—after awhile I will see you
again; perhaps I may have need of your help to save the
brave knight's life. God—be sure of it—will never abandon thee to such misery as this."

"Father!" she cried, "father, you won't let him be
killed!"

"I hope not; I believe not," replied Norbert, "but do
you obey me; go and sit down at home, nor leave the house
until I return. Perhaps you are the instrument in heaven's hand, by which the precious life of Messire Philippe
de Cornehaut is to be saved !"

Hearing these words, Dameroues wrapped her mantle
about her; her hands were crossed on her bosom, and her
eyes lifted heavenward as she stood supplicating the power
divine, to realize the promise jnst made by the canon.
Never had saint, aspiring to the glories of martyrdom, in
eyes or features an expression more celestial. She then
walked rapidly away, and Norbert went off in a different
direction. He reached Lienard's clos just as a band of
armed burghers were raising the trap-door. Simon and
the Seigneur de Pornes were at their head, and Payen was
there too.

Simon was in the act of speaking to the men about him—

" Don't go to amuse yourselves with taking him! As
soon as he reaches the top of the steps, drive your lances
into his breast, and cleave his head with your clubs. Do
that, and you will save us time, and some trouble too."

Norbert's voice broke out like the sound of a clarion
bearing a defiance :—

" Wretches that you are," said the old priest, " have yon
not supped full of your crimes yet ? can't you give them at

.least some semblance of law and right ? How long is it since knights are murdered in cold blood, and non-resisting ? I, yes, I; these sad eyes of mine have looked on most wicked deeds of men; I looked on while the excommunicate rebels as Laon were trampling down the body of their own Bishop Gaudry! but these very men, outcasts from holy church, and a disgrace to humanity itself, would have never dreamed, as you dt>, of butchering a prisoner spared by the sword of the battle-field 1 Withdraw!—begone hence; let no man dare to touch even the garments of the knight!"

Simon and the knight of de Pornes seemed not so much touched as angered by this second intervention.

" By the devil's gorge!" cried the gentleman, " I don't like sermons out of church. I' ll have no monk intermeddling with affairs of my own ! I' ll not have it I"

" The holy father spoke right, all the same," said Payen, " and, as I am a consul in this commune, I'm not going to have a murder committed here without knowing why. Monseigneur <le Cornehaut is an enemy of ours, that I know; let us put him to death publicly and openly, if needs must, and on the town square. It shall never be said that we murdered him for want of any good reason to execute him in sight of all the people."

Is there any man here that loves me?" cried Simon, looking round on the whole company. Payen at once replied—

" Every man of us loves you, every man of us loves the commune too; but every man of us loves his own soul, his eternal salvation, and his honest fame. Comrades, down with your arms, and let the chevalier be led to prison, and guarded well, until the executioner is ordered by us to strike off his head."

" You 'll not think of doing that, Payen, will you ? Don't

yon see that all Norbert wants is to save the prisoner's
life ?"

"That is nothing," said Payen. "The canon did very
right to come. I said nothing, but I was full of remorse,
and the thing shall be just as he may please to say. If the
knight of Cornehaut makes his escape, be it so; we 'll fight
him afterwards. He wounded me bad, to be sure, yet I'd
not be afear'd to meet him again, sword in hand. In fine,
I'm not going to have him butchered in this way ; I'm as
much of consul, and as free as you in this commune, and I
won't have the knight butchered just here, and that's all
of it."

" We must give up," said Simon, turning to Seigneur De
Pornes, and then looking on Norbert with a smiling countenance, that ill concealed his rage.

"You see, holy father, that we act as your will pleases
you to ordain. But you will remember that the verdict for
his death was rendered last night 1 This day, as soon as
our commune is regularly and legally proclaimed, Monseigneur Philippe will have to go and join bis forefathers !"

" What God allows, that you will do !" said the canon.
" For the present, I can rely on Payen's spoken word, and
to him it is that I commend the cause of justice and
right."

" Don't you be afraid, holy father," said Payen, firmly;
" may I never get your blessing, if one hair from the knight's
head shall fall to the ground here."

So saying, the burghers, at a sign from Payen, raised the
trap-door; and, as if the very sight of the prisoner was
offensive to their eyes, Simon and Baudouin withdrew.
Norbert gazed after them for awhile, and then, after new
assurances from Payen, he too went away in a different
direction. The people about took no notice of him, for
Monseigneur Philippe had at last made up his mind,

and was coming up the steps; but he came up very delibe-
rately.

When he reached the top he rubbed his eyes, for so
many hours passed in that outer darkness made the 6uddeu
flash of day blinding; at length he looked round on the
crowd, and spoke:—

" Well, well 1 have I had the nightmare ? I thought it
was all over with me ! Have you got your senses at last,
and are you agreed to talk about a ransom ?"

" Never hope for that, Monseigneur," said Payen. "You
are to die this day ; and if you have any arrangements to
make, it would be well to make them at once ; night will not
find you a living soul; and now follow me to your former
dungeon."

Monseigneur Philippe made no answer He had no wish
to bandy words with his conquerors, and he merely said to
himself: " So it seems Damerones could find no other way
to get me out of Joslin's claws." It was but a few minutes, and the chevalier found himself shut up in his first
prison again, not less than twenty feet down under the
ground. A new jailer—quite as worthy of his office as the
late M. Isengrin—turned the keys on him, and he readily
knew that a guard had been stationed above to keep watch
and ward over him.

"For once," said Philippe, "I don't see howl am to
get out of this—that is, if I am to get out of it."

The knight was down on his bundle of straw, with his face
between his hands; he heard a great uproar in the streets.
But let us quit the dungeon for awhile, and stop on the great
gaol-door step, and we shall see whole files of the workmen
coming in from the ramparts, where they had been busy
with shovel and pick all night long. The whole multitude
are buzzing or shouting, or singing, chaffing, coming and
going, as busy as a hive of bees hard at work. The appcar-

ance of the crowd gradually changes, and the whole scene puts us in mind of a Sunday. Everybody is dressed in his best; burghers, good old women, young girls promenading hither and thither in their finest gowns and frocks, merchants and artisans in their tight-fit or holiday hats; the whole mass seems metamorphosed, and the whole buzz, confusion, and noise have given place to a general feeling of solemnity. The carts are gone from the streets, and every spade, shovel, and pick was now clear out of sight.

The hour is come for the good people of Typhaines to be made acquainted with the new code of laws just drawn up by the consuls. They are now about to take rank with the powers of the time; their burgh, henceforth dignified with the title of City of Typhaines, is now about to be governed by regulations of their own devising and own choosing. True it is that, for the full and effective power of their charter of freedom, their consent and their acceptance is not the sole condition ; but just at this glorious hour nobody thought of that, for it was a rather disagreeable thought. The whole town is crowded into the great square, and to see their splendid attitudes, their nonchalant looks, and their haughty strut, a man would be apt to think himself in an assembly of a sovereign people.

The forum of the borough of Typhaines covered no great space, nor was it very regularly laid out. The surrounding houses had not been built in very exact lines on the street, and mostly consisted of one-story huts, with thatched roofs. In fact, the houses were few, and the hovels many. These hovels had left an open space or square between them of about two hundred feet long, by a width of from one hundred and thirty, in its broadest part, to some ten feet, where it was narrowest.

In front of the old abbey gaol they had erected a huge 6tage, or platform, furnished with a balustrade, and covered with blue cloth, draped in upholsterers best taste. A part of the town militia was drawn up in line opposite the great stage, leaving only a small guard at the ramparts. The militia too, as yet badly armed, exhibited not more than about a hundred men in light coats of mail, small iron head-pieces, without visors, and short swords and lances as heavy as they were long. Some two hundred of these bold warriors had bows and arrows, and were quite tine in their Sunday clothes. The balance had scythes, axes, flails, and other such agricultural apparatus as might readily be converted into muniments of war. Every troop had its officers, and not a soul was there to keep up any order or discipline; for order, discipline, and above all, silence, are more modern inventions. The women and girls seemed to have the highest opinion of those valorous patriots; conversations were going on everywhere between the spectators and the defenders of the good commune. The old men had been provided with benches in front of the stage, and the graybeards, as lively as the very boys and girls themselves, sat there laughing and talking at a great rate. As to the children—and the number at Typhaines was named legion—they had secured the very best places in the square for seeing at once, and keeping out of reach of their fond parents, especially the manual part of them. They garnished every roof, and clung to every chimney like those clustered tribes of live monkeys we meet with in an African forest.

After a long waiting, eager expectation and a variety of the usual episodes in a restless crowd, that are so very delightful to the mob, the five consuls of Typhaines made their appearance on the splendid stage. They were attended by their clerk, Baudouin de Pornes, and Anseau de Loysel, with ten men-at-arms commanded by the two seigneurs, and, further, by a trumpeter habited in the

Nevers livery, who was part of the ambassadorial suite.
The five consuls were at once greeted with the most tumultuous acclamations. Shouts of admiration, joyous
stampings, clapping of hands, there seemed no end to;
when the militia stopped shouting, the women took up the
hnrrahs, and as they grew weak, the children got the upper
hand; in fact, so great was the burst and outpour of joy,
thut it took nearly ah hour to get down to silence at last.

The popularity of the consuls was unbounded; yet the
love and confidence of the people was not the sole cause of
the grand success of the hour; it was the new costume that
excited the liveliest enthusiasm. Never, never had that
populace dreamed of haviug so splendid a magistracy at the
head of affairs, and their patriotism was increased an hundred fold as they looked on their superb chiefs. All the five
consuls wore magnificent scarlet robes, with furred collars
and cuffs; every man of them wore a long heavy sword, just
like so many knights; and over all was a violet cloth mantle,
and chaplets on their heads of the same hue. Through the
folds of their robes were seen their limbs in shining mail.
It is pleasing to think that the reader will thus readily
'comprehend the immense admiration of the good people of
Typhaines, on so magnificent an occasion. I might venture to add that the virtuous and yet determined look of
the five consulars, and, above all, Payen, who, with his
wounded arm still in a sling, stood bold as a lion in full
view of all the people, contributed not a little to the dignity and splendor of the consular costume.

At last, and there always must be an at last, the crowd
had got somewhat used to the gorgeous show, and then
Master Simon, taking from the reverent hands of the clerk-
of-council a huge parchment roll, proceeded to read aloud
the Communal charter.

"Ye good burgesses of Typhaines," cried Simon in a

ringing tone, " here is what we have thonght it fitting to
ordain in your behalf as the future code of laws for this
city.

" Every person in this commune swears to contribute to
the public defence. In case any one burgess should be
attacked or insulted, all other burgesses shall defend and
avenge him."

This article first—which was beforehand deeply engraved
in the hearts of all Typhaineers—was received with shouts
of admiration. The consul proceeded:—

" You shall pay into the chest of your seigneur no tax
but a poll tax, and he shall have no right to impose either
taille or corvee."

This article was saluted as warmly as Article I. had
been, and the clapping and cheering broke out again.

"Good people!" eried Jacques, "if you go on interrupting us so every minute, it will take Master Simon a
whole fortnight to get through the reading of our charter:
you should keep quiet, then, and listen quietly. If you
arn't satisfied you can say so when we *We* got through;
and if yon are satisfied, you can halloa as loud as you like
after it's all over."

This observation brought out plenty of cheers, and as
soon as silence was restored, Master Simon read on : " Typhaines burghers may intermarry with the daughters of
any serf whatever, saving those of the Church of Typhaines,
and such gentlemen as may have signed this charter on
oath taken. Whoever violates this article shall be reduced
to serfdom."

This provision drew a smile of satisfaction from Mon-
seigneurs Baudouin and Anseau de Loysel. The clanse had
been inserted by particular request of the Connt de Nevers
and those two knights, as well as the following :—

" No person shall be admitted as a member of this com-

mune who is unable to buy a lot and dwelling, or to build
one in the town; for, if a burgher should do any unjawful
act and then escape from arrest, it is just that the people
should take possession of his goods, as a penalty for his
misdeed."

Under this clause was concealed a measure the consul
thought it not fitting just now to specify—namely, a sure
means of getting rid of all pauper peasantry, a class of
but little use to the republic. Simon went oa through a
great number of other clauses, some touching matters of
trade, some artisans, and some the city police establishment;
next, followed numerous stipulations, the profound wisdom
of which was universally recognized, as they saw the venerar
ble graybeards on the front benches accepting them with
a grave nod of each reverend poll.

" A merchant having a claim, not paid at due, shall have
the right to proceed in person to levy on the goods of the
debtor, and pay himself out of the sales of the goods aforesaid, provided always that it shall not be lawful in him to
seize the wearing apparel and working tools of said debtor
nor his front door.

" Provided there should arise a suit at law between two
burgesses of this town, it shall be lawful, their several preference being made known, to fight a duel to the end that
the truth and right shall be by that means proved and established. The strongest man shall be adjudged victor in
the cause. In case one of the two parties to the suit should
refuse trial by battle, he shall be punished by a heavy fine."

This article appeared to give general satisfaction, for it
gave a gentleman-like air to the Typhaines men; but it
was followed by another that was not so favorably received,
especially by the gentler sex.

" A burgess may beat his wife, and his daughter, even if
a married woman; his sons and his valets, to the extent of

19

wounding only; in any case where such correction has
proved too severe, he may make oath to the effect that in
acting as he did his intention was good. The use of sharp
ground weapons of iron is for such occasion hereby inter-
dicted.

" In case a burgess should engage in a quarrel with a
serf, or even with a free mechanic, it shall be lawful for
him to call him thief, dirty dog, or to apostrophize him
with other abuse of like nature, but it shall never be lawful to strike him."

The charter was very long, and except for the communeers, would not have proved very interesting in every
particular clause. The reading of the document took up
several hours, and the sun was evidently declining to the
western horizon when Master Simon reached the closing
paragraph, which ended with these words :—

" The only thing, good people, that is now wanting is the
consent of the Abbot of Typhaines to our charter, and the
warrant of Monseigneur the King of France; but I beg
you to believe that we shall obtain both of these advantages
with but little trouble. Pon't vex yourselves at all about
these high concerns; it is enough for you to know that
Monseigneur de Nevers is our friend, and ready and willing to protect us against every and any enemy of ours. All
you have to think of is to live in peace at home as long as
order reigns at Typhaines, and to behave like brave men,
as you did yesterday, whensoever we summon you to the
defence of your liberties. It is ours to watch over your
rights; be you assured that we will in nothing fail to
secure that high end."

These words spoke, the meeting proceeded to the execution of the charter. It was to be solemnly sworn on a book
of " Hours" that Jacques laid on the front of the stage.
The book was open. The burgesses of Typhaines extended

their hands towards the volume, which the consuls, knights, and men-at-arms in like manner covered with their out-stretched hands, and the formula of conjuration was re-peated aloud by the whole congregation there assembled, multitudinous though it was. It was a scene of emotion—many of the people shedding tears of joy for the grand con-summation. Our own fathers can still remember the oath taken by the people at the Jeu de Paume, and they can never forget the enthusiastic weakness that drew tears from the eyes of so many dreamers, who thought they could see the heavens opening above them that day. The commnne-oath of Typhaines in the twelfth century exhibited a simi-lar spectacle, and a like sincerity. The ceremonies being at last fully accomplished, the consuls, in their brilliant attire—one they were henceforth never to put off, save in obedience to the public will—descended from the grand estrade.

"Tete Dieu!" cried Sire Baudouin, "you look quite pleased, Master Simon."

" I am so, and all the troubles of my whole life are at this moment fully rewarded."

" Are you like these good folks here, and do yon really think all those fine phrases so piled up by your scribe are going to keep you clear of the snares and the pig-headed obstinacy of your Lord Abbot yonder ?"

" No, not at all," answered Simon, looking alternately at the gentleman, and at bis impassible colleagues—"Not at all but this we do know ; we know what we have to live for, and to die for too."

" As for me," said Payen, " I have learned the meaning of commune now, and my eyes henceforth shall never look on servitude more ; no, never 1 No monk shall come to dic-tate his orders to me, and if the edifice we have here raised should crumble to ruin some day, I 'll never go out from the wreck to ask what 's next—never."

Jacques, Antoine, and Eudes approved of what their colleagues had said, and Anseau de Loysel at once began to jeer as if he had been listening to utter nonsense.

Monseigneur Baudouin resumed:—

" I am delighted to see how very happy you all are, and I now propose to conclude this joyous day by keeping our promise to the captive. Come, now 1 let's be merciful! poor Philippe de Cornehaut has languished long enough by this time in the bowels of the earth. Let's bring him up and give him the comfort of seeing the beautiful sun-shine as it is going down!"

"And we must hope," said Simon, "that Norbert the Venerable won't be here to stop us by breathing some tender scruples into a colleague or so of ours."

"If you mean me," replied Payen, "you are far in the wrong. All I wanted this morning was justice—and I want nothing else now. Come on 1"

The consuls, knights, and men-at-arms had reached the jail door. Lifting up their eyes, the very first thing they saw was Norbert leaning against the wall, his arms crossed and composed as a statue; he seemed to be waiting there for them. Near him stood a man-at-arms, a stranger, with his bridle rein under his arm, and leaning upon the sad-dled steed.

" What are you doing here again, sir priest ?" cried Si-mon. "You are abusing our respect for your cloth, and you are always tracking us 1 Don't interfere with our pur-poses again ! Christians though we be, you may perhaps push us too far !"

"You insolent vilain !" replied the priest, with the au-dacity that was a real element of his great influence; " what care I for your threats ? Are you here to accomplish your sanguinary projects on Monseigneur Philippe de Cornehaut ?"

" Certainly," rejoined Simon, planting his foot on the door-sill, "and yon cloud shall not have flitted across the sun's disk till our prisoner has felt the keen edge of our communal axe."

"As that is what you are thinking of doing, you might as well first hearken to what this messenger has to say to you."

The man-at-arms now stepped forward and said:—

" In the name of the lady of Cornouiller I come to offer you an exchange of prisoners."

" Prisoners?" and he laughed loud. "Prisoners, indeed I Go your way, friend, you are wasting your time. There 's 110 prisoner equal in value to ours. Tell your mistress that we will keep Monseigueur Philippe, and not only so, we mean to put him to death."

" In that case, I am charged to say to you that to-morrow morning in right of reprisals, we will set your daughter Damerone8· head on one of the donjon battlements at Cornouiller."

" Damerones !" screamed Simon, overwhelmed with terror. " Damerones 1"

"Master Simon," said Norbert, "Damerones is in their hands; and if you can't resist your blood-thirst, how can you expect the betrothed wife of Monseigneur to be more generous than yourself ?"

The consul made an effort to speak, but not a word could he utter; his eyeballs seemed starting out of their sockets ; he clenched his hair and tore at it—his head bent far backwards, and at last with a roar of anguish he rushed from the spot and flew towards his home

CHAPTER XVII.

FULK and the Abbot, without any great difficulty, forced
their way through the crowd of peasants and at length got
away from the monastery. A few well-given blows with
his battle-axe, and many more threats than hits with his
formidable weapon, had sufficed the honest squire to open
a track through the mob of assailants, and while his unfortunate master was clearing round Anselm a circle more
than thrice the longitudinal diameter of his trusty Rudaverse, Fulk laid hold of the Abbot's bridle and dashing his
spurs into his own roadster's flanks he launched at a gallop down the steep incline of the rocky mamelon, hoarsely
shouting "*Cornehaut! Cornehaut!*" A few crossbow bolts
and two or three arrows whistled by his ears, but all such
attempts proved useless and vain, for the arrows and bolts
were scattered on the hillside without harming either the
soldier or his ghostly companion.

The first and most terrible difficulty was now over; but
Fulk did not deceive himself at all in view of the fierce
exasperation of the communeers; he felt that his venerable companion must be exposed to the very greatest risks
uutil he could get beyond the frontier of the abbey domain ;
and so, he continued to push the horses at a high rate of
speed.

Fulk was an old campaigner; a man who had handled
dagger and sword in more countries than one ; who knew,
and knew well and on solid principles, the best way to

burst open doors, wrench out iron gratings, and scale stone walls; with the help of good friends of his own he had put to sac at least ten cities, fifteen fortified burghs, and thirty chatels, without counting in the Saracen Mosques and Tillages. A flight, fast though it was, or even a route itself if you like, was never enough to disturb such a champion's perfect coolness and presence of mind. Fulk was one of that sort of men who, in the most terrible circumstances, would be apt to merely say, "I have seen better times than this."

So, he seemed to have lost not a whit of his ordinary phlegm, and he had all his head about him as usual. In about half an hour, at a hard gallop, seeing no signs of a pursuit, he turned to the Abbot, who was quite as cool as he was himself, and said :—

" I say, holy father, are we near your boundary line ?"

" You *ve nothing to fear, my son," said Master Anselm, " they are yonder on that hill, where Seigneur de Pornes joins our lands. To be sure we run some risk there; but if you will take this path across the fields we can in an hour's ride reach one of Etienne de Galaude's vassals, where we shall be quite safe. Let the horses walk now; we ought to be very careful of them; and besides, it is not God's will that we should be lost."

Fulk at once obeyed orders; he put the horses at the trot after their long gallop; but the country was so flat, so devastated and deserted, and the enemy, if he should pursue, could be seen so far off, that they began to feel a sense of great security.

" By my faith as a Christian man, holy father," said Fulk, "I am not quite sure that it was right in me to obey Monseigneur Philippe's order: to save your life, and you are nothing to me; I left that good knight in the midst of a mob he 'll hardly get clear of, God help him !"

"Your master," answered the Abbot, with conviction, "is in no danger whatever. He has fought for Holy Church, and the Church will protect him. But if, by some impossibility he should have fallen, or is even now at the point of death, being taken prisoner, you ought to believe and trust that paradise is his—and he with nothing to regret as to this world."

" I Ve nothing to say against that," said the man, " but me ! me here, who have left my own proper seigneur, merely to take good care of a strange monk ! I don't think Holy Church is going to count me anything in this world but a traitor; just fit for all the claws of so many horned devils in hell. I'm confident I should not find a word to say against it."

"You," said the monk, "only judge by your worldly notions of these matters."

" Give me an answer, and don't go and comfort yourself so nicely about the misfortunes of a brave man-at-arms. The times we are living in are very bad times, Sir monk. Knights by the hundred are always on the road to get themselves killed by the Turks in Asia, while monks stay at home and fill their places. To tell you the real truth, I must say that I don't think much more of a monk than I do of a hazel-nut, and I don't believe one half the fine things people tell about them. Please remember too that I was once a page in the suite of the Comte de Sens, *surnamed King of the Jews* on account the protection he gave to usurers, and though it's true he did turn heretic at last, he had a good many very clever notions in that head of his."

^ The Abbot, exceedingly scandalized as he was by such *a speech, was about to give Fulk a very short dry answer, but he concluded the poor man talked in that fashion only because he was worried about his master, and not because

he wasn't a pretty fair Christian. He allowed him, therefore, to go on giving vent to his disgnst at the sitnation,
and Fulk finished his apostrophe as follows:—

" I don't say this to offend you. You are a monk—very
well, then, be a monk, if you like it best; but my master is a
brave cavalier, and if anything bad has happened I would
rather go myself to see about it; so then, let me know the
very first minute I can go and do my duty to him."

⁴ That conclusion," said Anselm, " just and reasonable
though it is, did not require you to vent your abuse before
you made up your mind about what you had to say. But
no matter; fighting men are rude of speech, and it's not
worth while to look to them for such gentleness as belongs
to clerics. All I have to do with you is to remember your
services to me, and as long as I live I shall ever pray for %
you. As soon as we come to the fortress I told you of,
you shall be free to go wherever you please."

"Free!" replied Fulk with a growl. "Very nice kind
of free, that—free to go and perhaps bury my master!
However, better late than never !"

The rest of the way was gone over in silence, and the
silence still held as the fugitives entered the fort.

Here dwelt a gentleman extremely religious and devoted to letters, for which he had a great taste. The second
named of these qualities was not absolutely rare at the period;
and Messire Jean Berniot, in his youth, that is to say about
his twenty-fifth year, had studied grammar at the Episcopal
School at Paris. He had even made himself sufficiently acquainted with theology to take great interest in the scholastic discussions and quarrels that were constantly breaking
out between the rival scholastic philosophers and their various adherents, the clerks in different parts of France. This
erudition of his, added to his military qualifications, had
gained him many powerful friends, and though he was far

from being a wealthy personage, he held his own along with many illustrious feudatories of the day, and among others he was great friends with le Sieur de Garlande, grand seneschal to King Louis the Sixth of France.

Abbot Anselm's coming under the guidance of a squire astonished Messire Jean very much; but the recital of his late adventures moved him very much more. He lifted his arms heavenward as he loudly deplored the wickedness of the communeers of Typhaines ; and then with the greatest eagerness offered the ecclesiastic his house, his men, and everything he could contribute to his service, his own person in the bargain.

" I expected no less at your hands, my dear son," said the Abbot; "but before you think about me let us, so it may please you, attend to this valiant squire who rescued me from death with God's help, and who is just now a prey to severe anxiety touching the death of his master."

"Squire," said Messire Jean de Berniot, "it is nearly dark, and you 'll get nothing by tramping all night long, and perhaps falling into the hands of the Typhaineers or Seigneur Pornes' people, a set of real brigands, infamous villains and rascals, just as their master is; promoters of all rebellions and atrocity. If your master is not dead, he is a prisoner; no, it will be time enough to-morrow morning for you to set off."

"I'm of a different opinion," replied Fulk. "As long as Monseigneur Philippe is in peril you won't be likely to see me amusing myself by going to sleep, or sitting down to a carouse. I mean to go at once."

"Halt now, my brave fellow !" said Messire Jean; "it may suit you to go and get your neck broke, but it does not suit me at all to risk my men's hides. You are fond of your master; very well then ; I 'ra fond of my soldiers. You know nothing about the roads, and you couldn't get on at all without a guide; hence, you see, yon are at my discretion. Surrender, I beseech you, my lad; get your supper; take a good sleep, and to-morrow, before day, you shall be guided to a place in sight of the abbey."

" It would be better for you," said the Abbot, "to hasten on to the Chatel de Cornouiller at daybreak. You will be far more serviceable to your master by telling the lady about all that has happened than you will by allowing yourself to be taken prisoner by the rebels."

" That '8 your advice—th£n persuade your friend to give me a guide to-night—at once."

"The holy Abbot needn't give himself that trouble for nothing; it would be putting his eloquence to waste; any man-at-arms that I might put on the road this night would be a man-at-arms lost to me. At such an hour as this every tramper in the whole land is out, and I marvel much that you got off as well as you did; and, upon reflection," said Messire Jean, as, throwing the door open, he halloa'd, " Ho, there, men! all of you! shut up the house with great care; inspect the crossbow strings ; put a stock of arms in the corridor to be ready to hand in case we should want them."

When he had given these orders the gentlemen returned to the hall, and Fulk, now fully convinced that neither prayers nor threats would avail anything, and acknow-ledging, moreover, the impossibility of finding his way in the dark, yet very angry and grumbling in his beard, and cursing all and sundry the monks and all their friends, went off and found a seat at the corner of the terrace in the open air, and swore that there he would stay all night long, and would have neither supper nor bed. The fact is that his grief and rage choked him so bad that the very smallest crumb of comfort must have stuck in his gullet.

At last, Messire Jean and the Abbot were left to them-

selves, and the Chatelain returned to the consideration of
the monies troubles, that far more concerned him than any
thoughts about Messire Philippe or his gruff old squire.

" Holy father," said he, " what have you resolved on ?
Will you stay here, and call around you all good Christians
in the neighborhood ? Don't it seem to you proper and
right to address a complaint to the Archbishop of Rheims ?
You are friends with the learned Alberic and his old
theologal. I have no doubt the clear justice of jour cause
will insure the support of all the Remoise prelates. While
the council is getting ready to launch its excommunication against Typhaines, I'll take care to warn the noblemen
hereabouts, and I think I can answer for it, you shall,
within a month, have at your service an army quite capable
of making every door fly open vo let you, in all honor, enter
into your own church and your own monastery. Such is
what has just this minute got into my head, and such as it
is, I lay it before you."

" Your good intentions are very clear," answered the
Abbot; " but, though you see me here now a fugitive and
robbed of everything, and though I may seem cast down
into the very lowest abasement and misfortune, you have
no real idea of the extent of my troubles. Had I nothing
else to do but carry on a war with my revolted peasants
and burghers, the measures you propose would be ample
for the purpose, no doubt, but behind Master Simon and
his accomplices stands a power that none of my surroundings could hope to contend with. The Count de Nevers,
your suzerain, for several years past, has been putting forth
certain claims, as he calls them, against the holy abbey of
Typhaines. He pretends that our lands are vassal to him,
and that their abbots owe him homage. You, my son, to
whom science hath imparted such magnificent gifts, you
must well know what a gross error there is in such a claim."

" Don't I know all about it?" said Messire Jean, much flattered by the compliment the Abbot had just paid him. "Who is there, that does not know that the lands and church of Typhaines were conceded, free of all claims, and independent of all vassalage whatever, to holy St. Procul, and that that gift, since renewed and confirmed by charter, is as clear and plain as the light of day itself? Eh ! truly! Monseigneur the Count de Nevers has not far to seek to find that out! It is perfectly easy to find the very documents in its charter now, all authenticated with sign and seal."

" Still," pursued the Abbot, " it appears that the Counts of Nevers have uever been satisfied with even all those proofs; and the odious and tyrannical claim I told you of, was first put forth by the present Counts father; yet the fact is that when he was on his death bed, he was not allowed to take holy Eucharist until he had first agreed to sign an Act of Repentance, an act that is still preserved in our registers, and begins with : ' *Suggeslionibus diabolicis* * and which he regularly executed. That whole piece is engraved in my memory; and only yesterday, an hour before the attack commenced, I was studying it with the utmost care and with the most thorough disgust at the crimes and perfidy of our adversary. Crimes, did I say ? Perfidy ? Yea, my son ! Scarcely had the old count closed his eyes, when his successor began to plot against us. For several years past the good and just right was maintained by a firm and faithful hand unscathed; but when the spiritual power of Typhaines fell into the hands of a wolf in the disguise of a shepherd, the Lord of Nevers reinstated his enterprises, and favored by the disorders of the times, he did succeed in setting on foot certain abusive usages, on which he now founds his most insolent pretensions.

"Just now, backed as he is by a certain cloth merchant,

20

a vagabond from no one knows where, and who by means of his title of kiug's burgher, has got a footing among our people there, the seeds of madness and sedition sown *by* him have sprung up among them. I tried, in vain, to oppose the spread of the mischief by gentle measures, by prudent reserve, by goodness of all sorts, and by generous presents. You kuow as well as any man what happeus when the idea of commune once gets into a burgher's head. I tried to open the eyes of my mainmortables as to the Count's projects. I have utterly failed. Nothing whatever could make the least impression on their stony hearts; they are rushing to destruction blindfold, under the lead of the demon who hath blinded the eyes of his victims. What more can I say ? The Abbot of Typhaines, menaced and torn from his sanctuary, is compelled to take flight, and you now see him before you like Jacob fleeing from the face of the wicked. Do you still believe that the Archbishop's protection is enough to rescue me from the hands of the violent? Do you suppose the seigneurs of this region, even should they make a coalition for my defence, to be powerful enough to restore my sheepfold, and that too in spite of the Count de Nevers, who alone is thrice or four times their superior in strength ? and, besides, who is to answer to me for their friendly intervention ? Is not the Seigneur de Pornes a robber, determined and always hot in pursuit of any plunder he can lay his hands on ? Is not his son-in-law's soul as perverse as his own, and as for all the rest of them, are they not as vassals to the Count, obliged to follow his banner against me under penalty of forfeiture ? And yourself even, my son—"

"I interrupt you, holy father; you have nothing to fear," said Messire Jean, " and what is more, I can help you. Speak, then ! and I will freely act, and Monseigneur de Nevers shall in nowise hinder me. It's true I am a vassal

of his, and I owe him service for this house I now hold
under him ; but, on the other hand, he is my man, for one of
his manors in Anjou, a manor depending on a hauberk
fief of mine; just as the King of France himself is at
once suzerain and vassal to the Count de Sancerre. I
suppose you will say that this just right of mine must give
way to Monseigneur de Nevers* numerous knights: not
at all—don't believe it. I, thank God, have some good
supports and have no fears for the legitimacy of my cause.
If Monseigneur should pronounce my lands here forfeit, I
would send him a like declaration as to his own, and he
knows well enough that our common suzerain, the Count
of Anjou, would defend me in my rights. Still, I must
confess that, setting aside all consideration of my own
position, the circumstances you have now detailed both
surprise and discourage me. Your situation is good for
nothing, and my notion about helping you is of no avail.
What will you do then ? In the names of all the saints,
tell me if you can discern any way of escape out of all this
terrible network of misery ?"

"I never had any doubt of the goodness of the God
whose servant I am," boldly replied Anselm; [14]and this
is the plan that my Good Master has inspired me with.
To the assaults of the bear I will oppose the teeth and
claws of the lion. I will go and demand snccor of King
Louis of France: I will depict all my misery before him.
They say he is a man both pious and magnanimous. Do
you doubt his willingness to welcome and serve me too ?"

"I know not," replied Messire Jean, "whether you will
find him willing to embrace a new quarrel, for he has his
hands full of them already. Ah! be is no poor soldier
like the Henris and Philippes, his predecessors! In their
day, as long as the barons of the Isle of France carried
their raids no farther than in sight of the ramparts of Paris,

those poor knights let them have their own way in fall
liberty. But it is quite a different case with King Louis ;
he is never out of the saddle; armor on his back, and
lance in his gauntlet; and I answer for it, he is a hardy
prince, who never complains of any trouble ; only I must
tell you he has a great deal on his hands, and I know not
whether he will hearken to you or no."

" No matter," answered the Abbot; "I 'll go to his city
of Paris and seek this king so active and valorous, and in
case he should refuse to hear, I will find out plenty of
people about him to force him to leud me his ear—yes—
even if it should be necessary to go so far as to appeal to
the Pope's legate himself!"

"Yours are brave and noble projects," said Messire
Jean. "You talk, father, like a man nurtured in learning,
and in the Spirit of God ! May you succeed ! To-morrow
morning I shall be ready to attend you on your way to
Paris; there I will conduct you to Etienne de Garlande,
and thence proceed to Anjou, where I must make myself acquainted with the Count's views before I return
to devote myself to your cause and lift my lance, if needs
must, against the Nivernais."

The conference was yet prolonged for a few minutes.
Messire Jean was a man of an elevated and hardy nature;
he knew all the greatness of the adventure the Abbot was
about to attempt. To invoke the royal authority against
one of its powerful feudatories—to excite active enemies
against that feudatory—to appeal to the thunders of the
church of the Gauls, was certainly, if he could succeed in
it, to be armed with very great power. In this, Abbot
Anselm gave proof of both his courage, and the expanse of
his views. His pallid features and hollow, sunken eyes,
veiled a heart that, for intrepidity and audacity would yield
to uo heart of knight or baron, were he ever so bold.

On the next morning at three o'clock, before the first ray of the dawn had glimmered in the remotest east, Fulk, with loud cries, had waked the whole house. Immovable in his brutal sorrow, he had refused every offer of food ; though, from a feeling of precaution, he had very carefully attended to the comfort of his good steed. As he led him out of the stable, and, grumbling the while, fixed the saddle on his back, the Abbot made his appearance, attended by Messire Jean.

" We are about to separate," said he to Fulk; "you saved my life, and I will never forget that you did so. If you find your master alive, bear him these express words. You defended the abbey of Typhaines at the peril of your existence, and the Abbot of Typhaines will think of a means to acquit that debt; though he is at present in a state of embarrassment, the day will come when he will bestow upon you, and that without wrong done to holy church, twice as much as the fief of Cornehaut was ever worth. Go, my son, I bestow my benediction upon you."

Fulk shrugged his shoulders and made the sign of the cross at one and the same moment. Thus mussing his piety and ill-temper into one, and then discovering a lad of some fifteen years standing near him, and looking at him quite curiously, he said:—

" What are you after, master rascal ? what the devil do you want, eh ?"

" Sir, squire," responded the boy, " I'm to be your guide, please, as far as Castle Cornouiller."

" Yes, it does please me ; but where's your horse ?"

" I hav'n't no horse," said the lad, " but I can walk very fast along by yours."

" I wish this miserable old house was squashed flat, and all the people in it! Such a guide as that! Pshaw ! Here, you, come here with you ; I '11 cure all that," and so leaning over his horse's shoulder, he opened his big hand wide, took in the nape of the boy's neck, and lifted him, as light as a feather, to the crupper behind, and without a thought of the child's grimaces " How now, which way ? right or left f "

" Left!" said the guide, very much alarmed, and clinging to Fulk as tight as he could hold. Fulk touched his war horse with the spur, and without a word of leave-taking dashed through the portal at a gallop. Half an hour later Messire Jean, the Abbot, and a dozen mounted cavaliers took the opposite road that led to Paris, leaving the fort in charge of a select though a small garrison. Messire Jean promised himself to employ the hours of their journey in the discussion with Anselm of certain theories of the Trinity, recently put forth at Laon by a canon of the cathedral there. Such was the pastime of the erudites of those times, long, long ago-

CHAPTER XYIII.

THE journey was speedily accomplished, and without the least accident; there was a truce of God at the time. In those remote ages there were no taverns or hostelries to be found on the roads, but for travellers of rank like the Abbot and Messire Jean de Berniot, the doors of all the priories, chapels, and manors were ever open to give them welcome. The story of the misfortunes of Typhaines excited surprise and indignation among ecclesiastics and nobles, wherever it was told. Master Anselm heard on every hand that certainly God was not to leave him in the hands of the Ty-phaineers, to be robbed of his seigneural rights, centurial as they were.

Cheered on in this way by the numerous evidences of good-will all round them, the travellers, toward uoon of the third day, came to the hills to the southeast of Paris.

It was but a small matter in those days that city, now grown to be so great—that is, if we compare its then condition with its present extent and magnificence; and yet civilization had elected it even then as one of its most active centres for western and northern Europe. On the top of the slope that descended toward the Seine sat the abbey of St. Genevieve, with its battlemented walls and towers ; lower down on the hillside the abbey of St. Victor, and Saint Germain des Pres seemed to emulate St. Gene-vieve in martial and ecclesiastical gravity. The remains of the still important Palais des Thermes recalled to mind the antique glories of the Gaulish Lutetia, and among those

illustrious monuments, groups of houses, scattered thick on
the hillsides, sprung up like mushrooms with new ones ever
rising all round about them. This was the spot where
science, among the clumps of tall trees, the vineyards and
meadows, was daily installing whole swarms of students
from every part of Europe; from Denmark, as well as
Italy, from Aquitaine, as well as from Germany. A love
for scholastic learning gathered in this particular spot, in
very savage looking and coarse lodgings, all these students,
too numerous for Paris to contain them. Here, too, came
the most illustrious masters, rivals of the chancellor of the
metropolitan school, to teach and develop their special doctrines upon this great neutral ground. In fact, the love of
learning brought in and daily magnified the crowds of students and teachers that laid the foundation of those vast
town-quarters, on the left bank of the Seine, where, even
to the present day, all the surroundings seem to put on a
claustral physiognomy.   *

After quitting that rustic slope, and crossing the Petit
Pont, they found they were in the city of Paris, partly inclosed with walls, with here and there a wide beach, flat and
pebbly, along which flowed the waters of the Seine. Here
numerous barques, come down from Burgundy or ready to
start on the up-river voyage, or going down toward the sea,
were moored to the shore. There rose the stores that con-
tained the trading establishments of the good burgesses of
the city of Paris, who were so fond of their river trade that
they afterward took the figure of a vessel as their blazon.
In another direction you beheld the stir and hurry of a busy
trading town, and along with many an agrestic remnant of
country life evinced in great flocks of poultry, geese, ducks,
droves of swine, vast piles of sheep iniquities heaped up
along the walls of the houses, to drain and dry, inqnining
the whole atmosphere with noisome smells. Clothes Hues

loaded with new-washed clothing, of every varied shape and hue, were swinging in the breeze, and groups of children were wantoning in the gutters, scarce watched by their coarse cross and grumbling mothers and nurses, save now and then by an angry growl, a smart slap on the back, or a severe shaking. Disorders of this sort are not to be seen in our days, hardly in the remotest and poorest of our French villages. Then, after coming out of one of these narrow crooked alleys, where the badly-aligned houses stood, some jutting far out, and others retreating far within the pavement line, with buildings—some towering high above and built half over the roofs of their humbler opposites —some, one-story houses, and others all new and gay, and smart as a bridegroom; some half rotted away, and covered with brown and velvet lichens and mosses—all of them garnished with little windows of little panes of glass set in their little leaden sasl^J'hen at last, I say, you came to a point from which WBant view might be had of the royal palace, or of the ancient abbey church of Notre Dame de Paris.

The Notre Dame of that day was not the sumptuous basilica that we now behold rising so pompously, with its innumerable stone carvings and traceries at the point of the island; nor was it the old Merovingian temple, built, as¹ twas said, on the ruins of an ancient fanum, sacred to the religion of old. Still, on her heavy and massive form, the *Bomane* metropolis of the time was none the less worthy of the veneration of the faithful. Like a noble and puissant matron she sat enshrined among cloisters inhabited by her chapter, and extended her supremacy far and wide and strong, over fifteen churches, all of which had found standing room within the very narrow circumference of the town. She daily threw open her nave, adorned as it was by the piety of kings, knights, and burghers, to a busy, hurrying, pious crowd, some promenading on the green lawns, and offeriug a grave contrast to the more regal and more mundane abode that was ever peopled with warriors and feudal servitors.

The reader should not, however, figure the palace to himself as a highly luxurious regal dwelling-place. Kings, in that age, enjoyed no great might of power, nor had they a great abundance of money, nor was it in their power to surround themselves with magnificent and sumptuous adornments. In that they pretended not to vie in splendor with their distant vassals in far-off Aquitaine. They, after all, were but lordlings who, suzerains though they were, yet were obliged to be very moderate and modest The chief ornament of a regal palace consisted in its garden, which was neither more nor less than a grove of planted trees, where on festival days the people and clergy of Paris were allowed to make their promenades; it is easy to conceive that the marvels of Le Notre flfll were not to be looked for in those times at Paris.

Such was the Paris of the day. It was all Paris, provided it may please you to add a small strip of ground, rather more methodically laid out than the student-bohcmia before described. This settlement began to grow up along the right bank of the river, and served as homes to the tradesmen and merchants who had settled themselves betwixt the fortified churches of St. Germain PAuxerrois and St. Gervais. You reached it by way of the Grand Pont, and you found there a far coarser and gross-looking crowd in the streets than the other more genteel quarters on the opposite shore. Everybody seemed eager in pursuit of gain on this side—of pleasure on that. Such was the Paris of that day, and yet we must call to mind the greatness of its renown throughout the world of that age. London was but a poor village, inhabited by mainmortable Saxons; Aix-la-Chapelle had lost its imperial prestige; Cologne and Treves, that had in former times been very powerful, could boast of none of that intellectual splendof that had crowned it with distinction in olden times; Rouen was rich, Thoulouse literary, Poictiers marvellous for the pleasures that abounded and superabounded there under the reign of the Guillaumes, of Aquitaine. Still, all these secondary glories, all the stars of second magnitude were far from shining with such far-reaching light as the city of Paris. Rome alone, of all the European towns, carried it over the French capital, on the banks of the Seine.

" It's growing late," said Messire Jean to the Abbot just as the travellers, debouching from le petit Pont, were getting into one of the narrow streets of the town. " If you will take my word for it, holy father, we had better go seek asylum from some of the good priests of your acquaintance here, and we will defer our visit to the Sire de Garlande until to-morrow. There *s hardly an hour of daylight left, and there's not time enough to reach him and have a very short conference with him."

" You speak well," responded the monk, "and as you justly say, I am not wanting in friends in Paris, friends who are very dear to me, and whom I can well call on for a welcome for myself and you too, Sir Knight. Come then, we will go for that end to Master Guillaume de Cbarapeaux."

" Oh ! what a happiness," cried Messire Jean in a burst of enthusiasm. " What a happiness for me to pay my respects to a man so holy—so great as he! I confess it has been one of my secret, my ardent desires to listen to the words of that learned Doctor. We are very unfortunate, we knights, ever engaged in the military affairs of the age and ucver having it in our power to attend as we could

wish to do, the public lectures of illustrious teachers like
him! but ever on horseback, lance in hand, we are compelled
to waste our lives in defending our domains and in reveng-
ing our insults and injuries. But let me see! What else
can I do ? Master Guillaume, as he is your friend, will be
an efficacious protector as far as the king is concerned—
for the king, it is said, is very fond of his company and
conversation, and that is a state of things far different from
our poor humble satisfactions."

" Tell me !" said Anselm, leaning forward on the saddle
and pointing with his finger—" say, who is that personage,
Messire Jean—the one there who seems to walk with so
proud a bearing as he moves forward with the crowd around
him ?"

" I do not know him," replied the gentleman ; " I have
not pranced along these streets for many a year, and I
don't know a siugle face I meet. The one you are pointing out seems like a person who must be a man of consequence in Paris."

The fact is that a personage, followed by a crowd of
people, and dressed in a sort of ecclesiastical costume, was
moving towards Grand Pont, with a sort of haughty and
sumptuous air of mundane pride that was by no means
pleasing to the ascetic eyes of our good Abbot. Clearly
the man couldn't be a priest, or at any rate a priest at all
diligent in the observance of any religious rule of life. He
was a youthful looking person ; his chestnut curls seemed
wantoning about his neck and shoulders as they fell and
rolled on his fine cloth robe; his hands were loaded with
gold and silver rings. He crossed the square with slow majestic steps, and his proud eyes glanced over the multitude
around, all hurrying and pressing to get near enough to
salute him as he passed by them. Behind him came on
multitudes of young students and even men of mature age,

many of whom were bending in deep respect while they addressed their questions, to which he lightly threw off answers that were eagerly collected and repeated and hearkened to with admiration.

" Doubtless," said Anselm, " this Master must be some very learned doctor; yet to me he looks so young and vain that I can hardly think him a truly learned scholar. Both you and I, Messire Jean, know how readily the foolish populace embrace and grow wild about many a shallow and lying oracle. Let us, however, get on faster. I am in a hurry to get under the hospitable roof of the dear friend of my youth."

Forcing their way through the press the travellers pursued their route, and at last arrived in the cloisters of Notre Dame. A passing cleric pointed to the abode of Master Guillaume de Chainpeaux, Archdeacon of Paris, well known as time long Professor of Dialectics in the Metropolitan Church. Crossing several lawns, many courts, besides threading narrow passages, they reached a door at which one of Messire Jean's men knocked.

I shall omit an account of the preliminaries of their reception. Besides, no sooner was the Abbot announced than his old friend hastened to meet him and embrace him with both arms, with warmest welcome. He issued orders at once for the proper entertainment of the knight, his followers, and their horses, who were all made as comfortable as possible.

"Well now," said he to Anselm, "you are come; you, whom I may name my soul's predilection—you are come to see a man broken hearted, a miserable being, visited by the wrath of God I You knew me, Anselm, once; you knew me when I was swollen with glory and pride, which, perhaps, was far too pleasing for the good of my soul— but I am punished now; crushed, yes, to the very earth;

21

and there is room in this heart of mine for your pious consolation, to bring back there some faint emotions of joy
again."

Thus the Master spoke, and the Abbot looked with
saddened gaze on the emaciated pale features and hollow
red eyes and bowed stature of the great archdeacon.

"Haven't I," said the Archdeacon, with a sad smile,
" haven't I been making rather free with the spoils of age?"

" Far too free," responded the Abbot; " but what is the
great misfortune that has changed you so ?"

"I will tell you the whole story, Anselm—I will confide
to your bosom griefs that I must conceal from every eye
but yours. You shall see the frightful depth of my fall."

In spite of his sympathy for his old companion, for the
man was at his side when they were attending the lectures
of the celebrated Manigold, one of the illustrious leaders of
that age; the Abbot, by nature and by duty above all
things else absorbed in the concerns of his community,
shivered, as he thought that sorrows like Guillaume's, if
they really did depend upon some temporal check, might
soon become his own as well. Coming to his bosom friend
in search of a protector, was he doomed to find him a
broken-down man barely able to sustain himself ?

" Tell me—quickly tell me all about you," said the Abbot. "You see before you a poor monk driven from a
church profaned by wicked hands, one who came hither to
implore your succor; tell me, soon, whether I can rely
on you; whether you can bring me to speech with the
king! or whether I must look elsewhere for help !"

" I know not," he answered, " whether you are talking
seriously or not; but if your words are to be taken to the
very letter, then you must know that I 'in still able to be
of use to my friends. My sorrows and misfortunes arc not
of the kind you seem to suppose, and I hope ever to keep

some part of the power I have long enjoyed and that I never have used, save for the good of the church. Let me know what it was that compelled you to quit your cloister, and you shall see whether I am the man to haggle about the terms of my succor."

Anselm told him the whole story. Ever since his flight commenced, he had everywhere met with willing and sympathizing auditors, but never yet had monk or knight taken so great an interest in his case as his new auditor. Archdeacon Guillaume, like all the eminent men of the day, had the very highest idea of clerical power, and considered it could never be too much exalted. According to him, it was vain to look for reason, gentleness, and a true spirit of equity, save with here and there an exception, but in the clerical classes.

" I have listened to you," said he, "with an anxiety that has almost made me forget my own griefs. I have but one word to say in answer, and that is that your cause is the cause of the whole church ; it is the cause of the Christian religion, and it is a matter of salvation that these monstrous innovations—called communes—should be put an end to. Time was, my venerable brother, when Christian peoples thought of nothing else but heaven ; or, filled with disgust and shame for their lives here below, they no more loved them than a man loves the chain, whose gilt surface lessens no jot of its odious weight. But now all is changed I Mainmortables, burghers, and serfs, all run into rebellion, not merely against their seigneurs, but against the very church itself. It imports, I tell you, to the salvation of the human race no longer to submit to such a state of things! And yet".   .   .

" Why do you stop ?" asked the Abbot, gravely, and laying his hand on his friend's. " Let me know what it is you fear; I am not a weak child to be frightened at a supposed danger ahead, and terrified into a state of helpless inaction. With the will and the courage to conquer in God's cause, I'm not the man to stop or to stay; no, not for anything here below l"

" Well, then, my friend," replied the Archdeacon, "you must learn that the men whose help you are to seek for are not the men to walk in the fair paths I could wish for them. In one word, the lord Louis himself does sometimes give his succor to those communes."

" I have heard that already," said the Abbot sadly, " and yet he is a pious prince, and a lover of justice !"

" No doubt," replied Master Guillaume ; " no doubt of that; but don't you know that lords, and kings too, ever suffer themselves to be influenced by circumstauces ? Such is the fact as to King Louis. At bottom he is no lover of rebel burghers, and he showed that when he marched in person at the head of his troops to put down the Laon com- mune, though he at first had upheld it. But since then, he has supported the Amiens men against their count, and the Soissons folk against their bishop. In fact, busy as he is just now making war on several barons who have been raiding the country about Paris, I can't say whether he will lend a willing ear to your complaints, and take part iu your quarrel."

" But my quarrel is his quarrel too," said Anselm; " and is it not clear that, if the peasants and serfs will go on set- ting up communes on baronial and church domains, it will not be long before they will set them up on the lands of lord Louis himself l"

" Perhaps so," said Guillaume; " but do you not see on the other hand that, however detestable those communes, they tend to weaken the nobles, bishops, and abbots ? De- priving them of their men lessens their resources, cuts them off from the control of cities and towns, and humbles their pride ? See you not, too, that money is needed to procure the king's charter; money to maintain it, and money, money to pay the suzerain's claims. See you not that, in this way the king gets his hand into the business of his vassals, and meddles with matters not his own ? This is the reason why—though he fully understands the iniquity of his conduct, Louis of France sometimes gives way; and for one commune that he forbids, he consents to the establishment of three or four."

" You will not succeed in frightening me," said the Abbot, squeezing his friend's hand. "I ever have before my eyes the desolation of our blessed Saint Procul, who looks down on his church, so shamefully despoiled of her rights, and accusing me, in the secret recesses of my own conscience. You must take me to the king."

" That I will do, most certainly," cried the Archdeacon, " and your courage but quickens my own. I think as you do, dear brother; God will not desert bis ministers, and Satan and his diabolical communes shall be driven back to the hell from which they were evoked by miserable wretches and false Christians. Eh, now! why should we be surprised at the monstrous innovations we mourn over, when the very foundation of all that's right—all religion and all learning are daily trampled under foot by an impudent, proud fool ?"

By this transition Anselm saw that the Archdeacon wag about to recount the history of his own misfortunes, and preferred to go on with his story, which had been broken off an hour before.

" You know," said Guillaume de Champeaux, " that for years I was devoted to the instruction of our students in the arts and sciences. Every one knows that in Dialectics I never had even a rival. For years I stood victor over the captious and lying demon who is ever striving to mislead the souls of Doctors, and cast them into the wildest heresies. Long surrounded and sustained by the zeal of my pupils, I continued my lectures in this cloister, and though I say it in all humility, I had reached the highest summit of all earthly glory, when feeling how vain is this world, I made up my mind to retire from it and provide for the salvation of my own soul; nevertheless, I still went on with ray course of public instruction, and my classes most certainly were not diminished in numbers. All of a sudden, while I was lecturing one day on Rhetoric, in the very midst of the assembly there appeared a young man, a student—just like any other man in the class, if not their inferior ! This demon, this serpent with a human head, impelled by some unaccountable madness, began to openly dispute against me; and whether it was that I had been misunderstood, or that I was confounded by his extraordinary audacity, I know not; only that, at the end of the discussion he withdrew with a conquering smile, and left me planted there in the midst of a dumb and terror-stricken audience!

44 My audacious contradictor, after his pretended victory over me, came here—here into this very cloister, where one of my best scholars—a man I loved, and had the utmost confidence in—was lecturing by my authority; he came here, I tell you, and the poor creature, seduced, won over or bribed, for aught I know, by the monster ravening for my destruction—yes, here, mfy agent came down out of the desk and made that fellow mount up and scatter among hundreds of imbeciles, maddened by his pestilent speech, the odious doctrines that were to overwhelm me forever!

44 It was not long till his name began to be whispered all about me; the few who remained faithful to me began to grow restless and uneasy about my silence under the pretended defeat. *Twas vainly that I strove to revive their courage by advice, and even by threats; they hesitated more

\

and more day by day, grew colder and colder, and I learned at last that I was daily insulted and calumniated in this very cloister; yes, here, where I had so long reigned supreme ! My profound retreat was attributed, not to my humility, not to my disgust at the world, but to a vile shameless feeling of submission and fear !

" Then, I must confess it, venerable brother, and I do it with tears of grief and shame, then I allowed my pride to mislead me; thinking I was quite in the right, I made up my mind to crush the rash man with a thunderbolt. I descended into the arena, I went there to look out for Abelard, and"—

Here the archdeacon bid his face in his hands and a burning blush flashed over the old man's pale forehead. He resumed his story and bitterly exclaimed, " Should you stay in Paris but a single day, you 'll be sure to meet with him."

"I have met him already," replied Anselm, "strutting along like a prince surrounded by an idolizing crowd."

" Yes, that was he," said Guillaume, "parading his insolence and affectation, seducing the humble, frightening the weak minded, scattering sarcasm and mockery, and so he will go on in triumph until the day, not distant, shall come when his madness will lead him to the dreadful abyss that yawns for him. As to me, what care I for what he calls his victory ? I yesterday received the cross and the ring. I am Bishop of Chalons, and will go in a few days, and forget the ingratitude and madness of mankind, who pretend to be lovers of learning, and yet turn aside from true scholars, and hearken open mouthed to the insipid divagations of a set of jugglers. It is no way surprising, brother, that in times when such enormities go unpunished, serfs and burghers should break out in open insurrection, and communes should be set on foot in the land 1"

Such was the expression of Master Guillaume de Cliam-peaux's cruelly wounded self-love. That celebrated doctor, in fact, had reached the painful crisis, wherein so many writers and poets, so many men of talents, are to find their fame eclipsed by some younger and more eloquent rival Ah, painful hour ! ah, sad necessity ! Happy they who, at least, find some consolation in their misery! Such was the lot of Master Guillaume, and yet the episcopate, though so elevated a dignity at that day, was an insufficient com-pensation for his popularity lost, and his shame endured

In his inner man, the Abbot took but a small share in his friend's chagrin. He looked at all that grief as a proof of weakness in a man whose extraordinary talents he, however, fully admitted. And so, sliding very readily into the track of consolations he felicitated him on his newborn greatness that was about to put it in his power to serve the cause of the abbey so much the more effectually.

44 Holy father," said he, 44 I think yonr city of Paris is just now agitated about a thousand various interests and a multitude of passions unknown to our provincial solitudes."

44 It is a gehenna," responded the archdeacon, sighing, 44 and to-morrow, after you have seen our lord the king, and the troubles that plagne him, perhaps, you will think quite as I do on that point."

Supper was now announced; the two dignitaries sat down with Messire Jean do Bcrniot, whose profound deference and enthusiastic admiration of the illustrious scholar infused a little gayety into Master Guillaume's melancholy soul, so that the new bishop that evening again saw somewhat of the early successes of his youthful years and a spark even of his former glory, though now deep sunk in dim and dark eclipse.

CHAPTER XIX

IN the twelfth century, it was not the fashion to sit up late at night: as soon as the sun had gone down and darkness began to prevail over the land, every body went to bed, particularly the burghers, a race of people ever famous for the regularity of their habits; their doors were closed and the kitchen fires put out as the last light failed out in the west.

Paris was sleeping now: the servitors of the canons were fastening the cloister entrance, and the beadle shoving home the bars of the city gates, as the bishop and canon each retired to his sleeping chamber, said the evening orison, and laid him down to wait until the morning dawn should come to make it lawful to live over again the life of that busy teeming world. The silence of the town was deep ; cries were now and then heard from the other side of the river, where there was a less peaceful population, and where the taverns were often kept open with guests drinking at the tables until daylight, to the great scandal of the honest city folk, who could hardly reconcile their notions of a true love of learning, a thing in itself so excellent and orderly, with a fondness for rowdyism and night brawling.

It was 6ummer-time, and the same fashion of the day that prescribed early bedtime required early rising as a rule of living. As soon, then, as the first morning beams began to venture themselves among the narrow lanes and alleys of the town, open flew window-shutters, and the good burgesses and their wives thrust forth their heads to snuff the morning air and bid good-day to the opposite neighbors; discuss the present state of the weather, and enunciate their final opinions as to the possible conditions of that important question for the rest of the coming day. The beadles rolled the grand portals of Notre Dame on their groaning hinges; the clergy and monks commenced the office of primes, or devoutly listened as they proceeded; the students were hurrying in from their remote scattered schools, to pursue their studies of the *Trivium*, that is to say, rhetoric, grammar, and dialectics; or to venture on the *Quadrivium*, comprising what they called arithmetic, geometry, astronomy, and music.

As the cloister gates of Notre Dame rolled open, the first comers were brutally repulsed by the zealous valets, shouting, and rather more than brushing their visages with soft and gentle fingers cried—

" Back 1 back with you, knaves 1 Place 1 place! place for the Bishop of Chalons-sur-Marne ! place for the holy Abbot of Typhaines I place, you vagabonds, for the Knight Messire Jean de Berniot 1"

Those three personages, in fact, at once made their appearance ; the two former mounted on good strong mules, and the third bestriding his war horse, and all followed by a band of clercs and laics on foot, chattering away or helping the cloister porter to put back the crowd, by the most efficacious if not the gentlest of remonstrances. But m those times there was nothing very disagreeable to the recipient of a blow, they were so common, and so great was the abuse of that current coin that nobody had any gainsay to it. Sensible people were quite satisfied with a proper rejoinder, when the blow had been rather rude, and no one ever complained of that; it was all fair and right.

The two ecclesiastical dignitaries and their military

companion came out into the dense crowd, either apostrophized by some of the rude pupils of Abelard, or greeted
by worthy burgesses on their knees, as usual, in praise of
the antique reputation of the archdeacon or profoundly im-
pressed, perhaps, by his new title of bishop, and in this
way the cavalcade stopped at last in front of the battlemented inclosure of the palace.

At that period the King of France kept no standing
army on foot—no hired soldiers were employed by him.
The return to the old Roman customs on that point took
place long after Louis' time. Whenever the lord Louis
had occasion to sojourn for a season in his palace at his
good city of Paris, he had no following about him, save
some of his barons, brought thither on affairs of business or on visits of ceremony or friendship ; all these, together with servitors from his own immediate domains,
constituted his main power: there was no equipage, no
luxury; the most that was aimed at was a moderate degree of comfort. Hence, we are not to conclude the scenes
we are about to witness to be the ordinary state of affairs in
the royal palace in peaceful times; for to do so, would be
to make a great mistake ; but let us pass through the outer
inclosure of the palace: the moment of our arrival is by
no means an ordinary one there.

" What ?" cried Messire Jean de Berniot, " is the king
setting off on an expedition ? I find a great many men-at-
arms in the court!"

" There must be something of the kind on foot," rejoined
the bishop; " I knew not that peace was seriously threatened just now; but, no matter, let us alight and go in."

The three friends quitted their saddles, and leaving their
animals to the care of their valets, passed through the low
narrow door, the only issue for the royal manor; ascended
the dark stairway, and at once found themselves in the

great hall, where they beheld the king surrounded with the
elite of his barons.

Louis VI., who was not yet known by the title of Louis
le Gros—but rather by that of Louis l'Eveille—Louis le
Battailleur, was standing by a massive oak-table, on which
were displayed a number of glasses and dishes, some silver,
some tin, and some of common earthen ware; he had a
gilt goblet in his hand, which he was holding out to a lady
in a rich dress, who, with both hands, was pouring wine
from a heavy ewer. Clinging on each side to her robe
were two little fresh-looking, rosy-cheeked boys: it was
Queen Adelaide of Savoy, and the children were her sons,
Prince Philippe and Prince Louis Florfes.

The king looked like a splendid and noble knight. He
was stout and strong, and though his lofty stature already
began to show somewhat of the wretched obesity that became the torment of his latter years, he, as yet, showed
nothing but the stout and intrepid warrior he was. His
tanned cheek displayed all the hues of health, and his eyes
shone with vivacity and resolution, and with not a little of
what might pass for penetration and cunning. Such to
the lord of Typhaines' eyes; such, in fact, was that king,
worthy of remembrance, who extricated the royal house
of France from its original poverty and weakness.

"Come, my dear!" said the lord King to the Queen,
" pour my last cup for me ; it shall be the stirrup cup; I
will then kiss you and the children, and set off with God's
help and St. Dennis'; and you, my valets, take care to provide wine for all these barons! I want them to go forth
joyful aud gay, to make their hands the heavier. But
God's splendor! Here is the venerable Bishop of Chalons I
Be welcome, holy father! I hope you are not going to
bring me new complaints against Master Abelard; for I
should have no time to hear them now."

" Monseigneur," responded the prelate, "I am come to confer with you on a very different subject. I bring with me the holy Abbot of Typhaines in Nivernais, who comes to implore your justice against the most odious acts of violence ever heard of in the world."

The bright face of the king at once changed to dark—and handing the cup to the queen, without putting it to his lips—

" I know all about it," said the king, speaking slow and low as if he wished to weigh every word and say nothing that might turn out to be dangerous. "My consin of Nevers and the people of the Commune of Typhaines have already sent me their messengers—what am I to do about it?"

" You," replied the Abbot coldly, " can refuse to support injustice, and you can crush out iniquity with your victorious arms I"

" That 's the way with the clergy," cried Louis, looking all round on the fifty or sixty armed nobles in the immense hall. " That's just the way they always talk—the moment anything happens to clash with their interests it 's justice that cries out help ! help I If they are assailed, it 's iniquity that is at work ! Ah, holy Abbot I there's plenty of iniquity and injustice besides what is troubling you just now."

"A king's duty," responded the Abbot, not at all disconcerted by the king's disobliging answer, " is to protect the Church. I find it so in holy writ and in the Acts of the Councils."

" And I," retorted the king, with a bitter smile, " I see rich abbots and bishops, with lands and serfs and subjects; but when a little money is wanted, it must be looked for in their strong boxes, whither every coin bearing our effigy seems to take instant refuge; and in the meantime we—yes, by Christ's death! yes we, King of France, we, suc-

22

cessor of so many puissant kings, have been by the violence of the age reduced to.a few miserable strips of land
out of the whole of our ancient heritage. Ha! brother, it
seems very much like jesting in you, to require my aid in
your squabbles with your own vassals, when you know I
am overwhelmed all the days of my life with the villainous
usurpations of my own vassals! You come and complain of
the loss of your power, you honest monks do; power, perhaps, you have no real right to, nor ought to have; and
yet you care not an iota for the miseries of kings! You
see me battling, ever battling, and at this very moment
taking up the time and making use of the loyalty of my
faithful barons to put down a false traitor who, not four
leagues away from my faithful city of Paris, has the audacity to revolt against me, and yet you have the impudence
to come hither and talk to me about your affairs. Don't
thiuk of it; don't think of such a thing, holy father. Wait
until Louis of France has reconquered the rights bequeathed
to him by Charlemagne; wait until Flanders and Artois,
Normandy, Guienne, and the Catalan marches acknowledge
him for suzerain ; wait till the descendant of Francus has
restored to his kingdom the full lustre acquired by his
Trojan ancestors, and then, you will be in the right to
come and lay your cause before me—I 'll weigh it then—
and, perhaps, heavier than suits you, in the scales of truth
and justice."

The majority of the lords in the presence appeared to
fully approve of this rude apostrophe. Some of them
clapped their hands by way of cheer, some laughed
aloud; while a few others, evinced by exclamations far
more energetic than orthodox, which even the presence of
the queen's majesty could not wholly repress, that they
thought the king had spoken well. Yet, notwithstanding
the rudeness of the seigneurs, and, doubtless, because of

that very rudeness, the clergy of the time had come to care but little for such opponents, so that giving the Abbot no time to make answer, Bishop Guillaume spoke out in harsh and crabbed tones as follows:—

" Such language as this is by no means usual as coming from a Christian king to God's servants on earth, and that too with the full approval of his rash counsellors ! I have heard before now, Sire King, that your mind does wander at times, but I never could have believed it unless I had seen and heard it myself. Consider, I pray, that Abbot Anselm's cause is the cause of the entire church of the two Gauls, and that until we obtain absolute and full justice we will defend it, as well as we may."

I do reflect, I do consider," said the king, stamping his foot on the floor, "that time is flying, the day passing away and our men getting impatient: my enemies no doubt begin to think I am growing timorous, and in the meantime are amusing themselves by ravaging our towns and devastating my people's fields. Come, my lords, to horse, to horse! Farewell, my dear! good-bye Philippe! kiss me, Louis! when thou art grown to be a man," added the king, lifting the child in his arms, " thou, yes, thou shalt be a brave knight, I hope. Come, my lords, are you ready ? As to you, my venerable fathers, believe not that I am wanting in respect for Holy Church, and to prove it I beg you to stay here with the queen—she will present you to Abbot Suger, who is fully acquainted with all my purposes; you can better come to a clear understanding with him than with a soldier far readier to wield the sword than brandish the tongue."

And King Louis saluted the two priests with a wave of his hand ; then, followed by his chivalry, he went down into the court-yard.

For awhile Anselm and Guillaume heard nothing save

the warlike ring of spars, the clash of arms, the rustling of swords in their iron scabbards, shouts and bursts of laughter; next came the tramp of the cavalry; banners and pennons of every shape and hue floated along by the tall narrow windows; the trumpets blared, and at last all was silent. Messire Jean had gone off in company with his peers.

" Madam," gently spoke the Bishop of Chalons, " Monseigneur the king has given us a rude welcome !"

" Don't mind it, my venerable fathers," replied Adelaide, with marked respect " Louis has a great many cares just at this moment; the Count of Chartres is at this very time making a new raid into France, and off there, toward Orleans, his men are ravaging and pillaging the whole country. But you should not be discouraged for all that."

" You are a pious Christian lady, madam," retorted the bishop, " and I am fully aware that in you God's ministers can find a sure recourse ; yet I am not quite sure that the same is to be said of the Abbot of St. Denis, to whom the king has just referred us. Though he is a monk, he is no strict observer of the rules of bis order, and I may say it without failing in charity, since it is a notorious fact; he keeps his hounds and his own men at arms, dresses sumptuously, and in the conduct and manuers he recommends to the king I see nothing bat frivolity."

Queen Adelaide was not one of the superior class of women. She was much attached to her royal spouse, was devoted to his children, and took great care of the internal administration of his palace as far as her power as its mistress went. Besides all this, she held everything that wore the ecclesiastical garb in the greatest veneration. Upon hearing the bishop's remarks on her husband's friend and minister, she felt herself unequal to a conversation so critical, and taking each of the children by the hand she spoke, with downcast eyes and timorous accents—

" I entreat you, holy father; I beg you to apply to Messire Suger: I know not what language he may hold on this subject or whether yon and Master Anselm will be content with his answer to your appeals; but if you will pray for me and these dear children, I will urge Louis to do all you desire to have done."

She left the hall, and in the course of a few minutes a servitor entered, to guide the two ecclesiastics to the presence of the Abbot of St. Denis, who had just that moment come into the royal residence from his monastic home at St. Denis.

"Think you," said Master Anselm, as they passed onward, "that we have any chance of touching the king's heart ?"

" His language was certainly not very cheering," replied the bishop, " and, as a general rule, it is true to say that Louis knows what he means to do; but his position is just now so unsettled, he is compelled to please so many different parties and to sustain himself by the help of so many different hands, and he so dislikes to raise up new enemies that possibly we may not succeed in getting him to change his mind as to what he is at present determined to do. But his confidant will, no doubt, let us know what we have to expect."

"As far as I have heard," continued Anselm, "he is a vulgar fellow, wholly given over to errors of worldly policy, and by no means to the true obligations of real piety."

"Yes," said the bishop, "you describe him well, and you have not been misled in regard to his character. I know not whether he may be converted yet, but for the present he has no views whatever, save such as a talented worldling might choose to make his boast of. He is, as you

perhaps already know, a man of low birth ; it's true he did
make very fair studies in letters, both sacred and profane,
and was King Louis' fellow student in their youth, and
that was the way he acquired his master's confidence. I
will not conceal the fact that burghers and serfs have good
reason to look up to him, as they do, for a zealous protector. He is fond of encouraging merchants and traders,
and attracting them to the city of Paris under the impression that a king may derive great advantages from their
residence in his dominions. He is fond of building too,
and sculpture as well. I describe him to you as he really
is, and with his good qualities too; for he certainly is
at times liberal to the monastic institutions of the country,
and takes great delight in the conversation of educated and
learned men. But all that is vitiated by the errors you
have heard of, and all I have to say is that I agree with
you—he is a vulgar fellow !"

The bishop ended his complex eulogy, or, if you like it
better, this chastened satire on the royal minister, just as
the guide, on opening a door, introduced the venerable pair
into an apartment where sat the celebrated statesman, who
has so long enjoyed the admiration and gratitude of the
people of his own nation and the whole civilized world.

The Abbot of St. Denis was, at that time, hardly more
than a young man, and as Master Guillaume had said, was
a person of great delicacy in point of manners and outward
appearances. His linen was scrupulously white, his monkish robe of fine woollen cloth was of the very best quality;
his beard carefully shaven, and his remarkably neat and
delicate hands were fairly coquettish ; all which were looked
on as reprehensible when seen in a monk—for even the
nuns of the day were never known to wear linen; as the
usual underdress, they wore drugget.

Seated in a large arm chair lined with serge, the minister

of the little kingdom of France seemed to have just finished a despatch, to which he was busy affixing the pendant seals. In the grosser ages of the world, employments are* always restricted in number, and an individual, though he might be an exalted personage, does a great deal of his work with his own hands. Hearing the footsteps of his visitors he turned, and seeing the two ecclesiastics he looked at them with a half haughty, half inquisitive gaze, and in a tone that was kind, or the reverse, just as it might please you to take it, he said—

" What may be your business with me ?"

" Sir Abbot," retorted Guillaume, in a tone of pedantic self-sufficiency, quite familiar to the old Paris scholastic, " this is the lord Abbot of Typhaines, who by the King's Majesty is referred to you concerning a matter of importance."

" Let him take a seat, and you as well," responded the statesman in a more modest tone of voice, and adding by way of official politeness: " The lord Abbot, no doubt, desires to give me an account of the recent occurrences in his fief."

" Do you know about that already ?" said Anselm. " It seems the king knows everything !"

"Yes," replied Suger, with a benignant smile, and looking aside at the parchment spread on his table; " yes, a messenger has just reached me with news of the whole matter there."

Anselm was much surprised at such promptitude, for he had no idea that an express could have reached Paris so soon ; he accordingly made no attempt to conceal his surprise, and at once proceeded to ask:—

" May I venture to inquire whether the rebels themselves have had the audacity to write to the king, or whether the

Count de Nevers has aided them by one of his scribes,
such as he employs in his own councils ?"

" That question is easily answered," said Suger. " The
Count de Nevers has forwarded his letters to us, and the
burgesses of Typhaines, in like manner; so that the reports are confirmed by both parties."

" The villains I" broke out the bishop, with a haughty
tone; " they crown their iniquity and rapine with impu"
dence inconceivable."

Suger made no reply; he only twiddled his abbatial ring
as he sat there, calm and cool. Now this coldness of the
royal minister was very afflicting to Anselm, for in that
very coolness he saw the ruin of his hopes from the king:
he began to comprehend how completely Louis and his
minister were subject to be led on by interests in utter
conflict with his own ; yet notwithstanding the discouragement, he was of a temper too firm and too resolute to give
way and hold his peace; accordingly, stiffening himself up
with an air of determination befitting his high ecclesiastical
rank—

"My lord Abbot," said he, "inasmuch as the odious
spoliation of the rights and property of the abbey of Typhaines is already known to you, I can hardly doubt that
your mind is made up as to the course yon are to take in
relation to it. On all hands I have heard much of your
prudence; I have heard it asserted that you are a man
well inured into the paths of wisdom, and that piety and
justice have never received offence at your hands : I adjure
you, then, to make known to me the part that is to be taken
by King Louis in this miserable affair."

"Your urgency is very great, sir," replied Suger, haughtily, " and I know not whether it is befitting one in my
position to make you an answer to questions so imperiously
propounded; were you a laic merely, I would most cer-

tainly do no snch thing; but the respect I owe to Holy
Church, to whom I, though an unworthy one, am a servant
as you also are, induces me to give you the information
you have asked for. The king is not willing that abbots,
bishops, and monks, nor secular lords either, should be
allowed to torment his poor people."

"I understand not," frigidly retorted the Abbot, "by
what right the lord Louis claims to meddle with the people
of my charge."

" He is your suzerain, Sir Abbot."

" Thanks be to God and his blessed mother Saint Mary,"
cried the Abbot, " the Church of Typhaines knows no
bonds of vassality—none whatever; no count nor bishop,
nor King Louis himself I none of them have a right to
command on my domains. We bow to St. Peter's Cross
alone : our clerical obeisance is due to the common head
of all Christianism, and to none other on the face of the
globe, before which the Abbot of Typhaines is as independent and as free as lord Louis the king himself. I
can exhibit the proofs—I have the charters—I hold the
concessions 1"

" How happens it then that so high and mighty a prince
should come hither to implore the aid and protection of an
impoverished king like the poor lord Louis of France ?"

" Holy Church, when she supplicates," replied Anselm,
" does not make herself a slave by that act. In her afflic-
tion she demands aid at the hands of her own children;
she does not on that account become subject to them—God
forbid !"

" But this is a question not of the church, it is an affair
of the lands of the burgesses of Typhaines. Let us not
get out of the true path, my lord Abbot."

" That distinction," roared Bishop Guillaume, reddening

with anger, [44] is almost a heresy; and I can, by the holy canons, prove that"—

[44] You forget," retorted the Abbot of St. Denis, with a frigid smile, " that you are not speaking to a laical feudatory ; but this discussion leads to nothing, it leads to no issue whatever. The Count de Nevers, by proofs good and valid, so they seem to us, establishes the fact that he is your suzerain : he takes the people of Typhaines under his protection, and at the same time commends himself, as well, to his proper seigneur, the King of France. The poor peasants have done the very same thing: that's all perfectly regular f "

[11] So," murmured Abbot Anselm, [14] it is not to a protector I am come—not even to an enemy—it is to a judge ?"

[44] You have said it," responded the minister, [44] and might it but please Heaven, I would I might see the day when that word, which seems to surprise you, should be the refuge and the law of every acre of laud from the Pyrenees to the Rhine ! Further, Sir Abbot, you appear to me to be animated by a degree of daring that really astonishes me. Are you then, indeed, so high and mighty a lord that it is repugnant to your dignity to give obedience to laws before which so many bishops and prelates loftier in rank and far richer and more influential than you can claim to be, have bowed down f If what you desire at my hands is the advice of a real friend I stand ready to give it to you : submit to the royal will, confess yourself a vassal to France; it will not be harmful to do so if, on occasion, you should be called on to defend yourself against attacks from the Nivernais."

[44] I!" exclaimed Anselm, in a towering passion. [41] What, II I go down on my knees to your master, when I have the right to walk even with him, at his side as his equal in rankl You little know what I am, my lord Abbot of St.

Denis, and you know not how gayly a child of the Lord chooses martyrdom rather than the sale, the cession, or the desertion of the very least of his jnst rights I I a vassal of France, indeed ? But I have heard enough ! This is not the only place where I can find snccor against my mutinous serfs. All princes are not robbers, nor do they all aspire to enrich themselves out of the spoils of our holy mother!"

"You are audacious, Sir Monk," replied Suger, as he touched the Abbot's sleeve with his hand. " But when a man has such a courageous heart as yours he at least deserves to know the whole scope of the dangers he is so daring as to face—read this."

So saying, he took up the parchment he had just sealed, and holding it open before Anselm, he pointed out the significant passages.

The Bishop of Chalons, seeing his friend's face grow pale, leaned anxiously forward. The parchment proved to be neither more nor less than a charter of franchises octroyed under the king's warrant to the good people of Typhaines, *fials et Men amez*, conditioned that they disavow the Abbot of Typhaines as their seigneur, take the Count de Nevers in his stead, and engage to pay into the Royal Treasury the sum of two thousand marks of silver, fine.

Anselm read the charter, thrust it aside with disgust and contempt, and then launching an angry scowl at the statesman, hastily quitted the apartment and hurried out of the palace, followed by the Bishop of Chalons as full of indignation as the holy father himselfi

CHAPTER XX.

THE two ecclesiastics exchanged not one word as they
traversed the streets of Paris. Each man, folly taken up
with his own ponderings, had enough to think about without breaking the silence between them. Each, according
to his special temper and position in the world, gave free
course to his reflections, and though the subject was one
of interest in common to both, the nature of their thoughts
was as different as the nature of their personal identity.

Master Guillaume did not seem to be very much surprised ; but the Abbot of Typhaines was deeply disgusted.
In King Louis of France's conduct he could see nothing
but a most horrible denial of justice, and the minister's was
pure and simple a scandal to the Church and the Catholic
religion itself. According to Master Anselm, all policy, of
what kind soever, that proved indifferent or hostile to the
interests of the clergy was worldly, reprobate, and satanic,
and situated as he was, attacked, and in some sort plundered over again, and that by an abbot like himself, by the
head of the most illustrious community in the kingdom, he
could hardly get rid of his feelings of horror and disgust.
It may be that at the present day, a man of his cloth and
of his opinions would, under similar circumstances, attract
but small sympathy; but it should not be overlooked that,
in the distant age at which our history transpired, the
bishop's precedence was equal to that of any feudal noble;
no doubt their claims were not in all cases as clear as

those of the conquerors, though they might well, and without too great a stretch of the imagination, claim to be rulers far more beneficent—and far less oppressive.

The clergy of the time were almost as proud of their learning as they were of their celestial consecration, and they despised the power of the laity as much as they dreaded it. Hence, Anselm could discover nothing less than barbarian injustice and detestable spoliation in the king's policy, and his minister's too.

He was irritated and indignant, but not depressed. Convinced of the justice of his cause, and fully resolved not to yield one inch of his lawful rights, in his single person he bade defiance to King Louis, even should he go £o far as to combine with his own regal force all the power of his feudatories to oppress him. His only difficulty appeared to consist in the choice of means for the occasion; it was important to act speedily, and every moment that should be lost for him, would be improved by his adversaries to their great advantage. In fact, he was not very thoroughly acquainted with the temper and disposition of certain great dignitaries, and so, unprepared to judge on the subject or count on their help. He had heard that the Bishop of Amiens, and he of Noyon had favored the cause of the burgesses, and that the communes that had been got up in their episcopal cities had been instituted with their consent and avowal. How could he know that other members of the prelacy of the Gauls, won over by such examples, would not turn a cold ear, or make open opposition to his efforts to reduce his insurgent peasantry to duty again ?

The two priests, then, being safe returned to Master Guillaume's lodgings in the canonial mansion, were free to converse and compare opinions without restraint, and Anselm freely opened out his whole heart to his friend;

23

demanding, too, such counsels as his wisdom and talents might suggest for the promptest conclusion of so difficult an affair.

While they were talking, Messire Jean de Berniot entered the apartment. The worthy knight had followed the king to a certain distance from Paris. In the palace hall he had met some of his old acquaintances among the barons there; and his fondness for chatting and scheming had decided him to get into his saddle, and, like others, go forth to see what would become of the expedition. He had quite made up his mind to have no hand in it, however, because as he was proposing to travel through the lands of the Count of Chartres, and he being himself a vassal of Nivernais, the lord king had no right to claim his aid and services. He had come back, after quitting the cavalcade, to inform his friends concerning their affairs, as far as he had gathered important information from various sources.

" You are at a bad pass, holy father," said he to the Abbot of Typhaines, and I have things to tell you that, 'pon my faith, have afflicted me not a little."

"Tell us at once," said the bishop. "You are well known for a careful, prudent person, Messire Jean, and you are better prepared to speak sensibly on the subject than any other person whatever; not to say that my venerable brother's learning is in any absolute need of any laical support; for I too have some claims in common with the lord Abbot! But—in fine—speak 1"

"I have seen the Nivernais envoys." •

"What! you have seen them; the miscreants?" cried the bishop, lifting his arms up in signification of the horror.

" I have both seen and conversed with them. I have seen the Sieur de Garlande too; in short, taking all that together with what I learned from my old companions, I am quite up to the level of the whole current of your business."

" Impart what you know then."

"I have to inform you that the Nivernais and Typhaines men, more fortunate than Monseigneur Abbot here, did not come to Paris empty handed; and to double their good luck, they came in at the very nick of time too, for the king happened to be greatly in want of funds just at that very moment."

" He is very often in that very case," said Bishop Guillaume; " bah 1"

" With such a recommendation as that," pursued Messire de Berniot, " they had no occasion, neither party, to display any great power of oratory; their rights were at once found to be sound and good and beyond all dispute; in fact, they were promised a charter on the spot; and so, they are about to start for home in the highest spirits."

" They haven't got as far as they think for," said Guillaume boldly.

The Abbot proffered no remark. He sat silent, his hands crossed on his bosom; his gray eyebrows all in a frown, with lips close drawn, and his whole pose indicative of inexpugnable determination.

" Say, my son," at last he spoke in low and gentle accents, " do you know the names of those same envoys ?"

" There are four burghers of them; hard looking cases too, they are; they seem to have a perfectly good understanding together, just like so many thieves at a village fair. The oldest one, the man who seems to be chief in authority, is named Eudes, an old fox; a brewer, I believe, and who has been, by your Typhaines-folk, elected as one of their jurats—wardens, or consuls, or peers—for the fact is I know not what titles that low scum delight in for their head men."

" Simon is not among them; you did not hear his name
mentioned ?"

"No, I am certain of that," replied the chevalier, "for
they told me all about the mission; that fellow Simon stayed
behind at the borough; which, by all accounts, will be in
the course of a few weeks thoroughly fortified just like any
real city. Those cheats of burgesses, from all appearances,
are as rich as Jews, and they are about to put up mansions
such as few of us poor gentlemen could ever dream of
indulging ourselves with. To eschew the services of the
abbey, they talk too of erecting a vast parish church, far
more splendid than your own."

" What impious creatures 1" cried the bishop.

"In fine," pursued Messire Jean, "it seems that the
borough of Typhaines is hard at work: walls, houses,
fortifications, and embellishments of all sorts are going up;
and in consequence of the laws those rascals have enacted,
the population is increasing at a great rate, and it will be
still greater as soon as King Louis completely gets the
burgh under his royal protection, and the Count de Nevers,
their suzerain, has fully concluded to protect and defend
them against all and every their enemies."

" Well then, well then," piously exclaimed Bishop Guillaume, " no more haggling ! It is not worth while. Your
cause is the cause of the whole Catholic Church, and the
Church must arm in your behalf. What, I pray, would
become of us all, should our serfs and burghers henceforth
forever break out in rebellion against our authority, and
strike bargains with princes who have no more conscience
than my shoe ? What would become of good manners and
public decency in case the lower orders should begin to
pay regard to the world here below, instead of employing
themselves, as they ought to do, in the pursuit of that

better part that leads to heaven at last ? Very well, then, all we have to do is to convene a council."

What, a conncil!" said Messire de Berniot; "truly that is a serious question, in times like these, when every man is busy in looking after his own private affairs. Do you think you could ?"

" I agree with the Lord Bishop of Chalons," said the Abbot. " Courage and firm determination, with Heaven's blessing, can do anything—everything. Let us seek for succor at the hands of our brothers of the Church : Heaven will not, nor cannot, give up her pontiffs and leave them helpless in the hands of such rebellious children of wrath. No; be sure of that. I shall yet see that villain Simon the most execrable of men; I shall see Lis friends, his supporters, his clique—yes, all the peasants and serfs in Typhaines crawling beneath my abbatial cross! They, building houses ! they raising ramparts ! they glorying in their wealth and their obstinacy! Let them glory 1 but believe me, with their own hands, yes, with their own hands they shall be forced to undo all they are doing this day, and so save, if possible, their poor souls from the eternity of torture they so richly deserve by their rebellion against Holy Church 1"

The light of the Abbot's eyes, that shone with the savage splendor of his enthusiasm, struck the chevalier and even the bishop with a feeling of awe. They both alike, deeply convinced as they were of Anselm's extraordinary sanctity, felt that he had read and interpreted the book of the future, in the very words he had just spoken; and the thought gave them redoubled energy for the accomplishment of the difficult task before them.

Indeed, the task was not an easy one; so, at least, it seemed. In those times, though councils were plenty enough and frequent enough, still it was not the fashion to

convene them for occasions merely special or personal, like
this of Abbot Anselm's. Where questions turned upon
some article of faith, some discussion on the Trinity, or
where some Doctor was to be denounced, nothing whatever
could be simpler than to convene a council; but the idea
of going into a quarrel with the King of France and one
of the most powerful of all his vassals, merely out of regard
for the interests of an abbot, was a thing as yet unheard
of. In spite of all this, the part assumed by our three
allies was well taken, and their resolution to go ahead was
too well settled to be shaken by anything. Their thoughts
then, were turned to the catalogue of such prelates as they
could best trust, and they did, in fact, go over the whole
list of the eminent clergymen of the Gauls. As soon as
they had concluded on the plan, they went forth and opened
their campaign by calling on influential personages, such
as the canons, abbots, doctors, and monks, deemed likeliest
to contribute to the success of their designs.

And so, we find the beginnings of the poor Typhaines
commune threatened with the terriblest attack possible for
those days of old. Just when the envoys were returning
in triumph to their rising town; at the very time Eudes, on
horseback, with the rest of the mandatories, was proceeding
up the High street, towards the commune council hall,
followed by the admiring mob, a horrible tempest began
to rumble in the far distance and roll its awful storm
clouds towards the vain and haughty town of Typhaines.
With that air of importance that, at his day and ever
since his day, was and is the distinctive characteristic of a
vain magistrate on public occasions, Eudes was proceeding,
accompanied by his colleagues of the embassy, at a solemn
and dignified pace, along the great thoroughfare. Their
very faces showed how cheerful they were over the successful accomplishment of their mission, and though they bad

not uttered a word as to the result, everybody, men, women, and children, were saying : [11] How fortunate 1 how ready the King of France was to octroy his charter! how delighted he was to hear of what his feal and well beloved people of Typhaines were thinking of doing; how his wife and the two sweet boys had eagerly insisted on signing their several names to the charter; and how the noble king, bold and debonaire as he was, stood ready to march at the head of all his chivalry to see justice done for the dear borough of Typhaines; borough indeed I—City of Typhaines !"

Eudes and the rest of the deputies, meanwhile, had been conducted to the council chamber we are already acquainted with as the place where we were lookers on at the time of Monseigneur Philippe's trial for his life.

Simon was acting as chairman. Payen, with his arm still in a scarf, and Antoine and Jacques were seated with him at the council table.

[41] What news bring ye hither from the good city of Paris, my brethren ?" said Simon. [14] Did you find the lord king debonair ? Did he kindly receive the presents you bore—did the Nivernais men behave with all honor, and frankly as they ought ?"

[44]All was for the very best," responded Eudes; [44]and truth to tell, we had few difficulties to overcome. In conformity with your counsel, we took lodgings at the house of Master Gerard, the king's armorer, and a great friend of his majesty, and of yours too. Out of love to your person, he made us heartily welcome, and as we followed his advice in every particular, our success was not long to be waited for; you see that we have been absent only a week from Typhaines, and have succeeded at all points." Eudes then drew King Louis' charter from his bosom, laid it on the table; the clerk read it aloud, and everybody evinced the liveliest satisfaction.

[41] See, my brethren, how everything smiles upon onr enterprise 1 everything goes on for the best. We ought now to take very good care to prevent Monseigneur de Nevers from assuming too many liberties with our commune. Let us by no means repeat the story of the horse that a learned monk at Cambrai once told me. [4] The animal was desirous to take revenge on a stag that had insulted him ; and to come at his adversary in a fair way to pay him off, he invited the man to get on his back: the stag was killed, of course, but the man refused to get off again.'"

[44] You see," said Payen,[44] that I didn't wait for this good advice of yours; the fact is I persuaded Monseigneur de Pornes and Messire Anseau to retire from the borough and go back to their own domain, where we could find them in case of occasion for their help arising. They hearkened to what I said, and it is well for them they did so, for their men-at-arms, and they too, began to get very ugly scowls in town. Burgher-folk have nothing very good to gain by having nobles too close neighbors; the two races are hardly well suited to live together."

[44]I see," cried Eudes, [44] that it's all gone right, ever since I went away to Paris. Your new-born liberty has made you all proud and bold, and even without protectors and friends,.you dare to speak out like men. As I crossed the foss, I saw, too, that the rampart is at least three feet higher already than it was the day I started on my journey, and as I came up the street I must have seen as many as twenty new houses rising, as if by magic, under the wands of hundreds of busy and delighted workmen! By the Lord, I never dreamed of a success so speedy as ours has proved to be. I assure you, I counted on seeing a good many weeks, nay, months of battle and strife, and the only security I had of dying a freeman, was that I was determined not to outlive our defeat. But how is this ? You

all listen to what I have to say, and yet not a man of you comes forward to take me by the hand, and assure me he looks on the situation with just the same confidence and joy that I do—what does it mean ? "

" You may be in the right—you are in the right, no doubt," said Payen, with a very solemn gaze as he looked on Eudes' visage, all lighted up with the glad prospects before him; " we here are ingrates almost, not to rejoice forever in such successes as you tell of. But you are under a mistake, Eudes, if you think we have such solid grounds of happiness. To make yourself really acquainted with the situation all you have to do is, to look at Simon there, and then you may guess at part of the truth at least."

As the blacksmith was speaking, Damerones' father quitted his seat and with an impatient gesture, turning his back on the company, strode to a narrow window in the council, chamber, evidently to conceal his features from his surrounding friends ; but Eudes had already remarked how pale and thin he looked—and now saw great rolling tears bedewing the dark'visage of his old friend.

" What is the matter ?" he asked.

Both Antoine and Jacques responded by a pantomime of gestures that seemed to mean sympathy or compassion for the cloth-merchant's distress. As for Payen, he merely leaned against the chamber wall in silence. After a few moments of utter stillness Simon exclaimed—

"Yes I our power is but a shadow ; our liberty a vain show—and while our good men are doing nothing day and night but shouting victory 1 no more lords! no more monks to obey I we here, who are obliged to be wise for their sakes, we know full well that we are constrained, enslaved, down-trodden, and insulted by a miserable power, which in one single moment of time can be started forth as the accursed mistress of all we have and hoped for. Thank fate, Eudes, that spared you the sight of our first deep humiliation."

"Though," said the consul, "my eyes did not see it, I will resent it, as much as you can. I, like yourself, am one of the leaders of the commune, and I have a right to know all that interests it. Speak otit, then, I will hearken—and I am no girl to break down for a single mischance, no matter what it may be; speak."

" Tell him all about it," said Simon, throwing himself into his seat again—"tell him the whole story." The cloth merchant spread out his arms on the council table, bowed down, and hid his head between them, and sobbed aloud with insupportable grief. So poignant was his anguish, that though its bursts had for some days been almost continual they struck a sort of terror into the hearts of the company around him, long accustomed as they had been to look upon Master Simon as one of the most resolute and indomitable of men. The people said, whisperingly, it must be a very great sorrow, an immense misfortune, a great and terrible danger thus to shake the firm soul of their chief, their counsellor, their bulwark; that spirit so highly tempered and yet so broken now!

Payen, with a degree of delicacy that his comrades, though perhaps as kindly disposed as he, yet far less nobly endowed than he, knew not of, detailed in a low tone of voice the whole story of Damerones' disappearance from home and her confinement in the dungeon of Chatel Cornouiller. Then, as far as he was able, explained the consequences of the terrible transaction; but Payen was very far from a full acquaintance with all the particulars, especially as touching Simon's part in the case.

Let any person try to conceive what must have been the feelings of the cloth merchant on finding that the devotion of his sweet Damerones, a devotion 110 less fanatical and

intense than his own private hate, had succeeded in sub-
stituting the beautiful head of his darling daughter on the
block designed for Messire Philippe's own ! What he had
felt, no tongue could tell: all ages of the world have their
passions; all have their peculiar impulses and tendencies;
all their own exaltations, and in some measure, their own
savageness; but savageism, exaltation, impetuosity, passion, all take on at different epochs different shapes, combine in different proportions, and give birth to different
ideas. To appreciate, therefore, what Simon felt, and how
he felt, one must go back on the ascending path of the long
gone centuries to study at the tombs of men who died ages,
ago. Let us refer to one, and the chief one : the consul
of the twelfth century was not the possessor of Junius
Brutus' soul; he loved his only child with a burgher's
loving heart; like a Christian; as a man does around
whose hearthstone are concentrated the home affections,
the most holy of all; and the deep-laid anguish that must
attend the final abandonment of a long-cherished longing
after revenge, would alone have sufficed to make him the
unhappiest of men ; for certainly he could not but hesitate
between his hoped for vengeance on Monseigneur Philippe
and the life of his child. But the events that had followed
Damerones' brave attempt, had also added to the consul's
grief and despair, for they came on like a host to assail every
fond interest of his heart, which, thus it appears, had been
touched at every its most sensitive point.

Canon Norbert having ascertained from the young girl
herself that she was willing to surrender as prisoner to the
lady of Cornouiller Castle, he at once consented to that
bizarre proposal. His impetuous and very singular temper
fitted him peculiarly to comprehend, to consent to, and to
promote them—and besides, lie was conscious that at any
moment his influence and his power were liable to wreck

in the inexpugnable will of the cloth merchant; in such a
case, he would be compelled to witness the death of the
crusader. He, therefore, had facilitated the evasion of
Damerones, and had even given her a slip of parchment
on which he had briefly, but peremptorily, traced a request,
or rather an order, to Mahaut, to treat the captive with all
becoming tenderness.

Bat, scarcely had Simon's daughter explained to the
chatelaine the whole of Monseigneur Philippe's danger, as
well as her own position in the affair, when the lady,
whether forgetful or disdainful of the canon's orders, commanded Damerones to be cast into the tower dungeon ; and
at once despatched, as we have already seen, a man-at-arms
to advertise him on how slemler a thread his child's life
was suspended—and she was in no jesting mood either;
never was reality more real: every drop of the burgber-
maiden's blood was not worth a single hair of Messire
Philippe's head, in her estimation at least. Beauty, goodness, devotion could not save her should Philippe be held
in peril of death. A few minutes of converse with the
Cornouiller man-at-arms was enough to make that quite
clear to Norbert; for Mahaut was his own penitent, and he
was fully aware of what that haughty spirit of hers might
impel her to do. As to the Typhaines consul, his well-
known hatred of the noble classes made it sure that they
too would show him no mercy. Yet, though it was so
hard for him to give way in either direction, he at last
yielded to much persuasion so far as to enter upon negotiations that ended in a full surcease for both Philippe and
Damerones. They both, one in the chatelaine's dungeon,
and the other in the abbey gaol, now found their existence
prolonged, but with the certain assurance that their lives
depended on the greater or less firmness and impassibility
of the boldest and gloomiest of the whole rebel horde.

Bat Simon, though carrying on negotiations with ^fahaut, flattered himself that he might even yet rescue his child without surrendering the captive crusader.

One dark night, guided through by-paths, he led a band of brave and devoted burghers to the very foot of the rock of Cornouiller, hoping to carry the donjon by surprise, deliver his daughter, and at the same time carry off the Lady Mahaut into Philippe's prison. Had he succeeded, sure it is that they would have had a sanguinary wedding-day ; but Simon's rage was redoubled when on raising his eyes to the donjon above him he saw that he was striving against an adversary as clear sighted as himself. The towers stood garnished with sentinels: his approach had been discovered; torches were flaming at every aperture in the walls: so that to give the assault would be mere madness. His hurried retreat was made with an accompaniment of hootings and invectives, and some of the enormous stones projected by the castle mangonels reached a few men among his rear-guard. The next day, the better to convince the consul that it was useless to try either force or cunning on the. lady of the chatel, fifty men-at-arms 6allied forth at daybreak to ravage and destroy the plantations and country houses of the Typhaines peasantry and burgesses. A large crowd of Cornouiller serfs followed in the train of the warriors, so that from the top of their ramparts and rising mansions the communeers looked out deploringly over their wide-spread fertile plain, where clouds of smoke gave assurance of the wide-spread desolation that followed in the track of that remorseless raid, which indeed came up within bow-shot of the walls. The people made a sortie, but were routed and driven back into the town by the cavalry ; after which exploit the men-at-arms repaired to the abbey on the rocky hill-top, where the monks wel-

24

corned them, cross and banner in hand, and saluted them
as defenders of God and Holy Church alike.

The thing that most astonished the consuls in this affcfir
was the numerous garrison at Cornouiller, and the quantity
of men-at-arms sent forth from the chatel to make the attack. A letter from the Maid of the Chatel soon told them
the secret. She had set on foot negotiation for the for-
mation of a league with fourteen of the surrounding seigneurs, who were willing to brave the Count de Nevers,
their suzerain, declare war to the death against the commune, and maintain Mahaut's quarrel with them.

CHAPTER XXI.

THE confederate raid had taken place in the morning of the day that brought Eudes back to Typhaines, from the mission to Paris; and although there had been no attack on the town walls, and the enemy had satisfied themselves with ravaging the whole neighborhood, it was clear that the lords of the league would not be content to let the matter stop just there. Mahaut's letter, too, declared the negotiations at an end, in consequence of Simon's night-attempt on her castle ; and she further declared that, provided Simon would not surrender his captive within eight days after the date, the charming head of his daughter should be sent to him in a box by the hands of some wretched serf, or thrown into the town from a balista.

Nor was that all; Simou's colleagues, who had for some time appeared inclined to sacrifice their animosity against the Abbot's defender to the very natural distress of their chief, now changed their minds; induced, as they were, to do so by the sight of their ruined farms and devastated fields, and by the confederation got up among the fourteen seigneurs of the region round about them. It was the unanimous opinion of the council that the malevolence and audacity of the fourteen confederates was deserving of punishment; that the commune ought to answer their defiance by a war to the death; and inasmuch as they now had a knight, ready in their hands, he should be put to death by way of reprisals—and *in terrorem.* Such was the subject of the deliberations in cabinet, and at the end of it Simon saw, with his mind's eye, the sweet rose of Typhaines lying a Corpse at his feet, as distinctly as if her bleeding form were already cast down on the ground before him.

This was the condition of affairs when Eudes returned from his journey bringing the charter, which at once restored in some small degree the usual calm to their troubled spirits; and as Eudes had not been an eye-witness to the terrible operations of the raiders, and had no share in the late violent agitations, and, moreover, being particularly devoted to his friend Simon, he joined Payen to oppose the ferocious longings of Antoine and Jacques. He was a man distinguished for good sense and gentleness; not sanguinary, and of a pacific disposition. Payen, who was a soldierly man, though a turbulent, was yet the most loyal of men: he desired the death of Monseigneur Philippe as much as any one of them, but he was still more anxious about the safety of Damerones, to save whose life he would, no doubt, have drawn his sword to rescue even that of the imprisoned crusader. But his remonstrances, though he pressed them through the entire morning, had all proved fruitless; he had two of the consuls against him, and Simon, who was in a state of stupor, had not a word to say in the argument. The advent of Eudes was, therefore, a fortunate incident.

Payen was earnestly engaged in relating, in a low tone, to Eudes, the story of the late events as Norbert entered the hall. Simon, still taken up with his dreadful grief and bathed in tears, took no notice of the priest's arrival, but when the canon lifted up his voice he shivered, ceased from weeping, and yet did not make any change in his attitude.

So, you are come together again, ye limbs of Satan ; ye dealers in treason, ye vipers athirst for gore! What new project is to come forth of your cabal ? How is it ?

and have you at last made up your minds, once for all, to offer your children as a sacrifice to your impious rage f Is the bold knight whom you hold in captivity to die at once ? Speak out! You have but one hour more; and as to the lady of Cornouiller, if you don't know who and what she is, I know her, and that right well. She will keep her word with you, and without any fail Damerones must die."

The consuls sat in silence, with downcast eyes, and afraid to decide the dread question.

Norbert resumed in the same solemn and scornful tone—

" Follow out your instincts. There is no creature whatever but must give way to their preponderant power. Show clearly forth to the world what you really are ! Christians? then spare blood-shedding! Children of Satan ? then pour it out in torrents! Act out your parts, and so display your real nature. But what good will you get by making a couple of martyrs more, to join the heavenly hosts above you ? The glad heavens shall open their shining gates to let them in, with hallelujahs and crowns and blessings and praises—but you—you, hell will pay the whole load of its heaped-up debt to you in disaster untellable, catastrophes leading to no end but there 1 No sooner shall the knight and the maiden yield up their last sighs than tempests and storms and whirlwinds of disaster and opprobrium shall rush on you from every quarter of the heavens.

11 What '8 the use of that big parchment signed and sealed with the hand and seal of the king ? Oh ho 1 Master Eudes 1 Is it you I see there ? So, you've come back and brought this rag, have you ? Why 1 do my eyes read aright ? Has that glorious King, Louis the Sixth of France, stained his fame by receiving you to his protection ? And so, then, you are all right, are you ? you feel all safe now, eh ! Poor blind creatures that you are ! You are henceforth free to

24*

work your will—and trample justice into the dust as long as you live!"

" The devil 1" shouted Payen, and he struck the table hard with his fist—" The devil! for he is the one we ought to invoke, I suppose, as you have handed us all over to him! I tell you these compliments and fine-sugared words of yonrs only scorch my ears ! I do most certainly respect and venerate you, holy father—no Christian can do other than that, for you are fully deserving of as much, and more; but I begin to grow less and less contented with your invectives. Heh! when a man wants to get something out of another, even an obstinate one, it is wisest to act not as you act As for myself, I confess I am just of your way of thinking about this affair, and here Eudes tells me he agrees with me too—we must let the knight go—we must do that Let us exchange him for Damerones, and by so doing compensate in some sort our friend Simon for his great services to the commune: We all know how hard it is to restore liberty to our enemy, and that the wrongs committed on us this morning ought to be avenged, but nobody knows what a day may bring forth. Messire Philippe, if set at liberty to-day, may possibly fall into our hands again to-morrow, and then, let him look out: his captivity won't be a long one. Come, let us decide at once and let the prisoner go."

Norbert, without deigning to answer the blacksmith's remarks upon his behavior, vigorously advocated his conclusion, and Eudes too made an argument against the very decided objection urged by Antoine and Jacques. Those two burghers cared very little about Damerones. They were both old men, both bent down with a weight of years, rich and childless; they had each lost by the morning raid a farm and their entire crops, and were greatly exasperated. The life of one chevalier and a girl seemed to them not

too much as an offset against all their sheaves and vineyards now to be replaced at heavy cost. Had their colleague the cloth merchant's thundering tone, that never fell
ineffectually on their ears, only sounded in behalf of mercy,
it is highly probable it would have won them over at once;
but Simon never stirred; he did not even raise his head
from where it was buried between his arms on the council
table ; and he took no part whatever in that animated discussion. He was too much agonized on account of Damerones and too indignant at the morning outrage of the
Cornouiller men to be willing to take an active part on the
occasion. He knew not how to choose. Whether out of
indecision, or whether it was punctilio, he had made up his
mind to wait for the action of the council, neither dictating
nor advising. His soul was all as if one throb, every sense
awake and startled; and with bated breath he followed
every phase of the discussion, sometimes deeming his
daughter must become the victim, and sometimes ready to
weep over his defeated hopes of vengeance.

Yet, and we have seen it was so, the soul of the burgher
of the twelfth century was a barbarian's soul! it was no
soul of an ancient Roman; and his child's safety was more
to him than any other earthly consideration. He was rejoiced then to hear Jacques, overcome by Eudes' arguments
and Payen's impetuosity, as well as the dark mystic denun-
ciations of the canon, rise to his feet and cry out—

" Yery well, then I since it must be so let the knight be
set at liberty—but before he goes he shall swear that he
will not bear arms against us. I know what he is, and
Payen knows it quite as well as I do, for he has felt that
vigorous hand. We have enemies enough on hand, without him to help them."

After a few words from Eudes the clerk left the hall, and
soon returned followed by the crusader. Master Simon

had now risen, and appeared to have recovered his usual gravity and composure, and as he stood there in his scarlet robe he looked on the scene before him—the severest and the most determined man in the whole assembly.

As to Norbert, all we have to say is that his face was illuminated as with a light-beam of the sublimest joy.

Monseigneur Philippe, now nearly recovered of his wounds, but somewhat broken down by his severe captivity, bent his knee to Norbert, who gave him the benediction, and then, before the consuls had octroyed the privilege of speaking, he threw himself carelessly on to a stool, and looking with inquisitive eyes on the people he exclaimed:—

" Ah well, how is it now ? are you going to put an end to the affair once for all ? No doubt the devotion of the poor burgher girl has won her a blessed paradise in heaven! and now you are about to butcher me too 1 Am I right ?"

" No, you are not right, Monseigneur," said Endes; " we have decided to exchange you for Master Simon's daughter."

⁴¹ On your Christian faith ? Are you telling me the truth now ?"

" Yery seriously—the truth. I tell you we are about to exchange you for Master Simon's child; but before you quit your lodging in Typhaines we expect from your courtesy an oath at least."

¹¹ An oath! and what oath I beg, sir bnrgher ?"

" An oath to take no part in any expedition against us— to enter into no league with our enemies, and further, to retire quietly to some place not less than ten leagues away from the walls of Typhaines."

¹¹ You can't think of such a thing," responded Monseigneur, with contempt. "If you want me to give you pro-

mises of some kind, ask one that I can keep. I am the affianced husband of the Lady of Cornouiller, and you hardly can suppose me such a base poltroon as to break my pledged word to her 1 and as she is at war with you, of course I must go on waging it on her behalf; of course I must. Besides all that, you have kept me in your dungeon here, and if I should fail to make you repent of that I would be a dishonored knight. Be reasonable—don't force me to take a false oath."

" He's in the right there," said Payen. " What you are asking of him is all nonsense—and I, yes I, though he treated me bad at the assault on the abbey, shouldn't be sorry to have a chance at him again in a fair held, where I would like to pay him back some of the hard knocks he gave me."

" Quite at your service, my lad!" resumed the knight with a smile ; " and blacksmith though you be, and nothing but a blacksmith, I see you have some very good notions as to what honor means."

Simon now rose to his feet and stepped up close to the chevalier; his eyes like burning coals, his fists and his lips and his teeth all hard clenched, as if he could hardly restrain his passionate desire to take him by the throat and slay him as he stood; with a half strangled voice said—

11 Go then ! go, since they say you must. You, no doubt of it, are no knight—no—you are an accursed sorcerer, a magician, an excommunicate wretch that has cast a hell charm on my poor idiot child I Go—go !"

11 Master Simon," interrupted Philippe, "is it customary with such as you to insult a prisoner? I am a better Christian than you are."

" Begone !" said the consul, grinding his teeth. " Go away, and since you will do so, make war on us—try to burn down our dwellings—assassinate us—all of us—and continue to carry on the infamous trade of your forefathers, every soul of them robbers and villains, a fit prey for Satan himself I"

"S'death!" said the knight, "thou liest, thou knave! Wretched serf, dost thou think the fear of death can make me quietly submit to such insults ?"

" No violence here, sir, tiger's whelp that you are ! I will not have your blood now, for that would be to shed my own unhappy daughter's; but know, and know well and truly, why I hate you, and why your death is both sure and near. I am a son of that unhappy warden of Cornehaut who was traitorously slain by your father; I am the nephew of the priest who was put to death by that same sacrilegious hand, and while I live I will give you neither rest nor truce I"

" How you talk!" said Philippe, with a shrug of contempt—and he took his seat again on the wooden stool.

"Am I free, my masters!" said he, "or are you making game of me ? That's all I wish to know. As for the resentment of a cloth merchant, that's a matter of perfect indifference."

The knight's very real indifference was not participated by the rest of the assembly. Norbert himself, who fully understood the strength of Simon's character, had been greatly moved by the agitating incidents of the past hour, and Simon's revelation of the causes of his unalterable hate clothed him, in some sort, even in the good saint's eyes, with a sort of excuse for all his violence, past and to come. The other burghers still felt most deeply the heavy griefs of their colleague, and fixing their eyes on him stood, expecting every instant to see him strike the knight dead with his heavy dagger, in a transport of blinding fury. But nothing of the kind occurred. Simon drew his hand across his brow to clear away the great drops of perspiration, and then, as if he had instantly recovered complete

possession of his presence of mind, coldly inquired of his
colleagues whether they had thought of the measures
proper to be taken in effecting the exchange of the prisoners : the affair, it is true, was not brought to a close by
their mere consent to exchange, for a courier must be at
once despatched to the Maiden of Cornouiller to make
known the conclusion of the discussion in council, and the
choice of a messenger was a difficult one. Who among
the burghers would dare to go out and affront the maraud-
ing bands, still doubtless in the field, and risk his neck over
and over again before he could reach the chatel on the rock
and the redoubtable chatelaine ? For an expedition a brave
man merely was not enough; what was wanted was a person not brave merely, but adroit, keen, subtle, and well
qualified to negotiate and to settle the terms of the exchange.
Luckily for all parties the question was promptly resolved;
for Norbert offered to go at once to Cornouiller; and it
was a very fortunate thing too, as probably he was the
only individual in the town that could take on him such a
commission as that. The truth is, that in all quarrels
whatever between the new communes and the nobles and
monks, it was too much the custom to treat all burghers as
seditious and rebellious folk and not as real belligerents.
Even after the settling of that point, there was yet another,
and that was to determine the exact method of carrying
out the convention, or, at least, to lay the programme before the lady chatelaine. It was a delicate and difficult
point, for on both sides it was supposed that the adversary
would not scruple to seize any chance whatever to get back
its hostage and keep fast hold of its prisoner as well. All
danger of that sort must be provided against.

After many *pros* and *com*, Payen proposed that Mahaut
should agree to a meeting, to be held next day, in an
open field half way between the tower and the castle.

The country there was a wide plain easily to be overlooked to a distance. Through the plain ran the little river that we have seen flowing beneath the bridge at the foot of the abbey-hill; and Payen proposed that each party, consisting of twelve men on horseback, not including the prisoners (on both sides), should advance to the banks of the stream, over which a bridge made of two planks only was to be thrown. He further proposed a stipulation, that neither arrows nor crossbows nor bolts should be brought on the ground by either party. As monseigneur, if set at liberty, would increase his side by the addition of one man, it must be further agreed that no horse should be led up for his use, but he might mount one belonging to any one of the men-at-arms. After the discussion and settlement of all these questions, which the old canon pronounced quite reasonable and proper, Philippe was led back to his dungeon with hopes of staying there only one more night, and the old canon, grasping his long staff, quitted the building and set off on the road to Cornouiller Castle again.

The appearance of a country where war has just left its blood-stained track is far otherwise sinister looking than any natural landscape, however sombre and awful. In this respect man's superiority over nature is terrible indeed: he creates scenes more horrible than precipice or deep and dark abyss, or bellowing and foaming cataract, or even a snow-covered desert, where the eye discerns in the frozen distance no living thing save a flight of famished crows struggling with flapping wing to win their way against the driving gale ! Such scenes are less terrible to the beholder than the most fertile lands, overrun by an army with fire and sword and remorseless revenge. Here, through the whole territory of Typhaines, he could find nothing but blackened ruins and trampled plantations. A few short hours had sufficed to destroy the labor of many years; the cabins were burned or torn to pieces; trees blackened with flame, their foliage all gone, seemed to lift up their wild, wierd, and naked branches as if imploring for pity—the shrubs all torn up by the roots and the vines broken down and their stakes all destroyed. Here and there a dead body or a mutilated limb might be met with among the general desolation, to show how cruel is war in its rage. As Norbert moved onward amidst these sickening sights, he could not find it in his heart not to turn aside from the path again and again to seek out some wounded or suffering serf, who might admit of having his wound dressed, or, at least be prepared through that good priest's ministry for his last long journey; he did, indeed, succeed in giving relief to more thau one poor fellow-mortal crushed and bruised under his fallen roof or beams, and who were still alive when he found them. But remembering that should he not reach the chatel in time, Mahaut was the woman to keep her word and put Damerones to death agreeably to her declared purpose, he sighed, as he felt constrained to choose between two such duties, and made up his mind, once for all, not to stop again for any cause, whatever its urgency might be; and so he went on at a great pace, his long staff in hand.

He at length crossed the Typhaines frontier and now was walking fast on the lands of Cornouiller, when he soon met with a party of men-at-arms headed by one of Mahaut's fourteen allies, who recognized him and greeting him reverently furnished him with a horse, by which means he soon afterwards reached Madame Mahaut's towers. As the afternoon was growing late, and his uneasiness on the score of Damerones was excessive, he had procnred from the commander of the party a man and horse, to be despatched with all speed to announce his approach to the chatel. It was perhaps no useless precaution, for night

25

was already down on the world around, as the canon passed
in through the outer gate, and went up to the great castle
hall.

It was the same apartment where we first saw the Lady
Mahaut surrounded by her women, and her noble vassals
as they were then listening with compunction to the pious
exhortations and counsels of the venerable priest and missionary from Treves, all saintly as he was. But the aspect
of the place was now greatly changed: on the immense hall
table preparations for supper had been completed; and at
the end of the hall Madame Mahaut was seated in the place
of honor, at the head of the feast, her servants all standing
duly arranged behind the seigneural chair. Order had
not yet been given them to go to the lower end of the table
and take their seats there. The fourteen seigneurs were
seated nearer to Mahaut according to their several ages,
the oldest being nearest the place of honor. Two elderly
gentlemen with long white beards sat one on each side
and neit to the noble maiden; the rest of the hall was
filled with armed vassals and vassal nobles, all free to partake of the lady's hospitable fare which was far more
abounding than elegant.

'Norbert's first glance at his fair penitent convinced him
she was not just then in a mood so humble and tender-
hearted as he had seen on other occasions. She, nevertheless, arose as he approached her throne, and kneeled
down, her hands joined and somewhat raised as he advanced to pronounce the benediction, and that ceremony
over, resumed her seat and pointed to a place for the holy
canon near her own.

" You are come back to my house, holy father," said she,
" and they tell me you bring good news with you. Can I
really count on Monseigneur Philippe's speedy arrival
here ?"

"Without the least doubt, my daughter," responded the canon, " you will see your affianced husband to-morrow; that is to say, if you but accept the conditions of exchange that I am charged to lay before you."

" I agree to them already," said she, " though it is a galling thing for a noble lady, as I am, to treat on terms of equality with a band of insurgent serfs. But you, father, who are a prudent man, tell me, I prithee, what I am to think of that mad creature of a girl you sent here as a hostage ?"

Madame Mahaut fixed a scrutinizing gaze on old Norbert's face, and as he made no reply, nor even seemed to understand her question, she went on :—

"Yes, father, what am I to think of that burgher-girl who, without compulsion of any kind, and entirely alone, passed my portcullis, though her father and his friends are bent on the execution to death of a gentleman to whom I am betrothed ? There must doubtless be some mystery in the matter that it behooves me to know, and I cannot, so it seems to me, do better than inquire of your holiness, who art the protector of my hostnge."

" Your hostage!" said Norbert; " did I send the maiden to you as a hostage ? I thought I sent her as a sister, rather, and I begged you to treat her with the kindness and respect due to virtue, as well as to common charity. What did you do with my orders ?"

" At Chatel Cornouiller," replied Mahaut, " I alone have a right to utter such a word as that; and I alone give orders here! and as long as my palm remains unclasped by a husband's hand, never will I receive orders from any person. Orders ? Indeed! My prisoner is in the donjon prison ; that's her proper place."

" Proud girl !" cried Norbert, in a rnge, " 111 break you like a reed—I '11 make you feel the sting of the Lord 1"

When these words of the priest were heard, a murmur ran through the whole crowded apartment, among the gentlemen assembled there, and one of the oldest of the nobles, whose seat was next to the lady's, cried—

"Upon my soul, these clergy-folk are growing Yery insolent! I 've seen the time when, for a lesser thing than that, a monk would have been tossed from the top of the rampart into the foss below." But old Norbert, who never was known to quail in the presence of a burgher man, was equally immovable in the palaces of the nobles, and so, going on with his apostrophe in the same supreme vein—

" Down on your knees, Mahaut," cried he, "confess your sin, and order the saintly maiden to be instantly withdrawn from your dungeon."

Mahaut did not quit her great lordly scat, but turning with a cold smile on the old seigneur who had so warmly given words to his indignation, she said: "Monseigneur, we must make sonic allowance to the exceeding worth of this holy personage; he always docs everything for the best, and if lie has made a mistake here let God be his judge—not we ourselves; and you, my men," turning to her vassals, "go you and bring the prisoner hither, since the canon appears dissatisfied with the hospitalities she has received at our hands. Possibly by bringing her face to face with him we shall be able the better to guess the motives for her strange behavior."

" In the behavior of Damerones, there's nothing strange, nothing whatever, nor did I ever refuse to tell yon everything about her, that I could declare without, violating secrets of the confessional. That young woman is a saint, and I have sealed her beforehand, though she knows nothing on the subject as yet, to become one of the lambs of the Saviour's flock. She this very day saves the life of

Monseigneur de Cornehaut, and by that good action has redeemed her own soul."

" Don't you think she will lose it, the rather ?" ironically inquired Mahaut. "I don't know much, or rather I don't kuow anything at all about the mad actions that follow in the train of a guilty passion ; but I have heard troubadours tell that they are many and wholly unbounded: the thing people call love, and which is accursed of God, may possibly inspire the hearts of such poor wretches with what may look like courage; and in the olden time such things even have been seen as women, utterly forgetful of the modest reserve appropriate to their sex and their low birth, as even to nurse hopes the most extravagant and insensate. I do not make these remarks for the purpose of accusing your Damerones, as you call her, for I really know nothing about her, nor do I imagine that anything less than a crazy brain could have led so ugly a creature as she is to nourish a pride so supremely ridiculous. I merely lay my poor thought before you, and now I beg you to give mo your counsel."

Mahaut now ceased talking in that constrained and frigid style, and grasping the arms of her lordly chair she bent far forwards towards the canon and went on—

" Know right well, Sir Canon, that had I reason to suspect even the true loyalty of Monseigneur Philippe, it wouldn't be for long that 1 would bear the shame of being a deceived maiden ? Never would I condescend to be his dupe; and traitors of all sorts should soon learn how 1 right my own wrongs. Hah ! indeed ! think you then that I here at Cornouiller, surrounded with armed men, dreaming of nothing but assaults, plunderings, and ambushes through night and through day for the life of a man who is not yet my husband, leading a most odious existence, and all that to the sole end of being cheated, cajoled, and insulted by a miserable adventuress brought in here, into my own castle, to lay snares for my simplicity ? Oh no, my lord Canon ; do not mistake me so far as that comes to; and if the Sire de Cornehaut counts on rewarding me for all the past by such compensation, he may stay with his burgher-folk and live with them if be likes. He can swap his buckler for the compter, or exchange his sword for a shuttle for all I care about it. I can find another spouse if I choose—let him make his election—and the sooner the better."

" Young lady 1" said Norbert in reply, " I thought yon had a sounder bead, and a riper reason than now seems to be the fact. The human heart needs only be opened for the admission of a single sin, and hosts rush in to fill every chamber of it. Put away all this violence and you will see the truth more clearly. As far as I can make out your meaning, you are here accusing Monseigneur de Cornehaut of engaging in projects of a nature most insulting to his affianced bride for the sake of indulging in a culpable at-tachment to another woman I I don't know whether in the present state of your mind and heart you can put trust in me so far as to believe what I might have to say on the subject."

"Yes, father I" cried Mahaut, suddenly changing the train of her emotions, and as humble now as she was arro-gant before. "Yes, father, only tell me that Philippe is not in love with that girl, aud that there is nothing between them—only swear me that, and upon my soul, and by my hopes of heaven, I will at once go and kiss her, not as a sister, but as if she was an angel just come down from heaven."

Norbert looked down at the flag-stones of the hall floor, and after a moment of reflection was just about to speak in reply when Damerones made her appearance, led as she was by the sergeants-at-arms into the great donjon hall.

CHAPTER XXII.

WHILE the poor crusader's imprisonment in the abbey gaol at Typhaines had been by no means pleasant or gentle, the dungeon in which Damerones had been confined was not more demonaire than the knight's she loved. Though it was not so savage a place as the one at Castle de Pornes, which, rumor said, was crammed with snakes and toads, and so dreadful that the very strongest of the people shot up there were never known to survive its horrors for more than five or six days, especially when the jailers happened to forget to send in water or victuals, it was bad enough at least to inspire some feeling of terror: the dungeon had been excavated in the solid rock far below the foundation of the great keep, and was so damp and dark that, though it was August, the place was as cold as a cellar, which indeed it was. There was not a ray of light there any more than there had been in old Lienard's deep underground ceil in Typhaines, where she had met and talked with Monseigneur, and dressed his poor wounded head for him. The only furniture in the hole was the bundle of straw that for time immemorial had been the sole couch now renewed for the bruised and aching limbs of the beautiful maid of Typhaines.

Still, it is true to say that if the borough dungeon had been lighted, embellished, and magnified by the firm courage of the chevalier, the horrors of the chatelaine's were victoriously combated and overcome by the high-souled devotion and amazing love of the consul's sweet child.

Still, brought up as she was, out of the horrible darkness
of that dreadful cavern, her hands yet bound with cords,
and into the light of the room, Norbert was shocked to see
how pale she was. A body when sustained by a vigorous
soul within may struggle for long, but it will grow weaker
and weaker; its generous internal monitor in vain points
out to it the ideal palm branches of virtue in the good and
the incorruptible; it hearkens; it obeys the brave counsellor
within, but it suffers, and nothing can prevent it from suffering ; and so, and in such circumstances, Damerones came
into the hall emaciated by a week of captivity; her beautiful
hair all dishevelled ; her garments all stained and befouled,
yet her face calm, her eyes serene, and her attitude distinguished for its noble tranquillity.

To be perfectly candid in our relation of the incidents
of this history, we feel constrained to say how harshly Mahaut had treated the devoted maiden, that sweet rose of
Typhaines. When the young girl first appeared in the
presence of the chatelaine with Canon Norbert's letter in
her hand, and told her in brief and simple terms that she
had come to give herself up as hostage, for the purpose of
rescuing Monseigneur de Cornehaut from imminent execution, the first emotion of the lady was to press her to her
bosom, even though she was only a burgher-girl; but a
rapid glance at the young person, her countenance, her
figure, her whole out look, instantly gave check to the
sympathetic emotion, and Mahaut very coldly proceeded
to interrogate her about the motives for a devotion so complete and bizarre. The poor girl's reserve, her very silence
even; an indiscreet blush that overspread her features;
and the downcast looks; all these had been felt like so
many stabs to the very heart of the jealous lady of the
chatel. Finding that interrogatories brought nothing but
imperfect or evasive replies, and that everything, every

step in the daring coarse Damerones had taken, was enveloped in mystery, she at once concluded to the very worst: her excited imagination carried her far wide of the troth, and she took it into her head that the consul's child was not only in love with Messire Philippe, but that the knight himself had proved to be by no means insensible to her affection, and that the righteous indignation of an angry parent had lent additional force to the motives that instigated the communeers to desire his death. Hence her very first thought was to cast her prisoner into the tower dungeon.

Mahaut now gave herself wholly up to the wild transports of this unfounded jealousy: wild, incoherent passions, doubts, even perfect certainty of the truth of her suspicions took place by turns and completely mastered her soul. Once, during the night, she sent for Rigauld, and despatched him with orders to put the young woman to death, and then suddenly revoked the orders and dismissed the forester from her presence. At times she made up her mind to let Messire perish at the hands of the rebels, and reserve for herself the pleasure of putting Damerones to death by protracted torture. Then again she could not bear the thought of leaving her betrothed husband to perish at Typhaines. Then again she conceived the bold idea of carrying the burgh by assault, putting the whole population to the sword, carrying off Philippe to the rock of Cornouiller and executing him and his paramour at the same instant of time. Again she as suddenly dismissed all these hateful projects and melted into tears, complaining and bemoaning herself aa the unhappiest of women.

All these passionate strivings of her soul were fighting and struggling in inextricable confusion within ; she yet, on the other hand, steadily thought out and resolved with unequalled skill and perseverance a plan for the prosecution of war to the death against the rebels in the town. She had, as we already are aware, availed herself of the negotiations set on foot by Master Simon, and at the same time had effected an alliance with the surrounding nobles, whom she succeeded in convincing that the existeuce of a communal autonomy in the neighborhood was a far greater peril to their material interests than any wrath they might perhaps arouse in the heart of their proper suzerain the Count de Nevers. By means of the money in her strong boxes she had raised a body of men-at-arms, reinforced her garrison, and, by firing her old seneschal's courage, had induced him to execute a successful attack on Messire Anseau's tower, which he carried by a coup-de-main, and so, by wresting one of his best fortresses out of de Pomes' hands, forced him to quit Typhaines and hurry home to the defence of his own estates. In this way the little twelfth century chatelaine hatched out in her brain, and in her soul—both alike active and impassioned—schemes, per- haps, as fierce as if they had been born of the genius of Catherine the Second, and, in fact, her audacity was not less than that of the great empress herself, though the limited extent of her dominions so dwarfed them in the comparison.

It was the return of her feeling of tenderness that made her bend in the old canon's presence, but all that vanished at once when Damerones stopped near her fauteuil. Nor- bert did not otter a word, and all the snakes in Mahaut's heart at once began hissing again.

She stretched forth her hand toward the captive maid, and with a proud imperious voice she spoke—

" Young woman," said she, "to-morrow you are to go back to your burgh ; the noble knight, whom you desired to rescue, will owe his life to your attachment—as his affianced bride, I give you thanks for that. I am willing even to forego my righteous indignation. It is, perhaps, the custom with people of your class to not blush for what disgraces them; be that as it may—you are to go home to your people to-morrow, and my wish is that you may be happy there."

" Had you waited, lady, for my response," said the canon, "you would not have uttered those arrogant words, which, though they cover you with shame, can leave no stain on the character of Damerones for purity and virtue. I now swear, since you have asked me to take my oath, that Monseigneur never entertained a thought of love for this pure maiden, and that he never spoke to her a single word that could, by any possibility, prove offensive to you."

Mahaut blushed, and smiled too. Hers was like Juno's joy when her immortal spouse had just sanctioned her Olympian will.

" How then happens it, holy father, that you made me wait so long for so simple an answer as that? Do you really care whether I complain and weep, or no ? Philippe is a noble gentleman, and you, my child, you are fair enough to please some peasant who will offer you his hand one of these days. Fair ? indeed ! but perhaps there is pride dwelling in your heart, and you think yourself above your station ? Though it may chance to be true that Philippe is no lover of yours, is it true that you never tried to win him ?"

At the beginning of this speech of Mahaut's, Damerones seemed perfectly quiet and composed, but was evidently troubled at the question that closed it; her eyes were at first downcast, and then, as if imploring his succor, they were turned to the canon, who was by no means insensible to the mute appeal.

"What concern have you, Madame Mahaut, with the private thoughts of a burgher-girl ? To be simple and foolish is not the same thing as to be criminal. It might, one would think, be enough for you to know that Damerones has saved Monseigneur's head ; and that, without the smallest personal offeuce to you. Is not the dreadful imprisonment you have subjected her too enough to hush down any rash thoughts, if any such, indeed, did ever win their way to the secret chamber of this poor girl's heart ?"

Mahaut bit her lip, looked hard and long at the captive before her, and as if she had at last made up her mind she said—

" Well, then, be it so ! I give my assent to the exchange, and I accept the conditions. But, instead of twelve knights, I will take only eleven, for I intend to be present myself on the occasion; and now let this young person have a seat among my women at the lower end of the table: you, holy father, I pray you, take a seat beside me here, and let us no longer hinder these gallant gentlemen from beginning their supper. By my truly, after the noble deeds they wrought this morning, it is, on the whole, matter of conscience to treat their hunger and their thirst as well as we are able to do. "

The entire company greeted the address of the chatel dame with delighted looks, and for a few moments nothing was to be heard in the hall but the clattering of stools that were hurried up to the table, the clank of mail armor, swords ringing and they clashing their scabbards against each other as their owners hastened to their places at table; then the clattering of knives, the clink of the drinking-cups against each other as the knights drank healths together. Everybody was too hungry to take time to carry on conversation, which was wholly suspended for a good long quarter-hour, and young and old alike never thought of talking until they had swallowed, in rapid succession, many a brimming cup—such bumpers as would

look very wonderful at our modern tables. Still, it must
be confessed that they did put a bridle on their thirst,
knights, squires, sergeants, and all, for they knew that
at Cornouiller, though only admitted there by the necessities of the war-time, they were in the presence of
the most rigorous and severest chatelaine in the whole
canton. Not an equivocal phrase, not a coarse jest, not
even an incipient sign of intoxication, would have been
pardoned by the mistress of the manor, who, in ordinary
times, habitually refused the visits of her neighbors, for fear
of remarks ; she being resolved that her name should and
must be kept spotless and unquestioned; besides, they had
begun, at that epoch, to treat the sex with that tenderness
and respect which was afterwards carried by the chivalry
of Europe to the very greatest height. Had there chanced
to be among all that crowd of mail-clad men with hearts
as hard as their steel covering, an insolent, twenty of
the giants about him would most certainly have pitched
him out of a window on to the scarped rock below; and so
it was that Mahaut and her women were surrounded by a
company of barons who composed a far more elegant, and
far more refined society than what might be expected to
be met with in a much more advanced period of civilization.

When the conversation at length began to flow freely
among the guests, no words were heard of a nature to
wound the delicacy of the female portion of the party at
table, or even of the Holy Canon of Treves himself; but the
talk was of wars and battle-fields; subjects familiar to women
and men alike, and from the highest down to the lowest
ranks in the assemblage: for seven or eight hundred
years it was the familiar, if not really the sole topic of
conversation in the rock-built castles of France.

Monseigneur Philippe's deliverance now seemed likely
to impart a far higher energy to the military operations of

26·

the lords of the Cornouiller league. Though he was not
the eldest, and very far from the wealthiest of the confede-
rated seigneurs, it was the most natural thing in the world
for him, as Mahaut's affianced husband, to take chief command in the confederacy—and again, he was a crusader;
he was just returned from his campaigns in the Holy Land;
he had not only fought the Paynim, but had scattered them
with the edge of his good sword, and that was enough to
give him marked superiority over the other seigneurs of the
Canton, which, moreover, was a thing not to be questioned
by dny person.

In the company at table there was one individual, seated
among the knights and squires, who made himself the object of much attention by means of his excessive loquacity.
He was a huge one-eyed man, who every now and then
struck the haft of his knife heavily on the table to mark*
as it were, the intensity of his affirmations, and who was
drawing a striking picture of the joy there would be at
the taking of Typhaines by assault. That gallant and
eloquent personage was none else than Fulk the Taciturn ;
but the fact is that the happiness he felt at the thought of
soon seeing his dear master had quite upset him.

" I suppose," said he to the squire in his neighborhood,
"that you don't know what Monseigneur Philippe is, and
how well he understands the whole business of carrying
on war. Oh ! we are going to do it in great style now, as
he is to come back to us; and those communeers will find
somebody to talk to when he does come. I give 'em but one
week more before their town is carried, their houses burned
down and pillaged, and if only what they say about their
wealth is true, I promise you now that all these knights
here will be made counts, every squire a banneret, every
man that is sergeant-at-arms a feoffed nobleman. Look
yonder; there's a man has seen my master, and he can tell

you how he manages his war-charger—yonder, that 's him,
that queer-looking fellow there in the corner, who sits staring at something with his stupid eyes. Halloa 1 Rigauld,
tell us what you think of Monseigneur Philippe."

The Abbot's forester, thus interpellated, seemed to wake
out of a sort of dream ; he replied in a few unintelligible
words to Fulk's apostrophe, and went on staring at the
chatelaine's women. There was a sort of terror-struck
look in his gaze; but no one paid any attention to that,
and Fulk continued to perorate with his neighbors and a
few knights near him, while Mahaut was quietly convers-
ing with the canon, the seneschal, and the two old gentlemen. The forester was so completely absorbed that he
didu't touch a mouthful of the bacon and oaten bread that
was set before him on his wooden dish. Open-mouthed,
and face as pale as a sheet, he seemed to be contemplating
some frightful object, and sat out the whole supper, without once budging; a circumstance that would certainly have
brought down a deluge of questions had it happened iu
any other company.

Supper being now at an end, all such as had no military
duty on hand for the night, went off to their sleeping places:
the canon was ushered to the oratory, whore a bed had been
prepared for him ; and Mahaut, after recommending, with
a sort of good-will, the prisoner Damerones to the kind
protection of her women, moved on towards her own
chamber. She was just about to open the door when she
found herself held back by her gown. The corridor was
so dark that the lamp in her hand merely served to show
how dark it was, and Mahaut, in her surprise, turning to
see who it was, descried the tall frame and wretched tatters
of Rigauld the game-keeper.

" What do YOU want *!*"

"Lady," replied the serf, "let me go into your room, I must speak to you."

Now, Mahaut, ever thinking about something, ever anxious, ever uneasy, with a head full of projects, imagined the forester had come to reveal some conspiracy, or treason; an ambush of some kind, or some weakness among her friends. She was well aware of the man's devotion to the Abbot, and, of course, to herself as well. She therefore did not hesitate, and entering the apartment   badehim come in, and then with her own hand closed the   door.

She took a seat and looked at Rigauld with a grave air.

" What have you to say to me ?"

" Do you know that woman in a blue frock that was at the supper-table just now, in the hall ?"

"Yes," said Mahaut, "itwas Damerones, the cloth merchant's girl at Typhaines; her I am to exchange to-morrow morning for Monseigncur Philippe, my affianced husband. Do you know anything about her ?"

Rigauld looked all round the room distrustfully, and then lowering his voice, said—

" Who do you take her to be, lady ?"

" Who do I take her to be ? why, for   MasterSimon's daughter, one of the commune leaders."

"You are mistaken; she isn't what she seems to be," said Rigauld.

"Are you gone out of your senses, you clown? or are you daring to make a jest of me ? Canon Norbert knows her—and he answers for her to me."

"Well then, Canon Norbert," continued Rigauld, "as well as yourself, has been duped by the devil, that's all. I tell you that person in the blue frock out there at your supper-table among your women, never budging, never eating one morsel, never speaking one single word, was anything but the girl you think she was."

"Who is she, then ?"

" Who is she ?" echoed Rigauld.

" Yes—explain yourself!"

" She—she, please God! she 's St. ProcuPs fairy . . . the spring over yonder!"

Rigauld looked so frightened as he uttered these words, evidently torn out of him by mere force, and spite of his horror, by his fidelity to the chatelaine, that Mahaut began to tremble too, and she crossed herself. But after a short silence and brief reflection she got the better of it, and cried out—

" What nonsense ! I know all about your encounter with St. ProcuPs Spring fairy; and it is a certain fact that it was through her we got wind of the Abbot's peril; but why should she come here and surrender herself prisoner in my hands ? Why would the holy canon assure me she was really and truly Master Simon's daughter? Of course you must know that the most powerful creatures of that kind are never able to disguise themselves from a priest's eyes—at least not very long. I answer for it, you are mistaken ! even if Damerones w^as to try to cheat us, she could not cheat Canon Norbert; you may be sure of that. You have been misled by some false resemblance."

" How came it, then," continued Rigauld, " that when I went into your hall and saw Damerones, she flushed up all red and put up her finger to her lip as a sign to bid me be silent ?"

" Did she do that ?"

" I am ready to take my oath she did, my lady ! I don't know whether the monks are liable to be cheated by devils or whether they ar'n't; but there's one thing certain, and that is, St. Procul's fairy is one of the worst kind, and the whole country knows about many a trick of hers that the patron of the abbey never could keep the folks clear of.

As to being cheated by her, why, St. Procul had to bear it a hundred times over, and he 'll have to bear it again too."

This argument was a strong one, and Mahaut, who had as long a list of the witch's pranks as anybody, could find not a word to say against it; and then too, upon reflection, it struck her as a very singular thing that both the fairy and Damerones should have taken it into their heads to fall in love with the knight, and with equal devotion too: to her it seemed out of the question for Damerones to have dared to strive in a question of love with her diabolical rival, and so she went so far as to conceive that one of those devilish tragedies must have been performed some dark night that we still now and then hear of in country parts. She began to suspect that the wicked sprite in a jealous fit had sucked out, while the girl was fast asleep, from one of those imperceptible wounds that they know how to make in the throat, every drop of blood, and then get inside and wear the dead body by way of disguise. As soon as the infamous cheat has answered its purpose the wicked goblin just walks out and leaves the carcass any-where by the way-side, as a thing no longer of any use. On such gloomy fantastic wings as these Mahaut soon rose up to a height of terror as lofty as Rigauld's own, who stood there with his teeth clattering and his knees knock-ing together with the horror.

For a time the chatelaine seemed to feel her castle-walls shaking on their rock bases as if they were about to tumble down to the plain below. She thought she heard voices in the corridors; jeering and demoniac bat-wings, fluttering in ironical impatience at the leaden window sash of her room; yet all these menacing appearances were mere fear-crea-tions; nothing really stirred, and those old walls and towers were destined to keep up their blackened stone-blocks for

ages to come above the country they commanded far and
wide around them

44 Hearken to me," she said; 44if, as you believe, and with
some appearance of truth too, that Damerones is the fairy
of St. Procul Spring, she*must be a fool of a fairy, indeed;
and her passion for Monseigneur must have turned her
very brain. She has had plenty of time, in the course of a
whole week she's been in my dungeon here, to tear us all
to pieces ; as she has done nothing at all of the kind, it's
clear she couldn't, and that's why she didn't do it, and
hasn't a bit of foresight; for by her own confession as well
as the canon's testimony, which can't be disputed, Monseigneur keeps on loving me just all the same. May be
she has not got any knowledge of the future; and they do
say Satan himself doesn't know a whit about it either, and
can only judge of it, and reason, just like any learned clerc.
But do you attend now to what I am going to say: do
you know a place called Rusquet-woods ?"

44 Yes," replied the man, 11 just as well as if I had planted
every tree in it myself. It's on the other side of the river,
where it crowns two of the low hills: the road from the
burgh that goes through it is so narrow that two men on
horseback can't ride abreast in it."

44 But, on the other hand, it's a good place for an ambush ?" said she.

" So good a one that in the other old Abbot's time, Seigneur de Pornes used to hide in it every year, at the Typhaines fair time, and never failed to get a fine booty out
of the foreign merchants that came to it, no matter how
big their escort."   %

41 As you know the place so well," said the lady, " you
must go and softly wake up the seneschal and tell him to
come to me at once; I wish to speak to him here. I will
give you both an order, which, if it should succeed, shall

give you your freedom, and a piece of land with a cabin
on it: now go; make no noise, and come back directly."

While Rigauld was away the damsel went to her *prie-
Dieu,* and with a fervor warmed by her inward excitement
paid out all the orisons she had learned since her childhood
days; nor did she neglect to make a vow to our Lady of
Chartres; and she exhausted every measure in her reach, to
secure Heaven's favoring smile before she would undertake
to succeed by mere temporal measures. By this method
of proceeding she in some degree recovered her tranquillity ; she gradually got back her presence of mind, and
glowing with the thought of the struggle she was about to
engage in, this terrible young chatelaine, whom men could
hardly have terrified, felt ready to go in cold Uood into a
fight with the powers of hell nself.

The seneschal now came in guided by the faithful Rigauld. There he had a very serious conference, ending in
an agreement that the old knight, accompanied with a
number of well-mounted sergeants-at-arms, the best armed
and bravest of the fief, should quietly set forth to the ambush in Rusquet woods and hide as completely as possible
in the closest part of the thicket, and wait perdu, until the
return of the burgher troops from the place where the exchange was to be effected. The seneschal's men were to
rush from their hiding places, and probably finding the
comrauneers off their guard, seize the maideu and convey
her back to the chatel. Such was the plan arranged by
Mahaut.

When the seneschal heard these orders he began to shake
his head, and confessed that, as far as he could see, nothing
could look more like an act of perjury, and to give things
their real names a shocking disloyalty. But the damsel,
who was expecting such a reproof, most pertinently remarked that, with demons and sorcerers there can be no

binding engagement; that common morals conld not be brought into question in the case ; and to conclude, directed Rigauld to tell his whole story to the old knight.

The forester obeyed, and such was the conversion operated by his tale upon the recalcitrant warrior that he at once agreed that no time was to be lost.

"You are quite in the right," said he to Mahaut, "not to allow such a creature as that to go tramping about the country; but if you will believe me, you would do very well not to let her come back here to the manor, where, as soon as she discovers that she is found out, she may, perhaps, do her very worst. Therefore I shall go and seize her at the ambuscade, tie her hard and fast, and as I cross the river throw her in with a stone fastened to her neck, and let her go to the bottom."

Rigauld swore that better advice never had been given, and the young lady, seeing nothing objectionable in it, gave her assent to the happy proposal of her faithful seneschal. The conference now broke up and they went off, Mahaut to her bedroom, Rigauld to the stables to see the horses saddled, and the seneschal to the donjon rooms where the men he had most confidence in were sleeping, and who had given proofs of their fitness by their behavior at the assault on Anseau's castle; behavior to make them fairly crow over their companions. Without the least noise, or any parade, the chosen troops soon quitted the tower, known only to the warder at the gate; plunged out into the dark, and went forward to reach their post before the first morning beams should begin to light up the slumbering world.

At the manor all was still and at rest save poor Damerones, who was kept awake and full of concern for Monseigneur Philippe's safety. Even although her deliverance seemed certain and near at hand, the consul's child, as everybody laboring with strong desires must, kept trem-

bling lest some unforeseen obstacle should be found to defeat the ends of her self-devotion. So great was her abne-
gation, and so sublime the power imparted by her love, that
she no more thought about the cruel imprisonment she was
now to leave, than of the terrible situation which she was
to encounter in the presence of her angry parent. What
was the hatred of the Damoisel of Cornouiller to her; or
the indignation of the Typhaines chief ? For herself, everything hinged on the single point whether the knight was to
be safe and happy ? Although she had revealed to her
father the hope she cherished of espousing, some day, the
gallant chevalier, and though in moments of calm she gave
herself up to the seductive charm of such notions—she now
thought no more about them. To rescue Philippe—to
know him free and safe—to think of him on his war-horse
and prancing free in the field like a knight, good and true—
that was her whole dream; that was all. She had put her
life upon a cast, and would have risked it again. She
would offer it, ever, to win this sole aim and end of a love
uuequalled.

Day broke at last, before she had once closed her eyes
in sleep. She heard the garrison trumpets that waked the
knights. The women in whose apartment the rose of Typhaines had spent the uight arose, dressed, and hurried off
to give their personal attention to the mistress, and then
Fulk soon made his appearance, beckoned to her with his
hand, and invited her to go down into the castle court-yard.
There she saw Mahaut seated on her courser, surrounded
by eleven cavaliers on their war horses; the ehatel&ine,
then without a word to the girl, pointed to a palfrey, upon
which Fulk seated her, and the good squire having got
his feet into his stirrups, and leading the pony that was
bearing his master's ransom, the entire troop moved off
silently, preceded by Norbert, marching on foot with his
long staff in his hand.

CHAPTER XXIII.

IT was noon; the warm golden sunshine came down ont of a high heaven of purest blue. The insects in the grasses of the plain were humming, and a few birds were fluttering among the branches along the river brink. From opposite sides of the widespread plain two troops of cavaliers were 6een approaching with lances and bucklers gleaming like so many particular fires. In the centre of the group from the manor rode Damerones, between the lady Mahaut and a knight; and Norbert walking close to her bridle rein. In the middle of the band from Typhaines, Monseigneur Philippe was seen riding a wretched mule, close watched by Payen at his side, and by Master Simon too, both covered with mail, wearing helmets, and draped with ample cloaks of a crimson dye. The men and their followers were as well armed and equipped as the knightly attendants of Mahaut herself.

The two coming parties detached each a scout, to see whether all the stipulations of the pact were completely fulfilled, and the videttes galloped up to the rustic bridge, earnestly reconnoitred the arrangements of the adversary, and hurriedly returned, each to his own band, who immediately moved forwards to the place of rendezvous. As soon as the Cornouiller and the Typhaines horse had got within fifty paces of the bridge, they halted at a signal from the aged canon, who at once crossed the river and invited Simon and Payen to accompany their prisoner

alone, to the foot of the bridge, while Fulk and Mahaut
were at the same time to lead Damerones to the opposite
end.

" How >s this ?" cried Payen, " a squire and a woman!
No, no, holy father! not so ; the consuls of Typhaines are
no traitors and miscreants, to show greater distrust than
their adversaries! As the lady of Cornouiller confides so far
in us, Master Simon shall go alone to meet his daughter; it
shall never be said that we are ignorant of courtesy."

"Holy father," said Philippe, "the clowns are great
scoundrels certainly, but I am sorry to see this blacksmith among them; he has the true heart of a genuine
man-at-arms. However, do not forget that my hands are
tied hard, and though 1 said nothing about it, Master Simon there did his work too well, and 1 am in a hurry to
be rid of these ligatures."

At tlfese words Payen drew his dagger and cut the
bonds; whereupon brave Sir Philippe most vigorously
brandished his fists, for the ropes were so tight as to leave
great bruised blue circles where they had been so long
hard tied; he then flew to the bridge. The first person
he saw at it, and it was quite natural too, was his betrothed
bride: a cry of joy burst forth as he rushed forwards to
kneel, seize her hand, and press it to his lips.

" Oh ! Lady—Oh, Mahaut I is it indeed you that I behold once more, after so weary, weary a time! How beautiful you have grown ! How charming I find you I Oh,
Mahaut I upon my salvation, lady, 1 never conceived of a
being so beautiful as you are ! Yes, upon my soul, by my
eternal hopes, lady, I love you with my whole heart, and
would die a thousand deaths rather than in the least particular break my plighted faith! I am well rewarded for
my faithful love, now that I gaze on you again, and you

looking more perfect than paradise itself 1 Oh, Mahaut! Oh, Mahaut!"

Uttering these passionate, half-sobbing effusions, Philippe's countenance was suffused, earnest, and agitated as he stammered his expressions; he seemed to have lost his wits, the poor knight; and it were not a mere figure of rhetoric to say, that merely to gaze on her, he thought himself in the seventh heaven.

On a sudden he heard Master Simon's hoarse voice like a thunder tone sounding close by him.

"Miserable wretch!" said Simon to his child; "come home to the family you have disgraced, to the town you betrayed! Come home to tears, and begin a course of penance never to end, for your baseness and wickedness !"

"Stop!" shouted Norbert—"Stop, Master Simon! I forbid you, in the naAe of my mission from the skies, to pour out on this dear girl the diabolical invectives of your hate. I '11 be there to watch you ! be you assured of that!"

Monseigneur Philippe, at Simon's first words, started up out of his ecstacy, and turned at once to Damerones, who stood with her arms crossed on her bosom at the end of the bridge stock still, gazing upon the knight with dry eyes, and with an expression so deep, so dolorous, so heart rending, that though not much of a physiognomist it greatly moved him : his idea was that she considered him forgetful of her services, and though he still held Mahaut by the hand, for he could not go so far as to let go of that, he said in a tender accent:—

" Farewell, young girl; never will I disown what you have done for me : my name is Philippe de Cornehaut, and never shall that name be stained by the meauness of ingratitude. Pray remember, and well remember too, that I shall never be perfectly happy until some occasion arises in which I may do you a good service; but I will try to

27

find out some way to keep my memory fresh in your heart, as an honest knight, as long as yon lire in this world. And yon, Master Simon," resumed he in fierce tones, " if I should once hear of you forcing one tear from your daughter's eyes, I promise you that I 'll break every bone in your skin, and knock every tooth down your throat;—however, that's a thing likely to happen, do what you w i l l a n d he broke out in a joyous laugh. Just as he got to an end with that harangue, he felt the weight of a couple of heavy hands upon his shoulders.

" And how about me ?" said Fulk. Monseigneur warmly returned his worthy squire's friendly greeting; for when a man has roamed half the world over with a true servant, suffered heat and cold, hunger and thirst, fought and conquered with him, there is ever a strong embrace when they meet again after a long parting. A"s soon as the knight's excited feelings had become assauged a little the old man went on to say—

" I took it into my noddle those fellows would bring you back bare-headed, like a prisoner, the miscreants that they are ! Now here is a helmet I selected for you at Cornouiller : you just be easy about it; it is a well-tempered one; I amused myself all yesterday evening hacking at it with my sword, and it never budged; and look here, here's a famous blade ! hang it to your belt 1"

" Poor Rudaverse I" said Philippe, with a sigh.

"Oh, we'll have her again," responded Fulk, with a perfect satisfaction in that belief. "Here, take me this lance in your grip. My souls! your arms are not so very nicely blazoned to be sure, but fact is, for want of a better hand, I—I painted them myself."

The giant was talking in quite a modest guise, and still bolding his master's hand, when—

" To horse !" said Mahaut in a sharp tone.

Monseigneur Philippe vaulted into his saddle with an ease and lightness that showed at least how little his late imprisonment had wasted his strength, and then, with a volte, he was at his mistress' side. He said, submissively : " It seems to me that you are vexed with me; you look so, to sny the least."

" Why ?" replied the damsel very dryly.

" Because you haven't spoken a single kind word to me since I came. Perhaps you are worried about all these nonsensical things I've been doing since my return. It's true, and I confess it, I ought not to have allowed myself to be taken prisoner; but after all, I love you none the less dearly, Mahaut."

"Don't trouble yourself about that," said Mahaut, "but merely answer me one question. What do you think of that Damerones ?"

" She is a very good loyal-hearted girl," said the crusader very simply.

"Very well; but the sight of her is very pleasing to you—is it so ?"

" Faith, it pleased me very much to see her in that dungeon at Typhaines."

" I suppose you will be excessively obliged to me, then, for telling you she's a sorceress, who was deceiving you at that very time."

" A sorceress ? Why, it's you that are deceived, not I; Damerones is a very good burgher-girl, and not a sorceress at all. I have known her for several years. Let's see! yes, she put me in mind that I used to see her when I was at Cambrai, making love to you, Mahaut."

Mahaut reddened with spite. Witch, fairy, or plain mortal, Damerones seemed more hateful now than ever. She resumed in an accent that she strove hard so to control as to give an idea she cared naught about it, and said:—

" Really ? Is she not a witch ? Then I am sorry for the orders I issued concerning her."

" See, now! you are always talking to me about Dame-rones, and not a word about your dear self or me either— pouting. Eh! my God! she saved my life, and — but that she is a burgher-girl, I really believe I am very fond of her; but talking about her all the time annoys me, now I have been so long parted from you."

" Well, we ll not talk about her any more"—looking half cruel, half jesting—" after we have shed a few tears over her tragical fate, we will never mention her."

" Her tragical fate ? I hope she may live many a year, and be happy, too ! But let 's talk of—about something else."

" Live happy ? Why, she*8 damned already, and that to all eternity! Live! she hasn't two hours to live, I guess."

" What does all this mean, lady mine ?"

" It only means that my men-at-arms, who are lying in ambush at Rusquet woods, are going to twist her neck and throw her to the bottom of the river—that's what it means."

"I bet you are joking!" cried Monseigneur, suddenly checking his charger.

" Never was I more in earnest," answered Mahaut,"and that's the very way, in my opinion, that witches ought to be treated."

The chevalier bent down his head—gave a sigh—red-dened in the face—grew agitated—then moved forwards to ride half a length to the rear of the chatelaine. It was apparent that a violent conflict was raging within him ; he greatly dreaded the anger of his arrogant fiancee, but could not make up his mind to let his benefactress perish. At last, he stopped suddenly—quickly raised himself up in the stirrups, looked back on the train, and meeting old Fulk's eyes, shouted with a thunder tone—

" Follow me, Fulk ! gallopI" Driving his rowels into the horses flanks he went off like a storm-blast towards the bridge he had lately left, crossed it at fnll speed, and drove on, followed by his faithful companion whose affection drew him after him, he rushed like a whirlwind into the open plain leading towards Typhaines. I shall make no attempt to depict the disappointment, wrath, shame, and despair of Mahaut, when she beheld this instant departure, for which, as a jealous lover, she assigned any cause but the real one. She sat on her saddle nullified, congealed— she looked like a stone statue surrounded by her ten companions, not less stunned than herself. And still the good knight tore on, and on, and Fulk had a sore task to keep within a reasonable distance of him. While straining his destrier after the knight, he little doubted his master had suddenly gone crazy, for, as he hadn't overheard the conversation with Mahaut and knew nothing about Damerones, he couldn't conceive what strange idea had got into Philippe's head to carry him back at such a rate towards the town where he had been so near to death on the block. He conjured up a thousand considerations, and of the very wildest, about a freak in which he could discern not one single element of common sense.

But before Fulk got up with the chevalier near enough to make him hear his voice, Monseigneur Philippe had gone over a great deal of ground. The plain was already far away behind him, and the hardy knight had rushed into the woods that formed the labyrinth of which Rusquet-pass was the centre. It was within a few hundred paces of that dangerous spot that Fulk at last got up with him.

" S 'death ! Monseigneur, are you crazy ?"

" Go to the devil! none of your preaching here 1 It's

2?*

quite enough to think what Mahaut will have to say when it 's all over. Make ready to give a matter of good cuts and thrusts."

44 Thrusts at the burghers ? They are twelve to two of us!"

41 No ! the Cornouiller men."

41 Ah, bosh ! I saw them when they went away last night; they count thirty at the least, and of the very best. Are they lying in ambush for the communeers ?"

44 Yes, and to capture Damerones, the burgher-girl you saw, and who rescued me from the edge of her father's axe. "

44 Eh ! Great God! your integrity is going to cost us dear, and perhaps we will do no good, after all, and get ourselves maltreated by both parties into the bargain. It would be better to halt here and think the matter over, and carry your succor to Damerones in some other way."

44I take the shortest way; if it don't suit you—you can go. Begone with yon !"

Fulk answered not a word, he only dashed his spur's rowel deep into the charger, who carried him at a bound right up to 44 front dress" by the knight. Just then they heard the rustling of fencing swords in the thicket, the clank of armor, horses neighing, shouts and imprecations most terrible. At the turn of the road, which they soon reached at a run, they saw the whole affair plain before their eyes.

That cut-throat looking spot was a small clearing, wider than it was long, and bounded by a dense growth of trees, among which were numerous large rocks that had often been used as a favorite place of ambush by the marauders and pillagers of the vicinity. The seneschal had stationed his men among the trees and thickets behind those huge boulders so as to occupy both sides of the narrow pass, with orders to rush out at a signal as soon as the Typhaines cavalcade should be fully engaged in the narrow defile; and when he at length saw that all was ready he blew one loud blast of his horn and the fray began. The pass being extremely narrow, the burghers, attacked on all sides, had but one of two things to do: they must either surrender, or suffer themselves to be cut to pieces; there was no other alternative.

The seneschal, who had no wish to have a fight to the death, in case he could succeed in his mission at a lesser cost of life, rode in shouting: " Surrender the prisoner, and your way shall be cleared !"

But the only reply made by Simon and Payen was to spur their horses against the steel-clad line; covering, the while, the path leading towards Damerones with their swords. Being well supported by their men, they made terrible efforts to break the line that barred their way; until, driven back by the men-at-arms, they had no other recourse than to fall back to the centre of the clearing. Simon fought with silent, desperate, solemn courage; he uttered not a word, but his blows fell like thunderbolts from out of a clear sky. In his hatred for the enemies of Typhaines, he found no reason for surprise at their foul perfidy and treason ; but Payen, who was younger, boiling, ever ready to rise to the height of enthusiasm, and passionate withal, poured out an unceasing torrent of invectives and curses upon those miserable violators of a sworn pact. Every time his sword rung upon helm or hauberk it fell intensified with a hearty curse. Beneath his iron coat his bosom was choking with rage and fury, and the energetic expression of his feelings seemed to lend tenfold more force to his stalwart arm.

Monseigneur Philippe came at full speed into this scene of furious heroic resistance resounding with the war cry of

Typhaines! Cornouiller! which were mingled with the
diapason of the battle: the knight's sonorous tones
blended with them the terrible shout *CornehaiU! Come-
haul!* and the first push of his lance tossed the old senea.
chal from his saddle feet uppermost in the air, as he flew
off in a parabolic curve to roll on the greensward below;
the good seigneur, who was looking for nothing of the
sort, might put one in mind of a ninepin centred by the
ball from a gay villager's vigorous young hand. Fulk did
better yet. One back sweep of his sword tumbled a man-
at-arms under the horses' hoofs, while with his left he
grasped another, who with his long knife in his hand
was trying to get at Damerones, by the throat, and not
knowing who he was, with a grip like a vice was on the
point of strangling him to death without scruple. Luckily
for Rigauld, the squire caught sight of his face, and
remembering the game-keeper's worthy sentiments, and
particularly his devotion to his master the Abbot, he let
him drop ; so that the poor fellow staggered and stumbled
with both arms thrown abroad, until he came at last to
tumble down on the stunned body of the gray-haired old
seneschal, and the shout *Cornehaut! Cornehaut!* rang
out cheerily.

Confusion now got into the Cornouiller ranks; yet five
or six of them pressed savagely on Payen, who had a hard
task, in spite of his courage and strength, to keep them at
a distance. Monseigneur Philippe spurred his charger to
Payen's side—

"Stand fast, bold burgher!" he cried, "I am your
succor 1" In times like that a man would accept succor
from the devil himself; and Payen, gathering renewed
courage and strength, seized his buckler with both hands;
he rose-in. his stirrups and dashed it with such violence on
a too adventurous soldier's head, that he stove in helm and

bone at a blow, and freed himself forever of that rash enemy at least: instantly grasping Damerones' bridle-rein he drew her onwards and placed her within a triangle of defence, of which he, the knight, and Simon constituted the points.

In spite of gallant feats of arms, in spite of the miraculous audacity of the chevalier, Fulk, and the burghers, it might be doubted whether the crusader's hot-headed enterprise could have been crowned with success had the reinforcement he brought up been bounded by the mere power of his hand ; for the fact is, that the Cornouiller men were three to one of their adversaries, and a reinforcement of two swords was not enough under such a disparity in the circumstances. The shout *Cornehaut!* did more to demoralize the assailing party than the resistance of the two intrepid men ; they knew that the knight was their mistress' affianced husband, and already their own half scignenr. They even began to question the part they had come to act out at Rusquet woods: when they saw the seneschal was down, and unable to issue an order, the situation appeared still more ambiguous, and under the uncertainty they began rather to put themselves on the defence, instead of attacking, and they no longer pressed their antagonists so fiercely. Monseigneur's falcon eye soon descried a gap in the line that barred the path to Typhaines and he bent over to Payen and whispered :—

" Take the young woman, and go off at a gallop."

The youthful consul understood and at once obeyed him. Simon, whose vigilant eyes were directed by turns to every quarter of the field, saw the move, and feeling it to be the decisive moment, *Typhaines!* he shouted, and away he rushed after Payen, followed by the whole of his remaining party. Philippe and Fulk remained to act as rear guard ; but that proved no very difficult task. As soon as the men-at-arms saw themselves dispensed of the necessity to exterminate their adversaries, or capture the whole troop they found so skilful in defence, they hurried to where their commander lay and got him on to his feet. The rest of the men, finding there was no more fighting to be done with the burghers, and only with Philippe and Fulk alone, did not care for the employment; and after a sort of pursuit that did not go very far, they let the heroes proceed to join their friends from the town, if they liked it, who, after all, were their most mortal enemies; and that was exactly what Fulk was thinking as the last Typhaines horseman disappeared in the distance.

"I am of a mind, Monseigneur," and he said it in a very cross way, " that I have been behaving like a man that 's not afraid of blows ?"

"Did I ever say anything to the contrary, my brave Fulk ?"

"I thought I heard something of the sort; but no matter now, as the fight is over and your Damerones all safe: what are we to do next, I should like to know?"

" Ah, yes ! that indeed !" said the knight, looking astonished the while, " I confess I had not thought about that."

"But it's worth the trouble of thinking about."

" Certainly 1" replied Philippe. " Let 's think about it at once. If we go on in this road we shall infallibly reach Typhaines, which is not very far off now, and is by no means the very spot where I, as I left it this morning, should have preferred to spend the night."

" Have you changed your mind yet ?"

" Not at all! While the fight was going on I saw, through his helmet bars, old Simon's eyes, with such a scowl at me, that sure I am, notwithstanding my help, he wasn't very far from handling me as roughly as I did some of Mahaut's poor men. No, no 1 I haven't the least wish to go back to Typhaines; my old lodgings there would be too ready to take me in again."

" H—m 1" said Fulk, " if we torn back, the company we jost now handled so roughly wouldn't, it's likely, feel disposed to give us good welcome."

" Very possible that, friend Fulk, but even in case we could manage to come to a parley with those brave fellows, I don't mind very much just at present to make my appearance before the chatelaine. I think I have done nothing but my duty; indeed, I'm sure of it; but Mahaut must be very much vexed, and I certainly have offended her; she has taken it into her head that Damerones is a sweetheart of mine 1 and so, all things considered, I believe I would rather not face her to day."

" That's just like you, exactly," replied Fulk. " When we were in Syria, Greece, Italy, you told me twenty times a day : 4 Ah 1 if I could only see *her* once more !' and now, when it depends on nobody but yourself never to quit sight of her as long as you live, here you are, it seems, wishing for nothing in the world but to keep clear of her ! Pshaw ! you 're just a mere baby. But for having those exasperated Cornouiller men between us and the chatel, I would halloa as loud as thunder let's go and get supper, and so to bed; we have had work enough for one day. Suppose the young lady should scold; can't you quiet her down ? Suppose you couldn't quiet her down; very well, then, let her quiet herself down, and she will get over it by morning. Now that's just what I wanted to say to you; but as we are situated here, between two gangs of wolves, I'm inclined to think the best thing we can do is to go into the thick of the woods, take off the bridles, stretch ourselves down at the foot of a tree, and masticate a mouthful of orisons to St. Julian by way of supper, for that's the only one we are likely to get this night. Eh I the good heavens ! I hope they will send us no more such wild notions in times to come as those that have had full swing this day."

" Fulk, you are cross;" said the knight, " and we are on the point of pulling each other's hair; for the fact is, I am not in the very best humor myself. However, I have got an idea that bull-head of yours would never have dreamed of, though perhaps I can make you understand it."

" Well, then, your idea, as you call it—what's your idea ? Idea, indeed!"

"We '11 follow this path until we come to the end of it, as if we were going on to the town; then, as soon as we get out into the fields, we '11 turn short to the right, and make our way to the abbey. Perhaps we can stay all night and get supper too. Who in the world is ever likely to think we have gone to take refuge so close to our enemies ? Perhaps, too, I might find Rudaverse again if we go, and I confess I never shall be more than half alive until I can get her in my hand once more, dear old thing 1"

" Oh! when yon talk that way," said Fulk, " I can understand why people do sometimes look on you as a reasonable being. Fact is, I haven't been easy myself ever since I missed poor old Rudaverse at your belt. Hey for the abbey then 1 It aint because the time there was a very agreeable one for me; but now the old Abbot's out of the way, they must have better suppers there than that infernal day we first went to it—may the devil fly away with it 1"

And so, chatting away, the knight and his companion in arms set off, taking good care not to travel too fast, and to allow time enough for night to come down and hide them under her friendly veil. In due and good time they reached the abbey-gate ; the lights of Typhaines were gleaming in the valley far below'; the monastery lay utterly silent and dark. They knocked, and getting no answer, knocked again—and again ; at last, through the cracks of the late ruined portal, they descried a lantern that seemed crossing the court-yard and coming towards where they stood; and their hopes revived.

28

CHAPTER XXIY.

THE sound of coming feet now approached the gate, and the two cavaliers saw the red beam of the lantern-light glancing beneath on the sill. A voice, broken and tremulous by fear, no doubt, now very gently spoke :—

" My good Christian men, if you are not Pagan Mahometans, go your way, I entreat you, and don't compel us to open; you will find in the borough of Typhaines everything any traveller can want for."

" Good father," responded the crusader, " we are gentlemen, and have nothing to do at Typhaines; open, then, for the love of God."

" I shall do nothing of the sort," answered the voice, "for what betwixt gentlemen and rebel burghers nobody knows which is worst for Holy Church, now-a-days. Heaven guide you, good people ; go your ways, and don't torment us any longer!"

Finding how obstinate the man with the lantern was, our good knight was on the point of an outbreak of his quick temper that would have done no good, situated as he was; but Fulk touched his arm, and summoning up a most seducing tone to show what very good folks they were standing outside there, he said :—

"Open, good father! if you do, you 'll not repent it; for we bring news of the father Abbot of Typhaines."

No answer was returned to Fulk's observation ; on the contrary, the light seemed moving off with the man that had it; but all of a sudden its glare shot down from the top of the battlement above and fell full on the two nocturnal visitors, and the brother porter, who had adopted this mode of making his reconnoissance, cried out with a delighted tone:—

" How! Monseigneur ! is it indeed you I see down there ? and you too, my brave, faithful Fulk?"

" Yes, certainly, we are both here—open the gate, will you ?"

" To be sure I will—yes, I'm hurrying as fast as I can. Bless my heart! these bars were never made to keep such as you out. Ah ! how glad the prior will be ! how all our fathers will rejoice! I 'll hurry as fast as I can; don't you be impatient."

In fact, and very quick too, the gate was flung open. The two horsemen entered the court-yard; the brother porter shut, locked, and barred the gate again and fixed the chain, and then, lantern in hand, guided the new comers to the refectory, where they found the whole community assembled.

Fulk and his master made their appearance just as the friars were about sitting down to their evening meal. Their refectory was a vast hall, with a low ceiling supported by two rows of immense heavy columns, rudely sculptured with bas-reliefs representing men, women, and animals; a large oaken table stood in the middle of the room, lighted by lamps suspended from the ceiling in numbers sufficient to light up the scene below.

Every monk arose at the entrance of Monseigneur, and the prior, quitting his place, advanced to pay his respects to and give good welcome to the knight.

" First of all, holy father, after the fight in your court-yard was over, did you find my sword that I threw as high as I could up in the air as I was being seized by the rebels V^y

"We did find that good weapon," responded the prior, "and not only so, but we deposited her in the chapel, where Father Nicolas was buried."

" Let me have it," said Philippe, and he sighed at the thought of Monseigneur Geoffroy. "My chief object in coming hither to ask your hospitality, was the hope of recovering Rudaverse."

" One of our lay-brothers will at once go for it, and it shall be placed in your hands within a few minutes; but in the mean time, please take a seat by me, and let your valiant squire be seated too, and when your hunger is appeased, you can tell us what news you bring of our father the Abbot."

"About your Abbot ?" cried Fulk, pouring out his wine, " we haven't the least word of him. I went off with him, as you must remember, as soon as the knight rescued him. He must have got to Paris, and beyond that we know nothing of him."

" Forgive our stratagem," said Monseigneur Philippe. "We could find no other way to get inside tho abbey; they were going to leave us out in the cold all night."

"I am the more ready to forgive," rejoined the prior, " for I have this very day had news from the Abbot, and excellent news it is too."

" Excellent—did you say ?"

"They are so,, I assure you," said the prior, "and I leave you to judge. The venerable Bishop of Chalons has given succor to our seigneur. They went, both of them, to Rheims, and the holy prelate who presides over that church turned a favoring ear to their protests and their complaints, and it was at once resolved to call a council. That council will open within a few days, and

is to have eight bishops and twenty abbots in session.
There's no doubt the Seigneur King of France and the
Count de Nevers will both be appealed to answer to the
council for their late conduct; and still more than that, the
Typhaines Commune is to be excommunicated."

" Hah! that's capital," said Fulk, and he poured out
another bumper—" will they haug the whole of them
burghers ?"

" Of course they will," said the knight; "but, father, are
you aware of the fact that the King of France has already
guaranteed the new commune ?"

" Oh, he *11 soon come out of his guaranty, and it won't
be the first time either, that I can assure you of."

" Come on! the thing is going all right; but how as
to me—aro they to give me back my property at Cornehaut? for the fact is I don't know what interest I really
have in the defence of your minster; if you are satisfied
with my services, you surely will give me back what belongs to me, and to nobody else ?"

The prior's eyes were downcast.

" It would ill befit such an one as I," said he, in wooing
tones, " to utter an opinion in the absence of my superior.
But, in any case, Monseigneur, you may feel quite sure that
the Church never did do a wrong to any living soul; and
that even where the-world judges too lightly from appearances, the spirit is vivified and enriched, though the flesh
is humiliated and plundered." .   .

"That's as much as to say," added'Fulk, "that they
don't intend to give my master any portion of his property.
Yery well, then! all I have to say in the matter is that as
soon as you have settled your business with the Typhaineers
you will find you've got a terrible bill to foot up with us;
that's all. As to the balance, I must say, this wine of
yours is very good wine."

"It's not worth while to talk of that matter just now," said Philippe, " for the present we are friends, and I must beg you to show me my chamber—supper is oyer, and I am in need of rest."

The knight looked sad and down hearted as he thus spoke. The monks supposed that thinking of his dead father and the loss of his estates might be the causes of his depression at returning to the abbey, which certainly had had a great deal to do in bringing him into difficulty; nor were they far wrong in that idea. At the very time he was told that his sword had been deposited on Messire Geoffroy's coffin, tears had sprung to Monseigneur Philippe's eyes, and would have burst forth from their lids but for the great effort he made to keep them down. The thought, too, of his tower at Cornehaut was a very griev-6 us one; but far more than all those, and it never quitted him for a moment, was the idea that Mahaut was offended and angry with him, notwithstanding his conscience told him he was innocent, and that he had done nothing but his plain duty—he still feared he might have, somehow, been in the wrong.

The knight was not a man endowed with the ready and subtle kind of intelligence that is equal to the coping with several different subjects at once, and following out any single one of them, without confusion, to the very end; but give him only time enough to think and he was as clear headed as anybody, and the fact is that after pondering long over the question with Mahaut, he had satisfied himself that his betrothed bride really considered him guilty of, at least, giving encouragement to Damerones; he therefore would have been willing to give anything in the world to procure tho assistance of some friend as fully convinced as he was himself of the perfect purity of his honor, yet eloquent enough to entirely extinguish every remaining doubt in Mahaut's heart.

The sight of Rudaverse, which was put by a lay brother into his hands as he entered his sleeping chamber, was to him a pleasing one; he kissed the dear old sword as if she had been Mahaut herself, could such a boon have been bestowed by that haughty and reserved damoysel; but he soon forgot Rudaverse again and fell back among his fears and anxieties.

As for Fulk, it was all right with him now that Rudaverse was found. He promised himself the satisfaction of furbishing her up with great care, and on that delicious idea fell asleep and snored until about midnight, when his master, who had not closed an eye, waked him to take the road to Cornouiller before the day dawn should come to make their departure visible to the watchmen at Typhaines and tempt those irreconcilable enemies to pursue him. The prior and his monks were busy at matins; so Philippe thought best not to interrupt them, and having saddled his horse with his own hands while Fulk was getting his own roadster ready, he mounted, reached the great gate, which, thanks to the porter, was very willingly and kindly thrown open, and they set out for the chatel.

Monseigneur Philippe and Fulk riding forth, both with helm on the head, visors closed and lance in hand, met with nothing on the way but a few swallows and one wild doe; and when they reached Rusquet Wood, saw nothing but the trampled ground with bloodstains here and there, left by the late conflict; the wounded and the dead, if there were any dead, had been removed; and so, the travellers went on until they came without any misadventure to the tower of Cornouiller.

They alighted in the court-yard, handed over their horses to the care of a page, and Fulk remained in the court without caring a fig about what the people, who had been friends with him in the morning, might have to say about the way he had handled them in the afternoon. The crusader went up to the upper hall of the donjon, and there found Mahaut, surrounded by her women, who gave him an icy reception. Though very much embarrassed, he took a seat near her and began to twiddle with some flocks of wool that had fallen from the distaff she was twirling, and finding that the maiden wouldn't speak—

" I am abont to explain myself very frankly," said he. "You are angry on account of what I have done; I assure you that you arc mistaken on the subject, and haven't the least reason to cast any blame upon me."

" It may possibly be as you say," replied Mahaut, very coolly.

" I do not know what your opinion on the matter really is," objected he.

" It is a very simple one. Yesterday you disobeyed me, attacked and wounded my people, and tore out of my lawful hands a woman who is a witch."

" But she isn't a witch at all."

" Suppose her an angel," said Mahaut, " if I wanted to get possession of her, it was not your affair to hinder me !"

" It would have disgraced me," replied the knight.

" Is it a very honorable thing for a knight to turn valet to a brazen-faced burgher-girl ?"

" Brazen faced or not," rejoined he, " she is no burgher-girl of mine, nor am I her valet; but for Christ's sake, my lady, can you have any notion that such a conversation as this can be pleasing to me ? Show me a kinder countenance, I implore you 1"

" Agreed 1 you are right," said she; " and perhaps I really have no cause to be vexed with you."

"Now do tell me what all this means; your words do not agree with your looks at all," said the crusader.

" It is five years, Monseigneur, since I last saw you,"

said Mahaut. " Many things may have happened since
that day. Setting forth with a soul filled with honor, it
may be you 've come back after losing it altogether. How
am I to know anything on the subject ? Perhaps you are
worried because you have allowed a bond to be made betwixt ... Eh! don't mind breaking any lien between us.
It wouldn't trouble me in the least to break it off."

Mahaut sat gazing at her lover—her voice as she uttered
the words was benign and softened and her eyes humid
and tender. Had Philippe not loved her, she would have
burst into tears on the spot and all her haughtiness and
pride would have broke down at once at the least proof of
his forgetfulness or indifference. But the brave crusader
made such a gesture of energy and passion jn an attempt
to repel her accusing words, that the chatelaine could
not indulge a single doubt as to her power over her lover,
and she then with a firm enunciation resumed:—

" Monseigneur, if you truly do love me, you can easily
give me a proof of it. I made war on the burgh of Typhaines solely in behalf of the Abbot and yourself. Now
that you are rescued, there is no reason why I should not
make peace with them. Do you wish me to do *so* ? All
the allies desire it"

" The devil take your allies," was Philippe's naive reply;
" you must never lay down your arms until the commune is
broken up."

" Do you really think so ?" cried Mahaut, taking his *
hand. " Well then, let us take Typhaines by assault—put
the town to sack and pillage—place Damerones in my
hands, who, I affirm it, is a witch, and who is trying to tear
you from me. Speak 1 will you have it so ?"

For the first time in his life Monseigneur Philippe, seeing himself so pressed, essayed, innocent though he was,
to evade the trouble by a trick.

" My lady," said he, is it an easy thing to do, to carry
the burgh by a ccnp-de-main ? I made a careful recou-
noissance of it as I came away from the minster this morning and found how well defended it is, and I fear an assault
would end only in covering us with shame."

" Want of success," said Mahaut, "is never considered
shameful, where success was impossible," and she spoke
with studied gentleness. " The bravest knights mount to
the assault again and again, four, yes five times in succession, before they succeed in carrying a rampart, but I never
heard they were dishonored by such obstinate courage."

" Typhaines is too strong," responded Messire. " If I
should assault it, I should only get your men killed for
nothing."

" I thought you was more in a hurry to avenge yourself
of your enemies I"

"Tu the devil's name," cried Philippe, stamping the
floor hard with his foot, " you are right, madam, and I
lay aside all pretences of any kind. What is it makes
me afraid of you, lady ? I, who fear no being else beneath
the moon ? Promise me to do no harm to Damerones and
I 'll sack the village for you."

Mahaut held her peace for a moment. She reddened
and turned pale by turns, and her clenched fingers were
tearing at the crimson fringe of her seigneural chair. She
was terribly agitated, but at last rose from the seat and
* strode up and down the hall. To her it seemed quite evident that the knight was cherishing a very different sentiment in his heart from any he was willing to avow, and
that such a feeling existed, nourished and stimulated by
the devilish arts, as she supposed, of the wicked Rose of
Typhaines, was drawing off from her side the man to whom
she had been so long and so truly faithful. Besides, she
was ever accustomed to see everything bend to her will,

and to see that no will whatever should rise in power above her own.

She suddenly stopped in front of the knight, and said—

"Monseigneur, you must be aware of what I have hitherto done in fulfilling the engagement between you and me. For the purpose of giving you an opportunity to win honor and fame, I insisted on your departure for the Holy Land in spite of my deep sorrow at the parting; and during the five years of your absence, I confined myself to the interior of my donjon without seeing any company, and thinking of you alone. In the mean time, many an honorable claimant for my hand had offered me an illustrious name, wealth, glory, and pleasure; but I preferred your distant affection to all the gifts of fortune, and my present solitude with it. Something, so it seems to me, is due to an attachment so great. Now that you are returned, and by some misfortune impossible to foresee, fallen into the hands of our cruellest enemies, I at once surround myself with armed men, and renouncing my solitude I quit the occupations of my sex and very nearly put on an armor of mail, and ... Be you, Monseigneur, judge between us, I beg you to be so; decide, if you dare, in favor of your obstinacy. For a tenderness so well proved what recompense have you offered me up to the present moment? Scarce do I see you, but you fall upon and massacre my servants, and rescue a miserable drab of a village girl out of my jurisdiction ! That is the way you prove your loyalty; and yet, if you still wish it, I will pardon you readily. Act in such a way as that Damerones shall perish. What is the life of such a girl as that to you, sir? In the cities and towns you have put to pillage you have been witness to the woful death of many a woman who certainly was far more worthy than she ? Give up Damerones, put her into my hands again, leave me at full liberty to punish her, and I swear to you I will forgive you and all shall be well with us as ever before."

Without losing time to reflect, Monseigneur exclaimed : " Mahaut! Neither for Damerones nor for any other human being could I ever have the thought to offend you. If you require oaths, lead me to the most sacred of relics; lead me to the venerated corpse of my redoubted father, and I will lay my hand on that noble knight's bosom, and without hesitation swear that in all my life long I never loved woman but you !"

" And Damerones ?" cried Mahaut.

"Damerones," replied the chevalier, "has twice saved my life, and certainly I will never be the cause of her death 1"

" And so you refuse to revenge your father, and to revenge yourself by attacking Typhaines 1"

" Not so, upon honor," rejoined Philippe, with a fiery tone. " I will assault Typhaines, and—please God—I will carry it; but then I will repay to Damerones the good she did to me, and if I do not do so(may I be treated as the meanest and basest of mankind 1"

" I love to hear you talk in that way," said Mahaut, slowly; " I at least discern very clearly the bottom of your thought, and as there is no way to clear your soul of the desire that offends me there, know that from this hour everything is broken off betwixt you and me."

" Broken!" despairingly asked the knight.

"Yes, broken, and by the Saviour's cross I swear it. I take back all the tenderness I bad vowed for you. From this moment forth you are to me nothing more than the vilest of men. You have betrayed me, you have deceived me 1 you play me off against a wretched girl, a magician, a fairy, a—I know not what; perhaps the most infamous demon that ever escaped out of the pit of hell! Begone

Monseigneur Philippe I go join that wretch I I give you back your pledged word, and put you wholly at ease; no doubt, sir, while you were in Syria, you must have turned Mahometan!"

Tears here broke off the words of that impetuous Mahaut. The chatelaine, sobbing, and ready to suffocate, threw herself down into her arm-chair, buried her face betwixt her hands, and gave way to boundless despair, which degenerated at last into screams. As to Monseigneur Philippe, terrified at such vehemence, he could hardly restrain himself from following her example, and answer sob for sob of the passionate maiden of the rock; but he made out so far as to renew his oaths, supplications, and passionate appeals; he put the lady in miud of the chaste and sweet beginnings of their mutual love in the Bishop of Cambrai's palace. He appealed to her own heart against her unjust anger, and said everything he could say to appease her. Unhappily, he was not an adroit speaker; he knew not that the heart repulses the frankest of remedies, and that when roused by passion, you must give it line, as to a fish that refuses to come in. Sure of himself, and in full confidence of his own loyalty, Monseigneur Philippe was not careful while making his own defence to say little enough on the subject of Damerones' virtuous devotion; such eulogies were discords for Mahaut's ears; to be brief, in spite of the very love that glowed and shone in every word he spoke, he succeeded in the course of half an hour, during which she spoke not a word, so well, that Mahaut ceased weeping ; looked hard in her lover's face with a cold resolute stare; rose up from her fauteuil and quitted the hall, ordering her women to follow her.

Monseigneur Philippe was greatly embarrassed. It is a difficult thing for human nature to exhibit equal enthusiasm in its outward and its inner man at one and the same

29

time. He began by handing himself over to the devil, with
all his heart, and Damerones and her good services with
him, and began to ask himself very seriously what was the
real meaning of all those charges about witchcraft, that had
been so perpetually rung in his ears.

" Decidedly," said he,"I may possibly be in the wrong to
swear so out and out that I would defend Damerones against
her 1 Damerones is all safe now behind her town walls, and if
I could by chance manage to carry them by assault, I could
give Fulk charge of her, and the damoiselle know nothing
about it. But what's the meaning of all this talk about
sorcery ! .   . I must have a talk with the canon about
thatl Ah, yes indeed, I never thought of it till this moment! The canon is the only man who can put me all
right on the subject. He is friends with Damerones, he is
friends with me, and Mahaut too. How came it that I
never thought of all that before ?"

Monseigneur Philippe was greatly in want of something
to brace up his courage; for it must be confessed that neither in Palestine nor in Typhnines gaol had he ever felt so
unhappy as he now was in Mahaut's chatel. He went
down the donjon staircase to proceed to the oratory; but
when in the court-yard he heard a noise of quarrelling,
which induced him to look towards the entrance gate—
and what was it he saw ? At first he could hardly trust
in his own eyesight.

Fulk, who had been laid hold of by a crowd of men-at-
arms, was, in spite of his outcries and protests, being
pushed by the shoulders and turned out of doors from the
fortified inclosure. His protests were all shouted forth in
vain, his calls for help were vain as well as all his demands
for explanation. Compelled to give way to superior numbers he had drawn his sword, but as the valiant squire was
bareheaded, he had a hard task to fend off the blows they

aimed at him, and so was forced, step by step, backwards to the gate. The men that were pressing on him had all the better heart for their work, seeing how roughly lie had handled them the day before at the fight in Rusquet Woods.

Thinking that it meant nothing more than one of those broils so common among soldiers, Monseigneur Philippe advanced a few steps and shouted with a voice like thunder:—

"You miserable scoundrels there 1 will you soon have done attacking my man in such numbers ? If any man has something to say to Fulk, all he has to do is to offer to fight him in a fair way; I answer for it, he '11 not decline to knock the whole of you over, if you *11 come on one at a time 1"

Monseigneur Philippe was greatly astonished to see that his intervention did not put an instant end to the struggle. On the contrary, the sergeants-at-arms pushed poor Fulk harder than ever, and now hootings and curses broke out against the knight himself! Highly irritated, he was about to chastise what he called the insolence of that low scum, when two of the gentlemen, Mahaut's allies, came forward with looks both solemn and sad.

"Monseigneur," said one of the gentlemen, "we know not why the damoiselle employs us as bearers of a message that afflicts us much."

" Never mind your message just now," replied he. " See how they are maltreating my squire there. Help me punish the brutes first—and I will then hear whatever you may please to say!"

"Monseigneur," continued the gentleman, "they have no intention to kill Fulk, but merely to expel him from the castle. The Lady of Cornouiller's orders will have it so."

" The lady's orders ? Eh 1 what has my squire done to deserve such treatment ?"

" Nothing at all; but where the master no longer abides, there the squire cannot remain. The Lady of Cornouiller charges us to say to you in express terms, that desiring to haYe no farther connection with rebel burghers, sorcerers, and their adherents, she commands you to quit her fortress on the spot."

Monseigneur Philippe was so stunned, so stupefied, at hearing these words that he stood still, incapable of uttering one word or finding any answer to make. His heart seemed to him so cramped that he felt as if he would suffocate—tears rose up to his eyes. He knew not whether it was anger or grief, that dominated him. He looked to the right and then to the left with an undecided stare; and impelled, rather by some kind of instinct than reason of any sort, he bowed to the two knights, moved towards the great gate, and made Fulk a sign to offer no further resistance, and follow him. He stepped across the threshold of his unjust fiancee, heart-broken, and miserable beyond expression.

In this way he stalked onwards followed by Fulk, who kept quietly asking him for some explanation on the strange affair; when, of a sudden, they heard the tramp of conning horses behind them.

They were the knight's and Fulk's chargers coming down the slope, driven forwards by the stable boys, who were cracking their whips to drive them faster down hill

CHAPTER XXV.

WHEN the burgher cavalcade, the evening before, re-entered the fortifications of Typhaines tired and out of breath with excitement and fatigue, Simon proceeded at once to his home, where we have seen him on other occasions. He did not go to the sumptuous mansion with its two towers on Weavers Street, for it was no nearer being finished than were the abodes going up for Eudes, Jacques, and Payen—he simply took Damerones to the old thatched dwelling we know of. In spite of entreaties and prayers, which at times seemed very near to coming to curses, Payen persisted in not quitting his colleague's side, and as the cloth merchant could not venture altogether to act out the part of imperious pre-eminence over his hardy colleague, he submitted, though with a bad grace, to the necessity of accepting his company.

On entering his door ho said to Jeanne : " Here, I have brought back your daughter; now that her life is safe I am going to make her expiate her crimes."

"Father," said Damerones, in tones soft though firm, " you treat me as if I was guilty, and you are greatly in the wrong. If, however, it seems to you just that I should suffer in my body for my sins and other faults, I make supplication unto you that you would put your trust in me to that end, and you shall have no reason to regret it, for you never can mortify my flesh so much as I intend to do myself."

" Look at her—the hypocrite!" cried Simon, " Bhe wants to seduce us again ! After tearing out of my grasp that tiger-cub of Cornehaut she is in hopes of evading the penalties she has so richly deserved ; bnt she will not succeed in that!"

" What good do yon expect from this violence," asked Damerones in the same placid tone, " and who can induce you to believe that I even dream of deceiving you ? If you should punish me with stripes, by privations of all sorts, by confining me in a dungeon, you '11 do no more, I repeat it, than I intended to do of ray own accord; and if you wish to know my motives I will not refuse to explain them.

" Speak, then—lying and faithless girl 1 thou enemy of thy father and thy city. Speak," said Simon, " and let us know what new trick it is thy spirit hath begotten."

"1 have just passed," said Damerones, " long days and longer nights in the dolorous solitude of a prison. It was there Heaven gave me to see my hopes and desires all naked before my eyes. I have learned to know how miserable they all are, and it is to the service of Ood that I now desire to consecrate my future existence."

This declaration seemed to touch .even Master Simon to the quick; Jeanne tenderly took hold of her daughter's band ; Payen, who when he entered the room had taken a seat in the far off shadow of the place, never moved. It seemed that this general silence had worked its influence on Damerones' feelings; on finding some little indulgence her soul softened down and melted with the emotion. She threw herself on her knees in front of her father, and spoke:—

"1 well know yon can accuse me of having ill recompensed your much affection for me, and yet, what is it I have done ? I saved Monseigneur Philippe's life ? Know you not that his death could never resuscitate our friends we have lost ? . . . Enough blood, father, has been shed on the earth. . . . Men are wicked 1 . . . God 1 how many inventions have they conceived to divide and reud asunder to attack and destroy each other! But, father, let us

not speak of such sad things any more—I will become a poor Clarisse. Yery well 1 I shall expiate my faults, and this one too among the rest."

Damerones uttered these words with a tone of voice wherein a faint smile appeared as if to suppress the rising tear. The savage burgher made no reply, and with crossed arms on his breast he appeared to be contending against the wild heart-throbs below them. Tender love of his child was, as we all know, a full swelling energetic sentiment in Simon's soul; it must well have been so, to enable him to struggle with the tempestuous passions to which the burgher had given up his whole life in its whole and every part. He was penetrated with grief as he looked and saw how severe her sufferings must have been. Damerones' fair countenance had grown thin now ; her great blue eyes begirt around with dark aureoles gave forth a splendor of beam they had never before been known to pour around, and her vague and dolorous smile served only to reveal the sufferings she would vainly strive to hide. Simon's heart was touched, but the wrath-fire that had for many days been smouldering in the deepest depths of his soul was not so easily to be quenched, as not at once to give place to a profound feeling of melancholy; and the consul, dissembling his real intention, made a stately gesture.

"To me it seems," said he, "that you have greatly fallen from your old high ambition. You used to dream of other things than celestial joys; and, if my memory serves, I think I have seen you filled with the insensate hope of participating in tbe donjon and the chivalric honors of the Sire de Cornehaut ?"

" I was wrong," said Damerones, very gently, while a painful emotion visibly flitted across her features—" I was very wrong; I knew not things that to-day I no longer ignore. But Canon Norbert spoke to me on the way; he showed me what the truth was; he laid open before me the very bottom of our hearts. I do not repent me of having rescued Messire Philippe from death, but I know that I saved him for another, and not for me. But, father, let there be an end to all this now, as there is no longer any question of a man who is nothing to me—not my brother, not my friend, not my . . . . (added she in a lower tone) my betrothed ! . . . I will be a Clarisse, and seeing that I am now detached from this world, you will grant me your pardon."

Payen, whom no one had appeared to be thinking of, arose from the corner where he had been sitting and approached Simon. The tall stature of the youthful consul, the mail that covered him, his crimson mantle, long sword, and tanned cheeks, hardy and bold, his whole outlook in fact gave him a warrior's look of which a nobleman might well be proud.

" Friend Simon," cried he, " I followed you here to protect your daughter in case your anger should happen to carry you too far. But now I am to take part against her. I am neither a gentleman nor a glib speaker, and it may be that my phrases will not be good ones; still, to tell the whole truth, I am in love with Damerones, and I will not allow her to lead such a hard life as that of the poor Clarisse^. Do you know, of a surety, my child," pursued the consul, turning to Damerones, " that the poor souls that enter that Order are obliged to fast all day long on bread and water, wear serge next to their naked bodies,

Bcarce sleep o' nights, and brnise and mangle their bodies with blows, no doubt, because they conceive it is not enough to drag themselves all day on their knees over the icy stone-pavements of their churches ? For great sinners, perhaps, such penance as that may be all right, and I see no harm in their taking all that trouble to turn their poor souls a little whiter or so. But for you, my child, who have nothing to complain of but a wildish head, the punishment is rather too severe. So now, Master Simon, here is what ought to be done—give me your daughter to wife. You once told me that such a proposal was agreeable to you; I am a burgher and a consul of Typhaines, wealthy, as you know, and able to do whatever I like, buy, or build even two more mansions superior to the one about which the whole town is daily paying its compliments to me. You will tell me, perhaps, that Damerones has been so silly as to think of marrying the knight; but what's that to me ? She is a worthy good girl, and 'pon my soul, though the knight is an enemy of the commune, and though I feel quite ready to give him back blow for blow if the chance should offer, if my head was as weak as a woman's, I could myself well love and call him peerless. After all, he has just saved the whole of us at Rusquet Woods. In short, Damerones is a child, and if you will order her to marry me, it's my opinion she 'll find more honor and profit too in obeying your command than listening to the foolish notions she's got into her head."

After this speech, Payen crossed his arms, stood looking at Master Simon, and waited to hear what answer his colleague could make.

In other days, to marry his daughter to the wealthy young blacksmith had been the favored dream of our cloth-merchant. His long and adventurous life had forced him to become acquainted with and to judge the characters of

too many different men, not to have made him skilfnl in the
science of physiognomy and disposition, and that science
had early enabled him to perceive in Payen an elevated and
noble nature, loyal in the extreme, and rarely to be met
with. Born in a noble rank, the Typhaines blacksmith
would certainly have made a man to rival even the audacious and brilliant courage of Monseigneur Philippe himself : cast by birth down into the burgess-rank he had
still, most promptly, comprehended and accepted too, the
exalted opinions and purposes of Simon, and was one of
the first men in the borough to conspire for the change of
the feudal institution of the abbey of Typhaines into a powerful and independent commune. Impassioned with the
theories he had embraced, he hated the gentlemen, in so
far as they proved to be enemies to his commune ; in other
respects, sensitive in the highest degree to everything
splendid and glorious, he had become captivated with the
valiant and loyal nature of Monseigneur Philippe, and
thought it no harm in Damerones to be struck with admiration as great as his own.

Beyond this the spirit of the blacksmith's inquiry did
not go. He had that simple, natural confidence in himself
as to never dream that the consul's child could refuse his
offered hand, now that to marry the crusader was become
a thing impossible.

But Simon was far better acquainted with the nature of
human passion, and with Damerones' heart. Tired as he
was of struggling, and ever failing in the strife, the consul
felt no heart to enter on a new conflict with the girl, which
he knew could end only in a new defeat. The very excess
of his sorrow, his disappointments, made it an imperious
necessity for him no longer to oppress her, but, on the
contrary, to raise her up and press her to his breast. That
austere and powerful soul of his was now the prey of a

sadden feeling of depression and discouragement that demands rest, and Payen's speech, by recalling him to a renewed and painful contest, sounded in his ears as a sad and lugubrious tone. He shook his head therefore sorrowfully, and taking his young colleague by the hand, spoke as follows:—

" I thank you, my friend, for your good intentions; in them I recognize the proofs of your friendly regard; but, believe me, it is better to let some time elapse before we speak together on these matters; the poor girl there who is gazing at us is still too far given over to her criminal thoughts. It is all a vain notion in her to aspire to the peace of the cloister life; I do not believe a word of it, and I should be angry at myself were I to send a woman so indisposed to honor and serve you, to your mansion here. Believe me, it is better to wait until the still glowing embers of her insensate projects shall have become extinguished and cold in her frivolous brain; it will be time enough to talk of a marriage when that is all over."

Payen looked suspiciously at his colleague. " I guess at your meaning," said he. "You prefer to keep Damerones, and punish her. That is your right, and there are many who would approve of your doing so. But I don't care about what you call justice; I love Damerones, and I will not suffer her to be afflicted. Should I learn, then, that the girl has been maltreated at your hands, I swear to you, Simon, though you are her father, I will come to your house and take her out of your hands, and make her my wife, in spite of you."

"My lord consul," interrupted Damerones, "your thoughts as to me may be very kind, but they please me not. My father is my master, and if he would kill me, who has a right to hinder him ? As to becoming your wife, think no longer of it; for, from this day forth I am a hand-maid to my God."

" What a crazy family !" cried Payen, as he stamped his foot on the ground. " I wasn't talking to you, and I don't want your opinion about it; it's your father's affair to decide what's right and proper for him, and mine to decide what is best for myself. So hold your peace, Damerones, I beg of you."

" Now all this is going to end in a quarrel," said Jeanne. " Be reasonable, master Payen 1 As my man says you 'U have to wait, why don't you yield to his wish about it?"

I told you about that, already," replied Payen ; " it is because I can see in the looks of him that he wants to mal-treat Damerones."

" You see wrong, then," answered Simon; " and as I do not wish to have a dispute, or any noise with a colleague, I promise you that my daughter shall be as free and as happy as she was a week ago—yes, a fortnight ago—nay a whole month ago, before any cause of division rose up between us. That I swear, and if you wish it, I will swear to it by St. Procul himself, the patron of our commune."

" Ah, that '8 the way to talk," said Payen, slapping his hand into Simon's big palm ; " and you, Damerones, good-night to you; try to be reasonable, and I truly swear for my part that when we are married, you shall have no cause to repent it."

Delighted with all he had said and done, Payen lifted the latch, and went into the street. He hadn't the least doubt that in two or three days Simon would send word that his proposals were accepted, and that Damerones—completely restored to her senses— would, as well she might, begin to count over the whole extent of her good fortune. Delivered fully over to these agreeable thoughts, the young consul, who was fond of ventilating his armor of mail, long sword, and scarlet mantle, on the high street, strode on towards Weavers' Street to inspect the works going on at his new mansion. He was soon met and joined by a crowd of some of the borough notables, who happy and proud to be counted as among a consul's familiar acquaintances, continued to attend him without being invited to do so, and to lavish the flattering speeches that are ever the certain revenue paid to all placemen.

As Payen and his friends now stood in front of the growing mansion-house—

" What a beautiful edifice I" cried one.

" What a superb front!" said another.

" As for me," said a small money-broker, " I have seen Milan, I have seen Florence, I have visited Arras, Bruges, Ghent, Liege, and the Rhine cities, and sure I am, when this structure is completed, it must eclipse everything of the sort ever imagined by the magistrates of those great towns; they never built anything so magnificent—not one of them."

" But this costs me very dear," murmured Payen, rather proudly, and with a smile to show how little he cared what it cost. " I will never rest content with it until I have received a visit in it from Monseigneur the Count de Nevers, aud even Lord Louis, the King of France."

¹¹ Is it your opinion then that either of those personages is likely to come ?" asked a craving news-hunter.

"Well, they say so," negligently and diplomatically responded Payen.

While these followers of the young consul were going into ecstasies over the opulence of the magisterial burgher, and calculating the honors that must inevitably crowd in upon him, there seemed to be some sort of emotion growing up among the outer ranges of the crowd, and with their acclamations to the one who was prime favorite with them,

30

were heard whisperings and suppressed accents, that told there was some rumor abroad among them of grave and serious import.

Those rumors soon reached and penetrated the group of Payees friends; and when he, who had been busy with the master mason charged with the execution of the fine sculptures on the faςade, suddenly turned round, he read on their visages the signs of a great consternation.

" Well, what is it all about?" inquired the young man somewhat astonished.

Oh ! nothing—nothing at all, or at most, only some small matter;" responded the little broker. "There is a rumor in the crowd that there's a Council met at Rheims to judge our cause, and that Abbot Anselm is omnipotent in it."

" Bah !" replied Payen with a shrug.

Just then a burgher came up, and humbly touching his cap, said—

" Seigneur consul, the city council are met, and request you to join them without delay."

Payen received the communication with all due dignity; and assuring the friends about him that he would keep them informed, as far as duty might allow, of what was going on at council, followed the messenger to the Commune-Hall.

Typhaines—that little city of the Middle Ages, which, though it had only within a few weeks past conquered its independence, was nevertheless just now at the very height of that kind of activity, so many examples of which are to be seen in all modern revolutions: only a few days had been required to effect a complete metamorphosis in the town; it had ceased to look like a vassal-borough attached to the abbey on the hill. The appearance οl the houses and streets had undergone a change; the population had

%

doubled, and the burghers had assumed an air of such pride, as well as luxury in dress, that you would not have known the very streets of the old vassal town. You met in the streets with none but wealthy burghers, dressed in good clothes, and wearing chaperones on their heads, either of fur or felt, and begirt with rich sword-belts and heavy daggers.

A commune in the Middle Ages no more resembled a municipal city in the seventeenth century than the latter does a modern one. Indeed, it was a real, though small aristocratic republic, governed by the wealthiest and most distinguished of its burghers, and whose whole territory was comprised within the circumference of its outer walls, its general interests being the interests of its members, and which looked on events of all sorts, provided they did not transpire within a league of home, with an indifference as supreme as if they were occurring in the remotest bounds of Germany. A commune of the twelfth century was ever trying to form alliances, to create a standing armed force, and open outlets and avenues for its commercial operations ; it forwarded and received ambassadors, and had no connection with the rest of France beyond a sort of conventional respect for the king, which was scarce more that nominal. As to the immediate seigneur, they acknowledged his claim of homage, and paid him certain dues as suzerain . . but always on condition that the town authorities would accept no refusal. Burgher towns, numerous enough and wealthy enough to conceive such a state of things, must have in time become sufficiently bold and warlike to push their pretensions as far as possible.

As to Typhaines, it was just now one of the completest models of the most turbulent of republics. Military ardor, enthusiastic love of liberty, greed for trade and money-making, fondness for social honors and distinctions, delight in novelties and in venturesome excitements of all kinds, so dear to people in rebellion, animated the whole scene. The ravages effected by the recent raid might be said to be already forgotten by the multitude. The Typhaineers were so sure of the eternity of their commune, had so little doubt of their own strength, were so vehemently in love with public affairs, that it was out of their power to dream of anything less than victory and success.

Yet, when Payen entered the Council Chamber, he did not descry such a cheerful self-complacent expression on the faces of the assembly as he had just left in the street outside. By Simon's side sat the Seigneur de Pornes, whose unexpected arrival, no doubt, was the reason why a meeting had been called. The wily visage of the cunning baron, like the faces of the rest of the members, was a rather disconsolate one.

" Colleague," said Simon to his young friend, " our enemies are threatening us in a way that looks dangerous."

" Yes," replied Payen, "1 have just heard of it They say a Council has been convened against us."

"And that's true," said Seigneur Baudouin, "and you haven't one single friend in the whole Council."

" What have we to fear, then ? Let us know it at once, as we have nothing to hope for!"

"You'll all be excommunicated, like so many Jews," replied the chevalier.

" Is that a thing to kill ?" responded Payen resolutely.

"We are not a set of Mahometan idolaters," said Antoine, " to make a jest of matters of this kind 1" and he crossed himself.

"No indeed," said Sire Baudouin, "for Monseigneur de Nevers, who is on bad terms with his bishop, already knows very well that you are the only party that's threatened; and if he should be put under an Interdict, his neighbors, who greatly admire his elegant lands, and his vassals too, many of them adherents of yonr Abbot, would be sure to turn their backs on him, or even treat him worse than that."

" So," said Payen, " Monseigneur the Count sends us word by you, does he, that he is going to give us up ?"

"Oh no, not that," said the chatelain confused; "but you ought to understand that provided the bishops and abbots in council should push matters to the extreme, the lord king will be forced to revoke his guaranty, and then Monseigneur will not be in force sufficient to enable him to stand by you. Oh, if he only had a few more troops ! but his men-at-arms are deserting day by day. He hns no money—and now I think of it, it wouldn't be a bad thing for you to offer him a small supply."

"We must have a clear understanding about that," said Simon. "We have already sent the count two thousand gold oboluses; he promised, and we have it here in the charter, a succor of knights and squires, but we haven't as yet seen a soul of them."

"You must be joking," replied Monseigneur Baudouin. " Am I not here, with my men ? And how did you treat me ? Messire Payen there, himself prevailed on me to retire from the town."

" It was out of pure friendship for you then," said Payen laughing: " your men were forever squabbling and fight-ing with people in the streets, and the end wonld have been that not a soul of them would have been left alive. If you '11 prevail on your count to send us a lot of men not so quarrelsome as your vassals, baron, we will give him two thousand gold oboluses more."

"Well said," cried Antoine.

" Agreed, and you '11 put in one thousand for my good offices in the matter. I think that wouldn't be too much.

But be in a hurry about it, for the count is really in want of the money.

" A moment (interrupted Simon)—a moment. We will engage to pay the money when the count has captured Cornouiller Castle, which troubles us too much, and not beforehand. For your portion of the booty we will agree to let you have the chatelaine; and you can marry her to your son, if you like; and in my opinion that's as much as you have any right to expect."

" Give me a merchant, when there's talk of a bargain," said Messire de Pornes, with the sleek look so peculiar to his visage. " Let your intentions be drawn up in writing, and I will set off for Nevers at once."

" That's a good notion," said Payen ; " but if we are to be excommunicated, I foresee already that our allies will turn their backs on us, and even in Typhaines we shall find traitors and people with weak knees; plenty of them. No matter, though. As long as any man is willing to fight he shall have me for a comrade, and if there's nobody else I 'll fight by myself. The Abbot never shall come back here, except he steps across my body."

There was not a man in the room but Simon to answer by a resolute look these brave words, and when the schedule had been drawn up and sealed, Chatelain de Pornes went off to join his followers, and the council adjourned, rather more silently than usual.

" We have a parcel of scoundrels to deal with," said Simon to Payen.

" Yery well, then ; we HI treat them as such, and I make it my business to take them in hand."

CHAPTER XXVI.

THE Canon had not been present at the fight in Rnsqnet Wood s. The truth is, that as soon as he crossed the river he quitted Mahaut's party and followed the burghers; but soon left them, too, to look after any poor victims of the raid, with a view to offer them assistance and religious consolations; after which he proposed to repair to Typhaines again and there carry out the plans his ardent imagination had inspired as to his grand work on the heart of the fair Rose of Typhaines. Of all the Saints of the time, and they were very many, setting aside St. Bernard and Peter the Venerable, St. Dominic and St. Francois d'Assize, Saint Norbert exerted tlfe greatest and most special influence on the population of that age and region.

He had come into France as a pions adventurer, filled with the idea that he could convert the wealthy prebendaries, whose licentious lives had proved to be a scandal for the whole church, and a danger as well: his success in that design was not very great; but by way of compensation, he did, by the vigor of his zeal and the impetuosity of his preachings, tame down the crowds of the laity who had refused to be frightened by his advice and his exemplary devotion, to the severest forms of religious penance. In the years during which our history is passing, in those parts of the country where St Norbert appeared, there was not a knight, a burgher, or a serf, but held him to be a real bona fide Missionary sent down from the skies. His oddities, the profound misery in which he persisted to live; and which would look so strange in our day, were but so many means for acting on the gross understandings of the age. St. Norbert was admired and venerated by the whole country around.

The Saint had deeply reflected upon Damerones' passion, and, above all else, had been struck by the act of courage by which the young maiden proposed to redeem the life of her beloved. That act seemed no more of a comedy in his eyes than it was in her own heart. In the manners and customs of that day, everything appears to have turned on some sudden fit of passion, and nothing could be more likely than to see Simon offer up his daughter as a sacrifice to his revenge, or Mahaut to follow his lead. Thus, though Damerones knew quite well what risk she was running by going headlong into the danger, her firmness inspired him with that secret esteem that strong minds never refuse to virtues that are real. Looking on the maid of Typhaines as a being altogether different from the numerous other women to whom he^abitually imparted spiritual instruction in that country, the old man had made up his mind to lead her on in the only path by which, according to his views, her merits could be so brought out as to work the full harvest of good to be expected from them. As he was despatching her to Cornouiller, he had already bestowed his primary lessons of instruction on the sweet child.

He showed her that her love for Philippe could not possibly come to a happy end; lie had proved that, by explaining that the knight was a son of the persecutor of her race; and so, he being divided from her by all those murders, she was better fitted to comprehend the power of the oath that bound Mahaut's and Philippe's life into one bond. She 6aw that, without an outrage, the geutleman could not possibly renounce a betrothal that had become consecrated during five years of absence, by what in the opinion of the whole province had been the very model of reserve and modesty among women. Nor did the Canon make any scruple about telling poor Damerones of Philippe's great love for the damoiselle, a love by the by she was fully aware of, as two troubadours had already published their poems on the sub* ject, and which she had got by heart. In fine, Norbert piled up before the poor child's eyes the most overwhelming proofs of the vanity of her hopes. He then went on to attempt to make her comprehend that she was reserved for another task ; that it was shameful in such an one as she to sigh and to suffer in behalf of the miserable happiness of an impossible passion.

Her heart pierced through with as many wounds as the Canon had launched out arguments, Damerones listened submissively, but silently, to the aged priest's counsels. Norbert reminded her that, according to God's will, the enthusiastic attachments of this lower world are incapable of returning a full recompense of reward. He sounded forth into her ears the then far-famed name of a woman, which has ever remained a celebrated one, who after astonishing the world by the depth of her devotion, seemed afterwards destined to enlighten it by the perfection of her virtues. He named Heloise's name, and proposed that it ought to be her noblest object and aim to live henceforth detached from all mundane things, and at the feet of the Abbess of Paraclete. In the mystic language so familiar to the theologian of every age, he boasted the sweets of penitence, the mysterious joys of austerity; he drew a picture, well conceived to seduce a passionate soul, of that bliss unequalled, boundless, and regretless, that overcomes the soul, the heart, the imagination, when abstinence, fasting, detachment from all things worldly, and from earth itself, have brought the insensate revolts of the will down to the very foot of the cross. He did not point out to her—though she saw it herself—that in existences of that nature, where all is nullified except an exasperated power to desire, and an immense expansion of the soul, even the endless reveries of a despairing love find, at last, a place where nothing comes in to put a check or set a bound to their free indulgence.

In spite of all, whether it was that her hopes—foolish though she knew them to be—still held her so firmly enthralled, or whether she could not find in her heart to think she must renounce of her own free will all that had made life—life for her—she departed on her journey, shaken, but not fully convinced, to present herself to Mahaut, her soul filled with dreams, and her will still undecided: she allowed too vivid a flash of her secrot to play around her features; and thus fell under the wrath of the proud fiancee, who had herself suffered quite too long not to have nursed her love until it had grown implacable.

It was in the dark prison at Cornouiller that the thoughts accumulated round about the soul of Damerones with such zeal by Norbert, awoke and began to hum and to buzz in a way to call her to a deep consideration of their real purport and value. The poor girl's anxiety concerning Monseigneur's fate during the eight mortal days of seclusion in the deep obscurity of her dungeon, disabled her from calculating the lapse of the hours that were prolonged by her impatience, and led her to suppose that her attachment to the chevalier, and consequently her resistance to the sacred will of the Canon, might well be punished by the death of the crusader. The idea was so horrible that it seemed as if true in its influence on her imagination. In great misfortunes we little doubt of what we most fear. In her despair, then, she asked herself whether she ought not to renounce a course so accursed of heaven. She wept, she sobbed, she settled the terms of duty, and the hours still flew on, and no one came to say that Monseigneur Philippe was saved. In fine, about an hour before the stone slab that closed her prison above was raised, she had gone down on her knees on the stone floor, and prostrated her forehead to the cold flags, and there took the solemn vow to obey the Canon, renounce her passion, and go bury with herself, within the convent of Paraclete, a passion as unhappy as the one which was already sleeping in that sequestered abode.

As usual, under great crises of the soul, as soon as she had pronounced her vow, she rose from her knees with a feeling of utter exhaustion, which she mistook for a feeling of complete rest. When her prison door opened, and the knight's deliverance announced so promptly after the making of her vow, she returned thanks to heaven that had not disappointed her expectations, and never for a moment doubted that Philippe's safety was a direct result of the work of her own hands. In this conviction she found a new source of strength, and a new reason to push her sacrifice to the last extremity, and made up her mind that as long as she should continue within the walls of Cornouiller, she would not utter a single word, for fear lest should she speak, even to Norbert himself, it might lead to a gush of her old tenderness, and to a giving way to the softer emotions of her bruised and aching heart. But for this apprehension of turning weak again, she might have spared Mahaut the poignant distress inseparable from a passion of love that believes itself betrayed.

During the entire ride to the foot of the bridge, she per. sisted in her silence, wholly absorbed in the contemplation of her sorrows, and given up to the interior tumults of her despair-enthusiasm; her outward appearance was one of coldness and constraint. Mahaut considered that stolidity as the criminal dissimulation of a corrupt soul; even Norbert interpreted it as the sign of a profound sorrow that was still clinging to its old hopes.

While the ceremony for the exchange of the prisoners was going on, Damerones had descried Messire Philippe coming forward; and when the gentleman, on speaking to her got no answer, he, too, was misled to suppose that the mournfal expression of her features, while she was inwardly taking an everlasting farewell, really meant a reproach of ingratitude ; though, in fact, she was breaking off forever the only bonds that now bound her to earth. To her it seemed that this last look she bore on her lover's countenance had drunk up the very last drops of human happiness in her bosom, and all the invectives of her old father fell unheard on her ears; and, indeed, throughout the entire march to Typhaines, she remained perfectly insensible to Payen's simple and natural evidences of affection. She didn't come to herself at all until the scene at Rusquet Woods, when she suddenly beheld in all the hurry of the heady fight Monseigneur Philippe, sword in hand, looking as redoubtable, as beautiful, and irresistible, thought she, as the valorous archangel Michael, when, with his flaming falchion, the immortal warrior assails and disperses the embattled legions of hell.

But now, Becluded in her father's dwelling, her only thought turned on the fulfilment of her vow. After he left the house, she held a conference with Simon and Jeanne, as sad for them as it was burning for her own poor stricken heart. She again explained her purposes, and swore that nothing in the world would induce her to give them up.

" If it must be so," said she, resolutely, " I will invoke the protection of the Canon and the population of Typhaines against your foolish opposition ; a Christian commune never can abandon the woman who desires to give herself up to the most high God !"

Simon had sapplicated in vain. He saw that his child's will was inexorable, and situated as the commune then was; as he himself was, indeed, he clearly comprehended that too protracted an opposition would bring him into suspicion with the religious portion of the community, and lend new arms to his own enemies, and the commune's as well. In utter despair, then, of preserving his onjy child, he was leaving the house with death in his soul, as word was brought that Seigneur de Pornes had arrived; and next, meeting with Norbert in the street, he accosted him humbly and submissively; how different from the boldness that in other days had shone out of his manly features! . . . but reiterated strokes of sorrow had at long last bent that intractable soul of the cloth merchant.

" Holy father," said the consul, " I presume that you are going to visit ray unhappy child. I implore you, take her not away from me ! You are a wise man, and very different from those priests who are moved by an inconsiderate zeal; you are not the man to desire to divide the happiness of men from the service of God. Does not the whole world know that 'twas you who dissuaded the good Count of Champagne from entering a convent, under the thought that he could better serve God by well governing his people than by praying in a cloister ? Leave me, I conjure you, leave me my only child!"

"Master Simon," rudely responded the Canon, "you talk like a laic, with neither wisdom nor reason. Go you and mind yonr own affairs, and don't meddle with what concerns you not."

The consul wrung his hands. He knew that menaces and excitement were powerless as weapons against the ancient priest, who, seeing how grieved he was, added in a softened tone—

" You speak foolishness, Master Simon, I tell you. You

31

are not consulting the best interests of yonr child. What I do you suppose that a soul cradled for years in an ambition so lofty can come down again to low and vulgar desires ? No, *you* ought to know what a heart is better than that. Damerones has been dreaming she would be the wife of a chevalier; she could never henceforth go down into a lower condition without ever blushing for shame. I know her; her soul is a great one, and she requires things far above her social rank. The cloister alone offers her what can serve to fill up the measure of that soul of hers. Go, Master Simon, go in peace; I take charge *of* Damerones, and I am not the man to act like a negligent pastor..   .

Now hearken to my advice on another subject. . . You know that I condemn and contemn the sedition of which the Typhaines people are guilty. The moment is near when you, their chief and leader, will have to render an account of your crimes. I know that powers you can never think of resisting, are conjured up against you. Take care of yourself! It is no pleasing sight for me to look upon bloodshedding!"

At these words Simon stood straight up; the disconsolate father vanished, and the consul of Typhaines was himself again.

" Holy father," said the burgher. " Thank you for your counsel. But, believe me, that I and my friends have no fears of the future; we have conquered our liberties, and think as you will of it, there is no power beneath the moon strong enough to wrest them away. Death, at the worst, is an ever open asylum, and we shall know how to find refuge there."

" Oh, obstinate race !" replied the old man, striking the foot of his staff on the ground; and without another word, he turned his back on the consul, and soon entered the abode where Damerones, seated by her mother's side, was trying to depict their approaching separation in a way less cruel, less dolorous.

The coming in of the Canon added new force to the instances and exhortations of the young maiden. Only a few words were wanting, and then the consul's wife gave in, for she trembled at the thought of standing out in opposition to the will of a man she looked on as the direct and special delegate of God himself; so that, after a few minutes she went forth to a corner of the garden where she might weep free and alone over her unspeakable loss.

Now Norbert was alone with his neophyte; with her whom he had introduced into a new line of thought—into a new era, and as he made her give him an account of the state of her soul, he was struck with the rapidity with which his counsels had blossomed and borne rich fruit in her heart. He felicitated Damerones on the occasion, and they agreed that within two days to come, she should silently evade the pangs of farewell to her parents; and so Monseigneur's unhappy friend, quitting her childhood's home, should proceed in company with the venerable old Canon to the convent at Paraclete, which lay at no great distance from the borough of Typhaines.

During the time Damerones was thus making ready to renounce the whole world, Monseigneur Philippe and Fulk, so rudely expelled from Mahaut's chatel, were mutually asking what was the fault, what the real crime that had brought such undeserved treatment on them. The knight and his companion retired into the very heart of the wood, and tying their horses to the trees, had seated themselves on the margin of a spring, where they gave themselves up to the most sorrowful meditations.

" The truth is," said the melancholy chevalier, " that I don't believe there ever was a more miserable being than 1 am. Ever since we came back to my native land, everything has gone wrong with me—and yet where is my fault f"

"It's no concern of mine," responded Fulk, "to know whether there has been any fault or no. The only thing I can think about is, that we are going to spend the evening without any supper, and that to-morrow morning we are to fall into the Typhaineers' hands, unless there should some good miracle happen. Women, it must be confessed, are a most abominable set 1 I thank God for putting my eye out at Cambrai, for that circumstance has dispensed me from the necessity of having anything more to do with them."

" How many misfortunes in only a few weeks 1" exclaimed Messire Philippe. " There's my father's death ; then the loss of my tower; next to that a most horrible dungeon, and to crown the whole, comes Mahaut's wrath 1 ah, that, indeed, is worst of all 1 Knowest thou why she treats me so ill ?"

"Know! Not I, indeed; I have not the least idea of it; no more than she has."

" Oh, yes; she has taken it into her head that I'm in love with the Consul of Typhaines' daughter, that little Damerones, that saved me from the claws of that old devil of a father of hers. He's worse than the devil, though!"

" Oh, you mean that little wicked thing they are accusing of witchcraft?"

This speech of Fulk's recalled to Philippe's recollection the urgency of Mahaut in always coming back to the impu- tation which had seemed to him to be merely an invective. Fulk had heard the story in conversation among the men- at-arms at the chatel, and edified his master's ears with accounts which, in spite of all their gravity, he could by no means make up his mind to believe in.

"No, no," said he, "Damerones has nothing to do with

hell; I should have to see a very striking proof of it before I could believe in that. She might be crazy, perhaps;
if she ever had an idea of making me forget my devoirs to
Mahaut, out of mere gratitude to her: she might save my
life a thousand times over again, and she could not succeed
in that. But if she is out of her senses, poor thing, she
ought to be pitied, and not accused. If I only could get
hold of that rascal Rigauld l He, the traitor, is the cause
of all the misfortunes that overwhelm me now."

14 Oh ! you are right there," exclaimed Fulk. " If I had
him in hands wouldn't I shake him till his infernal soul
would be too glad to squeeze itself out betwixt his two
d d lips l"

Now, just as if these charitable ejaculations had been
words of power, no sooner had the squire made an end of
uttering them than Rigauld, yes, Rigauld in person, made
his appearance in the path l Fulk uttered a cry of joy, for
he descried him before his master saw him; but a second
look showed that the forester was not unattended, and that
very likely the people with him wouldn't suffer him to be
mishandled without knowing the reason why.

Rigauld was walking on with a hasty step, head up and
face all joyful, in front of a numerous cavalcade. He was
dressed as of yore, and held in his hand, instead of his
crossbow, a very long javelin with a thin bright iron point.
Behind him, for no doubt he was the guide, came riding
on a richly caparisoned mule, his Seigneur Anselm, and by
his side Master Guillaume de Champeaux, Bishop of Cha-
lons-sur-Mame, and the good knight Sire Jean Berniot,
whom we are already acquainted with; then came on a
troop of clerks equally well mounted, and then about fifty
men-at-arms and sergeants on foot with long lances and
arbalists.

The sight of that numerous company that so suddenly

debouched from the woods, turned the course of Philippe's and Folk's meditations, yet they, neither of them, moved, and when the Abbot got up with them, they offered him no salute.

" Why, how's this !" cried Anselm; " is it indeed you, my son, that I find out here ? Praised be the Lord 1 he hath delivered you out of the hand of the impious."

"It's no fault of yours," answered Monseigneur Philippe, " if my head does stick on my shoulders—thanks to your d d abbey and you too, I have met with more misfortunes than tongue can tell 1"

" What do you mean, my son ?" asked the monk. " Whatever may have been the strokes of fortune, be you consoled, for Heaven deems that we have been sufficiently tried, and now everything is returning to good order again."

"No doubt," put in Messire de Berniot, "and as this knight is, I doubt it not, the valiant crusader who defended Typhaines so gloriously against the peasantry, he will be pleased to learn, together with the good news we bear, that the recital of his actions has covered him with glory at the court of our good King Louis."

All sorrowing though he was, Monseignetfr Philippe could not rest insensible to Sir Jean de Bemiot's speech; and after a short parley he suffered himself to be prevailed on, and 60 mounted his horse to accompany the ecclesiastical dignitaries, w^io insisted on knowing the cause of his isolation in that lonely Rusquet Wood, and the deep discontent that seemed to have overmastered him.

" You will go with us to the abbey ?" said Anselm.

" How, what ? Do you expect to get in there ?" said Philippe.

" What do you find to surprise you in that ?" asked Master Guillaume. "Don't you see what a following Messire de Berniot commands ; and do you imagine those burghers, stupid though they be, will likely be tempted to face the temporal censures of all these men in arms ?"

" You are right there," replied the chevalier, " and my surprise arises from the promptness the holy Abbot has evinced in thus changing his rout into a victory."

" It is always thus with the affairs of the Church," proudly returned the bishop. " None but the mad and the rash ever attack her; for, in fact, God has promised her an eternal triumph. So, my son, I would have you believe that though the Typhaines peasantry have been for a few days glorifying themselves in their revolt and madness, but a few days will pass before they shall be seen weeping together over the ruins of their commune."

" So mote it be!" rejoined the crusader, " but I none the less must remain robbed of my tower, and my domain, merely because it pleased monseigneur my father to disinherit me without the least reason in the world."

" You shall espouse the wealthy damoiselle of Cornouiller," replied Bishop Guillaume, "and the blessings our prayers will draw down on you will leave you nothing to wish for."

This ill-timed consolation brought on the recital of all the crusader's sorrows; but Anselm, altogether taken up with concerns far more sacred and, in his estimation, far more important, turned but an inattentive ear to the tale. The towers of Typhaines were already in sight, and Messire Jean interrupted the knight's explanation and doleances for the purpose of observing to the two prelates, that it was now time to redouble their precaution, lest they should be surprised by the burgh-people in case they should chance to have got wind of the approach of the cavalcade.

The bishop felt but little interest in the love and business affairs of Sir Philippe de Cornehaut the disinherited; he eagerly listened therefore to Sir Jean de Berniot's observa-

tions, and further remarked, how unseemly it would be for
the Abbot of Typhaines to re-enter his minster without
due pomp and parade. They therefore hurried Rigauld
forward to advertise the monks of their seigneur's return.

The party came to a halt; order was restored in the line;
the cortege was arranged and time allowed to the clergy
to dress the two prelates with their pontificals. When all
was ready, the troop issued from the wood, and the sentinels
at Typhaines sounding the alarum summoned the people
to the ramparts to see their cruelest enemies defiling in
front of them. First came on the trumpeters, with a band
of crossbow men on foot; then followed ten men-at-arms
on horseback, from whose midst floated out the banner of
the abbey. After these rode Abbot Anselm, coiffed in his
mitre and holding his abbatial cross, on a mule with a
caparison of cloth of silver; by his side advanced Bishop
Guillaume, whose episcopal vesture was sparkling with
gold and gems. Next they beheld the two knights, Messire Jean and Monseigneur Philippe de Cornehaut, between
whom marched the banner of the Bishop of Chalons. Fulk
brought up the rear; the rest of the infantry and cavalry
closed the march, with Messire Jean de Bemiot's banner
in the midst of them.

The crowd assembled on the town ramparts were smitten
with terror at the sight But, when they beheld how the
abbey monks were issuing in procession from the great
gate, rage got the upper hand of fear, and they broke out
in hootings and menacings, the only effect of which was to
bring back all Messire Philippe's hatred to the people who
had treated him so cruelly. Not a man left the town, for
the consuls had severely forbidden them to make a sortie.
Mingled with the distant din of the burghers, you might
also hear some of their prayers; many of the aged women,
seeing a bishop before them, went down in obedience to

custom, on their knees, while some of the men, who though they did not follow their example, were frozen with terror.

As to the monks, when they saw their Abbot again, they gave way to the most touching demonstrations of joy and love. On their knees, by the roadside, they kissed the hem of his robe, and the prior, who had meditated an address to be drawn up in solemn words, burst into tears as he gazed on his Superior.

Anselm reproved them mildly for an emotion unworthy of a band of Coenobites who ought to be insensible to every earthly emotion. Yet even he was not wholly exempt from a sort of tender heartedness. As he was passing in at the grand minster-gate Bishop Guillaume took his arm, and pointing to the Typhaines populace, who were crowded on the ramparts compact and uneasy—

"Yonder," said he, "are your serfs, and we will make them supple to the yoke of your authority."

The Abbot gazed for a while at the town below him, and tears filled his eyes.

" They are my children," said he, " and I am forbidden to bless them!"

He then went into the abbey, and as soon as the last cavalier of the band had crossed its threshold the portal closed again.

CHAPTER XXVII.

THE Seigneur de Pornes had left Typhaines, fully absorbed in his meditations. Monseigneur Baudouiu, of all
the knights of the Nivernais, was one who was most given
to meditation ; unfortunately, his reflections generally bore
upon the best means of hurting his neighbors. Like a
poet meditating an ode, or a musician dreaming about
some symphony, the cautelons chatclain ever had on the
anvil some more or less diabolical machination. His temper, too, was strangely affected by the success or the failure
of his plans. Had he succeeded well in some act of perfidy—had he led to a happy conclusion some infamous
snare, he became a most charming man on the spot, and
anybody might venture to accost him, and provided some
idea of how he could hurt you did not flash through his
brain, he proved to be the gayest, the most delightful of
good fellows, and witty and amusing to a degree.

To this uncommon amiability, and the extreme gentleness
and elegance of his manners it was, that he owed his influence with his suzerain, the Count de Nevers : repeated
proofs had been laid before the count of many reprehensible acts of Baudouin, but the count only shrugged his
shoulders, and always refused to treat the man harshly,
who helped him in all his affairs, and who, above all, was
sure to find money for him when he was hard pressed,
never worried him with advice, and with his keen, yet quick
face, could always make out to keep him in a roar of
laughter.

The day Monseigneur Baudouin left Typhaines, he was in a most particular good humor, for more reasons than one. The first was that, in a hunt of several days' duration after the serfs that had run off with Joslin, he had been so lucky as to get them into an ambuscade he had planned for the very purpose. He hung four of them, ripped up the bellies of two more, and being desirous, as he expressed it, to treat his favorite Joslin with special distinction, he had him 'tied to a powerful stag's horns, that soon tore the poor wretch into strips. These occurrences had transpired the evening before, and Monseigneur Baudouin grew so amiable and delightful over it, that at supper his daughter, son, son-in-law, men-at-arms, and all the servitors had been forced to laugh till they cried, over his funny account of the matter, and everybody saw that he was beyond any peradventure, the very best of fathers and masters, and that it would be wrong to hold him to a strict account for certain little severities that were natural to his temper.

His good fortune gave him next day a chance to deceive both his master and the Typhaines folk too. He had for a long time been persuading the count to support the burgher cause against the Abbot, and showed him how it could only serve to a considerable extension of his authority, besides bringing in a great deal of money. There was no use talking about the expense, inasmuch as he took it on himself to supply the commune with everything they might be in want of, out of the two thousand gold oboluses he had received in the morning; he counted on keeping a thousand for himself, and then make his master give him five hundred more to pay the troops he was thinking of raising, and whom he had not the least idea of paying, as he intended to let them live on the country, a thing most delightful to hireling soldiers, who are ever passionately fond of disorder. But suppose now all his plans should turn out wrong, what would be the consequence? Suppose his suzerain should declare war against him ? what then ? that was a matter of perfect indifference to the seigneur, for he knew that his castle was impregnable. Suppose they should excommunicate himl Monseigneur Baudouin, a rather rare case, was one of the strong-minded sort of people, and he concluded if they should proceed to such extremities as that with him, he would avail himself of the circumstances to pillage, annoy, and bring so many calamities on the people, priests, and monks, within ten leagues round, that they would be glad to reconcile him to the church were it but to secure a little rest. With all these agreeable perspectives before him, Monseigneur Bandouin was the luckiest, best-humored chatelain in the whole country holding from France, or, if you prefer it, from the great tower of the Louvre. Yet his happiness that day was destined to become still greater. As he was riding onwards with his escort, he met a knight called Messire Bertrand, who in fact was one of the fourteen confederates in Mahaut's league; an old wolf who, as he hadn't much to lose, gave Baudouin no particular motive to attack him. Messire Baudouin lived with him on terms which, if not good, .a thing impossible as to any neighbor, yet at least if there were any differences betwixt the two men, they were old ones and half forgotten, or too slight to hinder the baron from opening a conversation with him.

The first polite salutations being now past, Baudouin said:—

"It seems we are travelling the same road, Monseigneur, and yet this is not your road home."

"I am not going home," replied Messire Bertrand, "I am on my way to Nevers."

" To Nevers ? Eh ! you surprise me ! What is it you can have to do with the count our seigneur—you were in open revolt against him the other day, along with the lady of Cornouiller Castle ?"

" I was so, sir; but it appears I am not so now. The fact is, to keep you from languishing for the news, I am ready to tell you about all the events at Cornouiller from beginning to end, if you like."   .

" My interest in that matter is not very great in itself considered," replied the old cheat, " but when one is travelling along the road there's nothing shortens the journey better than a good story told by a wise and considerate man."

" As you are pleased to regard me as a wise and prudent person," said Bertrand,"I have to say that Mahaut has quarrelled with the Seigneur de Cornehaut her betrothed, whose love has been so much bragged about in the whole country these five years past. They were said to be the most attached couple, the fondest and most united of lovers ! Very well; instead of fighting the Saracens, and leading an elevated and noble life beyond seas, it appears certain the young gentleman has been busy at anything but heaving long sighs. So, those two people who were so remarkably fond, hardly had time to meet before they flew at each other like mad ! I do not precisely kgow what they said on the occasion, but the knight certainly did behave with the utmost brutality. He has cut her sergeants-at-arms to pieces for the sake of rescuing a burgher girl, who is no doubt his mistress; and to sum it all up he has been just turned neck and crop out of the lady's chatel. I am now on my way, in Lady Mahaut's behalf, to Nevers, to inform our lord the count that his vassal surrenders' herself to his mercy, renounces her hostilities against Typhaines, and requests his orders, which 6he intends to obey in every particular, and that most faithfully."

" You astonish and at the same time rejoice me much I"

32

said Seigneur Baudouin; " but how happens it that so many lords, about the lady of the chatel, and who all seemed greatly irritated against the Typhaineers, have changed their minds so suddenly when it was her pleasure to do so ?"

" Ten of them at least did quibble a good deal about it, and in a very bad humor too ; the rest, that is, two of my friends and myself, who never really took any interest in the war except for Mahaut's pay and the privilege of plundering, gave ourselves no great concern as to whether we should serve along with them or against them, for, in the present disturbed state of the country, it was out of the question to think of being neutral."

The sentiments of complete impartiality thus displayed by Monseigneur Bertrand were most readily appreciated by his auditor; with that quick wit Heaven had endowed him with he at once thought out a plan of action that he imparted to his fellow traveller, or at least as much of it as he thought best to disclose. The plan consisted in inducing the knight to add a simple phrase to Mahaut's message to the count, showing that the lady renounced her engagement to the disinherited lord of Cornehaut, and referred to her suzerain's wisdom the selection of a proper husband for herself. These few words, which would cost nothing to Messire Bertrand's eloquence, and still less to his conscience, the chatelain engaged to pay for with the sum of eight marks in silver, fine. The bargain was soon concluded, and all the words and conditions sworn to, they agreed to separate so as not to have the air of any private concert or agreement between the two barons. Monseigneur Baudouin took it on himself to direct the count's choice in such a way as to soon bring the affair to a close. He had no real conception of the circumstances that had led to Mahaut's sudden change of mind, but imagined that some misnnderstaudiDg tbat had hart her feelings very badly had induced her to behave in a way to allow him to make a favorable use of the opportunity. Although he never had been allowed to enter the castle, his greed for that splendid domain and its powerful chatel had induced him to make frequent inquiries as to the state of the lady's temper, which he knew was a very haughty and headstrong one. He thought of course that it would be best to be in a hurry about it, for violent tempered people are very likely to suddenly repent of their excitement and go back to their old state of feeling; so that Messire Baudouin trembled for fear some new freak of Mahaut's brain might interfere with the smiling prospects before him.

While the baron's perfidious head was busy turning his mingled hopes and fears over and over, Mahaut, quite given up to despair, had begun to get over the late bursts of her angry passion. Though so easily governed by her pride and resentment, she was really a devoted creature, and had loved the knight for so many tedious years she could not make out how all her legitimate hopes should have tumbled into ruin. Up to that hour she had gloried in her fidelity and constancy, and all she had suffered during her long isolation : for the uneasiness occasioned by the claimants for her hand, and the violent measures they had made use of to secure the possession of it, she expected to be fully rewarded by Monseigneur Philippe's inviolate attachment. But, alas I her betrothed had broken his plighted word I

As her anger went on growing colder and colder, her grief grew greater and greater, and she passed the whole day in tears.

Then, too, the rather violent discussion she had had with her confederates, began to make her doubt somewhat in regard to the justice of her own conduct in the matter. Used as she was to never bend or give way to anybody or

anything on a question where she had once made up her
mind, she had maintained, in the council with the barons,
her perfect right to give up the Abbot of Typhaines, if
such should be her good pleasure; but once she was
obeyed, she began to blush for the excesses into which
her wounded self-love had misled her, and for shame at the
thought of making an alliance with the men of Typhaines,
all which overwhelmed her with sorrow. She was next
tempted to despatch a messenger to the monastery to comfort the poor monks, and assure them she intended to be
perfectly neutral. Just as she was about to carry out that
notion, she reflected that people would accuse her of light-
mindedness, and even think she might have gone crazy:
next, she remembered that she had sent off Messire Bertrand to Nevers, and then, in her pride, made up her mind
to silently wait for the consequences of that rash and vio- '
lent proceeding; and, after all, the feeling that her tenderness had been betrayed, and her sacrifices ignored, was
even more poignant a distress than the memory of the
spotless fame over which she had so long watched with
most jealous care.

Thus was Mahaut far more to be pitied than her supposed rival. Damerones had been very unhappy, and was
still so, in spite of her exalted piety—in spite of her heroic
courage ; but she was sustained by thousands of cheering
thoughts: the wretched chatelaine had nothing of the sort to
lean on, for her impetuous passion had broken every support
to pieces. From the summit of her donjon she had looked
out on the departure of the very last of her friends, and was
now lonely; isolated with a garrison composed mostly of
mercenaries, in the very heart of a country torn by wars;
faithless to her devoir, as a woman of the noble class, as a
good Christian; suspected, no doubt, or soon to be so, of
protecting the seditious Typhaineers, and above all things

else, and worst of all—a widow—though au unmarried woman !

Who is there can tell how bitter were the tears poor Mahaut was shedding on the battlements of her strong chatel ? Who can give expression to her agonies; who name the shiverings that passed, like ice-bolts, among the quivering fibres of her heart! A thousand and a thousand times she wished she could die; a thousand times, in heartrending tones, did she utter the name of Philippe !—Philippe now forever lost to her.

Judging by her own heart, she felt certain that after the signal outrage of his expulsion from her own chatel, he never would return—never could pardon. Besides all this, she felt she never could receive him to mercy again. Thus it was all over, and that very evening she gave proof of the utter blindness in which her soul was held bound and captive by a causeless, but fierce jealousy.

Rigauld came in from the abbey, and brought two letters with him, one from the Abbot, and the other from Canon Norbert.

" Lady," said the gamekeeper, " Monseigneur, the Abbot, has sent me to inform you that he is returned from Rheims; that many of the knights who were here are now assembled at the monastery, and after a long conference between them and Monseigneur Philippe, he sent a messenger to the Burgh to request Canon Norbert to go to the minster and speak with him. An hour after that was done, they despatched me hither with these two letters, and with orders to deliver them, into your own hands."

" Give them," cried the chatelaine.

Seizing the two parchments, she went to the oratory to read them quietly, and alone, for she knew how to read; her uncle, the Bishop of Cambrai, had made her learn that science from the priests under his charge.

Norbert's letter, just like all the good Canon's eloquence, was nothing but fire and flame. It began by rudely scolding Mahaut for her inexcusable behavior. By breaking with her friends, and by outraging her betrothed, she had clearly shown to every judicious mind that she must be possessed by some malign spirit. Then he spoke of Damerones, and on that topic launched out into eulogies so great, expressions of admiration so enthusiastic, that every word he wrote to make the girl's innocency shine out clearer as to Messire Philippe, looked very much, to her, like a piece of special-pleading. He closed by threatening Mahaut with the whole weight of his anger in case she would not make haste to humble herself in the presence of such a splendid spectacle of sanctity in the individual whom she suspected of being her rival in love, and in case, too, she should fail to make, in a true spirit of gentleness and patience, the proper excuses to her betrothed husband, open the gates of her fortress again to her allies, and, in one word, undo everything she had lately been doing.

Had Mahaut been only a little out of temper, this missive of the old priest would have been of itself enough to make her carry matters to the very last extremity. When she began to read the Abbot's letter, her feelings were excessively hurt already, and that, no doubt, was the reason why she was so insensible to the wise and moderate language held by that good man, her once venerated guardian.

Master Anselm explained, and, as he said, confided to her clear and correct understanding a true account of the crusader's conduct; he took his part most discreetly and cautiously, yet he gently reproved Mahaut for a violence of behavior, the causes of which were purely and simply frivolous ones. He availed himself of all the Canon's arguments, but presented them in a better shape, and concluded his despatch by supplicating his pupil to return once more to her sound comraou sense, and no longer compro-

mise her happiness by unjust and hasty resolutions.
Then quitting this subject, that constituted the first portion
of his letter, but was far from being the largest part of it,
he proceeded to that which was much nearer his heart, to
wit, the neutrality which his god-daughter was said to be
thinking of between the abbey and its rebellious burghers;
he pointed out in strong terms how very wrong that would
be on her part, and conjured her to give up the thought;
and, to be brief, he pleaded so well, that he left the chatelaine fully convinced that all his solicitude in her behalf
looked to neither more nor less than the personal profit he
was hoping to make out of an alliance with herself.

"Cunning monk !" said she, as she tore his letter all to
tatters. "You think of nothing but your old abbey, and
you'd think yourself mighty smart if you could only deceive my simplicity enough to make me spend myself in
your cause, and reimburse the perfidious creature you've
been robbing, with my estate 1 But you 'll have no such
satisfaction, I assure you."

She ordered Rigauld to be called.

"Did you see Messire Philippe ?" said she.

"Yes," answered the forester; "I first saw him in the
chapter-hall at the abbey, where he was seated with the
Abbot, the knight, the bishop, the Canon, and the dignitaries of the convent. As I was leaving the hall, after I
got those letters, he followed, and drawing me aside, he
told me in just so many words, that I must assure you he
is innocent; that if you won't pardon his imaginary fault,
you will be the cause of his death; but as for him he will
love you as long as he lives, and, as he was saying so, his
eyes were full of tears."

Mahaut held her eyes downcast on the stone floor while
the forester was speaking, and was silent for some time
after he had made an end, and then stammered out—

" Tell the knight" . .

She stopped. No doubt some word of tender affection had risen to her lips; she was on the point of renouncing her severity and delivering her own heart from the thrall of its sorrow; but a fatal thought uprose.

"Answer me truly," said she rapidly, looking right into Rigauld's eyes, "did you hear Monseigneur Philippe, in the chapter-hall, in the court-yard, or anywhere else, name the name of Damerones ?"

The forester knew no reason why he should not tell the truth.

" Certainly I did," said he ; " he talked about her a good while, with Norbert and Monseigneur Abbot too."

" What did he say about her ?"

" Why, he said she was a devoted young woman; and but for her he would have been put. to death ; and to the last day of his life she would seem more worthy of respect, in his opinion, than a great many dames and damoiselles.''

In those words Mahaut could see nothing but an insult; she felt her heart carried away in a new whirl of indomitable and terrible passion ; she felt sure that the Abbot and the Canon too were attempting only to cheat her for the profit they hoped to make out of it, and that the knight was anxious about nothing in the world but his own estate.

"Rigauld," she exclaimed, "you will bear no answer whatever to Seigneur de Cornehaut. IMI have nothing to do with him all the days of my life, and I MI have him to know that never will I see him more. As to the Abbot and the Canon, tell them that I have put myself into my suzerain's hands, the Count de Nevers; he will tell me what's just and right, and I will obey him in every respect. Begone with you! and remember, you too, for your own safety as well as others, that any messenger, of what sort soever, who may come hither from the abbey, shall find my gates shat, and shall be shot with arrows at the foot of the wall by my archers."

Upon hearing this declaration, Rigauld stared at the angry dame in utter astonishment. His thick brain was unequal to the comprehension of how he, who for so many weeks past had had snch good lodgings at the manor, could so suddenly have turned into an enemy. He rubbed his ear, and after awhile spoke to his fearful interlocutress.

" My lady, seems to me there is great misfortunes in all this—I myself, for long, really thought Damerones was a real witch, but now it appears she is a saint, a real saint; and all the people in Typhaines, so they say, are stooping down to kiss her very foot-prints on the street—I don't go against that no more, for Master Norbert will have it that it's all a fact. Seems I must have mistook 1 but if I did, of course you mistook too as well as I. If I was in your place I'd let Messire Philippe come back, and Fulk too; 1 'd get married, and there'd be an end on't."

Mahaut deigned no reply to the gamekeeper, she merely pointed with her finger towards the gate. The forester went out at double quick, passed the barbican, and never checked his pace until he was fairly out of bow-shot. He was very sorry for these incidents, for he had got used to Cornouiller; he had been well treated at the chatel, and in the rear of the raiders had scrambled up a most capital booty in the suburbs at Typhaines. But after all, he loved, like the faithful vassal he was, the very least of the abbey monks more than all the knights and dames in the whole province. As soon as he got back to the abbey he repeated the whole thing in its native crudity.

There are many people who have suspected that the good forester, induced by some personal resentment, had made no really true report of his conference with the lady of Cornouiller, but that is not a thing to be even thought of. The very words she spoke were quite enough to convince the guests at the abbey that there was nothing to hope for as far as she was concerned.

Norbert, had he been still ou the spot, would have spent himself in savage complaints of the chatelaine; but that zealous and ardent personage had remained at the abbey only just long enough to fully vindicate and justify the whole conduct of Damerones.

Anselm was well acquainted with Rigauld's nonsensical superstition, and no long examination was required to show that Damerones was not the fairy of St. Procul's Spring. The sweet Rose of Typhaines, the cloth-merchant's child, in telling her story to the good Canon, had explained to him how the idea of warning Mahaut of the crusader's peril had crossed her mind; how she happened to think of Rigauld as a fitting messenger, he being the only man at the minster she thought she would trust; and how it happened that while searching for him she chanced to meet him close to St. Procul's Spring. She had been aware of the dull forester's mistake, and availed herself of his terror to spur on his zeal. These details did not and need not take up much time to clear up the whole business.

Norbert, then, had gone back to Typhaines, to the consul's, and warned Damerones that the time to depart was at hand.

" In the course of a few days," said he, " God alone knows what misfortunes are to fall on this unhappy and guilty town. You, Damerones, whom the Lord hath chosen to be one of the most cherished lambs of His flock, it is not fitting that you should stay and be an eye-witness to the ruin of your people." It was in the presence of Jeanne and Simon too, that the Canon thus spoke. Foreseeing the approaching departure of their child, that unfortunate man, torn between love for his daughter and love for his city, was constantly running from his house to the council chamber, and from that to his house again. He had hardly left the one for a few minutes when he was forced back again to the other—he was so uneasy he could not be quiet anywhere, for he was ever on the lookout for some horrible news. His instinct by no means betrayed him. He was at home when Norbert came in at his door to carry his child away.

Damerones went up to him and begged him to give her his blessing.

" Forgive me, father," she said, " I have been a heavy burthen for you to bear—I have not kept the faith I owed to you. I have failed in my obedience ; forgive me. I, too, have been unhappy."

Her voice was broken; yet she armed herself with firmness, though she could not restrain the gushing tears that rolled down her fair, now pale cheeks in spite of her

Simon took her hands in his own, while Jeanne, like her daughter, on her knees close by the bench on which the consul sat, looked like a thing inanimate. The broad bald forehead of the consul, furrowed with wrinkles, embrowned, his gray beard, all made him look the image of one of the patriarchs of the old law. He answered his daughter:—

" It is better for thee that thou shouldst go away, Damerones; but think of the life I am living I My people massacred ; my child devoted to the son of their executioner ; my city on the point of losing her liberties. . . . all the great and puissant of the land conspiring against one poor merchant I and yet, what harm have I done—to anybody ?"

" Come, Damerones," murmured Norbert in the kindest tone, and taking hold of his penitent's hand.

"One moment more, I implore you," said the father, with a suppliant look.

He gazed at his child ; he took her head and pressed it between his two trembling hands; looked again, kissed her violently, and then with the courage of a real despair pushed her away and cried, " Go."

" God save you, father ! and you, my mother 1"

She went out holding Norbert by the hand. This was the deciding instant in Damerones' life. It was, so to speak, the very instant in which she was to cast away all the hopes and joys of this existence below, to never know beyond it anything save the severities and rigors of her conventual cell. It is true, the Christian faith that actuated her tore asunder before her eyes a curtain and revealed felicity superhuman in the other world.

Nevertheless, Damerones was bathed in tears; all her enthusiasm was clean gone. She followed her guide mechanically, and the thought of never more beholding father or mother, nor any other thing she had loved in her youth, appeared to her stricken heart, armed with all its cruelty. As she went along the town streets, the burghers and the populace gathered about her; they kuew where she was going and what she intended to do. Norbert had cited her case as an example. The beautiful girl, the Rose of Typhaines, the very idol of all the gay and gallant and wealthy lads of the town, the maiden that Consul Payen had long ago announced as his future bride, had become the Saint for the whole country round, but she was insensible to all this public respect and affection ; the submissive and humble child had suddenly reappeared: though, she wept at the parting and had no thought but the thought of separation.

" Farewell, Damerones," said an old neighbor woman, her eyes streaming—" farewell; you will pray for me, for they all say you are a great saint now 1"

A young girl, a friend of her happier days, threw herself

sobbing on her breast. " Adieu, Damerones," she cried; " oh, remember us sometimes 1"

Norbert, the inflexible Norbert, scarce allowed his poor prey time to answer in brief words, full fraught with sorrows and attachment; he drew her onwards. The multitude opened for them to pass, and as they drew nearer and nearer to the town gate, the crowd redoubled their blessings and their last farewells. Payen suddenly burst through the throng, and advanced towards the village maid.

" Damerones, you are going to leave us 1 You will not have me to your husband 1"

" Oh 1 my poor Payen," exclaimed the poor desolate girl; "go and console my parents."

" To be sure I*11 do that, and I '11 do my best; but only see ! You are all in the wrong: I love you with a true-hearted love, and if you *11 come to me, you shall have nothing in the world to wish for."

" Farewell, Payen," interrupted Damerones, sadly smiling; everything about her, everything she beheld, everything that, within a few moments she was to give up forever, now became dear to her heart—oh 1 dearer than tongue can tell!

The consul still held the girl by the hand.

" Indeed !" he said, " you are wrong to go and leave us ; I would have given you every one of my keys! you would have been far more mistress than I master of our home, and as to my love, it was all your own; why go and shut yourself up in a cloister ? Is it because you was in love with the chevalier ? The thought of blaming you for that never entered my head, and never would. He is a valiant knight, and I wish I was like him."

Damerones squeezed Payen's hand harder than a simple " Thank you" seemed to require, and covering her eyes with her hand, hurried along, and went out through the

33

town gate. She walked on foe some time, sighing, in spite of herself, and striving hard to suppress the outcry that seemed as if it must tear its way through her bosom. Norbert, with manly tenderness and gentleness kept exhorting and encouraging her, and boasting of the celestial recompense of reward, whose treasure-house was being unlocked for her; but she made no response.

The two travellers had now left the boundaries of the town, and even the old abbey was soon to be lost to view behind the folds of the landscape. They were moving in a direction towards Champagne; it was there the convent of Paraclete stood, whither Norbert was guiding the maiden who, in his mystic language he had declared was born to become, at some future day, a bright Torch of love Divine. As they went on, they found themselves in the presence of Monseigneur Philippe, who, as well as his faithful squire Fulk, seemed plunged in deep melancholy, and engaged in some serious conference.

Norbert was the first to descry him.

" Daughter," said he to Damerones, "here your constancy has to bear up against one last assault—one last adieu—and the most painful of all, perhaps, is now in store for you. Be not troubled, and brave the snares of the demon."

Philippe, too, had now recognized the coming pair; he checked his steed, and leaning on his long lance, the heel of which he had dropped to the ground: "Well Damerones !" said he, tenderly: " you are going away to be a nun ? You will be an honor to the convent that receives you, for you have a good heart in your bosom, and I am sure you never could have wished that all the good you did for me should have been mixed up with so many misfortunes that are weighing me down this day."

At first, Damerones had made up her mind not to raise

her eyes to look on the man she had loved so long and so dearly; but her strength was not eqnal to her resolution. The non—and for the last time—was a woman, and a lover again. She was shocked to see how pale he was, and how great a change a few days had made in the warrior-like, bold, once so joyous traits of the crusader's face. She saw that his pale, thin features were stamped with the dolorous traces of watching and sorrow. His forehead, generally fair and smooth as polished marble, bore a slight wrinkle, his brows were contracted with reflection, and weighed down by a heavy burden of care.

"You are as unhappy as others who are guilty," she cried, with heart-melting tones; " but it cannot be that heaven will doom you to suffer. Take courage, Monseigneur, the lady of Cornouiller will suffer herself to be moved, and will learn the whole truth."

" I count not on it now, Damerones," replied Philippe, as he shook his head mournfully. " She has condemned me unjustly, and I shall never see her more. You, they tell me, are a real saint, my child, and I will ever love you as if you were my own sister. Go, then, in peace, and pray for my soul 1"

Monseigneur had no great talent at speech-making, or at holding his tongue when he ought; we have seen proofs of that already; but, though wit was wanting, he had all the delicacy of a great-souled man. His heart was as noble as his blood. He showed nothing whatever to even lead Damerones to suspect he was aware of her long-cherished love, and spoke to her with that air of patriarchal protection that was befitting speech with a burgher-girl.

The young girl again spoke—

" If, unhappily, the lady will not suffer herself to yield, what would you do ?" she said.

"Ah ! my child," responded Philippe, "that's just what

Falk was asking about a few minutes ago, as we were wandering along the roads, talking over my unhappy adventure. What would you have me do ? I came home from the holy land, thinking I had a father, a chatel, a betrothed bride, and it seems I have none of them at all. I am here like a *pastour*, free to wander, just like him, all night long over the lands. I have no more home than he has."

Here Norbert interfered with the conversation—

" My son," said he, " I know you are unhappy, and that, too, without any fault of your own. I cannot allow Typhaines Abbey to retain possession of your estate. No doubt your father had good reasons for doing as he did when he gave it away to redeem his sins; it was a good idea ; but he should have thought of you. On the other hand, it is known, and notorious, that holy father Anselm, the Abbot, has no right to despoil his monastery of a property that came duly and legitimately into his hands; and I will go so far as to say he has opened himself to me on that subject, which is a great trouble and sorrow to him. I took it on myself to write to the Pope and the Cardiuals on the subject, and their sense of justice cannot fail to soon cause your property to be restored, and yet the Abbot have nothing to reproach himself with as a despoiler of Holy Church with his own hands."

" Ah 1" cried Fulk, " what a brave Canon ; what a worthy Pope; what excellent Cardinals! *A* s for Abbot Anselm, he, on the whole, is a Very honest monk, even though to save his life he did force me to leave my master in trouble, fool that I was 1"

The knight appeared far more indifferent than his squire was to the Canon's good news.

"Father 1" said he, "I thank you for your good intentions ; but if they should give me back my castle, cover me with benefits, load me with honors, and I not have

Mahaut as I hoped, nothing in the world could make me happy, and all your charitable efforts would fail to relieve me of a burden of*sorrows."

"Mahaut will listen to reason," said Norbert in friendly accents. "You are a brave-hearted man, and you deserve to be a happy one; and so much the more because you ask for nothing but what is right. But if, by chance, the chatelaine of Cornouiller should continue to be possessed by the evil spirit, I will give you a counsel that may alike tend to the glory of God and your own. For the present I only ask you to have patience; and you, Damerones, follow me; already has this conference lasted too long."

" Monseigneur," stammered Damerones, " should you ever become the conqueror of Typhaines, and my father fall into your hands as a prisoner, pray remember that 'twas I that saved you."

" I promise you that," replied he ; " Master Simon shall never receive other than good at my hands, in remembrance of you. Is there anything else I can do in your behalf?"

" Nothing—no, nothing, Monseigneur. I am a nun, and have nothing more to do with things earthly... I ought to have none. Adieu ... Monseigneur ... farewell"—

She seemed to be hesitating—she appeared to want to say something she dared not express. Her eyes fell on Fulk; and then she suddenly untied a narrow gold band that she wore on her neck :—

" Here, brave squire," she said, " take this little present from my hands and keep it in remembrance of me. Be you faithful to your master. Ever love him. Whenever danger threatens, be you nigh. Never leave nor forsake him. Take heed that no evil shall ever befall him. . . . This I say for your own advantage, and in order that you may not at some future day be called to make answer to our God, for having acted the part of an unfaithful servant."

33*

She did not again look at Messire Philippe, bnt went on
her way. Whether it was that her soul was greatly shaken,
or whether it was that she felt constrained to appeal to
her whole religious sense, she folded her hands and walked
fast, and prayed fervently as she went. Norbert joined
her in prayer. They came to the top of a hill; she suddenly turned, cast a rapid glance towards him 6he had just
left behind, and then at once began to pray again, and so,
disappeared, with tbe Canon, behind the distant hill-top.

Fulk sat in his saddle, not a little touched at heart by
the penetrating, passionate gestures of the poor sad girl.
He held in his still outstretched hand the collar of gold
she had given, and could not very clearly make out why
she had given it.

" Bosh I" at last he exclaimed; " what a brave girl she
is! and in spite of the Damoiselle de Cornouiller's nonsense,
the fact is she did save your life, Monseigneur."

" It would have been better, a thousand times, if she
had let me alone to die there and then ! But as you say,
I ought not to think hard of her; she did her best for me,
and I hope she may be happy in her convent, for she is a
brave child, as you said, and would to God Mahaut were
but as tender hearted as she is I"

The conversation between the knight and his squire,
which had been broken off by the meeting with Damerones^
was now resumed, and incessantly reverting to the thought
of his misfortunes, and yet clinging fast to the smallest
shreds on which his hope still hung, the knight slowly
proceeded towards the minster; for though he was very
much irritated against that establishment and its Abbot,
there was something in Anselm's character that was so imposing that he felt bound to the cause in whose behalf he
had suffered so much. He would have blushed to abandon
what he deemed to be just and right on account of an

interest purely personal, no matter how great it might be. Hence, he had firmly resolved to continue faithful to the cause of the abbey, and postpone his declaration of hostility to her until after the town should have come back under the yoke of its masters.

At the abbey, the days passed on while waiting for the results of the Council of Rheims, which was to bring back everything into good order again. The bishop and Anselm, closeted with the prior, were receiving and despatching couriers and judging of the real news of the day, while the plain monks, who had nothing but rumors to jndge by, ran their theories fairly into the ground, being almost invariably far wide of the mark. Joy reigned in the sacred abode. The boasted liberties of the men of Typhaines were now suspended on a single thread: as the knight entered the chapter-hall, most important news was brought in.

Under the inspiration of Bishop Guillaume and Anselm the council had been composed of prelates well known as irreconcilable enemies of all the innovations of the age; men imposing by the high consideration of their Sees and their wealth as well. They were men whom the King of France was obliged to deal with most carefully, and whom the Count de Nevers might well fear.

To their secular grandeur was superadded the terrible rod of their ecclesiastical power, and it was impossible to brave either the one or the other. Hence the lord king and his prime minister too had made no delay in bowing to the very first injunction that commanded them to change their whole attitude in relation to the poor Typhaineers. The citation, addressed by the fathers in council to the hardy sovereign, had been received with all due humility, and Louis at once announced that he willingly submitted the entire affair to the discretion and conduct of the holy personages convened at Rheims. It may be, he was scheming the while, but the bishops and abbots were full as knowing as he. Appreheuding he might be intending to protract the business too long, they voted to send him a contribution in money, a kind of bait that no power in that age of the world had ever the least idea of not taking. King Louis and his minister, who had already been paid to uphold the charter of Typhaines, now eagerly accepted a bribe to overset it. Such was the sole policy of the day.

The convent had for two days been made aware that this great point was won ; but that was not all of it. The Count de Nevers had tried to get up a countermine, and had forwarded his messengers to both Paris and Rheims. At Paris the count's remonstrances had been answered by grand demonstrations of submission to Holy Church and invitations to his mandatories to proceed at once to the Council, which alone had power to decide all the questions at issue. The Nivernais deputies were received with *hauteur* by the sacred council; as it was at once announced to them that the Count de Nivernais must at once and for all renounce his iniquitous claims to the suzerainty of Typhaines Abbey and his friendship for the rebels, or worse it would be for him: the count was not powerful enough to make it worth while to buy him. The next thing was that the Abbot of Typhaines should be charged to engage his revolted burghers and serfs to return to their duty, and in case of resistance on their part, excommunication should be proclaimed, and should excommunication prove ineffectual, troops were to march against them from all quarters and ruin the rebels utterly.

When these facts were made known to Philippe he exclaimed—

" It's all well." Bishop Guillaume rubbed his hands in his delight; the good Abbot alone held his peace. He was carrying out the cause of his Church, and that he was resolved to do, but he mourned over the misfortunes that he foresaw must be drawn down on the rebels by their own obstinacy.

" And now," said Bishop Guillaume, " the only question left is, how to advertise those sons of Belial of the misfortunes that are hanging above their heads."

" That is a duty," added Anselm, " that belongs to me alone." As he said it a cry indicative of surprise and blame broke out in the assembly.

" How is this, holy father? Can you possibly be thinking of renewing your negotiations with those rebellious serfs ? Would you go so far as to compromise your sacred authority with the low people who have blasphemed it so openly ? Leave, yes, leave it to others to bend that fierce courage of theirs; they will do it as well as you can, and the dignity of the church of Typhaines can lose nothing by their intervention."

" Far be from me the weakness to hearken to your counsel," exclaimed the Abbot. " The question now is not how to keep up an attitude of mundane pride in victory. If the good right should prevail, it is the part of true charity to give check to the tears that cannot fail to flow. Not only will I make an appeal to my rebel vassals, but I will, in person, go and preach submission, give them promise of indulgence."

Nothing could turn the holy prelate aside from the determination thus announced, and which was particularly displeasing to Bishop Guillaume, a man charged brimful of respect for the church, and one never to relax his hold on the prescriptions of etiquette: still, Anselm had announced his resolution, that, no one could ever shake, and so, one of the knights repaired to the borough, accompanied by a trumpeter, to summon the consuls to a parley, in the name of their lawful lord.

The prior and bishop, who led the opposition to the good Abbot*8 design, relied fully on the hateful and violent temper of the insurgents to hinder the interview from taking place, and to prevent the negotiation from going beyond a mere summons to lay down their arms within a time fixed, or take the consequences. But these two great politicians found their hopes disappointed, absolutely disappointed; the Abbot's mandatory came back to the minster with news that the consuls had accepted the proposals for a conference, and stood ready at once to repair, if so it should be agreed, to the spot to be appointed, at the entrance of the stone bridge, and there hear whatever it might be that Master Anselm might please to say to them.

" Further," reported the knight, " I saw nothing of dark, sour visages I was led to expect, from the reports circulating on that subject among the monks. The men looked cold and determined, and not a soul, either in the streets, or the council chamber, offered me the slightest indignity."

" They are scared," said the bishop, smiling.

" I should be surprised at that," put in Messire Philippe ; " they by no means looked to me, when I saw them, like people either to be easily astonished, or to turn weak-kneed."   *

"Perhaps," said Master Anselm, "it has pleased the Lord to touch their hearts."

"Bah!" rejoined Monseigneur Philippe, "they are too hardened for that."

" Be it as it may," pursued Anselm, " let us give thanks to the Saints for the happy thought, which they alone could have breathed into their hearts, to accept of our conferende; and you, Messire, who have just seen them, return, I pray, and say unto them that it pleaseth us to acknowledge their courtesy, by accepting their proposal to have an interview at once. In the course of an hour we shall be at the bridge with our friends: let the chiefs of the poor commune also repair to the same spot."

The whole abbey was in motion as soon as the news got abroad of the coming event. The formalists condemned, while the hot heads approved, the proposed plan ; the vindictives—and there were some of that class among them—were furious about it. What, in fact, would be the consequence, in case the Abbot, by his eloquence, should really make a powerful impression on the hearts of his insurrectionist vassals! There would be no such thing as pillaging Typhaines! burning Typhaines to the ground ; no such thing as a general sack and loot! pleasure, profit, and all, clean vanished and gone! It was a matter to make the mercenaries weep! Nevertheless, as I stated before, all was- motion, agitation, chatter, behind the walls, and in the great court-yard of the sacred abode. Here was a fellow busy furbishing up his casque to make a finer show in the Abbot's suite there; another swallowing his hasty-plate of soup, for fear of spending the whole day fasting, for everybody opined the interview must take up a great deal of time.

It was visible from the minster that the town was fully as much excited as the abbey population. Women and children, and even men were seen hurrying to the rampart to gaze up at the venerable institution, and talking fast about what they saw, and what they thought. In fact, curiosity, emotion, and anxiety about what was to come to pass that great day, were at the height. And, what a strange thing! neither party appeared to have the least distrust as to the intention of their opponents. Neither side had even offered a proposal to secure the bridge against a coup-de-main; the number of men in attendance on each had not been settled, nor even mentioned. It all went on simply, rapidly, and by a sort of carrying away; they

looked as if in a hurry to have the thing over. Ah, ha!
the burghers were scared about their excommunication I
Were they ? They were terribly afraid of the coming
push of pike ! Oh, ho! However all that was, towards
two o' the clock in the afternoon the abbey-cavalcade issued
forth from the grand portal of the sacred fortress. The
Typhaines consuls, notified of the proceeding by the
shouts resounding from the rampart, passed out from the
town walls, attended by a crowd of their people. In the
whole band not a helm, not a hauberk, or buckler; not a
halbert or lance was to be seen. They were even bareheaded, and wore no armor that day but their swords.

" What is this we are doing ?" cried Master Anselm at
such a sight. [11] When these people advance so peacefully
to give us greeting, why all this parade of warlike arms and
cavalry. Let the sergeants-at-arms go back to the abbey :
let our knightly brethren alight from their chargers, and
the venerable bishop and I will advance open-handed to
meet these poor people."

"You are right," said Monseigneur Philippe, who was
first to leap to the ground; " we must never let an enemy
exhibit confidence greater than our own."

"Monseigneur," muttered Fulk, "you know nothing
about it: stick to your horse and your lance."

" Hold your tongue, and be off at once with the courser
and penon."

Fulk's only response wAs by shrugging his shoulders. As
soon as they beheld the change taking place in the band
from the monastery, and the men-at-arms wending their
way up the hill, with the pages leading off the war-horses
and carrying their master's bucklers, the Typhaiues population sounded their applause, and uttered most enthusiastic cries and shouts; on hearing which Abbot Anselm said
to his companions—

" The poor people are not yet perverted ; we shall briug them back without being obliged to chastise them."

He had reached the foot of the bridge just as he uttered the words. The consuls and their retainers advanced upon it at the other end. Simon, Eudes, Jacques and Antoine were there, but not Payen ; he was wanting.

Approaching the Abbot, Simon bent down as if he was about to kneel. Anselm, seeing all his sacred hopes on the very point of being realized, stretched forth his hands and opened his mouth to speak words of concord and union, when the consul, quickly rising, drew his sword and struck a blow at the Abbot's head that knocked him senseless to the bridge floor, and shouted, *"Aid! Aid! Typhaines! Typhaines! Death to the monks!"*

Like a thunderbolt he rushed at Monseigneur Philippe, who was at the Abbot's left, and utterly stunned and stupefied at the act, stood with his hands abroad, without even seeing the coming blow. Eudes, Jacques, and Antoine had all drawn their swords; the burgher troop did likewise. The town gate continued to pour out streams of men, who now were clearly enemies indeed; and the whole hateful band bore, like a pack of famished wolves, on the astonished and disarmed cortege of the venerable Abbot, on the bishop, the priests, and the monks, shouting " *Typhaines ! Typhaines ! Death to the monks !*"

CHAPTER XXVIII.

It is certain that at the beginning of this outbreak not
a soul among the Abbot's followers had any clear notion of
what was going on. Anselm lay stretched on the ground
motionless, with a cut on his head that poured out streams
of blood to empurple the stone pavement of the bridge, and
yet people not more than two paces in the rear of him kept
asking—What's the matter? what is it? Monseigneur
Philippe had seen the blow struck, and instantly after it,
Simon rushing at him sword in hand ; and yet, at first he
had no clear conception of the incident. Such a stupefac-
tion as that could not last very long without great risks,
and, fortunately for him, it did not last long; the good
knight recovered his presence of mind soon enough to leap
two paces backwards, and then dart to the right, where he
drew Rudaverse from her scabbard, and then fearing naught
from Master Simon, nor the devil himself, he shouted in a
ringing tone, " *Cornehaut! Stand fast!*"

At nearly the very same instant the knights, squires,
and monks had all recovered their senses, and every sword
was gleaming in the air; the monks who, as having nothing
to do with such affairs, were only in the way—made a hurried retreat to the rear-guard, and the fighting men came
to the front, so that in the course of a minute the fight
was regularly begun, to the vast disappointment of the
burghers, who found themselves surprised in their turn.

The conflict, at first, went on round and over the prostrate body of the venerable Abbot, and they fought as the Greeks and Trojans of old did over the body of Patroclus; Simon, who had proudly pressed his foot on the unfortunate prelate's body, was driven backwards by a heavy blow that Philippe struck on his shoulder, and which forced him still further to give back : one of the pages seized the opportunity to run to the front and raise the unconscious Abbot, and bear him to the rear out of the fray.

In the mean time Philippe and the consul continued to press each other with the greatest vigor, but the crusader had evidently got the upper hand of his valiant opponent. Furious as a maddened bull at the sight of the venerable priest's flowing blood—a sight that carried him to the highest pitch of indignation and rage—he lost all remembrance of the promise he had made to Damerones. His sword, that valiant Rudaverse, heavy though it was, in his hand weighed like a rush in a pastour's palm. She vibrated, and danced, and flashed like live lightning round Simon's head, shoulders, and arms, and often on the bright blade that the courageous Typhaineer opposed in fence. She fairly looked like a dancing demon, and her clickety-click was enough to make the stoutest man turn pale. At last, with a back-handed swing she dashed Simon's blade into fragments, and *Cornehaut* was his war-shout as he rushed on to seize the bruised and streaming frame of the hardy consul.

Philippe raised his adversary's body in his terrible arms, and pressing him on the edge of the parapet, was on the point of heaving him in the dark deep stream below. Simon uttered not a word, and his face wore a smile of blended rage and contempt. Philippe bethought him of Damerones—

" I '11 pardon you for your daughter's sake 1" and he let go of him.

"You are a madman," bellowed Fulk, close behind him, and at once stooping down over Simon, who had not had time to rise, he took hold of him again. In the meanwhile Philippe had found it necessary to make bead against Jacques, by whom he had been struck with a dagger, though the point glanced on the polished scales of his armor. One sweep of Philippe's good sword tumbled the consul to the ground, and when he turned, Fulk and Simon had both disappeared. *

" If but that miscreant has only not dragged my poor squire to the bottom of the river with him ! He must be a demon! However, I did keep my w'ord to Damerones 1"

The battle was lost to the burghers, and very simple was the reason why.

Fulk, the man of precautions, and of little faith in others' good faith, had prevailed on the sergeants-at-arms not to retire too far from the place of conference at the bridge. He made them mount the knight's chargers, and it was in that way that at the first sign of the disturbance he brought up his strong reinforcement at the gallop. The cavalry charge drove the communeers in at all points, though they seemed, as by a sort of enchantment, to have become instantly supplied with lances, battle-axes, and sharpened stakes, and would unquestionably have overwhelmed the small knightly escort that had remained on the bridge ; but, as I already stated, Fulk's distrust was well placed on that day.

Still, we ought not to believe that, in spite of the fall of two of their consuls the multitudinous Typhaineers, though repulsed by the men-at-arms, resorted to a cowardly flight. No; the madmen were forced only step by step to the town gate, and made head with such fiery energy that they were very near recovering the advantage ; but, though they were constantly receiving reinforcements from the burgh, and they did receive very many; and thongh they were powerfally assisted by the clouds of crossbow bolts from the town rampart, the men-at-arms also grew most rapidly by the coming up of their companions in the abbey, and they came up at a run. At length, one last vigorous charge by the cavalry drove them back to the wall, and the mercenaries seemed as if they would enter the town with the retiring crowd. Monseigneur Philippe, by a superhuman effort, had wrenched away one of the draw-bridge chains, but Payen made a sudden sortie with a fresh company, struck the chevalier a heavy blow on the head with his battle-axe, that he reeled and stumbled, and the draw-bridge head was at once standing upright in the air.

" Good ! we *11 pay you another visit," said Philippe : he beckoned a trumpeter to him, made him sound the retreat, and marshalling his troops, recrossed the bridge, on his way to the abbey. He not only thought it useless to get his men shot to death from the walls, but as he had no ladders, he knew that an escalade was not to be thought of; and, besides, he was anxious to know what had become of the venerable Abbot and his faithful Fulk.

The scene inside of the walls was a very different one.

"We have had a very bad time of it," said Antoine to Payen. " The rascally monk is dead though, I hope; the rest of them got off, and Simon—"

" What of Simon ?"   *

" Simon has disappeared, and Jacques is killed."

" To the devil, the whole of you !" exclaimed Payen, as he wiped his bloody sword, and thrust it back into the scabbard. " You are a set of traitors, all of you, and I told you how it would be ! You have disgraced the commune !"

"Fool, that you are," rejoined Antoine, in a rage; "if you had gone with us, instead of hearkening to your stupid scruples, we should at this hour have been revenged, aud

34*

safe too. With Simon to help you, we should have made
an end of that scoundrel of a Cornehaut, and the commune
wouldn't have had an enemy left."

"Nonsense!" rejoined Payen, as he stamped his foot
upon the ground—" nonsense ! I am ready to die for the
commune, but never, no, not even for her, will I be guilty
of an act of infamy. Your project and Simon's was a
scandalous one, and must ever be one accursed of heaven ;
and I firmly believe has lost the commune, while a true
and honorable courage would have been able to save her
completely."

" After all," responded Eudes, with a jeer, " the Abbot
has got his head clove open; he's dead, any how, and that
makes one monk the less for us. *Long life to the Commune !*"

Payen turned his back on him, and went away, nor did
he meet any smiling faces as he strode on. Not one of the
customary acclamations was to be heard. Everybody knew
how opposed he had been to the treasonable plan of his
colleagues, and though they also knew he had just saved
Typhaines from being captured and sacked, he was accused
of caring very little about her; his popularity was stone-
dead.

When Payen became convinced it was so, the thought
struck him to the heart. Ho stopped, and folding his
arms across his manly breast, turned and faced the crowd
that was following him, not silently, but mutteringly.

" What do you want ?" he haughtily asked.

" Death to all cowards! down with the traitors! long
life to Simon!" were exclamations that were now heard,
but only from the outer ranges of the encircling mob, though
the nearest of them merely stood and stared at him, without a word said. Payen marched directly on to the press

that at once opened and gave him way, until he met Eudes
and Jacques on the street.

" What's the meaning of these shouts, my masters ?"
said he. .

" The people are not satisfied with you."

" Nor I with the people. I thought I was in command
of a body of brave men—not a gang of assassins!"

Payen unhooked his scarlet mantle, his consular cloak,
and dashed it down to the pavement at their feet, and
turned 'his back on them. Murmurs and threats now broke
out like mad; but he paid no attention to them whatever.

" Silence! my children !" cried Jacques in paternal tones;
" be composed. Our lord King Louis and the Count de
Nevers, our faithful allies, will make it all right. Even
should the decision of the council be adverse, which I don't
believe, it will be broke by the Pope. It is far better for
you to be governed by people that really love you than by
faint-hearted folks !"

" Long life to Jacques I Long life to Eudes!" they
cried. Payen, as he heard the shouts, merely shrugged
his shoulders, to mark the intensity of his contempt, and
went home to his own house. What a condition is that
of a city, when its victorious enemy is marching on it and
its ruin inevitable ? It is like an hospital for the insane ;
and so it was with Typhaines. From that moment onward,
Eudes and Jacques, a couple of stupid dunderheads, hardly
fit to guide themselves, and whose only merit had been their
complete obedience to Simon, were to become, at that very
moment, absolute masters of the commune. They tried
to blow up the popular courage with the most absurd
schemes and hopes. Sometimes it was Suger, the king's
minister of state, who was marching in person to the succor
of Typhaines, at the head of a thousand lances. Sometimes, it was the council, that had been won over by the

burgesses sent to them by the consuls to induce them to
favor the commune. Twenty different sorts of nonsense
per hour stimulated, and then disheartened the public confidence. In fact, common sense had fled the town. From
time to time troops were seen marching to the ramparts to
stare at the monastery on its rock above them, and as they
gazed and gazed at the silent walls, they gave a loose to
their conjectures as to what was going on inside of them.

In the first place, and the most important too, the Abbot
was not dead, Simon had missed his aim. Next, Simon
himself, by a sort of miracle, was not lying at the bottom
of the river; for just as Fulk was on the very point of casting him over the parapet, he had become illuminated by
a flash of thought, not of clemency, for that was a kind
that ever proved very confusing to the honest squire's
brains while busy in a struggle, but it was a refined idea
of vengeance, that to him smacked of divine inspiration.

He dragged his prisoner, now exhausted by loss of blood
and nearly choked to death by his vice-like grip at the
throat, he dragged him, I say, out of the tumult, and calling a couple of soldiers who helped him to tie the poor
man, they took him on their shoulders and hurried him
off to the abbey, where the redoubtable burgher was instantly and faithfully deposited in the abbey dungeon, to
the intense admiration of the monks. Bishop Guillaume,
above all, could not sufficiently express his high satisfaction
at the capture of the cloth merchant, though to be sure he
was still in doubt as to the fate of his friend the Abbot.

Ah ! if but a compassionate angel, the same one, no
doubt, whose address once turned aside the blow aimed at
Isaac, had not been there to make Master Simon's hand
swerve, the thread of the Abbot's life would have been
mercilessly cut, and he would have received in heaven the
recompense of the truth and the right for which he would

have died the death of a martyr. The blow did swerve, and though the wound it gave was a deep, it was not a mortal one; but the Abbot remained wholly unconscious during the whole of that and the following day.

Fulk, whose rather unmerciful habits his master was aware of, was surprised when his master expressed some surprise at his conduct in the matter, and did not need any pressing to explain to the knights in presence of the bishop and gentlemen, while at supper, how it had come to pass.

" The fact is," said he, " I do believe my holy patron Saint, who when in the flesh must have been some remarkably wise clerk, did inspire me at the very nick of time. Only think ! as I was holding Master Simon on the parapet, my right hand on his throat and the left at his legs to give him the somersault, I suddenly remembered the day when the Abbot was standing in the court-yard beside Sir Geoffroy's dead body, then lying on the pavement; the Abbot foretold, iu the merchant's hearing, that he should do penance some day for his crimes, in that very court-yard. Of course I had no notion of going against Heaven's decree; so I brought the fellow up here, and now it depends on these illustrious Seigneurs to say whether I was in the right or not."

"So right," exclaimed Bishop Guillaume, [11] that the Abbot's prediction shall be brought to pass on the instant. It is possible that our illustrious friend may die this night of the wound he got at the bridge; and it is even possible that his goodness might induce him to forgive his assassin ; if you believe me, my lords, the predicted expiation ought to take place on the spot."

They all, with one voice, applauded the prelate's proposal ; and the abbey-court soon presented one of those strange scenes that are stamped forever on the startled imagination of every beholder of them.

Night had now come on ; moonless; stormy; starless: a
tempestuous wind was moaning or howling among the
towers and along the corridors. Men-at-arms in their
iron armor, monks wrapped and hooded, valets with flaming pine torches in their hands, stood ranged around
the court-yard.

Four powerful brothers brought in the Abbot lying unconscious on the stretcher, his head bound up in bloody
wrappings; four of the squires, in like manner, came in
with a bier on which lay Sir Geoffroy de Cornehaut in his
coffin ; one already a prey to the grim destroyer, and the
other carrying on a feeble resistance to his pressing attacks.
The two ghastly burdens were set down in the midst of
the knights, facing the Bishop of Chalons-sur-Marne, who,
bareheaded in the storm, and grave as the occasion, stood
president of the terrible court.

When all was ready, a guard of soldiers was despatched
to bring in Master Simon from the dungeon. He was
ordered to kneel; but took no heed to the order, and said
not a word. The men-at-arms then bent his legs by force,
and held him down on his knees before his two victims.
He uttered no complaint, and held down by the iron hands
of the soldiers offered no resistance. His was thg face of
a stoic—his eyes were bold; but he neither braved nor
supplicated his victors and judges.

" Simon I" spoke out the bishop, "you have come to
the end of your crimes. Your murders, your rebellions,
your most base and cowardly treason have dragged you
to this spot. Behold ! see yourself on your knees before
your Seigneur the Abbot of Typhaines."

Simon did not even frown; he looked at the Abbot's
body on the stretcher, and seeing that it moved not, something like a disdainful smile seemed to swim over his hardy
impassive features.

" The Abbot still lives, and will live," said a knight.

Simon seemed not to hear this refutation of his last hope.

" Now look again," said Bishop Guillaume, " this is the dead body of father Nicolas—the Seigneur Geoffroy de Cornehaut."

Simon looked towards the coffin. A new smile sat on his lips, and for this once he opened his mouth.

" As for him," said he ... . but he stopped as if his determination to see all, and suffer all, was now fixed and unchangeable. He repelled the temptation he felt to triumph before his victors* faces, in the death of the Baron of Cornehaut, his terrible enemy; and he held his peace. A shiver of rage ran through the ranks of the men-at-arms, and the two valets that held him on his knees pressed him harder down—they almost stretched him on the stones.

In solemn tones the bishop resumed—

" The hour of pride is past; the time to repent is come. Here, thou proud man! thou impious murderer, thou standest humbled in presence of thy victims, and before the faces of these gallant men 1 these pious coenobites, who stand gazing on thy countenance ! Thou bearest witness that the spirit of prophecy did, once at least, visit the lips of holy Abbot Anselpi. Rise up, now, or rather let them lift thee up, for thou art become a slave, and hast no longer a will of thine own. Holy Church repudiates and denies you, and delivers you over to the secular arm. "

" Good," exclaimed Fulk; " the secular arm 1 I suppose that means us soldier-folks. The secular arm is going to give a good account of this villain. The monks took up the stretcher and the bier, on which lay the unconscious Abbot and the dead baron, and forming in procession two by two, moved solemnly and slowly away, carrying their wounded Superior, to whom had thus been paid an act of homage he would undoubtedly have refused to accept, had he been conscious of the proceeding, and along with him the corpse of the late father Nicolas. The knights, squires, and men-at-arms remained and drew up in a circle close around the prisoner. The council of war for the trial of the cloth-merchant was now convened.

Monseigneur Philippe was the first to speak. It was not much in his way to make a speech, and we have seen that he was never inclined to make an abusive use of his eloquence, but for this occasion he broke his rule, and had his reasons for it, too.

"Seigneurs," he said, "you, as wise and honorable men, are about to pronounce a verdict on this Master Simon before you. It is your right to do so, and I think there is none to gainsay it But for myself, I pray you allow me to abstain from taking any share in his trial. A vow I made, forbids me from pronouncing an opinion on this burgher's case; should I cast my vote against him, I should look on myself as a perjurer and an ingrate. To be brief, I refuse to pronounce a verdict in his trial."

" As you please, Monseigneur," replied one of the oldest of the knights: "pray withdraw to yon corner, and without uttering a word, look on, if you please, to see how we shall decide."

" Willingly," rejoined Messire Philippe, and he took a stool that one of the soldiers offered him, and seating himself a little way off in the shadow, prepared to watch the peripatetics of the scene about to be accomplished, and that was not likely to take up much time. He sat facing Master Simon, who was now on his feet again, with his scarlet cloak all torn to strips, hanging about him. His grizzly hair was all tumbled and glued up with the dried blood of his wounds; and he stood with arms folded across his breast. To the eyes of a friend he looked like a being wholly intrepid; to an enemy's eyes, his was the face and attitude of a braggart and an insolent.

" You stand accused of many crimes," said the gray-headed knight, who, by right of seniority, had taken Monseigneur Philippe's place as president of the council of war.

" I will enumerate them for you, and you are allowed to make a brief defence if you choose to do so."

" Neither brief, nor long," said Simon, in a rude voice. "I have nothing to say to you; and you may use your pleasure, as to me."

" Are you resolved ?"

" Resolved," answered the consul.

" These are your misdeeds," resumed the knight. " More than twenty years ago, you forced your mistress, the lady of Cornehaut, to quit her castle halls. You impelled the serfs of the place aforesaid to set up a Commune, and in a state of open rebellion, you fought at their head against your liege lord.

" When driven away from Cornehaut, you assisted the burgesses of Amiens to rise in insurrection against their seigneur, the bishop, and fought among the rebels.

" When received at the burgh of Typhaines by holy Abbot Anselm, you again excited the burghers and serfs against their lawful seigneur. Father Nicolas was murdered by your direction; you have headed the revolt, and you have been its principal leader; in fine, you made a traitorous attempt to assassinate your benefactor the Abbot, at the very time he was thinking of granting you a pardon. Are you seriously resolved to make no defence and tender no answer ?"

" Resolved !" again said the consul in the same insulting tone.

" Then I will take your votes, Messeigneurs."
    35

The council held a brief consultation, in an under tone;
it was as brief as might have been expected, and the
knight turned to Simon.

" Burgher 1" he said, "you are condemned to die on the
spot."

He made a contemptuous gesture for his only answer.

" Has anybody got a rope 7" asked Fulk.

"Here's one I . . . . here's a better one I"

"If it's only strong enough !" muttered the squire, as
he advanced to the prisoner and made a sign to the sergeants-at-arms to lead him to the abbey-gate.

At that moment supreme, the crusader approached him.

" You are about to die," he said, " and though your sen-
tence is a just one, I have not been forgetful that you considered it a duty to take vengeance on my father and myself for the death of your relations. In addition to that,
your daughter saved my life, and I now, in her name, ask
if I can do anything to assauge the bitterness of your last
moments ?"

" Yes," replied the consul; " leave off speaking to me;
for in the world there is nothing I so utterly detest as
yourself."

Monseigneur Philippe, greatly scandalized, withdrew
muttering—

" Discourteous brute I " and he abandoned the condemned man to his executioners.

At the abbey-gate, looking towards the town, there was
a stone gargoyle that projected some five or six feet from
the eaves. By means of a ladder, two of the soldiers
climbed up to the fatal support; their comrades below had
been equally expeditious, for Master Simon, stripped of his
mantle and hauberk, and naked to the waist, was already
standing beneath with the rope round his neck. Though
the Commune of Typhaines and its adherents might be

properly looked on as excommunicates, the Bishop of Chalons, considering, he had received no official advices on that point, took it on himself to send a monk to Simon to assist him in his last moments. Simon inquired whether they could furnish him some other confessor, not belonging to the abbey, and upon receiving a negative answer, said he had no need of any one. The soldiers upon the gargoyle had commenced hauling on the rope, and Simon's body slowly rose into the air. The acclamations of the men-at-arms and convent servitors became deafening. In a moment it was all over. The body was left hanging in front of the abbey, and the first beams of the morning sun would disclose it to the terrified gaze of the people of Typhaines.

[11] Good 1" said Fulk, and he winked his only eye. " One basilisk the less."

Thus ended Simon, cloth-merchant, consul of the Commune of Typhaines, one of the most arrogant revolutionists of the twelfth century.

CHAPTER XXIX.

THE morning following this execution found the Bishop of Chalons-sur-Marne in one of the halls of the monastery, seated by the bedside on which the venerable Abbot was lying, and there attended by certain of the convent brethren endowed with skill in surgery, who were eagerly engaged in lavishing on their wounded Superior all the resources of their art, with the utmost tenderness and affection. The holy priest had recovered his consciousness, yet his weakness was extreme; but that did not prevent him from questioning his friend on the recent events. Bishop Guillaume held a parch men t-roll in his hand that he had just received.

44 Well, well, venerable brother," said he,44 God hath not forsaken us I The church is triumphant, and impiety is overthrown and cast down. The Council of Rheims has been dissolved, after completing the measures proposed by your wisdom. The Excommunication has been proclaimed; this parchment is the official act; and it now depends on you to fulminate it, in case the rebellion should hold out; what is more, the Crusade is to be preached throughout all Champagne, in Burgundy, and the Isle of France, against communeers and their adherents. We cannot doubt that this lair of assassins and robbers will return under your authority, and purged, too, of the wretches who have been carrying on war against you."

44 Yes," replied the Abbot feebly, 44 the immense mercy

of the Divine Being hath come to my aid; henceforth the hour for firmness and courage hath passed and that of mansnetnde is come. I hope I shall be found, not to have dishonored my dignity at the time I was despoiled utterly, and wandering and fleeing like a doe from the pursuing wolves. Now that the Lord hath restored power to my hands, it is a duty to act with gentleness to the people who, once subdued, are become my children again. Words of excommunication, I trust, shall never issue from my lips. As to the crusade, let us strive to avoid the use of it, and let the menace exert its power, and let us not put it to the last test; it would make my heart bleed to see the burgh put to the sack, and delivered over to all the horrors of war. Believe me, in spite of yesterday's treason, I have not given up the hope of making those mistaken unfortunates listen to reason, and that even Master Simon himself, on finding the impossibility of a successful resistance, will counsel submission, and himself submit to the necessity of the case."

" I verily do believe, venerable brother," responded the bishop, who was exceedingly surprised, " that your charity would induce you to pardon even Simon himself for his execrable crime 1"

"And why not ?" answered Anselm, with a smile, " ought we, without some great necessity, to will the death of the sinner ?"

" Happily for us all," rejoined Master Guillaume, " your men-at-arms and your allies, less debonair than your holiness, took it upon themselves to execute justice upon that villain." He then recounted to the Abbot all that had occurred from the time he had received the stroke that deprived him of consciousness at the Typhaines bridge. The old Abbot drew a long deep sigh, closed his eyes, and began a prayer. All the people around him immediately followed his example, and the prior had orders to have the proper office performed for the repose of the soul of the deceased consul. Quite a useless precaution, as Fulk showed, for it was his mind that that same soul, gone off with quite a stout packet of crimes, did of right and without remission belong to a very different place from one of rest

Be all that as it may, it was plain to be seen that the Abbot deeply regretted what had been done. Whether it was that he felt it a useless thing to complain, or that it was not quite befitting in him to hurt the feelings of his friends by further recrimination, the pious monk said nothing more in regard to the hasty verdict of the court-martial, with which he had neither lot nor part; but, he issued a formal order that, until his cure should be completed, all acts of hostility against the Commune should be suspended. No one dreamed of disobeying him, for his firmness was a thing well known to all.

Anselm did not, however, allow matters to take their own way. He held long conferences with Monseigneur Philippe, who that very same day was sent as a messenger to the borough to speak words of peace to the people. Anybody but the crusader would have been far from any wish to go back into a town where the recollections of it were so disagreeable, the danger too so great; but the crusader would have felt dishonored to refuse such a mission. Besides, the Abbot had rightly judged, by sending him, that the tigers there had turned into sheep. In fact, the first effervescence, once fairly at an end, had been followed by the deepest discouragement; a sort of reaction had taken place iu the Commune, hardly less violent than the despair that had led the consuls and the great mass of the population to the horrible idea of massacring the Abbot and knights while the friendly conference, as proposed by the good priest, was going on at the bridge.

The only difficulty was that this violent reaction had begun to decline again. Simon, incontestably the very ablest man in Typhaines, had clearly understood, the evening before, from the reports brought in from various quarters, that resistance might indeed be kept up for a while, but must inevitably come to a surrender at last. There was nothing seductive in the idea of drawing a crusade on the burgh: every body knew that in such cases rebels were treated as conquered countries, as infidel, Pagan, Mussulman: the harsher this treatment the better it seemed. Simon and his friends had set their last hopes on the stroke they had planned to give at the conference, and thought that success in that signal audacity, by freezing the Typhaines monks with terror, by depriving the league of a chief so redoubtable for strength, fame, and activity, might indeed postpone for long, if not forever, these last great perils, and restore to the King of France and the Count de Nevers both the power and the will to act in behalf of the Commune.

The whole scheme had failed. Simon was taken prisoner. Payen the brave *par excellence*, after he had with abhorrence repulsed their treasonable project, had none the less saved the town from a surprise, but he had abjured his office as magistrate and gone home to his house, where[1] he still remained close shut in. Jacques and Eudes were still left; they were two poor fellows, most miserable supports for such times. Simon having disappeared from the Commune, the soul that enabled them to think w^s dead too; they never did any one thing but take his advice and follow it. When morning broke and exhibited on the horizon the swinging corpse of the great consul—that was the last stroke. Howls of grievous pain ran along the ramparts, went down into the town, passed through the streets, and spread out over the squares.

As Monseigneur Philippe rode towards the councH-hall
he saw none but people squatting at the feet of the wails,
and all bedewed with tears. The desolation had no bounds,
as the rage had had none.

The chevalier's conference with the magistrates turned
altogether to the advantage of peace. The more the crusader pressed and advised them, the more the two men lost
their wits, and saw the fumes of their old ambition vanish-
ing away into thin air. Had they had nothing to lose by it,
there is reason to believe that they would have held a very
different kind of language, and clung to their dignity at
the risk of seeing the town carried by assault and delivered
over to pillage. But, as we well know, they were both
wealthy and both avaricious; therefore they chose to be
reasonable, though the conditions imposed must have seemed
hard to submit to.

In the first place; the Commune was to be abolished, the
people going back under the old system of rule, and the
refugee serfs all to return to their several glebes. In the
next place; the burghers were to be held to pay all expenses caused by their rebellion; among others, the pay for
the men-at-arms the Abbot had now hired to serve him for
the space of two years; that is to say, provided the conduct
of his vassals should not, in the mean time, give rise to any
disturbance. Again, the ramparts were all to be levelled
and the ditch filled up; the houses constructed in town,
with towers and pignons, and all houses showing forth the
burgher-pride of the communeers, were to be demolished,
and the old fashioned abodes reinstated in their old places.
On these last-named points Monseigneur Philippe showed
them that the Abbot was fully resolved to be inflexible; for
he would not agree to allow the spirit of resistance to feed
upon any monuments of the rebellion.

Jacques and Eudes, with many a sigh, and hearts very

heavy, consented to everything. They merely asked permission to consult the population, being unwilling, so they
said, to bear the whole burthen of responsibility for acts
of that kind. The Seigneur de Cornehaut granted the
article as just and proper, and the burgesses were convoked,
by sound of trumpet, to a meeting in the same square
where they had sworn to die for the Commune. The question now before them was, to set aside the Commune; not
to die in defence of it.

It is natural to suppose that the new aspect of the square,
and the crowds gathered in it, was not like the one we saw
there on a former occasion. In the first place, many of the
old thatched houses that were there then had disappeared
and given place to handsome structures, which, to be sure,
were not yet finished, but nevertheless displayed, in certain
of their portions already completed, and in the height of the
scaffolding, how sumptuous had been their owner's thoughts
on architecture, and how wealthy, too, they were. Instead
of the old humble buildings whose thatched roofs we once
looked upon, here are beheld nothing but tourelles, pignons,
and on some of the façades of the burgher-folk, the stone-
cutters had made a beginning of the figures of Adam and
Eve in conference with the serpent; further on, our first
parents doing penance for their first greed; or other subjects taken from the New Testament, such as C»6ar's-
pence; or moral scenes, the application of which it was
easy to make out

Ah ! but how sad were the multitude, though those mansions shone out so brilliant! Nothing was to be heard on
every hand but moans and groans and stifled sobs; and as
Jacques, mounted on a stage, which for this particular
occasion it was not deemed worth while to drape, gave
signal that he desired to speak; the entire audience, that is
to say, women, children, and burgher-men, all broke out so

loud with sobs and moans that for some minutes the consul, who was himself overcome with the public emotion, could not even begin to pronounce his discourse—so that good Monseigneur was deeply touched with sympathy for the general sorrow.

" Come, come, now, my children," said the knight, in a half severe tone, " we are not met here to weep, but to come to a decision such as becomes a set of reasonable men. As to myself, I cannot see, putting myself in your place, that you can do better than choose either to go on with an accursed rebellion on the one hand, in which case you will be all cut to pieces, and inevitably damned afterwards, every mother's son of you; or on the other hand, make an end of yonr nonsense at once, and submit to your lord Abbot, who, I assure you, has no wish to be a hard master. I am even authorized by him to say, that in case any of you should prefer to quit the town, he shall be allowed one month to arrange his business affairs and then go avay* But, s 'death! make up your minds quickly, for I take little delight in all this moaning and groaning; it makes my ears ache."

Jacques now rose and said :—

" Friends and fellow-burgesses, you have now heard what this worthy knight has thought fit to say on the situation of our affairs, and you know he spoke truly when he told us that further resistance on our part is a thing wholly out of the question. It is yours to decide what ought to be done, for I have no advice to give you on the subject. I have nothing more to say, except that Eudes and I have both resigned our offices as consuls."

" My friends," said Monseigneur Philippe, "I am waiting for your answer. Your lord Abbot will take into account any good grace you may show in the act of returning to duty and obedience."

To carry on a discussion of questions of treaty with a multitude is to lay one's self open to the strangest freaks.

"Long life to Cornehaut I God bless Cornehaut I" they roared, and few among the populace failed to join the hurrahs.

"Well, now!" said Philippe to the two consuls, "you have grown reasonable at last! don't you think so ?" And he could not suppress a smile of contempt. " My mission is at an end, I suppose ?" ■

"Yes, Monseigneur," replied Eudes in a piteous tone; "but may we now venture to ask you what is next to happen to us ?"

" Nothing, nothing at all," responded the knight. " The father Abbot will prove very merciful. The only thing is that you will have to contribute, rather more than some of the rest of you, to the pay of the abbey-garrison, and if it was any business of mine to give you advice, it would be to put away all your scarlet ensigns, take off your mail-coats, and dress yourselves in a way becoming honest and good burgher-people, and first of all set to work with hammers on your new houses."

The two burghers bowed and waited on the crusader as he proceeded towards the first barrier. They did not speak a word as they marched along.

"By holy cross!" cried Monseigneur Philippe, gayly smacking his hand on Jacques' shoulder, " I've a notion, my good fellow, that when you and your comrades had me down under that Isengrin's axe over yonder, you little thought how it was all to end—nor I neither, that I do Bwear! But I have nothing to complain of now."

The two burghers raised their hands up towards heaven, and then looked steadily on each other's faces. Rage, humiliation, and grief—every frightful sentiment of the wildest anguish was depicted on their visages.

" Can't we resist ?" murmured Eudes in broken tones.
" Is it not better to fall by the swords of our enemies than
to be butchered to death with a thousand lesser stabs as
tfe are doing?"

" How can we resist ?" retorted Jacques, " not a soul of
them would obey us now. Didn't you hear them cry long
life to the chevalier ? Perhaps Payen" . . .

" No, no; I 'll have nothing to do with Payen ! ... he
called us a gang of cowards and assassins, and never will I
forget that, as long as I live. He was always opposed to
us in the council, and I'd rather obey a thousand monks
than that scoundrel's pride. If we must bend our necks,
comrade Jacques, at least let us not yield them to one of
our equals."

"I agree with you in that," said Jacques, " and so good-
bye—neither you nor I know anything of what's to come.".

What was coming was to submit to their *dech&ance* from
the consulship : the populace too were glad to get rid of
them, for not a soul spoke to them as they stalked along
homewards, an evidence of their fallen state that was very
grating to their feelings, for it is a hard thing to soon get
used to the loss of place and distinction.

As they were about to hang him, the soldiers tore off
Simon's cloak; Antoine had been buried in his mantle, at the
bottom of the river ; Payen had disdainfully cast his down
on the street pavement; Eudes and Jacques took off theirs,
with weeping eyes, and carefully packed them away, without the least hope of ever wearing them again, but fully
resolved to have the pleasure, now and then, of opening the
coffers and gazing at them. They then, to bring everything down to the level of their real condition, at once
began the task of demolishing their rising mansions.

On the evening of that solemn day, it was not without
emotion that the towns-folk looked on to see several of the

Typhaines monks walking through their streets: it was a very novel sight; and the reception they gave to their former masters, now restored to their rights, was both timid and servile ; yet when they found how kind and conciliating they were in speech and manners, they began to grow enthusiastic about them. The monks boasted a great deal of the lord Abbot's sweet and gentle disposition, spoke of his wound in a way to comfort gvery body, and related, in a rather gloomy way, perhaps, the story of Simon's death ; it was not the fault of the good fathers that Simon had died; but it all came of those mercenaries, who to make the best of it, had spread a report that Simon had died blaspheming like the very worst Mahometan. The monks failed not to tell all the poor folks they fell in with, to come up to the abbey next morning as in the good old times, and .have a taste of the nice convent-soup that would be in waiting for them; to the women they tendered the long absent sweets of their religious counsels. The men were promised a high-mass for the next day, to be followed by a *Te Deum*, and the exposition of St. Procul's Annulary. The burghers were in perfect ecstasies over the kindness, merits, and virtues of the Abbot and his recluses, and from that very moment they never could succeed in making out how it was they could be such a set of fools as to allow themselves to be drawn into a rebellion against such excellent, such worthy seigneurs. Being now converted, they at once began to cast about, to find out some way of doing honor to themselves and at the same time show their affection to their masters. They held a consultation; some proposed to kill Payen, but one of the meeting suggested that the blacksmith had openly protested against the murder of the Abbot; of course he must have been secretly planning in the good seigneur's favor, and of course it wouldn't be well

36

to lay their hands on him. At once the shoot broke out,
"Long life to Payen I long live Payen I"

The next idea was to play some bad tarn on Eades and
Jacques, but the prudent part of them found it an easy
matter to show that far from being a thing pleasing to the
monks, it might very well happen to irritate them, for don't
you see, it was Eudes and Jacques that were the very first
of all to advise the communeers to submit. Well, then, what
can be done ? for we must do something—it will never do
to let such a splendid evening pass without doing something of some sort. As the consuls had quit, the bailiff not
yet appointed, and there being no authority of any kind,
the good people of Typhaines were left entirely to themselves and their good inspirations; somebody cried out:—

Hurrah for Jeanne, Simon's wife, let's go and give her
a ducking I"

The thought was a roost luminous one. The entire mob
rushed off for the street where Damerones had resided.
The door was standing wide open; nobody at home.
They tumbled everything topsy-turvy and no person came
up to stop them. Jeanne was gone. Let us, without delay, here state that, some days afterwards, Rigauld camo
across her dead body out in the woods, half devoured by
the wolves; a most singular thing, that might put one in
miud of the old saying, that that sort of animals are in the
habit of eating each other.

We will now return to the good people of Typhaines,
who found themselves sorely tried for want of something
to do. Most unfortunately, it had been clearly made known
to them that there was no plausible reason why there
should be any hanging done; and so, for want of that
delight supreme, they had to go to work on things inanimate, and away they gayly went and at once commenced
the demolition of the ramparts.

On the following morning, the prior, as the Abbot's representative, came in with the men-at-arms to inangurate the new bailiff for the borough. He was received most admirably; they hugged his mule's legs, and if he could have trusted to people's wishes, he would have given his very frock for so much sacred relics. The prior, as part of his duty, traversed the streets and everywhere saw that the Abbot's ordinance concerning sumptuosity in dwelling-houses was in a fair way of being consummated. At one of the mansions, he and all his attendants were profoundly astonished to find that instead of being in a process of demolition the workmen were actually going on with the building.

What's the meaning of this ?" inquired the prior of some of the notable burgesses about him.

"Alas !" they humbly replied, "this is Payen's house; we thought he was better disposed to obey our seigneur's orders than this comes to."

" Bring the man here," said the monk, " and let me tell him what his duty is."

Some of the soldiers entered the house and found Payen there, in his blacksmith's dress, and eating his supper.

" Here, you peasant," said the soldiers, " come out and make your appearance before the lord prior of Typhaines."

" I have no seigneur but the king," replied the black-smith, " and if the reverend prior wants to see me, he can come here and do that."

" The day of insolence is passed," they replied, " you are nobody now, sir peasant, and if you won't follow us with a good will, we '11 force you to march."

" In case I should knock out your brains, both of you," said Payen, looking askance at an enormous sledge-hammer within reach of his hand, " I should not by that restore the

Commune; I should not find Damerones again—and so, I will submit and follow you."

" Sire monk, what do you want with me ?"

" No doubt you have forgotten the lord Abbot's order ? Your house was to be taken down!"

" Never with my consent," spoke out the bold burgher.

In that case it will be demolished without asking you; but think of it; you are forcing me to employ a useless rigor."

The rigor will not be without its use," replied Payen, and he scowled fiercely at the crowd,[41] for it will prove that there was one Communeer of Typhaines who resisted to the last"

" Have the house taken down," said the prior to the sergeants-at-arms.

The word was given, and the builders immediately began the demolition. The populace lent their hands to the operation and it was marvellous to see how rapidly the work was done. Payen stood by; contemplated the scene of destruction; heard the mob laughing and jeering, and saw the walls tremble, then topple down, without once ehanging his attitude of cold contempt.

" Am I a prisoner ?" he asked.

" Not at all."

" Then I quit the burgh; and hearken to me, sire monk: you and your Abbot have not been hard, for conquerors as you are; you might have done worse; but these miserable people of Typhaines have been too cowardly; they might have done better."

And as this bravado drew down a storm of threats—

"Ah!" cried Payen, raising his clenched fist, "you wretched howlers—let not a soul of you recover his courage! I promise him he will make a miserable proof of it. . . . Place ! make way for me while I pass !"

"That," said the mercenaries, struck with Payen's martial attitude, and already well aware of his reputation for bravery, "that's the stuff to make a man-at-arms of I Pity such a man should be a burgher."

Payen was gone. He had returned to his old residence, and there shut himself in. No one doubted of his determination to avail himself of the permission granted by father Anselm to withdraw as soon as the seceder could realize his property, and they were right. The only man who had loved liberty without hating anybody, and served her without treason or relaxation, could not consent to live among a people whom he now regarded as cowards and scoundrels. Besides all that, he was now very much disabused on subjects once most cherished by him. The Commune was dead, and very dead.

The prior went back to Father Anselm's bedside to report what he had seen, heard, and done, and Bishop Guillaume, whose ardent zeal would have willingly hearkened to the violent counsels of the military, now fully agreed with his old friend that, next after proper firmness, gentleness was to be esteemed neither a weakness nor a mistake. The learned prelate departed the next day, quite proud of the part he had taken in this grand affair, and of the success that had crowned his efforts. May it please Heaven that Master Abelard's reputation may never annoy him more ! but it did continue to follow him for a long time; indeed, down to this very day it beclouds his glory. Apart from this misfortune, Master Ouillaume de Champeaux was a fortunate prelate, and the See of Chalons was honored by his science and virtues. The day after the prior's visit to Typhaines, Monseigneur Philippe approached the Abbot's bedside, and announced that he had come to take his leave.

" Why, my son ?" said the venerable monk, rising on his elbow. " Take a seat by me, and listen to what I have to propose; perhaps the result of this conference may be to convince you that the melancholy that sits on your brow has no business to be there; and what is more besides, that there ought to be no question of a separation betwixt you and me."

" I wait your orders, holy father," said the crusader, somewhat surprised.

The Abbot softly laid his hand on the young man's arin

CHAPTER XXX.

"My son," pursued the Abbot, " though the days we have, of late, lived in and the tempests of adversity that have howled around us were most terrible, yet, with God helping us, we have passed in safety through the dreadful trials, and now, nothing is left for us but the pleasing task to show how great is our love, and how lasting our gratitude. Among all those who have given us good aid and comfort in such sore afflictions, you certainly do hold the highest place, my dear son; still, I must say, that my personal respect, my admiration and gratitude, are no meet compensation for your eminent services to this abbey, and to God's holy church."

"Ah, holy father," answered Philippe, mournfully, " speak not to me of rewards, for I desire none. I wish no temporal recompense for what I have tried to do in that behalf. I want for nothing; nothing in this world . . . now."

"But, my son," rejoined father Anselm, "your marriage contract with the damoiselle of Cornouiller is by no means certainly broken off. It cannot be that a mere transitory fit of anger, utterly causeless as hers is, should lead my ward Mahaut to violate the pledged faith she has kept so long and so truly—and which has my fullest, my most entire sanction. All that is needed to convert your betrothed from her present resolution, and renew her long, faithful affection for your person, is but a little prudence. Mahaut's present paroxysm of anger will gradually become a great calm again: the waters of the sea, which, though they may be lifted up into mountainous waves by the lashing tempest, always become smooth and calm again, as soon as the storm-w.ind grows lull. Hearken, then, to the plan I have laid out for you : Bishop Guillaume has already intimated to you that the Church of Typhaines has sent a petition to Borne for liberty to restore your entire property, and I doubt not in the least that his holiness will yield to the solid reasons I have alleged in my letters, and that he will at once grant me the boon to reinstate you, my son, in your ancient heritage. But that is not all it is proper I should do as a sufficient acknowledgment of your services. Down to the present day the abbey has ever been without an Avoyer; the country having been undisturbed, seigneurs and peasants alike have respected her power and rights throughout the whole region around her; but times are now greatly changed—they are hard upon us; and though we have come off victors in the late strife, it is the dictate of prudence not to slumber upon our successes. You, then, shall become our Avoyer; you shall keep on foot for our defence, one hundred lances and three-hundred crossbowmen ; and to make it easy to defray the expenses of so large an establishment, you are to receive as your fiefs from our hands the four castles of Maisonriche; Bresuay; Coq-Hardi and la Taille, with the lands on them depending. It's unnecessary for me to tell you that, together with your ancestral domain, these new acquisitions will, with the domain of Cornouiller, to be added by your union to Mahaut, make you the wealthiest seigneur in all the marches of the Nivernais."

Monseigneur gratefully pressed the aged prelate's hand, but he slowly moved his head in sign of negation.

*' I most clearly perceive," said he, "that your good-will

to me is great, my father; and as for my ownself, I do thank you for it, and will keep it, a precious memory all the future days of my poor life. But upon what, and on whom, does the full realization of all these flattering projects depend? On an angry woman, my lord, and one, too, who will not be even just to a man who loves her far more than the whole world beside. If Mahaut persists in her hatred, far from becoming the abbey's Avoyer, I will go—I know not whither, to seek some remote corner of the world, and there to lay me down and die."

The poor knight spoke under the deepest conviction, and what he said was certain and sure, for the *punctilio*—the point of honor—at that day was, ever to win the palm* of constancy, and especially constancy in all love questions. The Abbot saw there was no use in combating so intense a sentiment as that—and all he did was to gravely and mechanically nod his head, and dismiss the true-hearted knight. A few minutes after the interview was over, the prior of the monastery, by Anselm's orders, was on his way to Cornouiller, and it may well be supposed he was bearer of a message of peace.

The prior was received at the castle-gate without any difficulty, and then admitted to the interior of the donjon ; but his surprise was extreme when, instead of finding himself in Mahaut's presence there, he stood face to face with Monseigneur Baudouin de Pornes. The worthy monk was near falling over backwards with the shock; but Messire Baudouin, assuming a most agreeable manner and tone, reassured the messenger as far as he possibly could—

" How happy ! how rejoiced am I!" said Sire Baudouin, [41] to receive a visit from the reverend prior of Typhaines I Ah! I am well aware, father, that you have felt some doubts as to my devotion to that holy house ! Some little misunderstandings, certainly, did spring up between us;

yet I have heard, with the highest pleasure, that the rebels
have submitted at last! The wicked wretches had spread
a report through the country that I was one of their allies—
why, they actually stole several of my own serfs from me !
Bosh I don't let's talk of them; I'm too delighted to welcome you to my Chatel de Cornouiller, indeed I am."

" Your castle ?" cried the annoyed prior.

" That is to say, my son's chatel. To-morrow he is to
be united in marriage to Madame Mahaut."

"But, have you bethought you, Monseigneur, that the
lady is the reverend Abbot's ward, and that he has not as
yet conceded his assent to the union ?"   •

" Pray be undeceived, father," replied Messire Baudouin,
" his reverence the Abbot is no longer my lady's guardian.
Upon her own demand, the Count de Nevers, our suzerain,
has received her under his protection, as was his right to
do ; and his kindness has induced him to approve of this
union, which is most gratifying to me."

"Might I be allowed to have speech with Mahaut?"
asked the poor prior.

"No;" was the baron's peremptory answer; "she's
busy—or—perhaps—she's asleep."

To such a reply as that, there could be no gainsaying, and
so, the monk bowed, and deeming his mission at an end,
returned to the castle gate, accompanied however by the
baron, lavishing on the missionary numerous civilities, the
kindest, the most respectful, and politest in the world.

He returned to the abbey and communicated the result
to Father Anselm.

There were various rumors abroad afterwards in relation to that singular affair. It was said by many persons,
that while the prior was conferring with,Messire de Pornes,
Mahaut was restrained by main force from going into the
hall to meet him : others asserted that the treatment mea-

sored out to the monk was in full accordance with her own free will; while those who knew her best, insisted that such a blind obstinacy as that was a thing impossible to be supposed of any human heart.

It was said that she certainly had placed all her property and her person too under the protection and control of the Count de Nevers; but, that the Seigneur de Pornes had been so cunning as to hurry to the castle in good time; for a few hours later, and without fail too, she would have changed her mind in regard to Philippe; that no sooner did she set eyes on her old enemy, than she started as if waked out of a wild dream, and tried to expel the baron from her walls, but without success, because the cunning nobleman, suspecting some possible change in her temper, had got in in force, and instead of going out like an idiot after coming in like a thief and a robber, he was now able to talk in the tone of a master.

Whatsoever, among all these various explanations, may be the real truth, there is no one now left to tell. It remained a deep and hidden mystery, and must ever be a mystery. It is known, however, that from the time of her marriage, Mahaut led a life of severe seclusion; receiving no visits, except those of a couple of ill-famed barons, who were her father-in-law's intimate friends. The baron took up his quarters at Chatel Cornouiller, under the pretext of supervising his dear children's affairs, who, so he said, were too much devoted to their mutual affection to mind their real and most important business: he took good care to keep up a stout garrison at the place, and maintained watch and ward of the very strictest.

Never was Abbot Anselm, though greatly concerned for his former ward, allowed to approach her presence. It was evident that no person conld gain admission without Messire Baudouin's sanction, by any means short of carrying

the strong Keep by assault; an enterprise rather too hope-
less while the baron was there to hold it

In fine, we have to state that Mahaut died quite young
and childless; her father-in-law adjudged the succession
to himself in right of his son, her husband. Rumors so
sinister had got abroad about the treatment the poor lady
received from the hands of those wicked people, that the
peasantry even told how her ghost was seen walking during
dark and tempestuous nights on the summit of* the lofty
donjon; and that they had heard her shrieking for help
amid the roarings of the storm-wind, and exclaiming in
heart-rending tones, " *Cornehaut! Cornehaut!*"

Monseigneur Philippe could certainly never have heard
anything of those dreadful stories; for, if he had heard of
them, no doubt poor Mahaut's sad fate would have been
cleared up some way or other. He, as soon as the Abbot
had told him of the prior's visit to the chatel, at once summoned faithful old Fulk, ordered the horses to be saddled,
and took leave of father Anselm, with many thanks for
kind intentions to-him-ward, but still averring that he
would not avail himself of them. It was a dolorous
moment for the good old Abbot of Typhaines to see him
depart. Being a man of great energy and devotion, he
had, too, as we well know, a most tender heart, and Monseigneur had won it wholly. Of course, then, he often pondered over the absent knight, and was ever anxious to
learn what had become of him, till one day, about four
years after his departure from Typhaines Abbey, there
came a knight Templar from the Holy Land to demand the
surrender of Monseigneur's family estate: that personage
had joined the Holy Temple Order; to which he had made
a full and free gift of all J>is worldly goods, whatsoever
and wheresoever. What to him was worldly property,

thenceforth forever? Was not his lineage about to cease
in the world, as soon as the last breath should pass out
from his lips ? He was to leave no posterity behind at
his death ! and his sword and helm, so he ordained, were
to be buried with him in the last narrow house whenever
it might please his Maker to loose him from the bonds of
this human life !

Pilgrims, returning to France from the distant lands of
Palestine, deeply imbued, as they well might be, with admiration and respect for these knight Templars, so brave !
so single-hearted ! so patient! spread throughout Europe
the high fame of the commander of the Templars, Sir
Philippe de Cornehaut, won, as it had been, in the course
of so few lapsing years ! He, so they told, was the very
column of the Order and the glory of the true religion,
Roman, Catholic, and Apostolic.

Exploits of his were told of, that seemed to surpass the force of any human thought. Among other
things, they told how he and Fulk, his good old squire, a
few leagues away from the town of Joppa, had once scattered, like so much dust, a whole Saracen corps of two
hundred horse, commanded by the soldan's own brother,
whose head he clove by a flash of old Rudaverse; it is
unhappily true the while, that the Emir's mamelukes had carried off the valiant squire's head with a falchion's sweep,
and that was a great sorrow set in Monseigneur the commander's heart I He loved his faithful servitor as if he
were an own brother to him, and always accepted his counsels, having long proved how wise, sincere, and disinterested they had ever been.

After he had wept over, and, to his very best, taken vengeance for his humble friend, ne made choice from among
his lay-brothers of the Temple-Order, of a person named

37

Payen, wbo, in many a rencontre, had lent him a valiant support. The commander and his squire were said to have had long private conferences together, and that after they were over, and they both came forth, they seemed always sad and dolent. But that was a very plain story for us, who know those old days, when they both received wounds incurable. The commander used to talk on those occasions about Mahaut, who, away off, far away yonder in the little district of Nivernais, was spending her life in a living martyrdom ; the other spoke of Damerones, whom his fancy drew as kneeling at Heloise's feet, a true and holy Saint, at Paraclete. The one pondered on his life as a nobleman, now forever lost, his ancestral line broken, and soon with him to disappear, from the world's face forever I the other conjured up to fancy's eye the once loved Commune, and bemoaned most bitterly, and with many tears, too, the vices and crimes of his once loved friends. The two templars never quarrelled ; on liberty and on love, they neither were known to have any* sentiments whatever, for all such thoughts were quelled for evermore in their sad bosoms. Their death was sublime. It-happened. on that heroic and fatal day when King Louis le jeune so covered his name with glory. The Christian array, driven in at every point by the innumerable squadrons of the misbelieving Paynim, had fallen like a ripened harvest beneath the arrows and falchions of the Pagan hosts. The commander of the Temple-Order, Sir Philippe de Cornehaut, and the brother Payen, were last seen standing alone on a rock, where they continued to fight as if on the summit of some tall tower. They had strewn the space around their last refuge with the dead and dying bodies of the Saracens, and finding that the great cloud of their assailants was ever swelling and growing and darkening; their hauberks and helms and bucklers, too, all beaten in and broken, with none but the ruined fragments left, they both comprehended that their last hour was come. They now swore they would never surrender, or fall alive into the hands of the Mohammedans. Tired at last of seeing their comrades slashed and slain by the two Christian giants, the sons of Islam withdrew beyond the sweep of their swords, and did just what the soldiers of Marsil once did to Roland the Paladin, and brave Archbishop Turpin, of Rheims; they stood off at a safe distance from their redoubtable foes, and rained on the two soldiers a storm of arrows and javelins.

"This is the last of it," gravely said the commander to the squire. "We shall not spend the rest of the day with the ladies; still, brother Payen, we should think of our souls. It is time to do so now."

The two templars, without paying the least attention to the hurtling tempest of missiles, went down on their knees —face to face—on the rock, holding their sword-crosses before their eyes. They then began to confess their sins to each other; but Payen had hardly begun his penitential recital, when a long zagaie came whistling on, struck him on the left temple, and cast him dying on the spot. Monseigneur Philippe went on devoutly with his orison, but had no long time to wait; he, too, fell: but he yet had strength enough left to drag himself close to the brink of the rock, where it rose perpendicular to the flowing river below, and then to toss his tru6ty old Rudaverse into the air: it rose and rose, and then plunged deep into the wave, and was lost to sight forever, unstained, unsoiled by the touch of an infidel hand. This last effort over, the good knight laid him down at length on the rock, and with a murmured *Jem Maria!* before the inrushing, bellowing wave of the Moslem soldiers coaid reach him, his last breath was drawn, and so he died. An Egyptian sheick, who had been an eyewitness of the gallant defence of the templars, refused permission to cat off their heads, and gave orders for an honorable burial.

The Troubadour.

The beautiful spring delights me well,
   When flowers and leaves are growing;
And it pleases my heart to hear the swell
   Of the bird's sweet chorus flowing
     In the echoing wood:
And I love to see all scatter'd around,
Pavilions and tents on the martial ground;
     And my spirit finds it good
To see on the level plains beyond
Gay knights and steeds caparison'd.

It pleases me when the lancers bold
   Set men and armies flying,
And it pleases me too, to hear around
   The voice of the soldiers crying:
     And joy is mine
When the castles strong besieged shake
And walls uprooted totter and quake
     And I see the foemen join
On the moated shore, all compass'd 'round
With the palisade and guarded ground.

Lances and swords and stained helms,
  And shields dismantled and broken,
On the verge of the bloody battle scene
  The field of wrath betoken,
      And the vassals are there,
And there fly the steeds of the dying and dead:
And where the mingled strife is spread
        The noblest warrior's care
Is to cleave the foeman's limbs and head
The conqueror less of the living than dead.

I tell you that nothing my soul can cheer,
  On banquetting or reposing,
Like the onset cry of "Charge them," rung
  From each side, as in battle closing
      When the horses neigh,
And the call to "aid" is echoing loud,
And there, on the earth, the lowly and proud
        In the foss together lie;
And yonder are piled the mingled heap
Of the brave who scaled the trench's steep.

Barons! your castles in safety place,
Your cities and villages too;
        And Papiol! quickly go
And tell the Lord of "yes and no"
That peace already too long hath been.

www.ingramcontent.com/pod-product-compliance
Lightning Source LLC
Chambersburg PA
CBHW030951110726
47900CB00004B/1217